UNBROKEN
FAITH

BOOK NINE OF THE CASTLE FEDERATION
BOOK THREE OF THE DAKOTAN CONFEDERACY

UNBROKEN FAITH

BOOK NINE OF THE CASTLE FEDERATION
BOOK THREE OF THE DAKOTAN CONFEDERACY

GLYNN STEWART

FAOLAN'S PEN
PUBLISHING
faolanspen.com

This edition published in 2023 by:

Faolan's Pen Publishing Inc.

22 King St. S, Suite 300

Waterloo, Ontario

N2J 1N8 Canada

ISBN-13: 978-1-989674-46-8 (print)

A record of this book is available from Library and Archives Canada.

Printed in the United States of America

1 2 3 4 5 6 7 8 9 10

First edition

First printing: December 2023

Illustration by Sam Leung

Faolan's Pen Publishing logo is a registered trademark of Faolan's Pen Publishing Inc.

Read more books from Glynn Stewart at faolanspen.com

1

LKI-598 System

18:00 January 8, 2740 Earth Standard Meridian Date/Time

THE PROBLEM WITH OPPORTUNISTIC PIRATES, in Vice Admiral Anthony Yamamoto's unfortunately considered and experienced opinion, was that because they were *opportunistic*, they wanted to be able to go back to regular trade afterward.

Which meant that, as a rule, they *left no survivors*.

The fighter pilot turned fighter group commander now turned *task group commander*—and he wasn't sure he'd ever forgive his boss for that—stood in what had been the crew gymnasium of the mining ship *Penelope's Fault*.

Fault was a permanent resident of the LKI-598 System, an uninhabited and uninhabitable waypoint star on the edge of the Dakotan Confederacy. Most of her crew had cycled in and out about every six months, according to the files they had, when a big interstellar transport came through to pick up the results of their labor.

A lot of people, including *Penelope's Fault*'s owners, had made a great deal of money from the mining ship. Unfortunately, *now*, all four hundred and ninety-odd members of her crew were dead. The

Dakotan Confederacy Marines who'd boarded ahead of Yamamoto weren't even sure how *many* people had been herded into the gymnasium before the pirates had opened fire with machine guns.

"Any sign of survivors at all?" Anthony asked flatly. His voice was tense, which always turned his accent even more Scottish. The tall Japanese man certainly *looked* like his famous ancestor, but he'd been born and raised in Scotland on Earth.

A planet now a hundred–plus light-years away and, unfortunately, a mortal enemy to his new nation.

Life was funny like that. Not that he was finding much funny today.

"We restored atmosphere before we brought you aboard, sir," Major Omiros Iordanou told him. "There was no air aboard... for at least a month."

The big Kretan officer was wearing full-body powered combat armor. So was everybody *else* in the charnel house that had been a gymnasium, except for Anthony, who wore a standard shipsuit. Which functioned as an emergency space suit, so he wasn't in any danger.

He wasn't the only non-Marine aboard the ship, either. They'd brought several dozen computer and forensic specialists over from the Dakotan Confederacy Navy carrier *Saratoga*, all under the careful watch of the carrier's starfighters and the battlecruiser *Iroquois*.

But he'd needed to see just how bad it was with his own eyes.

"Computer specialists are tearing into the systems as we speak," Iordanou continued. "We should know as much as possible about *Penelope's Fault*'s killers before we leave the system."

"What I want to know, right now, is *where are they?*" Anthony said grimly. "And I suspect I'm going to be sadly disappointed on that front."

He took one last look around the massacre, then grimaced and strode out of the gymnasium. Iordanou followed.

"Our best option is probably to send the ship into the damn star," Anthony told the Marine. "Give these poor bastards all the sendoff we can manage."

"I don't expect to find much in the computers," his subordinate replied. "On the other hand, every time I poke at just what the hell our pirates would have been doing in LKI in the first place, I get all hopeful that they might come back."

"The problem is that after two years, we *know* Brillig is a goddamn mess," Anthony pointed out. The Brillig Sector, like the Dakota Sector and the Meridian Sector, had once been a six-inhabited-star-system subdivision of the Terran Commonwealth.

Dakota and Meridian had survived the collapse of the Commonwealth's communication networks over two years earlier by allying and forging the Dakotan Confederacy. *Brillig* had disintegrated into anarchy on an interstellar level. The sector fleet had broken up, and the star systems had stopped talking to each other by *any* method.

It was starting to return to a semblance of calm, but Brillig would forever be four independent systems and a two-system *problem*, not a multistellar government. Not unless one of the expansionist Successor States scooped them up, anyway—and everyone *else* who shared borders with them seemed to think that aggravating the second-largest of said Successor States was a bad idea.

The Dakotan Confederacy wasn't going to conquer the former Brillig Sector themselves, but one star had joined the Confederacy— and Dakota had the ships, Marines and diplomats to make anyone *else* think real hard about looking greedily at the Sector. Especially now that every star system in it was back on the interstellar communication network via *Dakota*'s q-com switchboard.

"And if you were swinging back and forth between, say, Brillig, Blyton, and a couple of our stars, LKI-Five-Nine-Eight would be a good place to stop and catch up in safety," Iordanou observed. "Not a *great* plan, as I understand it, but a place to hide away from prying eyes can be more useful than a faster trip, I imagine."

"Sometimes," Anthony conceded. "I'm going to check out the computer center and see what the analysts have found." He tapped the side of his head, a universal indicator of the neural implants they all had in their skulls.

"I'm keeping my ears open; let me know if we find anything."

———

Penelope's Fault was smaller than any interstellar ship, but that wasn't saying much. The Class One mass manipulators needed to create the Alcubierre-Stetson FTL drive cost a measurable percentage of a star system's GDP *each,* and a starship needed a minimum of four.

No one built starships smaller than "the largest they could." That metric changed over time—the two ships in Anthony's task group had both been the largest available when built, but *Saratoga* was "merely" eight hundred meters long and forty million cubic meters or so… while *Iroquois* was over *seventeen* hundred meters long, with a volume of over *eighty* million cubic meters and a mass of over twenty-five million tons.

Fault was an oblong brick just over half a kilometer long and about two-thirds of that thick. Her sublight engines were crap, but she wasn't intended to be much more than a somewhat mobile base for the extractor ships that were tearing through LKI-598's asteroid belts.

There was plenty of space for the several hundred Dakotan Confederacy Marines and Dakotan Confederacy Navy specialists to vanish into the dark and foreboding corridors. The Marines had restored atmosphere, but gravity was still only present in key areas.

Gravity systems were fragile at the best of times and didn't handle being abandoned for an unknown number of months without maintenance or operation particularly well. Plus, the mass manipulators and exotic-matter coils that underlay any gravity system were the highest-density value items aboard a sublight ship like *Penelope's Fault*.

Most of them were probably gone.

Still, as Anthony approached the mining ship's main computer center, his implant told him that there was a gravity field present. His shipsuit was automatically adjusting his boots to allow for the seventy percent of a gravity that an emergency generator was putting out—and his neural implant threw up both the location of said generator and of the heavy-weapons team covering the entrance to the center.

The Marines were finding the dead spaceship as unfortunate as he was. A pair of the armored soldiers was following him everywhere, which he figured was reasonable there!

The woman in charge of the guard detail saluted as he approached, metal clinking softly as her gauntlet touched her helmet.

"Admiral, computer center is secure," she reported. "We've got a portable power source and a bunch of specialists bringing the systems online and poking through them." She paused. "Your pet Crow is here, too."

Anthony did not *quite* roll his eyes at that.

"Agent Rogers is not anyone's *pet*, Sergeant," he observed. "But I'm glad they're here. Their skills will come in handy."

"Of course, they will, sir," the Marine confirmed. "Should I clear you in?"

"Please." He smiled. "Do you need to see my identification?"

A notification in his head told him she had done the network equivalent of just that a moment later, checking his implant ID codes against the implants and codes that Vice Admiral Anthony Yamamoto, Dakotan Confederacy Starfighter Corps, *should* have.

"You're clear, sir."

The multi-barreled heavy penetrator cannon hadn't been pointed at him at all, but its crew ever-so-subtly moved the heavy weapon to point *away* from him at that declaration.

Anthony nodded his approval to the Marines and strode forward, letting the Sergeant open the door for him with only moments to spare.

The computer center was the first place he'd been aboard *Penelope's Fault* that had full lights. They probably *could* have put the lights on full in the gymnasium, but Anthony rather appreciated that they *hadn't*.

If there had been any massacred innocents in the computer center, they'd been removed before he got there.

Instead, the bright lights shone down on dozens of semi-crystalline towers of molecular-circuitry computer cores. There were particular patterns and shapes to the cores that told even Anthony, whose interest in technology normally began and ended with starfighters, that those cores were old. Probably obsolete and, if nothing else, very, very cheap.

Two dozen Navy techs in their maroon-edged black uniforms were swarming over the systems. Most of the cores appeared to be online, but no one was using *Fault*'s own systems to access them. Several mobile computing setups had been linked in to act as relays, but as

Anthony walked into the organized chaos, he could tell that most of the work was happening in his people's implants.

He wore the same duty uniform as the techs, but where they had maroon lapels on their jackets and piping on their shipsuits, *his* uniform had the dark indigo blue of the Starfighter Corps. The colors were part of the small but clear changes made when the Dakotan Confederacy military moved away from using Terran Commonwealth uniforms.

Still, over half of their personnel had served in the Commonwealth's military, but the failure of interstellar communications and a few *political* issues had led to the Confederacy's independence... almost two years ago that day, in fact.

The odd person out in the mix saw Anthony and walked over to him as the Admiral approached. Unlike everyone else, Agent Jessie Rogers didn't salute. They were, theoretically, civilian—though the Dakotan Confederacy Reconnaissance Organization was arguably *paramilitary* and certainly worked with the Navy.

Rogers' uniform had no piping at all. The only sign of any department was the lapel insignia they wore—where the Marines wore a coyote, the Navy wore a dolphin and the Starfighter Corps wore an eagle, the DCRO agent wore a silver crow.

Anthony figured the nickname might have been inevitable, but he had to admit that the Confederacy's new intelligence agency had definitely courted it. For their part, Rogers was even taller than Anthony, dark-haired, with a beak of a nose and pale skin that might have led to crow comparisons *anyway*.

"Admiral," they greeted him. "Looking for more nightmares?"

"My stopover in the gymnasium guaranteed those," Anthony said grimly. "Tell me you have something. Or that you will." He made a gesture encompassing the entire room. "I recognize that this isn't a fast process."

"*Penelope's Fault* isn't a warship, Admiral," Rogers pointed out. "Step this way."

Anthony followed the Crow, his Marines trailing him by a discreet few steps.

"The Navy folks are still poking through details and running full analyses, but they have a process to follow," Rogers told him. It wasn't a criticism, Anthony had to note. Just a statement. "I don't. I have an *objective*."

"Please tell me that objective was finding the assholes that did this."

"Oh, it very fucking much was," the Crow told him. "And while I don't have any *promises*, Admiral, I know a lot more about what happened here and our potential opportunities than I was afraid I would."

Even through the sealed pane of the spy's shipsuit helmet, Anthony could see a smile that *definitely* belonged on a carrion bird.

"What did you find?" he asked.

"Somebody on *Fault*'s crew was a paranoid, paranoid, *paranoid* bugger," Rogers observed. "If I thought they'd survived, I'd be organizing a queue to give them great big thank-you kisses."

"Agent."

Rogers chuckled.

"They had a secondary sensor cluster set up, running a completely separate set of hardware, software, everything," they told Anthony. "And while I'm sure some of the engineers had to know where it was, the *pirates* didn't. So, when they fucked up all of the sensors and did a purge of the files, they missed everything on what was probably meant as an audit trail."

"Do we know who they are?" Anthony demanded.

Rogers made a gesture and a three-dimensional image transferred to the Admiral's implant.

"*Great Chicago Fire*," the Crow told him. "Fifty-five million cubic meters, big ass motherfucking transport that does a round-robin loop between what was the Brillig and Dakota Sectors.

"They've been doing this run for almost twenty years. *Fire* was probably one of the first civilian fifty-fives ever built. She's been through a few crews, a few captains, but her route hasn't changed much. Not even when the Alliance fucked our coms."

"But she's big enough to give a lot of people a damn headache if she gets opportunistic," Anthony guessed grimly.

"Digging into the records we have from Before, she's got expanded shuttle capacity and a quite-capable anti-meteorite-impact system," Rogers pointed out. "Latter, at least *officially*, is all popgun lasers... but let's be fair: *popgun lasers* can fuck up a merchant ship pretty handily, and it's not hard to reconfigure shuttle-handling gear to handle starfighters, is it?"

"No." Anthony expanded the imagery with a thought. "Do we know what she's been up to the last two years?"

"On paper, the same damn thing she was doing before. A lot of ships with these regular routes stayed on them, just getting more cautious. Seems *Great Chicago Fire*, though, was part of the reason everyone was getting more cautious.

"Mapping her against known pirate issues definitely pops a few positives. Nothing solid enough that I'd even flag her for investigation, but given that I now have detailed sensor footage of her launching two dozen old Scimitar-type starfighters and a flotilla of assault shuttles at a ship where everyone turned up *dead*... Well, I don't *need* to flag her for investigation, do I?"

"Fuckers."

Rogers was a spy and, ultimately, had no law enforcement authority. The DCRO was allowed to run counterintelligence operations *inside* the Confederacy on very strict rules—and among those rules was that the final call for a lot of things came down to planetary law enforcement.

Anthony Yamamoto, on the other hand, was a task group commander in the Dakotan Confederacy Navy—even if he was a Starfighter Corps officer—and that gave him some rather significant law enforcement authority, especially when it came to piracy.

"So, where are our Chicagoan friends now?" He looked around the room and swallowed a spike of anger. "For that matter, do we know when this happened?"

"Seven months ago," Rogers said instantly. They coughed delicately. "The Crows *may* have arranged for your patrol to get updated to include LKI after *Fault*'s owners raised the question of having lost their ship."

"We'll talk about why that's a terrible idea later," Anthony said warningly. "But we're here and we found them. So, now we find *Great Chicago Fire.*"

"So, one of the advantages of an audit-trail sensor package like this one is that it just… keeps running," Rogers told him. "Which means we have sensor data up to about six weeks ago, when the backup power finally failed. Combining that with the records from back home on *Fire's* course, I *think* she's headed back into Confederacy space about now.

"I think she's using this system as a stopover point, a place to go through their loot and consider their next steps," the spy continued. "And if all of that adds up, I believe we may be about to get lucky."

Anthony gave the agent another repressive look.

"Jessie?" he asked.

"I figure we've got a fifty-fifty chance the bastards are going to show up here in the next twenty-four to forty-eight hours, Admiral."

That was better than Anthony had dared hope for.

"Keep on those computers with my people," he ordered Rogers. "If we might have guests, I should get back to *Iroquois.* Because with the evidence you've just said we have, if they come visiting… they are *not* leaving."

2

LKI-598 System
23:00 January 8, 2740 ESMDT

IROQUOIS'S naming and classification were complicated, to the point of being a running joke in the DCN. The first of six eighty-two-point-five-million-cubic-meter warships under construction when the Confederacy had seceded from the Terran Commonwealth, she was officially on the Confederacy Navy's list as the name-ship of her class, one of two *Iroquois*-class battlecruisers now in their order of battle.

She'd been *laid down* as a *Da Vinci*–class battlecruiser of the Terran Commonwealth Navy, as part of a secret shipyard expansion intended to act as a reserve against exactly the kind of catastrophe that had befallen the Commonwealth.

It was not, in Anthony Yamamoto's opinion, the Alliance of Free Stars that had destroyed the Commonwealth. The enemy had merely destroyed the communications network linking together the Commonwealth's star systems.

That had forced the Commonwealth to sue for peace and would have inevitably led a number of star systems along the outer edges of the nation to secession and foreign invasion. What had *destroyed* the Commonwealth was the Commonwealth itself.

First, the ever-tightening grip of the Unity movement had made it impossible for many systems to even raise concerns with central authority, leaving those systems primed to look for an escape route. Second, the very *existence* of the Marshal role, delegating military officers the Senate's executive authority inside a limited area of space for a limited time, had left a far-too-neat framework for Sector Admirals to become warlords.

Lastly, that same far-too-neat framework had ended up being applied at the level of the Commonwealth itself, with the man tasked with the war *against* the Alliance taking over the entire government as Imperator. That, and the orders Imperator Walkingstick had given to try to hold things together, might not have doomed the Commonwealth overall... but it had certainly driven the Dakotan Confederacy into their declaration of independence.

And part of the prize had been the six eighty-million-plus-cubic-meter warships under construction. Whatever the TCN had intended to name them, Dakota had named them for Old Nations tribes on Earth—battlecruisers, battleships, and carriers alike.

Anthony's only *complaint* about *Iroquois* was that she was so much bigger and more capable than *Saratoga* that he simply could not justify commanding his task group from the carrier. *Saratoga* carried his only bomber squadrons, but a full *third* of his regular fighters were aboard the battlecruiser.

And her ridiculously modern command spaces were hard to resist. As the Vice Admiral considered the situation and their potential chance for revenge against *Penelope's Fault*'s killers, he was seated in a command seat that had four variable-sized monitors positioned around it to support the feeds he was getting through his implants— but that seat was suspended in a hologram that rendered the walls, floor and ceiling of his flag bridge invisible.

His people and their stations were suspended in deep space, an illusion of the void outside *Iroquois* that doubled as a full-system tactical and astrographic display. Icons marked the position of his two starships, the four ten-ship squadrons of Katana starfighters flying

Carrier Area Patrol around the task group, and the wreck of *Penelope's Fault.*

The rocky planets and asteroids of the LKI-598 System weren't marked with icons, but a thought would bring the zoom in on any of them and provide detailed information on any given rock. The system required the crew to have modern neural implants, but every spacer in the DCN *had* those.

It was impressive technology, and at that moment, it was telling Anthony Yamamoto that his people were alone in a star system that had limited economic value except for some rocks unusually rich in superheavy metals.

"Q-probe network is spreading," his operations officer, Commodore Amos Peña, told him. "We have a sub-thirty-second delay out to fifteen light-minutes now."

There had been a time that a fleet would deploy enough q-probes—quantum-entanglement-communicator-equipped sensor probes—to provide *real-time* data across a bubble at least a light-hour out from the ship.

A single warship or two-ship group like Task Group *Iroquois* would have settled for sub-ten-second delays to about thirty light-minutes, meaning that no point in that bubble would be more than three million kilometers from a q-probe.

But the Commonwealth's q-coms infrastructure had been destroyed, and the Confederacy lived in the shadow of that catastrophe. Thanks to rapidly expanding production facilities and outside help, the Confederacy Navy now had enough entangled q-com blocks to deploy dozens of q-probes... but not the *hundreds* Commonwealth Navy doctrine had called for.

"Are we seeing anything in that bubble?" Anthony asked. "Our Crow is telling me that there is a decent chance that we might see the people who hit *Fault* come back through, thinking they had a safe place to sort out their loot and conceal it before heading into star systems where questions will be asked."

"Nothing yet," Peña said with a disgruntled snort. "I haven't had a chance to go over the records Rogers said they looked at. Until my people confirm what they said, I'm not buying it."

"We don't need to buy it, Commodore," Anthony said, giving his senior subordinate a level look. "We need to do our jobs and find the bastards if they do show."

"Our eyes are open; our probes are spread wide." The ops officer spread his hands in a shrug. "Biggest question is what do we do if they show? They're not going to be right here, and we've got almost four hundred people aboard *Penelope's Fault* still."

"Plus two squadrons of fighters in space," Anthony agreed. "No, we'll need to loop Captain Waterman in if you haven't already briefed him. We'll leave *Saratoga* in place and take *Iroquois* out to pin our pirates down."

Commodore Aku Waterman—addressed as *Captain* aboard his ship —was *Iroquois*'s commanding officer. Unlike most of the Dakotan Confederacy Navy's senior officers, he'd never been an officer in the Terran Commonwealth Navy, instead rising to his current rank in Gothic's security forces aboard sublight guardships.

Anthony suspected that politics had played a huge part in Waterman transferring from the defense forces of the third-most-popu-lated system in the old Dakota Sector to take command of the first eighty-million-cubic warship commissioned by the DCN. Still, Waterman was his flag captain, and while Anthony wasn't quite sure what he *needed* from a flag captain, the other man hadn't left him actively disappointed.

"He's received a basic update of Rogers' findings," Peña told him. "Should I advise him to get the ship ready for action?"

"If *Iroquois* isn't already prepared for action, we're in real trouble," Anthony said with a chuckle. "But yes, let's—"

"Contact!"

The single word barked aloud was only the beginning of the report from Anthony's analysis teams. More data flowed into his neural implant and onto the displays around him as every officer and analyst's attention shifted.

Alcubierre emergences were *very* visible. The entire point of the Stetson stabilizer systems was to stop them unleashing so much energy that a starship arrival was an inherent catastrophe. Thank-fully, an *un*-stabilized Alcubierre Drive created a bubble of warped space that was utterly destructive to anything contained within it.

Since the bubble contained its own drive systems, that meant that an Alcubierre Drive without Stetson stabilizers tended to be short-lived and extraordinarily energetic. Even with the stabilizers, though, the collapse of the drive field was a massive burst of radiation and energy clearly visible at significant distances.

As that initial burst faded, the q-probes around the contact were able to get a clear view of the ship from multiple angles.

"Contact is a freighter, fifty-five million cubic meters. Energy signatures suggest a moderate-mass cargo load, estimate fifteen million tons. Profile, size and mass are consistent with *Great Chicago Fire* as identified by *Fault's* records."

"And ours?" Anthony interrogated.

"Checking now... Yes, sir," the Commander running the numbers confirmed. "CIC is still checking some details, but they make it over a ninety percent likelihood we are looking at *Fire*."

Anthony was pulling the information into his own head and displays as the analyst spoke. *Great Chicago Fire* was at the outer edge of their probe bubble, almost sixteen light-minutes away around the arc of the star system.

A mental command opened a battle-command network, looping Waterman in with Peña and the rest of Anthony's key officers.

"CIC makes that our target, people," he told them. "I mark it at forty-five seconds since emergence, and time is fleeting. Time lag is sixteen minutes, almost exactly. Suggestions?"

"Depending on how much attention they're paying, they may already know we're here," Peña warned. "Neither *Iroquois* nor *Saratoga* have our sublight engines online, so we are harder to detect than we might otherwise be.

"But if they're specifically checking out the area around *Penelope's Fault*, they're going to notice the shuttles and starfighters."

"They haven't done anything yet to suggest they know there's anything going on," Waterman replied. "I recommend we move immediately, sir. Under full Alcubierre, we can reach their position in just under sixteen minutes.

"Regardless of their reaction, we can't change that time frame, and the sooner we move, the sooner we're on top of them—they *will* detect the A-S activation, but not until approximately the same time as our arrival."

Over longer distances, the trip would be more definitely faster than light, but the Alcubierre-Stetson accelerated at roughly one light-year per day per day, or approximately one hundred and thirty thousand gravities. The *average* over sixteen light-minutes was faster than light, with a peak of over twice lightspeed, but the activation itself took long enough that it would be seen around when they arrived.

"There's no point in waiting," Anthony agreed. "Does anyone have any reason we should not immediately go after *Great Chicago Fire*?"

"Do we have enough grounds to attack like this?" his legal officer asked.

"We have video footage from *Penelope's Fault* of *Great Chicago Fire* launching starfighters and assault shuttles to carry out a boarding action of the mining ship," Anthony replied. "I believe that more than suffices for us to demand her surrender so we can sweep her computers for more information?"

Tallulah Akecheta was a Dakotan lawyer who had only joined the Navy eighteen months earlier. In the six weeks she'd served as Anthony's legal officer, he'd found her inclined to challenge *everything* he did… and yet he found she had a surprisingly good head on her shoulders, and her refusal to fall into what the *Commonwealth* Navy had regarded as normal was good for all of them.

"I would like to review that evidence, if possible, sir," Akecheta told him mildly. "But if your description is correct, then that evidence suffices for us to *blow them to fucking hell.*"

Anthony smiled thinly. Someone, he suspected, had seen more of the footage from *Fault* than was really wise.

"I think we're aligned, then," he told his people. "Waterman, get your ship on the move. Bardakçı, you'll remain here to provide security for Fault and the search teams."

Commodore Gulshan Bardakçı's virtual avatar nodded grimly, *Saratoga*'s CO clearly having seen that coming.

"We've got your backs," he said calmly. "I doubt they're going to decide to cause trouble, but we'll watch the flock while you deal with the pirates."

The entire conversation had taken place in a virtual link, even the people in the same room subsumed into their implants—and so had taken under thirty seconds of real time.

"Make it happen, people," he ordered.

———

Iroquois was part of an entirely new generation of ships equipped with an entirely new generation of Stetson stabilizers. The four Class One mass manipulators that underlay her Alcubierre Drive weren't much different from the same systems a century or even two centuries earlier, but how large a ship could travel with a given drive was decided by how large a stabilized bubble could be created.

Saratoga would probably have been intimidating enough, though despite her positron lances and her starfighters, she was actually *smaller* than the pirate ship.

When the battlecruiser plunged back into reality in a blaze of bright-blue Cherenkov radiation, her presence alone made most of the points Anthony would have wanted. She was *thirty million cubic meters* bigger than her prey and crashed back into unwarped space less than half a million kilometers from the pirate ship.

"Target has electromagnetic deflectors!" someone snapped. "Contact has starfighters in space; running identification programs now."

"Get me a strength number on those deflectors," Waterman ordered before Anthony could say a word—and the Admiral swallowed his own reaction.

His job had ended when he'd given Waterman the order to take *Iroquois* into action. Commanding the battlecruiser through this fight was Waterman's job—though if the pirate ship's deflectors were powerful enough, even the battlecruiser's megaton-and-a-half-per-second main antimatter cannons might not be able to hit at this range.

"They're an anti-fighter screen at best," the battlecruiser's tactical officer reported. "We are inside our effective range."

"Fire a warning shot," Waterman said. "Full power, lance one, right across their bow."

A moment later, the computers drew a stark white line on Anthony's displays as one of *Iroquois*'s mighty positron lances spoke, making the reality of *Great Chicago Fire*'s position all too clear.

"Let me talk to them," Anthony said mildly. "Do we have a time on their ability to reactivate their drive?"

"At least ten minutes still," Peña told him.

An icon popped up on his implant, telling him he had a channel to activate at his command. Another icon in his vision told him where the pickup was, and he focused on it calmly.

"*Great Chicago Fire*, this is Vice Admiral Anthony Yamamoto aboard the DCN battlecruiser *Iroquois*," he told them. "We have reason to believe you were involved in an attack on a ship we located in this system. You *will* stand down and prepare to be boarded by Dakota Marines.

"If you do not, we will destroy you before you can enter FTL. Surrender now."

He sent the message and leaned back in his seat, watching as fighter squadrons blazed out from *Iroquois*'s launch bays.

"Get the fighter squadrons headed straight for her," he ordered. "They're more able to disable her than *Iroquois* is, and if she doesn't surrender, I still want to take her intact."

"We can probably manage that from here," Waterman pointed out.

"If we hit *Great Chicago Fire*'s antimatter engines with a *fifteen-hundred-kiloton-per-second* heavy positron lance, there won't be enough left of that ship to do spectrographic analysis on, let alone board and retrieve systems from."

His flag captain chuckled.

"Major Iordanou requests permission to deploy assault shuttles," Waterman told Anthony. "She seems a bit, uh, *peeved* at these people."

"Get the shuttles in space, but keep them in the lee of *Iroquois* until they either surrender or the starfighters have neutralized the defense," Anthony replied.

Iroquois was moving toward the freighter at a gentle and high-efficiency fifty gravities. Her *starfighters,* on the other hand, were screaming across the intervening space at five hundred gravities.

"Incoming response, sir. We have a live channel."

"Connect it to myself and Captain Waterman," Anthony ordered. At just over three seconds' total lag, they were close enough for a reasonable conversation.

The woman who appeared on his screen looked like someone's grandmother, a gray-haired woman shrunk somewhat by age and time. For all of her venerability, though, she was clearly hale and hearty—and something in her near-black eyes told Anthony he *definitely* had the right person.

"What is the meaning of this, Admiral?" she demanded. "*Great Chicago Fire* is flagged to the Tau Ceti System and flies under the authority of the Terran Commonwealth. We have done nothing requiring or allowing the Confederacy to engage in this kind of brutish behavior. We will not allow ourselves to be bullied!"

The implication, of course, was that any action against *Fire* would potentially be an act of war against the Rump Commonwealth, the remnant of the Commonwealth under the control of the Imperator.

Which was… quite the line of bollocks. Especially given the information that was scrolling across Anthony's implant, coming from both Jessie Rogers and Tallulah Akecheta.

"I presume I am speaking to the Captain of *Great Chicago Fire,*" Anthony said calmly. "I am surprised, Captain, by your claim of Tau Ceti registry, as you reported a *Blyton*-system registration when you docked in Gothic last week.

"Regardless of your system of registry, however, the general laws of space recognize the LKI-Five-Ninety-Eight System as being part of the jurisdiction of the Dakotan Interstellar Confederacy," he continued. "As such, if we have grounds to believe you have been involved in high crimes and misdemeanors, we have every right to halt your ship for search and examination.

"Your arrival in this system—a system home only to a murdered mining ship—is questionable enough, Captain, but I also have to note that the starfighters you have deployed are *illegal* for civilian possession in both Confederacy and Commonwealth space. Also in Blyton space, if you want to change your story on your registration," he added.

"The presence of your starfighters alone justifies our boarding and inspection of your vessel. You *will* stand down, Captain, or I will order my starfighters and this cruiser to fire into your vessel as necessary to render boarding safe for my Marines.

"Choose."

"I am a citizen of the Terran Commonwealth and I will *not* be bullied!" she barked.

"Then you will be compelled," Anthony replied. He cut the channel and sighed.

"Fighters are to target *Chicago Fire*'s engines," he ordered. "If possible, let's try not to vaporize the whole ship—but, frankly, I understand the risk of firing positron beams into—"

"Sir! New transmission!"

"Well, did she wake up?" Anthony asked aloud. "Reconnect us."

The *location* of the video was the same, a standard civilian bridge with minimal decoration. The room was spacious enough, with each console having plenty of room—and, Anthony suspected, enough space to hide consoles managing such things as weapons and fighter direction.

The person standing in the center of the pickup was different this time. The person facing them was a Black woman. She still wasn't young, but she was clearly *much* younger than the Captain.

"I am Chidi Steiner," she told Anthony, her voice trembling. "I am the purser and third officer aboard *Great Chicago Fire*. Um. Um." She swallowed, trying to find words. "I have implemented a security lockdown on the bridge, and I *think* I have shut down the defenses. I have *definitely* shut down the Alcubierre Drive.

"If you are prepared to guarantee clemency for..." She swallowed again, then repeated herself. "If you are prepared to guarantee the lives of the seven surviving bridge officers, we believe we can trigger a full lockdown of *Chicago Fire*, which will allow your Marines safe boarding."

Anthony concealed his grimace inside his head. Even Dakota, the capital planet of the Confederacy and driven by a judicial culture of *restitution before retribution,* left the death penalty on the books for truly egregious crimes.

Piracy wasn't actually one of them… but *mass murder* was.

"I am prepared to guarantee that the death penalty will not be considered for any member of *Great Chicago Fire*'s crew that lays down their arms and surrenders *now*," he told Steiner grimly. "Anyone who resists my Marines will be met with lethal force, and anyone taken prisoner by force of arms *will* suffer the full weight of Confederacy law."

"That is… enough," Steiner said quietly. "We will lose communications. I am about to kill power to the entire ship."

Anthony didn't even have a chance to respond before the channel cut off—but the sensor feeds were clear that she wasn't bluffing.

He exhaled a slow breath and considered the situation, then shook his head.

"Send in the Marines," he ordered. "Have the fighters provide close cover, just in case."

"You think it's a trap?" Waterman asked.

"I think we cannot afford to assume it isn't."

3

ANTHONY KNEW where his skills lay. He could coordinate a starfighter strike in his sleep, manage the morale of a hundred high-ego fighter flight crews with ease, and even transfer those skills to the command of a two-ship battlegroup with around twelve thousand people under his command.

He knew nothing useful about Marines and boarding operations, so he kept his mouth shut and his hands to himself as Major Iordanou and her people stormed *Great Chicago Fire*.

Still, he thought he had been keeping an eye and ear on things, which meant he was a touch discomfited at being called down to one of the shuttle bays for a *surprise* from the Major.

Each of *Iroquois*'s two secondary shuttle bays held between forty and sixty small craft, which meant they were cavernous voids exceeded only by the main starfighter flight deck and a couple of key engineering spaces in size. With most of the small craft in space, shuttling Marines and prisoners back and forth from the pirate freighter, much of that space was even *open* at that moment... and surprisingly empty.

Enough prisoners had been hauled aboard the battlecruiser that he was expecting to see a lot more Marines as he entered the open bay. He was expecting more *people* in general, which made it swiftly clear that either *this* bay wasn't being used at all for the operations on *Great Chicago Fire*—or that Waterman and Iordanou had temporarily diverted all of the ops to the other bay or the main flight deck.

A single assault shuttle—still a Terran Commonwealth Marine Corps Pelican-2730, though the DCMC called it a Heron—slowly drifted into the bay on momentum alone as Anthony joined the small group of Marines forming what he recognized as an honor guard.

"Here, sir," a Master Sergeant, the only Marine in dress uniform instead of power armor, told him. She was indicating a specific point, presumably where the honor guard would guide whoever they were waiting for to.

"What's going on, Sergeant Clover?" Anthony asked. "The Admiral is not supposed to get *surprises*, Master Sergeant."

"Fucked if I know," the Marine noncom said. "Major told me to prep an honor guard and be ready for you to join us. Whatever this is, she didn't want it on the radio."

Anthony nodded silently and took the indicated spot. His own shadows, two Marines in armored dress uniforms like Master Sergeant Clover's, took up flanking positions behind him as the bay's mass manipulators used gravity fields to gently pull the shuttle down to the deck.

The first people off the shuttle were much what he was expecting, a quartet of his own Marines, still in powered armor from the board action.

The *second* group of people, however, were something else entirely. They *moved* like Marines, but they wore undress uniforms that had clearly been lived in for days at least. Their lack of dress didn't stop the four soldiers from spreading out into a protective box, surveying the shuttle bay for threats, and clearly hoping against hope that Anthony's people *were* friendly.

"VIP security detail," Sergeant Rosenberger, the senior Marine in Anthony's detail, noted in his implant. "Uniforms suggest military, but I'm not familiar with them—but the doctrine and pattern are private security."

That was more than *Anthony* could have picked up from how the four troopers had moved out of the shuttle and taken position. They were, he noted absently, armed—but the weapons belted at their waists were clearly *Dakotan* stunners.

Iordanou had clearly equipped them to allow them to fulfill their bodyguard role but hadn't wanted to allow an actual *threat* to *her* Admiral. Which begged the question, of course, of *who* the newcomers were bodyguarding.

The answer followed the source of the question, as a helmetless but still power-armored Major Iordanou exited the shuttle behind the bodyguards, escorting a pale and clearly injured man who appeared to have escaped some accounting guild's magazine covers.

The stranger was almost as tall as Anthony, the Admiral judged, but had the gaunt and sallow build of someone who got neither enough light nor enough food entirely by choice. Or at least distraction.

From the state of the suit he wore, it *had* been impeccably tailored, and the ragged mix of stubble and goatee on the man's face had probably been impeccably groomed. Something had gone very wrong for the stranger, but he straightened as he saw Anthony.

He then winced and collapsed back into the somewhat-hunched position around his side.

"Admiral, I need to introduce you to Envoy Andreas Weaver of the Weston Republic," Iordanou told Anthony as she led the man up to him. She produced a small black folio from the storage of her armor and passed it to him.

"All of his documents are on the chips. We validated them as best as we could aboard *Great Chicago Fire*, but a full check-in would require q-com access, and I wasn't sure we could risk revealing his presence by sending a transmission.

"*Someone*, after all, managed to set a pirate ship on his transport."

It was possible, Anthony reflected, that the pirate ship had just randomly found and ambushed an Ambassador coming to the Dakotan Confederacy. Possible… But then, *he* wouldn't have been expecting anyone to come to Dakota from the Weston Sector.

Assuming this Republic was anchored on the old Sector, that put them almost two hundred light-years away, a third of the way around the Old Commonwealth.

"Admiral… Yamamoto, yes?" Weaver asked, straightening more carefully. "Your Major has the rough precis of my role, yes. I am tasked to act as Ambassador to the Dakotan Interstellar Confederacy on behalf of the Weston Republic.

"I am Vice Admiral Anthony Yamamoto," Anthony confirmed, letting his burr stretch for the gentle reminder that he was *far* from as Japanese as he looked. "I am in command of Task Group *Iroquois*. I wasn't expecting to encounter any diplomats aboard a pirate ship."

"As you can imagine, one presumes, I was not aboard *Great Chicago Fire* voluntarily," the Weston man said. "Our transport was overrun by these… *people* about two weeks ago, on the outer edge of the Desdemona System.

"The details are not relevant at this moment," he continued. "I can share them if you wish, but I must apologize. I am fatigued and our captors were… not gentle, even after they realized that killing me was neither wise nor profitable.

"I *must* speak with your political and military leadership as swiftly as possible, Admiral. I bear news and dispatches of the utmost import." He sighed, wincing as he accidentally moved too far for his ribs.

"For now, Envoy, I think you must see our ship's *doctor* as swiftly as possible," Anthony suggested. "Once you have been cleared for more intense conversation, I want to know what's going on that brings you all this way."

And while the Envoy was being seen, Anthony needed to regather his ships. There hopefully wouldn't be too much left to do aboard *Great Chicago Fire* and, well, they'd learned everything from *Penelope's Fault* they could.

Even if Weaver's dispatches weren't as important as the man

figured, they had a duty to deliver the Ambassador to Dakota. And, conveniently, that was the next place Anthony's task group was supposed to go anyway.

Though they *had* missed Confederacy Day and the rest of the parties that would be taking place that day.

4

Dakota System
10:00 January 9, 2740 ESMDT

As the parade float—Fleet Admiral James Tecumseh could think of no better descriptor for the open-topped vehicle—pulled out into the tree-lined streets of Dakota's capital city, Táálaʼíʼtsin, he reflected on how thoroughly he'd been played.

In the distance, he could see the immense kilometer-tall shadow of the Lonely Tree itself, the massive Dakotan greatwood that anchored the largest city on Dakota. Closer in, though, all he could hear were the cheers of the crowd as he headed toward his wedding.

When his fiancée, Dakota's elected planetary First Chief, had suggested they get married on Confederacy Day, he'd agreed on the impression that they would use the distraction of the festivities to have a nice, *quiet* ceremony.

James knew, without any false modesty, that he was a *good* tactician and strategist. There were people who were better than him at both in the universe, but they weren't common. Unfortunately, his wife-to-be appeared to be one of them.

His wedding wasn't being concealed under the festivities honoring the second anniversary of the decision to declare independence from Terra. It had been made the *centerpiece* of the festivities, and there had to be twenty thousand people lining the route as his float made its way to the foot of the Lone Tree, Táála'í'tsin itself.

"Count is thirty-two thousand and rising," a clipped voice said in his mental ear, as if Shannon Reynolds had followed his thought. The ex-Commonwealth assassin had declared herself his bodyguard a long time before—and while her *official* position hadn't changed, everyone who knew anything knew she was also the operational chief of the Dakotan Confederacy Reconnaissance Organization.

Right now, the Crows were in charge of security for the Confederacy Day festivities, including James's wedding. And somehow, despite being calmly seated in the car behind him, Reynolds was running the whole affair.

"I don't dislike crowds or public speaking," he sent back silently. "I'm an *Admiral*, for crying out loud. But this is... something else."

He waved to the crowd as the float turned a corner, the back of his mind linking to *one* of the datafeeds Reynolds was receiving. That feed overlay the security measures on the crowds around him.

Thirty-two thousand civilians lined the streets, cheering the man the Confederacy's leaders had made a *mascot* of their freedom—a role James chafed at but couldn't argue at the need for. Except... No, he followed the data on the feed and chuckled to himself.

Thirty-two thousand civilians lined the streets *he* was following to Táála'í'tsin. *Another* twenty-odd thousand were lining the avenue that Abey Todacheeney, First Chief of Dakota, was taking to the tree.

No man could make Admiral without enough of a competitive streak to be pleased he'd drawn the larger crowd than his wife-to-be. There were, of course, downsides to that—but his security overlay reassured him somewhat.

There were Marines and security officers scattered through the crowds in covert body armor. Concealed sensor platforms swept the whole affair for weapons, while rapid reaction teams with assault shuttles and aerial fast movers lurked just out of sight.

For that matter, James knew that the battleship *Choctaw* hung in a powered orbit directly above the city. Commodore Erzsébet Mašek wasn't even being *subtle* about the positioning of the kilometer-and-a-half-long *Cherokee*-class battleship. She was *visible* from the surface, though at a distance where he could block out the shadow with his thumb.

"Everything is as secure as physically possible," Reynolds told him. "Do you think for one second I would let you be out here if I thought someone could sneak a sniper rifle in?"

"Someone can *always* sneak a sniper rifle in," James replied grimly. "The risk is just worth it. Abey and I need to be seen, whether you and I like it or not."

"If you want, we can record all this and send it to Earth," the assassin-turned-bodyguard suggested. He could *hear* her sickly sweet smile as he waved to the crowd. "This is *exactly* the kind of voluntary adoration the Imperator wants—and *he* spent decades cultivating a cult of personality to get half of this.

"You just did the right thing and are more beloved than he'll ever be. Might just kill him with apoplexy and save us some effort."

"Let the news media handle that," James told her. "No assassination attempts, no matter how indirect. We are not technically at war with the Rump."

Reynolds snorted.

"Has anybody asked *them* their opinion of that?" she asked drily. "*They* were the ones who sent a fleet *here*, after all."

They were also, unfortunately, not technically at *peace* with the Rump either.

───────

Tááła'í'tsin was unlike anything James had ever seen before coming to Dakota. He'd seen Dakotan greatwoods and even the Lone Tree now—if nothing else, the city of Tááła'í'tsin was woven through and intermingled with an entire *forest* of old- growth greatwoods, even if none of them approached Tááła'í'tsin in scale—but they were unique to his new home.

The largest of the trees there was the biggest on the planet and, he suspected, one of if not *the* biggest tree known to humanity in the galaxy. Over a hundred and fifty meters wide at the base, the "shadow of Táádła'í'tsin" created a zone clear of other trees roughly half as wide as the tree itself was tall.

As he understood it, the original planetary government had talked about putting the government buildings in that shadow. Instead, though, they'd declared the entire area a park where no permanent buildings were ever to be erected.

The shade of the monster tree limited what could grow there, but it also made the space muffled and comforting. A careful intermingling of both native Dakotan plants and Terran plants wove around flag-stone patios and hand-carved wooden benches and statuary, creating a public space both immense in scale and intimate in effect.

The intimacy, he supposed, was somewhat lost as fifty thousand people closed in behind the two separated parades and began to fill the plazas. At first glance, only the gentlest of suggestions and lines were in place to control the crowds, too—though the visible lines were backed by virtual avatars gently inserting themselves into everyone's implants.

The Marines were more visible there, clad in gorgeously bedecked dress uniforms carrying polished gold coyote insignia on both their lapels and the almost-never-worn dark-green peaked caps. While it might appear that each Marine was being expected to watch a line a hundred meters wide, everyone—including, James presumed, the crowd—knew there was a lot more to guard the lines than those widely spread decorated troopers.

Five Marines were waiting for him as the parade float came to a stop, headed by Major Arlene Revie. The young woman had headed his bodyguard detail since the declaration of independence and would stand at his back today.

Reynolds fell in with the five Marines, James's escorts wordlessly forming a hexagon around him—as a blinking set of pale gold arrows appeared in his vision. His implant had received directions as to where he was supposed to go.

"Well, Admiral, shall we go make an honest man of you?" Reynolds said with a chuckle. "And don't worry; my orders are clear. If you try to run, we're to be *subtle* about dragging you to the altar!"

A set of drums led the rhythmic stomping of thousands of feet as James's bodyguards led him to the hollow at the very base of the tree, where a tiny group of people was waiting for him. Only years of training and some key cybernetic augmentations gave him enough situational awareness to be aware of anyone other than the woman in the white suit standing in the center of the dell.

Abey Todacheeney was, in his admittedly biased opinion, the most gorgeous, sensible, intelligent, thoughtful, brilliant and amazing woman ever to be elected head of state for an entire planet. She was a stockily built woman at least a decade younger than him, with black hair that hung to her waist and dark eyes that looked clean through the soul of everyone she looked at.

Her white suit—the latest in fashion on Dakota these days, as they didn't have enough of a communication link to Earth to regularly follow Terran fashion—matched the core feathers of her headdress, though the coordinated tones only drew out the riotous colors of the *rest* of her headdress.

James would admit that his connection to his own Shawnee heritage had been weak at best when he'd arrived on Dakota, but the planet's people were driven to sustain as much of the Old Nations' culture they'd brought with them as possible.

He didn't understand what all of the feathers and tokens in his bride's headdress meant—only that each and every one of them meant *something,* and that Abey herself had little or no say in what was included in the headdress.

There were only two such headdresses, including Abey's, in the hollow they were using for the core ceremony. James only had eyes for Abey, but he was *aware* of the delicately built form of President Quetzalli Chapulin, the head of state for the entire Confederacy and the *officiant* for today's ceremony.

As he crossed the hollow toward Abey, his bodyguard party split to smoothly take up positions around the outer edge of the plaza. They almost certainly *had* rehearsed the maneuver, and James found himself delivered unerringly to a spot directly in front of Chapulin, facing Abey Todacheeney in the shadow of Tááła'í'tsin itself.

"Hey," he whispered as he half-consciously reached out to take her hands.

"Hey yourself," she told him. "Looking good."

James was in the full dress uniform of a Confederacy Admiral. He probably *could* have designed it to be whatever he wanted it to be, but in practice, it was a shockingly white version of his normal uniform.

"You too."

A soft drizzling sound began to echo down from above. It was raining, James realized, though all that made it through the shelter of the massive tree was a slowly descending mist.

Chapulin cleared her throat brightly as the stomping and drums came to a crescendo and then cut to silence.

"Shall we begin, my friends?"

5

Dakota System
14:00 January 9, 2740 ESMDT

THE ACTUAL WEDDING ceremony itself took about fifteen minutes, but it was four hours later before James Tecumseh and his new wife finally found themselves with a moment of peace and quiet for more than a traditional public kiss.

Not that they had time for more than a slightly more passionate private kiss, even though their combined staffs had split off to give them privacy—and would probably fight to the death to *protect* that privacy.

"Your grandmother looks happy," Abey told him when they came up for air. "And smug."

"The last conversation she and I had before we lost the q-com network was about how I should get married," James admitted with a smile. "And I'm *still* not entirely sure how she got from Terra to here... and I'm not asking too many questions!"

From his conversations with Nizhoni Tecumseh since her arrival on Dakota, it had been a smooth and painless extraction. Given that there was *no way* Imperator Walkingstick hadn't ordered James's family watched, he could only imagine how much work Reynolds' people had done to pull that off.

"I'm glad the Crows did it," Abey said. She was still holding his hands and he was *not* taking them back. "Neither of us could order it, not really, but I know you weren't comfortable with her being on Terra."

"I…" James trailed off, glancing away from his wife—the word sent happy tremors through his heart and stomach—for a few long moments. "I did not and do not believe that she was in danger there. James Walkingstick has honor. It is a flexible honor, one prone to fits of convenience, but it exists.

"And harassing my grandmother would never have served his purposes."

"I'm *still* glad she's here," Abey told him, pulling him in closer and leaning her head on his shoulder in a moment of softness he doubted she'd show in public.

"Me too."

He was about to ask what the next thing on their ridiculously packed schedule was when his implant chirped inside his head.

"Tecumseh." His response wasn't aloud, though he knew Abey would recognize the signs of him linking into an implant call.

"Sir, I don't think there are *words* for how much I hate interrupting you," Senior Chief Petty Officer Sallie Leeuwenhoek told him. "And the wonderful collection of Admirals you have as a staff have, of course, dumped that responsibility on me."

"I suspect, Sallie, they dumped the *choice* on you," James told his personal steward, the woman who ran his life and had helped arrange at *least* a quarter of his wedding—despite several *hundred* people being involved in said arranging. "Because they knew you'd make the right call.

"What's going on?"

"We have two alpha-priority requests for communication," she told him. "That actually… uh… *are* alpha priority, I think. One is Admiral Yamamoto. The other is… Mister Glass, sir."

James grimaced. *Mister Glass* was a high-level covert operative for the Castle Federation, first among equals of the Alliance of Free Stars whose victory over the Terran Commonwealth had led, seemingly inevitably, to its collapse and his current position.

They were also the only reason the Confederacy had started rebuilding their q-com network as quickly as they did. Even with Glass's covert assistance, the Confederacy had slowly fallen behind the Rump Commonwealth in the penetration and availability of FTL coms… but the Federation's supplies had turned a critical moment in Dakota's favor.

"I have Glass trying to contact me," he told Abey. "Is there somewhere here we can set up a call?"

James figured Glass knew perfectly well it was his wedding day. The man could damn well talk to the second-most senior member of the Confederacy's government.

And since the building they'd taken temporary "shelter" in belonged to the planetary government, he figured Abey could tell him where to find a secure conference room.

"Tell Yamamoto to be patient," he instructed Leeuwenhoek. "He is *almost* my highest priority, but I *did* just get married, and one of the… oh… *two* other people who might have been able to interrupt me also called."

———

After over a year of working with the man, James Tecumseh had made enough quiet inquiries to be sure who, roughly, "Mister Glass" actually was. The main conclusion he'd drawn from that was that the man had done an exemplary job of staying out of the Commonwealth's files on its key enemies! But he was also reasonably sure that he was talking to one of the senior Admirals of the Castle Federation's Naval Intelligence operations.

He just wasn't entirely sure which one, and the level of editing he could guess at when Glass's image appeared above the desk didn't help. The space Abey had commandeered belonged to a senior treasury officer for the planetary government, which meant it had fully secure local coms systems that they could use to relay up to *Choctaw*.

The battleship carried entangled blocks for both the Confederacy's new q-com network and the Castle Federation's existing network. The latter had helped keep the Confederacy intact over the last two years, and while they were less *essential* now, James figured having a backup coms system relaying through a switchboard a few hundred light-years away didn't hurt!

They wouldn't *trust* it as much as coms they controlled themselves, but if something horrific happened to the new communications network, they'd still have a backup. The Confederacy's new network was structured around more, smaller, switchboard stations than the Commonwealth's had been—but even the TCN had thought they had enough backups.

And they'd been wrong.

"Admiral Tecumseh, First Chief Todacheeney," the holographic Glass greeted them. He was an elderly man, with a nearly translucent white goatee and no other hair. Age appeared to have done a number on the spy, and James didn't trust the Federation man's apparent infirmity one millimeter.

"Mister Glass," James replied. "I hope this is important. This is not exactly a day I was expecting to be interrupted."

"I know. Congratulations to you both, by the way," Glass told them. "I imagine my *personal* wedding gift is buried under some vast pile of presents from assorted well-wishers, but I assure you it *does* exist."

James was unsurprised that Glass knew about the wedding. He was mildly surprised that the man had sent them an actual wedding gift—though he did believe the spy that said gift existed.

"Thank you," James said carefully. "Though I imagine we're using a covert and secured communication channel for more than just your best wishes."

"You're right." Glass smiled. "First, I should tell you that we won't be using a covert channel for much longer." He paused, clearly gauging their reactions. "The Senate and Assembly of the Castle Federation voted this morning, my friends, to fully and formally recognize the Dakotan Interstellar Confederacy and to normalize our diplomatic and interstellar relations.

"I imagine that Ambassador Florentine will have some fancy gift worthy of my government when they arrive in Dakota in a few weeks," he continued. "I will admit that the formal recognition is a major relief off my shoulders, as we will be able to *officially* provide much of the support we've been keeping under the radar for the last twenty-odd months.

"Also important to recognize is that this is a coordinated recognition," Glass said. "The Coraline Imperium, the Renaissance Trade Factor, the Star Kingdom of Phoenix and half a dozen single star system states that matter to *me*, if not you, have also agreed on that recognition and normalization.

"Congratulations are in order." Glass's smile widened into a very pleased grin. "You are the *first* Successor State of the Terran Commonwealth anyone in the Alliance of Free Stars has chosen to recognize."

"That's... huge," Abey said quietly, reaching over out of the hologram pickup to squeeze James's leg. "That opens a lot of options once we speak with this Ambassador Florentine. And the timing of it on Confederacy Day seems..."

"Intentional," the spy told her. "It, of course, *seems* provident and portentous, but this is interstellar politics. We make our own portents."

"I figured," she replied.

"So, congratulations on your wedding," Glass said. "Your wedding present from the Castle Federation is formal recognition of your star nation. Ambassador Florentine will have quite the list of position papers to present when they begin discussions. Trade agreements, potential military-aid pacts. All kinds of things."

"We've come a long way."

"You have. But I do have one piece of grimmer business to discuss," Glass told them. "You are aware of the courses taken by Admirals Rao, Morris, and Verity, yes?"

James grimaced. Vice Admirals Harendra Rao and Celestine Morris had commanded sector fleets for the Commonwealth. Rear Admiral Surinder Verity had been a more junior officer, commanding a deployed task group.

All three of them had become exactly what everyone had feared of TCN senior officers when the Commonwealth had collapsed: warlords, using the ships and troops under their command to seize entire star systems as their own pocket empires. Rao and Morris had bitten off more than they could chew, from what James had heard, where Verity had leveraged their initially smaller force to violent perfection and now controlled half of the sector they'd started in.

"Warlords and pirates," he told Glass. "Traitors to their oaths and their uniforms." He sighed. "The last can be applied to myself and most of my officers, too, so I can't complain *too* loudly."

"But they are warlords, dictators of fourteen star systems between them," Glass told him. "And it is, now, between them. According to our intelligence, they have united their forces and territories under the label of the Triumvirate.

"We don't know what their plans are, and frankly, they are on the far side of the Commonwealth from us," the spy continued. "They are even less in our zone of attention than the Confederacy—we had eyes on the Stellar League, after all. Now... they may be the greatest threat the stars of the former Commonwealth are going to face.

"If I thought I could point them at Walkingstick and no one else, I'd think they might be useful. As it is, though..."

James looked at Abey and shook his head slightly.

"They're a long damn way from us," he pointed out. "*Earth* is closer."

"I suspect, though I don't have information on the coreward regions of the former Commonwealth to say for certainty, that what happens with the Triumvirate may well decide *everything* about the fate of the Successor States," Glass told them. "So, I'm attaching all the information we have. Consider it a courtesy warning, Admiral, First Chief.

"The Triumvirate is not and will never be a threat to the Alliance of Free Stars. But they are in a position to shape the future of the Successor States... and I can't help but think you're not going to like the direction they'll take it in."

———

A few more pleasantries and then James and Abey were on the *next* call. The disadvantage of having interstellar communications back,

James reflected, was that urgent things really *could* interrupt every-thing, even from almost thirty light-years away.

Yamamoto looked like he'd been waiting patiently enough, though James didn't know the other man to *ever* look impatient.

"Anthony. You *know* what today is," he pointed out.

"And we're about ten minutes from having to leave," Abey added. "Neither of us gets large open gaps in our schedule, especially today. So, this *better* be important."

From her tone, Abey had very carefully scheduled this private time. James had fallen into work brain dealing with it all, and only the edge to her voice made him really recognize the interruption.

He suspected he was going to pay for that later, though Abey was *generally* understanding of that kind of slip.

"Some of it could wait," the Vice Admiral conceded, bowing his head slightly to Abey. "I... um. I didn't consider the issue of inter-rupting post-wedding time."

Anthony Yamamoto, James reflected, didn't understand how rela-tionships and romance worked in general. James had seen that in action over the last two years, and this *wasn't* the first time the other man had accidentally stepped all over someone else's romantic plans without realizing what he was doing.

"Well, you already have, so talk quickly," James ordered.

"Okay." For a moment, Yamamoto seemed nonplussed, then he seemed to mentally shrug and forge ahead. "We successfully inter-cepted and captured a lightly armed freighter that had been engaging in piracy along our border with the former Brillig Sector. While we're still in the process of interviewing prisoners and so forth, I've made the executive decision to detach *Saratoga* and Captain Bardakçı to finish prisoner rendition.

"*Iroquois* will warp space in six hours, en route back to the Dakota System at maximum speed. Estimated time of arrival is early morning on the twentieth."

"That's at your discretion," James said quietly. But it was unex-pected for Yamamoto to split his task group, even if the Starfighter Corps Vice Admiral *was* eager to return to his regular not-quite-desk job. The short-term task group command had been *James's* plan, adding some key seasoning to the officer who was going to be commanding Dakota's Starfighter Corps for the next few decades.

"We have a complication and that's why I'm contacting you," Yamamoto replied. "Turns out that our opportunistic pirates were either working for the Rump Commonwealth or stumbled onto some folks the Rump and others would pay richly for.

"Their most recent capture was carrying a consular mission from the Weston Republic. Envoy Andreas Weaver was apparently on his way to set up a permanent embassy with us—and the conversation I've had with him suggests there's going to be an immediate request of some kind."

Yamamoto shrugged.

"His documents check out, and he's asked to speak to our civil and military leadership as quickly as possible. What I wasn't so sure of, I'll admit, was whether to reveal that we had enough q-com capability for him to have a live virtual conference *now*."

Technically, control over the secrecy of the quantum-entanglement communication network *was* in James's hands. In this instance, though, he shook his head with a side glance at his wife.

Using that descriptor for Abey still made his heart skip a couple of beats.

"Holding an Envoy from another Successor State incommunicado for eleven days is a *political* decision, Admiral, not a military or operational one," James warned. "We can run the call by President Chapulin, but... frankly... I don't see any reason *to* keep that secret. We're about to open the network up to broad civilian usage.

"Let's not start off an international relationship keeping secrets that are going to be obvious inside a few weeks," he concluded. "Send an official request to the Cabinet for an audience for your new friend and let the administration sort it all out."

"And you can do that without us," Abey said sweetly, smiling to take the sting out of her words. "The Cabinet will want to meet with the Envoy and we'll be there. But I think that's all you need us for now, right, Anthony?"

Even Anthony Yamamoto could take *that* hint.

"Congratulations and good luck with your marriage," he told them with a chuckle. "I'll see about the Cabinet call, I suppose."

Abey cut the communicator with a gesture and looked darkly at James.

"I think I screwed up," she told him.

"Love?"

He *watched* the single word soften her stressed shoulders.

"You wanted a quiet ceremony. *I* wanted to use our wedding, however personally important, to secure the traditions and pageantry of our new nation—and demonstrate your loyalty and reliability to our people once more," she said.

"But with a *quiet* ceremony, I could have justified taking the two of us somewhere without communications and actually having a honeymoon in hiding somewhere."

James laughed softly as he took her hands.

"My love, my Abey, my wife," he told her with a smile and a kiss. "*Neither* of us is capable of actually stepping away from our duties for that long."

"I know," she conceded. "But I know Anthony Yamamoto too, almost as well as you do. *He* thinks this is war. And I know you too damn well to think that *war* isn't going to steal my husband away right after the wedding."

He winced.

"A bit early to fear that, isn't it?" he asked.

"Maybe," she conceded. "But I know *you*, James Tecumseh. If the Weston Republic calls for help, do you have it in you to let their call go unanswered?"

"That decision is no longer mine," James said after a moment. *He* didn't, not really. But he would obey the orders of the President and Cabinet of the Dakotan Interstellar Confederacy.

She sighed and pulled him to her. He embraced her tightly in turn, and they were both silent for a long time.

They both knew she was right. He wouldn't make the call, but the Cabinet would *listen* to him. And just as James Tecumseh knew he could never pull Abey Todacheeney away from the planet she led, *she* knew he couldn't be detached from his people and his fleet.

6

BETWEEN CONFEDERACY DAY and his wedding, James had been up very late the previous night. He and Abey had been *supposed* to have the entire day after free from work, but when the first diplomatic contact from another Successor State happened…

He suspected that Chapulin had pushed the meeting until late in the day by Earth Standard Meridian Time—thankfully, *roughly* aligned with Táála'í'tsin's twenty-four-hour-and-sixteen-minute day right then —to give him and Abey *some* quiet time.

That time was sadly now past and he was back in his normal working dress blacks. If he was attending the meeting virtually from the spare office in Abey's apartment, well, that was hardly relevant when the man presenting was aboard a starship in warped space twenty-six-odd light-years away.

Abey was in the *main* office in her apartment, also attending virtu-ally. The "apartment" in question was the official residence of the First Chief and occupied an entire floor of the complex administration and residence building that wrapped itself around eleven greatwoods on the north end of Táálaʼíʼtsin.

The suite was *bigger* than his quarters aboard *Krakatoa*. While the *Volcano*-class carrier he used as a flagship was smaller than the new ships, she was still nearly a kilometer long. The builders hadn't skimped on the spaces for a flag officer aboard her.

Still, the virtual reality he was immersed in put him in the main Cabinet meeting room in the Confederacy Building. Built as the Commonwealth Dakota Infrastructure Center, the Confederacy Building now served as the central administrative hub of the Confederacy's government.

In the illusion, he joined sixteen politicians—including his wife—around a large table made from a single slice of greatwood trunk. Some of the politicians were physically present, but he figured at least half were holographic representations like him.

Not that it was possible to tell from inside the virtual reality he occupied. He was vaguely aware of the office he was *actually* present in, but that awareness mostly came from the fact that Abey's German Shepherd mix had decided that his feet were cold.

All twenty-plus kilograms of Sherlock were wrapped around James's legs, which made it impossible to *completely* tune out his physical location. Tradition said the First Chief adopted a shelter dog to keep them humble, though he suspected that at least *half* of the thought process was to get an animal to provide emotional and moral support for the job!

James knew every one of the politicians around the table, one Minister for each of the fifteen systems of the Dakotan Confederacy. Twelve were from the original Dakota and Meridian Sectors that had voted to form the Confederacy two years ago the previous day.

The other three were from Testament, Chatham and Corellia, three systems that requested to join the Confederacy. Corellia was from the old Brillig Sector and part of why the Confederacy paid so much attention to that region.

Testament and Chatham were from the Icon and Oregon Sectors, systems close to the Meridian Sector that had found themselves looking at overly eager Stellar League conquistadors and condottieri and decided they needed bigger and more-local friends than Terra.

All three system governments had all but *begged* to join the Dakotan Confederacy—and given how opposed the core government of Dakota was to expansionism, not much less would have led to their voluntary annexation.

From James's perspective, it was relevant that they'd brought exactly *one* capital ship and zero warship building slips with them. None of the three new systems was *poor*, per se, but they hadn't possessed immediately useful military assets.

Right now, though, they added to the collection of locals arranged around the table and facing the spot where the new Ambassador should appear right about... then.

Envoy Andreas Weaver made a surprisingly good first impression for someone who'd just been a prisoner, James judged. He wore a perfectly tailored suit that looked like it was freshly cleaned and pressed and had an impeccably-groomed short goatee and neatly clipped hair.

"Thank you all for seeing me," he began. "I am Envoy Andreas Weaver. I bear documents confirming my position as an Ambassador Plenipotentiary for the Weston Republic." He grimaced helplessly.

"Unfortunately, the quantum communicator I had for staying in touch with the Republic was destroyed by the pirates who kidnapped me," he noted. "I have no ability to contact Parliament or the President to provide additional confirmation."

"We have reviewed the documents forwarded by Vice Admiral Yamamoto," Chapulin told him. "We are prepared to accept your bona fides based on them, though I must note that they seem very light on details of what you are expecting to accomplish here."

The President, a former Terran Commonwealth Marine despite her delicate build and height, gave Weaver a small bow.

"I am Quetzalli Chapulin," she introduced herself. "I am the directly elected President of the Dakotan Interstellar Confederacy. These worthies are my Cabinet, Ministers with assorted portfolios whose primary task is to act as the representatives of their systems at this level.

"Each is in continuous communication with both their system delegations in the Assembly and their home governments," she continued. "In the case of First Chief Abey Todacheeney, she is *also* the head of state of the Dakota System."

Chapulin smiled with amusement.

"We consider ourselves lucky when Chief Todacheeney can join us," she noted. "The one *non*-politician here is still a regular part of this Cabinet and would have been present even without your request to include our military.

"Fleet Admiral James Tecumseh leads the Dakotan Confederacy Navy, the senior of our three armed services," Chapulin concluded, gesturing to James.

Presumably, the introductions for the other fourteen Ministers had been sent directly to Weaver's neural implants, as no one else seemed to feel *slighted* at the lack of verbal introduction.

"Your request for Admiral Tecumseh's presence suggests that you are here for more than simply trade deals and interstellar relations," Minister Sanada Chō rumbled. The representative from Shogun served as the unofficial vice president and first among equals of the Cabinet's Ministers.

Some of that, James suspected, was due to the man's sheer presence. It was impossible to miss that Chō had been a planetary champion sumo wrestler—and anyone foolish enough to miss that his bulk covered both an immense amount of muscle and an incredible brain would swiftly learn their mistake.

"As interstellar trade begins to find a new normal in this difficult time, we in the Weston Republic have taken the opportunity to learn who is left of the former Commonwealth and which other states have taken shape from the wreckage," Weaver told them. "I am one of several Envoys sent out to make contact with the key Successor States to build new diplomatic and trade relations."

The Confederacy had been engaging in similar research, James knew. There were, prior to the news from Glass, anyway, ten multi-system Successor States to the Terran Commonwealth. Including the Rump Commonwealth itself, which still controlled roughly a third of the hundred inhabited star systems and three hundred claimed stars of the Old Commonwealth.

Three of those states had been the pirate nations that James had been warned had merged into the Triumvirate. That would bring them down to eight, he supposed. He had known the Weston Republic existed, after all.

"As I'm sure you are aware, the Dakotan Interstellar Confederacy is the second-largest of the new Successor States taking shape, after the remnant Imperial Commonwealth itself."

That was… a politer description for the Earth-centered rump state run by Walkingstick, James figured. Though the Rump certainly *claimed* it held the full power and territory of the Old Commonwealth and wouldn't accept *either* name.

"The Weston Republic, consisting of the entire former Weston Sector, was until very recently the *fourth*-largest of the Successor States," Weaver told them. "The Emerald Commonwealth has not necessarily *officially* declared themselves independent, but they are most definitely *not* taking orders from Sol."

The Emerald Commonwealth, like the Rump Commonwealth, was still claiming to be the real Terran Commonwealth. Officially, their central government was an emergency continuity-of-government committee.

Given that the members of the Emergency Committee were still, after two years and almost certain communication from Sol and the Star Chamber, claiming to *be* an emergency organization and holding near-dictatorial control over nine star systems, James trusted them even *less* than he trusted Walkingstick.

He suspected *they* were relying on the fact that the Emerald and Persia Sectors were directly between the core sectors controlled by the Rump and the Alliance of Free Stars. Attacking them would be a clear threat to the people who'd just *beaten* the Commonwealth.

Not that the Alliance was going to tolerate their crap for very long. Given that the systems closer to the Alliance—including *half* of the Persia Sector—were officially independent and under the protection of the victors of the war, well…

It wasn't going to take many missteps on the part of the Emerald Commonwealth to find themselves with Castle and Coraline supercarriers on their doorstep.

"You say *until recently*," Chapulin said. "I take it something has changed that is relevant to this discussion."

"Ten months ago, the Republic found ourselves in a nasty border conflict with what used to be the Crimea Sector and was then the Crimean Free Oblast under Admiral Celestine Morris," Weaver explained. "The war was... rather inconclusive. It was neither formally declared nor formally ended, but Morris stopped prodding our security outposts around the Saskatoon System and seemed to leave us alone.

"Our military commanders figured that we'd delivered a sharp-enough rebuff that the Oblast figured they couldn't get anything useful from us without losing ships Morris couldn't replace."

"If anyone is wondering," James interjected, "the Crimean Free Oblast is basically a warlord state, run by Admiral Celestine Morris. She *was* the Crimea Sector Fleet commander Before we lost communications, and she swiftly moved to secure control of the entire sector as her personal fiefdom."

She'd been more successful at it than some others.

"It *was*, yes," Weaver confirmed grimly. "The only system in the Crimea Sector that wasn't part of the Free Oblast at that point had been seized by forces under the command of Admiral Surinder Verity.

"I don't know if the two had conflicted outside of that, but from our perspective, Morris has achieved with diplomacy what she failed to achieve with force. She has united her forces and her systems with those under the control of Surinder Verity."

That lined up with the warning from Glass, and James grimaced.

"And also those of Admiral Harendra Rao in the Archon Sector?" he asked.

"Yes," Weaver confirmed, looking surprised. "Your intelligence is better than I dared hope, Admiral. Even we were taken completely by surprise by the unification of the three pirate warlords. We have no idea what deal Admirals Rao, Morris and Verity have cut, but the

Archon Sector, the Crimea Sector, and two systems of the Oglaf Sector are now under their control."

"Two of the other systems of the Oglaf Sector are under the Rump's flag," Hjalmar Rakes told the rest of the Cabinet. The Minister for Krete had slowly stepped into the role as the head of foreign affairs for the Confederacy—a role, so far as James could tell, that generally involved being transparent enough to the Assembly that Reynolds could continue to work in the shadows.

Foreign affairs was very public and open. *Intelligence* was much less so, even as the Confederacy tried to build a tradition of transparency in all forms of government. The deal, so far, was that the DCRO would be very open with the Assembly as to *what* it was doing and how much it cost—while telling them as little as possible about *where* they were doing it and *who* was doing it.

"The other two are independent, which I regarded as impressive enough *before* hearing about this new unity among warlords," Rakes noted. "Our information on the Triumvirate, Envoy Weaver, is quite limited."

And James was very glad he'd passed on the high level of Glass's warning to the rest of the Cabinet.

"Our intelligence is a mess," Weaver said bluntly. "So is our situation. I'm a week or so out of date at this point, but just before I left Weston, we were presented with an ultimatum: surrender to the Triumvirate within thirty days—or be taken by force."

He spread his hands.

"We are outnumbered in both ships and stars," he conceded. "But there was no question that we would concede to such a demand. I and several other Envoys were already on our way to the other Successor States, but the ultimatum added a new urgency.

"All of our Envoys are traveling by rented accommodation on civilian shipping," Weaver warned. "I left Weston forty-two days ago and was only expecting to arrive in Dakota a week ago. Now I understand my final transit will be around fifty days."

"Vice Admiral Yamamoto is doing everything he can to get you here on time," James said.

"Admiral Tecumseh, I have nothing but the greatest of praise for

Vice Admiral Yamamoto and his people," Weaver assured him. "I am not sure if the pirates were planning on selling me to the Triumvirate or Terra, but it seemed very clear that my life and personal liberty were going up for auction. Instead, thanks to Yamamoto and his people, I am on my way to Dakota to complete my mission.

"And the core of my mission is very simple," he told the Cabinet. "In the long term, the Weston Republic wishes to establish an embassy and open negotiations for trade.

"But for us to be able to sign trade treaties, we must *exist*. The Triumvirate's ultimatum ran out twelve days ago with no response from us. While I lost coms with home a week ago, I can only assume that the Saskatoon System is now under attack, if it has not already fallen."

He looked down at his hands, then up at the Cabinet with dark eyes.

"*My home system* is likely in the hands of the Triumvirate as we speak," he told them softly. "My government will have had no choice but to yield the system, fighting as hard as we can, to buy the time necessary to call for help.

"The Triumvirate's combined forces badly outnumber us. If we are to remain free, we need friends and we need help. The Commonwealth was born, long ago, on the concept of mutual security and protection. While the Commonwealth itself has fallen, all of our systems were part of that structure once.

"We all believed in standing together against the shadows of humanity's darker nature. The *nation* we once shared is gone, but that principle, that concept, that commitment… That stands; that can still live.

"If we make it live. Our ancestors decided to stand together against this exact kind of tyranny and evil. We of the Republic know we have no call on you. No bonds of oath or treaty. Only history and the faith of those who were once siblings."

He spread his hands.

"We can demand nothing. Only ask that you honor the faith and the ideal upon which the Commonwealth was built. Let the shadows and failings of the Commonwealth die—but let us honor the principles for which it was built.

"I ask, on behalf of the Parliament of the Weston Republic, that the Dakotan Interstellar Confederacy send ships and soldiers to help us defeat this attack upon our sovereign stars and our innocent citizenry."

7

Dakota System
20:00 January 10, 2740 ESMDT

THEY SENT Weaver away with no immediate answer. James Tecumseh knew what his own soul called out for, but the Confederacy had its own troubles. Its own enemies. No one in the Cabinet would turn down Weaver's impassioned plea, but they could not give him an immediate answer.

As soon as the Weston Envoy had left the virtual call, though, every eye was focused on James and he sighed.

"Well, Fleet Admiral, you know the question I'm about to ask," Chapulin told him with a chuckle. "*Can* we?"

"When I first took command of Sector Fleet Dakota, I told my officers there were two types of problems before us," James said quietly. "Those that justified the *entire* fleet and those that couldn't justify *anything*. That was an inherent problem of our position then.

"Our strength has improved. Our enemies have been managed. But there is *no way* we can send the entire fleet to Weston."

There were files and information that were always to hand for him, especially when he was talking to the Cabinet. A thought suspended dozens of holographic images in neat rows above the middle of the table.

"We have had three sources of ships to date," he told the Cabinet. "First and foremost, the original Sector Fleets and the survivors of the Clockward Fleet. Seventeen ships in total. Secondly, we have captured certain units from the Terran Commonwealth and had multiple ships defect to us over the last two years."

He shrugged, highlighting a second section of the fleet.

"Including *Intrepid* in that category, we have picked up eight ships along the way," he observed.

Intrepid had been in the Testament System and had pledged her loyalty to the government there, joining the Confederacy with them. One *Saint*-class battleship had carried Walkingstick's demand that James turn the Dakota Sector into a warship foundry for the Commonwealth, and that battleship had been seized. Four ships had defected in the wake of Walkingstick's assault on Dakota, and two more cruisers had shown up on their own at various points over the years.

"Lastly, we have the ships that have commissioned from Base Łá't-s'áadah here in Dakota," he told them. "Six ships, each larger than anything else in our order of battle.

"In total, we now command a fleet of twenty-nine interstellar capital ships. The problem is that the Rump Commonwealth still commands over a *hundred*. Walkingstick hasn't wholly made good his losses here or even kept up with his losses elsewhere as he has slowly expanded—but the replacements he *does* have are sixties or eighties, more powerful than the average ships in his previous fleet.

"Our best guess puts the Rump Commonwealth in control of thirty warship yards," he continued. "At this moment, I believe every one of those yards contains an eighty-million-cubic-meter warship at some stage of completion. The entire rest of the Commonwealth combined didn't have thirty warship slips when we lost the coms networks."

The warships were replaced by the map of the Confederacy, with new icons marking *their* shipyards.

"Thanks to assistance from the Stellar League, we have been able to acquire a sufficient supply of Class One mass manipulators to complete the six ships we had under construction," he noted. "And given the economic strength of the Confederacy, we have expanded our yards in a way that Walkingstick doesn't need to.

"We now have sixteen capital-ship yards," he reminded them. They'd also doubled the *civilian* shipbuilding capacity of the Confederacy along the way. They added two more yards to Base Łá'ts'áadah, the complex at the eleventh moon of the gas giant Virginia. Four yards had been built in the Shogun and Meridian Systems as well, leaning on the industry of the three wealthiest systems in the Commonwealth.

"Frankly..." He sighed. "We all know building sixteen ships is already straining our economic resources. We won't be able to maintain a forty-four-ship fleet. What our exact final strength will be is something we're still discussing, though the grim truth is that the cost of maintaining an eighty-million-cubic-meter ship is not as much higher than that of a twenty-five million cubic meter ship as you'd think."

And there were more *Paramount*-class carriers and *Assassin*-class battlecruisers in his order of battle than he really liked. He needed them right now, but he'd happily scrap two of those ships to keep an eighty in commission.

"It will be at least another year before the first of the next wave of new ships is ready," he warned. "So, the important number right now is twenty-nine. With twenty-nine starships, we need to see to the security of fifteen star systems in such a way that the Rump Commonwealth, who have a *hundred* starships, does not decide we have become an easy target."

"So, you do not believe we *can* help the Weston Republic?" Chō asked, the big man's voice quiet and grim. Almost sad, even.

"Even if we could, the Republic is over a hundred and sixty light-years from us," Patience Abiodun—the Minister for Arroyo and Social Works—pointed out. While Abiodun was often quick to plead poverty on the part of Arroyo, the Confederacy's poorest system, *poverty* on the scale of a star system in the Old Commonwealth would leave many other star systems green with envy.

"The resources necessary to extend our strength that far are needed here," she continued. "Envoy Weaver tells a wonderful and heartwarming story of unity and ideals, but we must see to the survival of the Dakotan Confederacy first, before all else."

James waited silently as a few others laid in their opinions—not quite an even split, he noted, with the weight coming down on *not* intervening—before finally answering Chō's question.

"The question raised, which Minister Chō repeated, is whether or not we *can* help," he reminded them.

Chapulin nodded to him, a silent gesture that still swiftly brought the rest of the Cabinet to quiet and attention. The Cabinet would argue with the President—loudly, endlessly, and gleefully—and that was its *purpose*, but they were a surprisingly aligned body for all of that.

"We can," James told them, smiling at the surprise he saw. "A year ago, we could not have. Now I estimate we can spare a *small* force. The vast majority of our most modern ships must remain here, but I believe we can justify deploying a fleet of four ships.

"My initial impulse is to wait on Admiral Yamamoto's return and anchor that fleet on *Iroquois* and *Saratoga*," he continued. "I would want to attach a second carrier, either a *Volcano* or a *Blackfoot*, and either one of the older battleships or two of the older cruisers."

The only cruisers in the DCN worth deploying on their own were the two *Iroquois*-class ships. The *Ocean-* and *Assassin*-class ships were thirty million cubic meters or less, among the oldest and weakest ships he had.

"Could four ships make that much of a difference?" Rakes asked. "We are talking about a pirate fleet anchored on the third-largest of the Successor States now."

"And one that is attacking the *fifth*-largest," James replied. "You have as much access to our intelligence as I do, Minister Rakes. How many ships can the Weston Republic muster?"

"As of our last information, nineteen," Rakes told him. "And before you ask, we estimate the collected strength of the Triumvirate at *thirty*."

"We do not need to make up the entire shortfall between the Republic and the Triumvirate," James told the Cabinet. "The Triumvirate must see to its own defenses, and we are not looking to shore up the Republic across the board.

"Our purpose will be to put four starships at the inflection point. There, where the odds will be *far* more even, I believe our ships will be enough to turn the tide."

He smiled.

"We must also consider, after all, the fact that we are not the only people the Republic will have asked for aid."

It was clear that only a handful of James's fellow Cabinet members had followed the consequences of Weaver being one of *several* such Envoys sent out.

"They contacted both of the Commonwealths, at least," Chapulin agreed. "Our intelligence suggests that the Emerald Commonwealth won't get involved. It's too far away and the Emergency Committee's hold on power requires the impression of major threats on all sides. That is not an impression that can be maintained by sending ships away to deal with other people's problems.

"The question, I suppose, is what will *Walkingstick* do."

James sighed.

"For every reason you can think of and more, Walkingstick will send ships," he told the rest of the Cabinet. "He will send ships to influence Weston politics toward reunification. He will send ships to weaken the Triumvirate for a campaign to retake their stars by force. He will send ships to *make us look bad*… and he will, even as he justifies it privately with realpolitik, do it for honor.

"Walkingstick believes, in his heart of hearts, that he is our Cincinnatus, our Washington, and if we would only let him, he would save us all," James concluded grimly. "He will send ships. He might well lead them, which might make the gesture even more powerful.

"Either way, if the Commonwealth deploys forces to help the Republic, it eases our own burdens. And… for all of the harsh truths about the Rump Commonwealth, Imperator Walkingstick is a dictator imposed on a democratic system *that still mostly functions.*

"The Triumvirate are *not*. They are military dictators ruling states where the democratic structures have been broken to the whip and the yoke." James shook his head. "They are expansionist, aggressive, and their only national goals are the aggrandization of their leaders.

"They are *exactly* the type of threat the Commonwealth was forged to stop. The Commonwealth is broken, yes. But today, we"—he gestured around the virtual room—"must decide if the faith between the *systems* of the Commonwealth is to be abandoned with it."

"No," President Chapulin said quietly. "I do not believe it is." She met his gaze and then glanced around the rest of the room. "We will keep that faith," she told them. "Unless someone can come up with a *damn* good reason we should betray worlds and systems we shared a flag and a government with all too recently."

"We all know I'm biased with regards to arguments James makes," Abey said cheerfully, which earned her chuckles from the rest of the Cabinet. She and James had engaged in at least one take-no-prisoners argument across the Cabinet table over financing for the fleet versus domestic programs.

Even *James* felt they were occasionally a bit too ridiculously in love, but that didn't mean they *agreed* on everything.

"On this, though, he's made every argument I would and then a few more," she told everyone. "But he has missed one: who are we? Who do we want the Dakotan Confederacy to be?"

She smiled, the same brilliantly clever expression that led James into the awkward position of being married to a senior member of the government he served.

"Is the Dakotan Confederacy a nation that stands aside when people ask for aid? Do we *want* it to be? Can we *allow* it to be? The answer to all of these questions is *no*. For the same reason we could not bow to a military dictator imposed from Terra, we cannot stand by while others suffer.

"*The only thing necessary for evil to triumph in the world is that good people do nothing,*" she quoted. "We cannot do nothing… and our Admiral has made the case for what we can do very clear, hasn't he?"

8

THERE WAS A LOGIC, James Calvin Walkingstick reflected, to the old Roman tradition of a triumph. Returning victorious from a four-month-long campaign felt like it required more celebration than turning his ships over to the yards in Sol and an extra-long night's sleep!

Emerging from his bedroom into the main space of his quarters, he saw that his steward had laid out breakfast and coffee in the last few minutes—even the coffee was still steaming. He really wasn't sure he deserved the man... but then, he'd made *damn* sure his steward was well compensated and taken care of.

The number of people the Imperator of Terra could trust to prepare his food was disturbingly small. Even now, twenty-five *months* and change after Walkingstick had found that title dumped on him, some of the realities still chafed.

He'd barely taken a seat and picked up the coffee before Jean-Marc Parris, the steward in question, stepped back into his living room.

"Admiral, the Senators Burns are here to see you," Parris told him.

"Think I can sneak the coffee in before you send them in?" Walkingstick asked with a chuckle—but he waved off Parris's response before the French Command Master Chief Steward could say a word.

Parris held the highest noncommissioned rank the Terran Commonwealth Navy *had*, and he held it for damn good reason. If he was telling Walkingstick that the Burnses were there before he'd finished his first coffee, it was urgent.

"Send them in and make sure we have food and coffee for them," Walkingstick told his man. "Assuming I'm remotely presentable, that is?"

Walkingstick was an immense man, tall and broad-shouldered with carefully maintained muscle and long dark braids. Every aspect of his appearance spoke to his Old Nations heritage, and decades of practice meant that even stepping into his living room, he'd made sure he met a minimum standard.

Helped by the fact that Parris had laid out a full working uniform for ease of dressing, of course.

"You're acceptable, though depending on what the Senators want, we may want to dig up something prettier," the steward noted. "Let me know?"

"Jean-Marc, you've eavesdropped on every meeting I've had for twenty-two years," Walkingstick said drily. "Why would I pretend you're not going to listen to this one?"

"Because there are proprieties to observe, Imperator Walkingstick," Parris replied in a prim tone only truly old-blood French could manage in Walkingstick's experience.

"I will bring the Senators in," he continued. "And make sure they have food as well."

———

Senators Michael and Hope Burns were the two elected senators—as opposed to Assembly Representatives—that Alpha Centauri sent to the Star Chamber, the Interstellar Congress of the Terran Commonwealth.

Michael Burns was the man who had hung the "Imperator" title on

James Walkingstick, though that had been more a matter of imposing the *name* than changing the reality. By the time he'd used the title for the then-Admiral, Walkingstick had already been standing in the Star Chamber, surrounded by Marines.

They were old friends, and Michael Burns now served as Speaker of the Interstellar Congress—and the only reason he wasn't *President* of the Commonwealth was that the Congress had formally rolled *that* role into the status of Imperator.

It wasn't like the President had been doing much *before* Walkingstick had marched Marines into the heart of the Commonwealth's democracy.

Both Burnses were Black, with the husband as broad-shouldered as Walkingstick with short-cropped pure white hair. His wife was easily twenty years younger, a tall and elegantly framed study in contrast with her husband.

They were, in their own way, as key to the survival of the Commonwealth as Walkingstick himself. In the current environment, their power base was critically dependent on him—but he was doing everything he could to *avoid* the kind of ugly purges his sort of rule had seen in the past.

That gave the two civilians some sense of safety in his presence above and beyond their value to him. They took seats across from him without asking permission, then thanked Parris as the steward brought them coffees.

"How was Tallulah?" Michael Burns asked as Walkingstick finished his own coffee and eyed the two politicians.

"Bloody and muddy, metaphorically at least," Walkingstick said flatly. "Fredericka Waters made me miss James *fucking* Tecumseh. Is it crazy that I'd rather fight a competent enemy than a brainless goddamn butcher?"

"I... somehow doubt that Waters was a *brainless butcher*," Hope Burns pointed out. "She *did* successfully secure control of two-thirds of a sector, which required her to bring her entire Sector Fleet along into piracy with her."

Walkingstick grunted.

"There are officers who are perfectly competent at every other aspect of the job but whose idea of clever strategy is *assemble a hammer and beat people with it*," he observed. "I'm fond of a hammer as a tool when it's the right time for it. When outnumbered three-to-two with a violent insurrection ripping through your territory and your logistics pipeline..."

He grimaced.

"I don't know how Waters kept her people together, but she brought eight starships and two dozen sublight guardships right at us like *she* had the numbers edge," he told them. "We lost two cruisers and a battleship in that mess, and the last I'd heard, General Petit was requesting another five divisions to deal with her holdouts and the damn insurrectionists."

The rebellion against "Queen" Waters—formerly Vice Admiral Waters of the Terran Commonwealth Navy—had *asked* for Commonwealth intervention. Even so, only about two-thirds of the rebels had laid down their arms when Waters' appointed minions had surrendered in the face of Walkingstick's battle fleet and General Salvador Petit's Marine divisions.

General Petit—now the military governor of the Tallulah Sector—had brought thirty divisions with him. After losses and reinforcements, the man had *half a million* Commonwealth Marines under his command as he tried to impose order and peace on a sector that had either never left the Commonwealth or begged them for help.

Walkingstick hadn't expected gratitude, but it would have been *nice*.

"Thanks to General Krizman, we're aware of his situation," Hope Burns told him. "Four more star systems returned to Unity isn't nothing, Imperator. And most of their population seems glad to have us back, according to the administrative people we're moving in."

"Because, of course, the bitch *shot* every Commonwealth bureaucrat she could find," Walkingstick growled. "Matter-antimatter annihilation is too good for some people."

Michael Burns chuckled.

"You want the good news or the headache first, James?" he asked.

"I could use some good news," Walkingstick admitted. "Waters and her people have left me feeling like I walked through a pit of tar."

"Your campaign in Tallulah might have felt like a mess saving ungrateful locals, but it *has* brought four more systems back into Unity," Burns told him, echoing his wife's words. "Almost as importantly, though, it didn't take much massaging at all to make you and the Commonwealth look damn good doing it.

"Waters' campaign and her citizens' call for our help have boosted our profile across the full Commonwealth. We're pushing uphill still, in a lot of ways, but Waters really helped demonstrate what Unity is about."

"I hate to think that monster served our purposes," Walkingstick admitted, "but if we can use it, let's use it."

"Oh, we have used it," Hope Burns said with a cold smile. "Getting polling data from across the full Commonwealth remains difficult, but we're seeing some of the difference already in our diplomatic discussions. People are starting to warm up, realizing that there *are* threats out there.

"We're not quite at people knocking on the door to come back in, but we're getting there. We're now up to two non-core sectors entirely in Unity."

Walkingstick had held on to the Core Four and the Serenity Sector with both hands and a not-inconsiderable amount of bloodshed. Without the immense industry of the twenty-four star systems that made up the beating heart of humanity, rebuilding the Unity of the full Commonwealth was impossible.

Serenity, on the other hand, had been the second of two sets of secret yards churning out the new eighty-million-cubic-meter warships outside the Core. And while the Alliance had *obliterated* the official shipbuilding capacity of the Commonwealth, the secret yards of Project Hustle had survived.

One set, unfortunately, had been in Dakota. The others were in his hands.

"Time and demonstration of what we are prepared to do for them," Walkingstick murmured. "And what we will do *to* them, if we must."

"Which brings me to the headache," Michael Burns told him. "An Envoy arrived from the Weston Sector two weeks ago, claiming to represent a new Republic there."

"We're in enough privacy here, Michael, that we can dispense with the careful phrases of our public posturing," the Imperator instructed. "The Envoy speaks for the Weston Republic. We aren't going to *officially* acknowledge the existence of any of the so-called Successor States, but we need to work around them."

Until he could deal with them. And Weston wasn't on top of his list for that. There were others who were clearer *problems* that he'd deal with first.

"Envoy Yeter Milburn of the Republic, then," Michael Burns allowed, "is here to ask for our help against a group called the Triumvirate. Rao, Morris, and Verity have—as you predicted—combined forces. The Republic expects them to move directly against the Weston Sector in short order."

Prediction wasn't quite the right word for that, Walkingstick reflected, and that meant there was a conversation he needed to have. His agents in the Triumvirate had told him the alliance was coming. Now it was time to see what kind of leverage those operatives had.

"So, when they can no longer defend themselves, they come to us," Walkingstick said. "As expected, I suppose. We will answer the call, of course. And lay the groundwork for other tasks."

"We've talked before about social license," Hope Burns reminded him. "If we can save the Weston Sector from the Triumvirate, that unquestionably gives us social license to invade and re-annex the systems under the Triumvirate's control."

"And some heavy levers to pull with the Republic itself," Walkingstick agreed. "Potentially, that will even leave us in position to deal with Emerald."

He *really* wanted to deal with Emerald. It was *easier* to deal with the explicit warlords, the Navy officers who'd taken control of systems and sectors at the point of a positron lance. Emerald's *political* dictatorship, though, bothered him more.

Everyone, he reflected, had their own biases about what was a bigger problem. Part of it, he knew, was that when military officers used force to exert control, there was no question of the illegitimacy of their power. His own situation was more mixed than most, because he was still mostly working inside the structures of the Commonwealth.

He'd taken control of the *Star Chamber,* but the Star Chamber still ran the Commonwealth. Sort of. Necessity was the mother of hypocrisy, after all.

The so-called *Emergency Committee of the Terran Commonwealth,* however, had none of the legitimacy of the Star Chamber and the Imperator they'd involuntarily appointed. The Emerald Sector's Committee was made up of a mix of local bureaucrats and planetary governors that had declared themselves the continuity of the Commonwealth to maintain order in their region.

Walkingstick couldn't begrudge them that, but it should have quickly become clear that the Commonwealth had survived and that they should return their allegiance to Sol. Instead, the Committee had declared the Star Chamber—specifically, the Imperatorship—illegitimate and claimed *themselves* as the true government of the Commonwealth.

And they'd refused to hold elections or carry out any other aspect of the democracy of the Commonwealth for two years. The two-dozen-odd members of the Committee were just as much dictators as he was —more so, in many ways, as the systems that remained in Unity *had* held elections.

"If we can knock off the Triumvirate, bring the Weston Republic into the fold semi-voluntarily and then smash the Emergency Committee's pretensions, we'll be over halfway there," Michael Burns said. "*Well* over. The Triumvirate and the Republic hold twenty systems between them. If we bring in the Committee's nine, we'll be back over sixty star systems. Only Dakota will remain as a secessionist state of any weight at all."

There had been one hundred and five significant inhabited star systems—with populations of over a billion—in the Terran Commonwealth, with about two hundred systems with smaller populations that were also part of Unity.

The only systems anyone was actually *counting* at that point were the significant ones. When those fell into line, the outposts, mining stations and fledgling colonies in the surrounding stars generally came with them.

"The main Expeditionary Fleet has been worked hard," Walkingstick said grimly. "We could probably rearrange things and send... thirty, forty ships to deal with the Triumvirate. But I think that might draw too much attention to the wrong things."

"We need to be *seen* to act and we need to *act* decisively," Hope Burns told the two men. "But the reality is, yes, if we send a fleet large enough to overrun Republic and Triumvirate alike, we're probably going to make people worry about aggressive expansion on our part."

"And while I hate to draw attention to the shadows, we *need* a key fleet in Sol and at other systems in the Commonwealth," her husband continued. "Our control of our own stars is solid, mostly, but there are those who would take advantage."

"The Alliance brought a fleet all the way into Sol," Walkingstick said. "The home system's aura of invulnerability is gone. As Hope says, we must be *seen* to defend her with a might that cannot be overcome."

He sighed.

"The solution is relatively simple, I suppose," he told them. "We send a smaller fleet, under my own command. As with the campaign against Waters, I must act and be seen to act, to provide the symbol of the Unity we have given up."

"You will need to meet with Envoy Yeter Milburn," Hope Burns said. "Whatever decision you make and whatever force we deploy, we need to be seen to listen. To act because we are asked to, not because we are out to reconquer everyone."

"The story and the image are everything," Walkingstick agreed. He didn't *like* playing this game with people who *had been* part of the Unity of the Commonwealth. He still knew how—he hadn't built the cult of personality that had delivered him the command of the Rimward War against the Alliance and then the Imperatorship without knowing the moves.

"Unless Milburn says something I don't expect, I have a solid idea of what I'll be able to take with me," Walkingstick observed. "We don't have enough of the eighties to risk them, unfortunately, so they'll remain with Gabor.

"It will take some time for us to get enough of the fifties and sixties cleaned up and rearmed for this," he continued. "But we should be ready to move before the Weston Republic falls."

Michael Burns snorted softly.

"For our purposes, coming to the rescue of a defeated Republic might work better," the Senator pointed out.

"Perhaps," Walkingstick admitted. "But too many people would die, Michael, and while I am prepared to spill lakes of blood to preserve and restore the Commonwealth, I do so to *avoid* spilling oceans.

"And if the Republic falls to the Triumvirate and has to be retaken…" He shook his head. "I will break the Republic myself if I must, but fewer will die if we can manage to see the Republic only fall *once*."

He studied his two political allies carefully and smiled.

"I will meet with Ms. Milburn," he confirmed. "Until then, how have you found working with Gabor and Krizman? I need the four of you aligned if I am to risk being away from Sol."

And balanced against each other, civilians on one side with Navy and Marines on the other. The Burnses, running the Star Chamber and the Commonwealth civil service between them, were a more unified front than Admiral Mihai Gabor, the current deputy chief of the Terran Commonwealth Navy, and General Pearle Krizman, the General Commanding the Terran Commonwealth Marine Corps.

On the other hand, of course, Gabor and Krizman had all of the guns.

9

WHEN HE WAS BEING honest with himself, Walkingstick *adored* the pomp and pageantry of his position and his career. Even when he'd been a "mere" Commodore commanding a battleship with a crew of several thousand, careful use of staging and costuming had helped maintain his authority and build his following.

That skill had served him well over the thirty years since, and it was absolutely *essential* to maintaining his authority now.

One of his most useful tools in all of that was the Atlantic Elevator Platform itself. Despite its intentionally mundane name, a pure descriptor of the massive oceanic structure's purpose as the anchor of the mid-Atlantic orbital elevator, the AEP served as the heart of the Commonwealth's government.

Several of the massive flotation tanks, cavernous empty voids used to keep the station above the surface of the Atlantic Ocean, had been repurposed as immense spaces to serve as homes for the Senate and Assembly of the Interstellar Congress of the Terran Commonwealth. An incredible amount of effort and decoration had gone into those spaces, and the half-millennium-dead architects who had revamped the platform in the twenty-third century hadn't stopped there.

The Platform, after all, served as the anchor for a series of immense cables that stretched all the way into geostationary orbit and beyond. Parts of the core structure rose a full kilometer into the air to frame and protect those cables—and other parts descended all the way to the ocean floor, just over thirty-five hundred meters below the surface.

The dining room he'd selected for tonight's endeavor was in the latter sections, suspended a full kilometer beneath the surface of the Atlantic Ocean, where the only light came from the Platform itself. This was as deep as the truly *usable* portions of the Platform went, but a reinforced transparent bubble had been installed to serve as an impressive backdrop to a private dining space, traditionally at the disposal of the President of the Commonwealth.

Since the Star Chamber had transferred all of the President's powers to the Imperator, that meant it was at *his* disposal, and it didn't take much work to make *that* backdrop impressive.

Gleaming white marble flanked the window behind Walkingstick, and a long table stretched inward toward the center of the structure. He sat at the head of the table, with a handful of carefully selected guests—Senators and Representatives from the Star Chamber—spread out around the room as Envoy Yeter Milburn entered.

Milburn was a dark-skinned woman wearing a pale pink suit and a matching turban-style headwrap covering her hair. She didn't seem particularly taken aback by the backdrop as she and her two neatly suited aides entered the room—even though they'd been escorted down by Marines.

"Envoy Milburn, I am delighted that you can join us," Walkingstick told her. "Please, you and your people can take a seat, and dinner will be served shortly."

Jean-Marc Parris was as enamored and capable of pageantry as Walkingstick himself, and the Commander Master Chief Steward appeared out of nowhere with a pair of uniformed junior stewards.

Of course, in *this* space, the "junior stewards" were Chief Petty Officers in their own right. Each of the Chiefs gently guided Milburn's aides to seats at the far end of the table—while Parris himself led

Milburn to the head of the table and a seat at Walkingstick's right hand.

Inside the transparent bubble, with a clear view of the seemingly infinite darkness in every direction. The Weston Envoy stepped out into the space with only the tiniest of hesitations—but hesitate she did.

Not that Walkingstick blamed her. *He'd* made sure only Parris was in the room when he'd taken his own seat for the first time!

"I'm uncertain of the protocol here, Imperator Walkingstick," she told him as Parris led her to her seat. "Should I bow? Salute? Prostrate myself?"

The Weston Republic, it seemed, had equipped their Envoy with a sharp tongue.

"*Imperator* is, at its core, a military title, Ms. Milburn," he told her. "I am no absolute monarch to require formal groveling. Please, sit."

She obeyed, ignoring the table and the plates as she continued to meet his gaze, her eyes trying to burn into his soul.

James Walkingstick had faced worse and responded to her focused regard with a small smile.

"Monsieur Parris has prepared a fine dinner for us all," he told her. "Shall we wait for the food to come out?"

"I am not certain this meeting required a meal at all, Imperator," she replied. "I have been in Sol for fifteen days, and my patience and time both run thin. My link home tells me that we are under attack."

"The pirates of the Triumvirate, yes," he agreed mildly. "It does raise an interesting question, doesn't it, Ms. Milburn?"

"Which is?" she replied.

"From *my* perspective, you are from the Weston Sector, member worlds of the Terran Commonwealth that I am tasked to defend," he said. "Except that you sit here with us, claiming the prerogatives of a foreign diplomat.

"If the Weston Sector is now the Weston Republic, making you the Envoy you claim instead of merely a courier... then the Weston *Republic* are no members of the Commonwealth and we have no obligation to protect them.

"If we grant you your titles and prerogatives, Envoy Milburn, then the question becomes *why* should the Commonwealth leap to the defense of a secessionist state, of worlds that threw aside our shared mission, our Unity, at the first hurdle?"

"That is a discussion for the Commonwealth to have with its conscience," she replied calmly. "Along with the question, I suppose, of *why* so many worlds fled if our mission was so shared and connected?"

Walkingstick chuckled and gestured her to the plates the stewards were serving.

"Eat, Ms. Milburn, and reflect on my words," he told her. "The question stands and I'd ask you to answer it before the night is done... but not yet."

She probably *had* several canned responses, but he wanted her to *think* about it and answer the questions he'd asked instead of the ones she was expecting.

———

Parris had outdone himself. The stewards didn't serve just one meal, prepared for everyone. They served each diner a *specific* meal, planned for each of their dietary needs and restrictions.

Envoy Milburn, Walkingstick observed, was not merely vegetarian but what he recognized as either Jainist vegetarian or something derived from that. Her meal included neither meat nor root vegetables.

And because Parris understood *exactly* how Walkingstick was handling this particular negotiation, the Imperator's entree was a carefully prepared version of the classic steak and potatoes. *Rare* steak, at that, that visibly bled as he cut into it.

Not quite to Walkingstick's taste, if he was being honest, but that was hardly the point.

As the plates were cleared away, he turned his levellest regard on the Weston Envoy.

"Well, Ms. Milburn?" he said. "I asked, at the start of this meal, where the Weston Republic stands."

"That was not exactly the question you asked," she murmured.

"And yet." He smiled. "I spent my adult life, Ms. Milburn, fighting for the cause of Unity. To bring new worlds and new peoples under the protection of the Terran Commonwealth, where our democracy, ideals, and economy could uplift them all into a solid, protected, and stable future.

"*Forty-six years,*" he intoned, the words ringing through the entire room. "For forty-six years, I gave the Commonwealth and the cause of Unity everything I had. And then, as soon as there was a moment of resistance, the smallest of hurdles to that cause, I watched the nation I swore to serve, the people we had done *everything* to protect and enrich, shatter as those very people betrayed the Unity we fought for.

"And now... Now that you face a *new* hurdle, you come back to us. You broke faith with the Commonwealth, and yet you ask us to keep faith with you."

She raised her head and met his gaze.

"That we stand in this room and that I make my case to *one man* tells me that we did not break faith with the Commonwealth," she said bluntly. "The Commonwealth we shared died the day you put on that eagle instead of an Admiral's stars."

Walkingstick touched the golden eagle he wore on his collar instead of the stars of an Admiral. It was the sole sign, on a day-to-day basis, that he *was* more than "merely" another senior flag officer.

"The Commonwealth was already falling apart when I became Imperator," he said. "The excuse is handy for many, I suppose, but it falls a bit flat when entire sectors were in open revolt and the Star Chamber itself was already ordering kangaroo courts and summary executions."

Of *him*, in particular, though he'd short-stopped a few other examples being made when he'd taken control. His own purges, as much as possible, had involved forced retirements and the occasional jail cell.

"But regardless of your reasons and your claims, you have returned to Terra," he continued. "The first challenge and you return to us."

"We come to you seeking allies, to stand against a common foe," Milburn said. "We are not here to kneel to a faded memory of a broken nation. We are here to stand in the reality and recognize that Commonwealth and Republic alike cannot see the Triumvirate grow in power.

"We would have you fight alongside us, to prove that you are better than your enemies claim you are," she insisted. "There are perhaps discussions to be had around the future of the Commonwealth, but this is not the time for them. As we speak, the starships of the Triumvirate lay siege to the Saskatoon System. Triumvirate soldiers have stormed the cloudscoops at Lafleche. Innocents have died and more are at risk."

"No force in this universe can save Saskatoon if the Republic cannot protect themselves," Walkingstick told her. "That star system will fall."

"We know. So, we are here, speaking to you and asking for your help."

"You broke faith with the Commonwealth, Ms. Milburn," Walkingstick told her, rising to his feet with all of the physicality his immense frame allowed. He *loomed* over her and a table of politicians that hadn't bothered to say a word to him or Milburn the entire evening.

"The entire Weston Sector broke faith with Terra," he continued. "You betrayed your oaths, breached treaties and promises a quarter-millennium old, and now you *ask us for help*."

He raised a hand before she could speak.

"You broke faith with us," he repeated. *"We will not break faith with you."*

He smiled and he *knew* the expression was terrifying.

"Weston calls for aid and the Commonwealth *will* answer. I will lead a fleet *myself* to the rescue of your stars, Envoy Milburn. We will drive back the Triumvirate. We will liberate Saskatoon. And maybe then, when you have seen the strength of the Commonwealth's faith, you will reconsider the weakness of *yours*."

10

Dakota System
20:00 January 19, 2740 ESMDT

DAKOTA WAS A GENERALLY PLEASANT WORLD, with the vast majority of its continents not only habitable for humans but friendly toward them. Even on a pleasant world, though, there were places that could be regarded as a step above.

Teotihuacán was that place on Dakota. A plateau rising from the sea a few kilometers from the main coastline, it was shielded from inclement weather by the mainland and a rocky peninsula. But where the mainland was rocky broken terrain, Teotihuacán descended smoothly to sun-warmed waters on three sides, ending in sweeping expanses of white-gold sand.

Up the gentle rises on top of the plateau, an almost-entirely self-contained ecosystem had flourished with few predators, none of which were large enough or daring enough to threaten humans.

The Confederacy of Nations that governed Dakota had set strict rules around the island to protect that unique ecosystem. The island had been protected from any serious development, with the inevitable resorts mostly actually built *inside* the cliffs on the north side of the plateau, giving the rooms epic vistas across the open sea.

And the same government and partner corporations that had made certain Teotihuacán's ecosystem was protected had made certain both that the tourist numbers were kept low to protect the site *and* that it did not become merely the playground of the rich and powerful.

James Tecumseh suspected that the government held on to a certain number of the island's access slots for itself, hence it being made available for the First Chief's honeymoon, but otherwise, getting onto the island at all was run by a lottery system.

There were different tiers of resorts and rooms a tourist could choose between once they had an access slot, but *everyone* on the planet could register for the lottery. A certain number of spaces each year were underwritten by the planetary government, too, making sure that Teotihuacán was truly a place where *everyone* could theoretically come visit.

He and Abey were in a luxurious suite at the highest level of the northern cliffs, and he was seated cross-legged on the balcony, looking over the sea on what he knew had to be their last day.

"Working again?" Abey asked as she joined him. She took a seat on the lounger next to him, positioning herself clearly in the corner of his vision.

He turned to smile at her, taking in the full gorgeous vista of his new wife. The view on the balcony was quite different compared to the view *from* the balcony, but both definitely had their appeal.

"No, actually," he said. "I know I've been working more than you'd like. More than *I* was planning, but…" He spread his hands in a helpless shrug.

"You're taking four starships on a twenty-seven-day voyage the day after tomorrow," Abey conceded. "Some preparation is essential."

"Unfortunately, yes," he agreed. "We will save some time by only bringing *Iroquois* from Yamamoto's task group, though that raises its own issues."

"Issues you're solving by inserting yourself and *Krakatoa*?" she asked. She shook her head at him, wrapping a strand of long black hair around a finger. "You don't *have* to command every deployment your-self. With four ships, wouldn't Yamamoto make more sense?"

The current planned strength of Task Force Six, the force James was taking to the Republic, was the battlecruiser *Iroquois*, the carrier *Krakatoa*, the battleship *Adamant*, and the strike cruiser *Black Sea*.

One brand-new ship, one modern ship, one older ship and one functionally *obsolete* ship. But *Black Sea* brought forty Katana starfighters and twenty Longbow bombers, where *Iroquois* didn't carry any bombers and *Adamant* didn't have any fighters at all.

"Anthony is an excellent officer, one of my strong right hands and a critical component to the Confederacy Navy," James said slowly, still basically ogling his wife. "He is also, like *all* of our officers, badly inex-perienced for his rank and authority. As a CAG and as the commander of the Starfighter Corps, I have the utmost faith in him.

"As an independent task force commander? Both he and I would prefer he stay closer to home." He shook his head, looking down as he put his hands back on his crossed legs.

"It's also about image and the... *weight* of what we are sending Weston," he continued. "We could, in some ways, send one of my subordinates if we were sending a dozen ships."

He chuckled.

"Of course, we don't *have* anyone else I'd want to give command of a dozen-ship fleet to," he admitted. "But sending four ships, we need to add a name they'll know to it, an officer senior enough to convince them that we mean business and that we have their back.

"If I thought there was another option to meet that call, I'd have asked the Cabinet for input."

"The Cabinet and DCN Command have a flexible balance," Abey noted. She shifted the lounger over so that she could put her feet in James's lap, her skin cool against his own sun-warmed flesh. "I'm sure if someone thought you were *wrong*, we would have raised the ques-tion, but we do trust you to handle the military side of things."

James smiled and shifted around to begin to gently rub her feet.

"Which I appreciate, even as it terrifies me," he admitted. "It wasn't that long ago you decided to seduce me to have a leash on the local potential warlord."

80 | UNBROKEN FAITH

"Please, James, by the time I *actually* seduced you, I knew that wasn't really necessary," she purred at him. "The thought was in my mind, yes, but I became pretty familiar with the stick up your ass."

He chuckled, nodding. For a few long moments, he continued to work on her feet and shins, soothing muscles that were already relaxed.

"I'm guessing that *you* were working," he suggested. That was the most likely reason she'd expected him to be doing so. Planetary heads of state, even sub-sovereign ones, didn't fully get away from work anymore than Admirals did.

"Yeah." Her amusement faded. "It's hard to enjoy our honeymoon when I realize just how many people are working to keep up even the pretense of relaxation."

"Seventy-two Confederacy VIP Security personnel, one hundred and twenty-five Marines, four assault shuttles, sixteen helicopters and three atmospheric fast interceptors on standby."

He doubted Abey needed the list, but it had hung around the back of his mind for most of the last ten days. A *lot* of people were working to keep them safe and secure while trying to impact Teotihuacán's general population and clientele as little as possible.

That was one reason—of several—that they hadn't left their suite much.

"Our time is almost up, I suppose," she whispered. "Neither of us was as good at keeping out of the loop as we were supposed to be, anyway."

"I'm out here to watch the sunset," James told her. "I think we should watch it together."

Iroquois would arrive in less than twelve hours, at which point his honeymoon was very definitely over.

"I really wish I could convince you not to go to Weston yourself," she told him, shifting the lounger around again so she was sitting next to him and taking his hand. "For selfish reasons, yes, but also because I think the Confederacy needs you. I don't like risking you."

"A ship is safe in harbor... but that's not what ships are built for," James murmured. "I am of value to the Confederacy because I act."

"You're of value for more than that, my love!"

"Fair," he conceded. "But the point stands, Abey, that I do the most good *by* acting and being seen to act. Like it or not, it is *my* name that carries enough weight to make four ships seem like enough."

"Can four ships make a difference for them? Even with you in command?"

"I can't make four ships feel like a hundred," James said. "But I think that we're bringing enough to turn the tide. And to make sure we come home."

"That part isn't optional, just so we're clear," she told him firmly. "You *are* coming home, with all of your people!"

He nodded silently.

Both of them knew that was a promise he couldn't actually make.

11

Dakota System
12:00 January 20, 2740 ESMDT

"WHAT'S *IROQUOIS*'S STATUS?"

James Tecumseh suspected that Commodore Waterman was still in the process of catching up, but there was no sign of that in the man's expression as he looked around the virtual conference.

"We're in the process of switching over key personnel groups," Waterman reported. "Ninety percent of the Alpha swap teams are off, including the entirety of Flight Group Twenty-Seven, and we're in the middle of coordinating the loading of the Fox swap teams, including Flight Group Thirty-Two."

Despite James's determination that they *could* spare four ships for this mission, the Confederacy had spent most of its short history desperately short on ships. Hardware needed maintenance and updates and hands-on care—but it still lasted and endured better than the organic bits.

The "swap teams" had been the solution. Training up their enthusiastic corps of new volunteers was an ongoing problem, but James had been able to assign every ship approximately a hundred and fifty percent of its list strength.

Divided into six teams, those expanded crews cycled every month. A given team—Alpha team, for example, aboard *Iroquois*—would spend four months on active duty aboard their ship, followed by two months in training in Dakota.

New recruits, volunteers, promotions and transfers were, as much as possible, integrated into the team at the start of the two-month training cycle, giving them two months of practice with their immediate colleagues before ever going on an active mission.

It wasn't perfect—there were core crews anchored on the command staff that couldn't be cycled the same way—but it seemed to be working so far.

"What about supplies and munitions?" Rear Admiral Young Volkov asked. She'd been *Krakatoa*'s Captain when James had found himself creating an entirely new fleet from scratch, and now she'd risen to serve as his new Chief of Staff and Operations Officer.

His *old* Chief of Staff, Rear Admiral Madona Voclain, was commanding a two-ship patrol group much like the one Yamamoto had found Weaver with.

"We were being careful with our fuel and food stocks on the patrol," Waterman told them. "We were only down to eighty-six percent on both, and we've been fully replenished since arriving."

James nodded to Waterman and looked at the other four starship Captains. The reality of the scale of modern warships meant that three of his four "Captains" were full Commodores—he was being *very* tempted by the Castle Federation standard of moving *Captain* up one tier to be the equivalent of a TCN junior flag officer, but he was hesitant to change *too* much of the TCN-derived structure his people were used to.

Commodore Patricia Jack now commanded *Krakatoa*, James's flagship and Volkov's old ship. She'd been Volkov's XO before, which created a potential friction point James needed to watch. Volkov was the task force ops officer, not *Krakatoa*'s Captain, now. That was something for him to watch.

Adamant was commanded by Commodore Morley Werner, who

had joined the DCN as captain of *Mediterranean,* one of James's original *Ocean*-class cruisers. He was one of the few officers James had who was definitely experienced enough for his role—though he'd be moving swiftly into a staff role if this mission went well.

Lastly, and least well known to James, was *Black Sea*'s commanding officer, Captain Chinweuba Bull. Earth-born like James himself, Bull was a gaunt-looking Black man who'd been recommended for his role by the strike cruiser's previous commander and Admiral Jessie Modesitt, the commander of the Confederacy's Meridian Fleet.

James didn't know him, but he came well recommended.

Vice Admiral Anthony Yamamoto had, for all intents and purposes, *declared* that he was coming along as Task Force Six's CAG, and Vice Admiral Ove Bevan, James's Intelligence Officer, brought the meeting up to seven senior officers.

The ship captains and command staff of Task Force Six. The people tasked with crossing a third of the Old Commonwealth and fighting a war at the other end.

"We've got a hell of a job ahead of us, people," James reminded them. "But we have almost no information about what is going on at our destination. Envoy Weaver expected an attack on Weston space within a week of the expiry of the Triumvirate's ultimatum.

"That ultimatum came due twenty days ago. By now, it is a reasonable assumption that the Saskatoon System has not merely been attacked but has fallen to the Triumvirate," he concluded. "And while I am not drawing the civilians' attention to the point, we have to understand that there is a chance that this war will be over by the time Task Force Six arrives.

"From the moment we leave this star system until we arrive in Weston, we will be in warped space for twenty-seven days. Very few of our crews, even our veterans from the pre-secession TCN, have spent that long under Alcubierre Drive."

James had, as part of the setup for a disastrous operation in the stars *past* the Alliance. That mission had gone badly enough that he'd ended up *allied* with a Castle Federation task group to take down the very people the TCN had sent him out to work with.

Losing modern warships to pirates was frowned upon by just about everyone, even if the pirates successfully blindsided you.

"As I understand, the biggest risk is boredom," Waterman replied. "We can keep that at bay, I'm sure."

"For longer than you might think but not as long as you might hope," James said. "Remember that you can see *nothing* in warped space. At least we will have q-coms home and with the other ships of the task force."

"What happens if we get there and Weston is in the hands of the Triumvirate?" Volkov asked.

"That depends." James shook his head. "Most likely, though? We turn the fleet around and we come right back home. We are taking a task force to war. We *are* risking these ships, but we cannot afford to lose them for nothing.

"If the Weston Republic has already fallen by the time we arrive, we aren't bringing enough ships, firepower or Marines to liberate them. At that point, we probably aim Walkingstick at them and stand aside."

That got him a few chuckles, but all of the humor faded into a grim examination of what *that* would look like.

"Walkingstick is almost certainly going to be there," Admiral Bevan warned everyone. The blond man looked thoughtful and a touch exhausted. "Not just his ships but, given his most recent patterns, *him*. Our information says that Admiral Tasker was *supposed* to be leading his troubleshooting expeditions, but since she died here… Well, every time a major force has left the Rump Commonwealth since, Walking-stick has commanded it himself.

"And frankly, outside of his attack on us, he's mostly made himself look good doing it."

"That's because there are people like Fredericka Waters in the galaxy," Yamamoto burred at them all. "And my early impressions do not put the Triumvirate on much higher of a pedestal."

"It appears that Rao, Morris and Verity have a better concept of both strategy and long-term planning," Bevan said. "However, they don't appear to have registered the fact that the slow and steady restoration of the q-com network has created a new dynamic.

"We *can* now call for each other's aid. I don't think they're going to like seeing us show up—and if the Rump has sent as many ships as we have, it's going to start looking very ugly for them, very quickly."

"And yes, I agree with Intelligence's assessment," James said grimly. "Walkingstick will be there. And we will, people, be *very, very* polite to the TCN at that point.

"We are not and will never be allies of the Rump Commonwealth. But there is a high chance that we will both be allies of the Weston Republic, and while we are in Republic space, we will respect that."

"We need to make damn sure the crews know that," Waterman observed. "A few grams of prevention should save us a few dozen administrative punishments. Warnings will go a long way."

"It better. We can barely afford this war," James warned. "The last thing the Confederacy needs is for *us* to start another one."

12

Dakota System
16:00 January 20, 2740 ESMDT

"WELCOME ABOARD *KRAKATOA*, VICE ADMIRAL YAMAMOTO."

"Thank you, Colonel." Anthony returned the salute of *Krakatoa*'s Commander, Aerospace Group, Colonel Avedis Maeda. "She's the closest thing I have to a home these days."

The short, dark Colonel grinned at him.

"Closest thing to a home a lot of us have," Maeda agreed, "what with a lot of our homes being under Walkingstick's boot. Starfighter Corps Chiefs are seeing to your quarters on the flag deck, but the Admiral didn't put anyone else in them."

"Nah, Tecumseh knew putting me on a flagship of my own was temporary," Anthony told his subordinate with a chuckle.

Anthony Yamamoto and more than a few others were Admirals of the Dakotan Interstellar Confederacy, but no matter what any of them did, there was only one "the Admiral" in the DCN and its associated services. There might be more full four-star Admirals as time went on, but Anthony was *quite* sure there'd only be *one* "the Admiral."

James Tecumseh wasn't perfect but the DCN knew who its founding father was.

"I was surprised by that," Maeda said softly as he fell in beside Anthony.

No one was bothering to give the Vice Admiral *directions*, clearly assuming that if Anthony had somehow forgotten the layout of his ship in the last six weeks, he could fake it through his neural implant.

"The Admiral felt, and I conceded begrudging agreement, that to command the Starfighter Corps, I needed more experience in command and to understand what our task group commanders were dealing with. Since I had the rank and experience, taking command of one of those groups served the purpose quite well."

Anthony snorted.

"We didn't expect me to wander into the political shitstorm of the year."

"We're not quite out of January," Maeda reminded him. "I'm sure it won't be the *worst* political shitstorm of the *entire* year."

"We're taking twenty-one thousand spacers, pilots and Marines to the coreward side of the Old Commonwealth, beyond any reasonable hope of tactical support from the rest of the Confederacy, and poking our noses into someone else's war," Anthony replied. Frustration *always* made his burr thicker, and he waited a second as Maeda processed the accent.

He was about to repeat himself more clearly when the Colonel nodded.

"I'd like to think that's as bad as it gets," Maeda finally said. "But after the last two years, I have to assume that it can and will get worse. I have plans to get the fighter wings worked up—and since we now have enough q-coms for inter-ship exercises even while warping space, we can exercise with *Black Sea*'s and *Iroquois*'s flight groups."

"Good," Anthony told him. "We don't have good intelligence on the order of battle of either the Republic or the Triumvirate at this point, but we can assume that they're going to have more starfighters than we're bringing.

"We're going to have to make up the difference with skill and train-ing." He grimaced. "Not even necessarily experience, as I suspect the

Triumvirate's pilots have seen just as much fire and brimstone as we have."

"Or more," Maeda warned. "*We* have only fought when people came to us. They've been looking for fights. Some of them with each other."

"Let's hope those are fracture lines the Admiral can find a use for," Anthony told the other man as they reached his quarters. "I'll be good from here, Colonel. I'm pretty sure I know the code for my own door."

"As you wish, Admiral." Maeda paused. "Do you know when we're shipping out?"

"Not decided yet," Anthony replied. "But my understanding is *as soon as possible*, so pretty much immediately upon everyone being fueled up and having the right crews aboard."

Taking the ships a month's flight away was going to throw a wrench in the careful team rotation the DCN had built, but Anthony *hoped* that someone in the DCN Personnel group had thought that through and double-checked.

Grumpy spacers were one thing, but if his *flight crews* got prickly, well… Those people were flying around with immediate access to guns that fired antimatter!

————

The lights inside Anthony's quarters were off, but he didn't even need to turn them on to realize he wasn't alone.

"You know, you're getting predictable," he told the darkness—and mentally instructed the room to bring the lights up to a middling level.

"Predictable is dangerous in my profession," Shannon Reynolds told him. The assassin-turned-bodyguard and espionage chief was seated cross-legged on the dining table in the front section of his quarters. "Though I do have an understanding with your Steward."

"I'd hope so, at this point," Anthony agreed as he crossed to the table and pulled out a chair. Despite the fact that she was in his quarters, he noted, Reynolds was wearing a bathrobe, and he had a solid idea what the woman was wearing under it.

There weren't *that* many pansexual oversexed aromantics around, in his sad experience, and very few people who didn't fit in that category really understood the degree to which Anthony Yamamoto did *not* understand relationships.

Reynolds was in that category and that made things… comfortable. If this *was* a relationship—even after two-plus years, Anthony wasn't sure he'd put that label on it—it was so open he could fly a starfighter through it, but it was *comfortable.*

"Welcome home," she told him, fiddling with the belt of the bathrobe. "I'm coming with you lot to Weston, if you weren't sure."

"You generally go where Tecumseh goes," Anthony pointed out. "I presumed. How was Teotihuacán? I haven't been myself."

"Too many people seemed to think that *I* was there to have a vacation because my main principal was there to have a vacation," Reynolds replied. "I mean, I wouldn't turn *down* an excuse to have a horizontal week with the First Chief, but she's sadly monogamous."

Anthony chuckled.

"A week with Tecumseh would be more, ah, vertical, would it?" he asked.

"Depends. I suppose he'd be even less likely than you to let me tie him up."

"I wouldn't know," Anthony replied. "I am and always have been in his chain of command, after all."

"A rule that makes sense, even if it's occasionally damn inconvenient," Reynolds told him. For all of her cheerful sexuality, he barely registered her starting to move until she was perched on the edge of the table, facing him.

The petite blonde woman moved like a big cat. She was a predator in human shape, one that had decided he made for more fun as *recurring* prey.

Fortunately, that worked for him—and the angle made it clear that she was wearing *exactly* what he thought she was under the bathrobe.

"You ready for the mess we're going to see in Weston?" she asked. "Back channels suggest some real mucky shit went down, and they had an… *odd* transition to self-governance. I'm pulling some old favors to get details."

"Folks from that life still talking to you?" he said. "I wasn't under the impression CISS was overly happy with you."

CISS—pronounced "kiss"—was the Commonwealth Internal Security Service. CISS's job had been to stop *exactly* what had happened with the fall of the communications network. They'd been infiltrators, spies and assassins—covert operators working to keep the various internal activist movements in line by any means necessary.

Reynolds herself had been tasked to make sure James Tecumseh didn't go rogue. In the end, she'd gone rogue right alongside him.

Anthony was *not* arrogant enough to think that his sleeping with her had impacted that at all.

"CISS is dead," she told him. "Probably half has rolled over into the new Commonwealth Bureau of Information, acting as spies and forward agents for the Imperator's people. Of what's left... maybe two-thirds went dark, dead or just retired. Probably a sixth of the old CISS, though... we picked our sides and they weren't with Walkingstick."

She chuckled.

"And, frankly, we're enough of a bunch of clinical psychopaths and sociopaths that we're still in contact with the ones still working for the Rump. So, yes, folks are still talking to me. We don't tell each other anything that will hurt our current sides, but people like the Triumvirate?"

Reynolds gently shook her head while hissing softly.

"They are the absolute worst-case scenario, the boogeyman we used to justify some of our worst stunts," she said. "Frankly, I didn't think anyone was *actually* going to go that bad."

"And then we had Waters. And a few others where Walkingstick has done the universe a favor."

"The Triumvirate at least understands building for the future. So did Waters, but something went wrong in her head once she realized Walkingstick was coming and she couldn't stop him."

She sighed.

"Anyways, work, back to the question: are you ready for this? We're going to have at least three different allied states working together, a minimum of one of which is going to be measuring everyone else for a knife and a coffin. Walkingstick isn't going to send people to Weston out of honor and the good of his heart, after all!"

"We'll be ready," Anthony promised. "Not least, both Tecumseh and I are prepared to listen to *you*."

She sniffed melodramatically.

"Listen, if not always execute on my suggestions."

"The Admiral is never going to kill people to avoid *potential* trouble," Anthony told her. "Nor am I."

"Probably a good thing," she conceded. "Though there are days I *swear* just listening to me would avoid trouble down the road."

"Or create more. Tecumseh seems to make allies of people *I* thought we'd have to kill, let alone people *you* thought we'd have to kill."

Reynolds chuckled and shifted a few centimeters forward, sliding off the table into his lap and somehow leaving the bathrobe behind.

"Now, it says terrible things about me that that line of conversation doesn't turn me off," she purred, "but I'd rather something a *touch* less bloodthirsty before you get inside me. How was your task group command?"

13

Sol System
09:00 January 21, 2740 ESMDT

"GRAB A SEAT, PICH," Walkingstick ordered the subordinate who'd just stepped into his office. Pich Misra headed his intelligence wing and was supposed to be briefing him. Even if his last call was running long.

"I'll just be a moment."

He turned his attention back to the virtual call he was on, leveling an unusually harsh gaze on Admiral Mihai Gabor, the commander of the Commonwealth Home Fleet and his main military deputy.

"There are eighty-six warships in this system," he told Gabor. "*Eighty-six*. Another twenty-odd under our command, once more readily drawn upon by q-com. And we're discovering that we can't muster a twelve-ship expeditionary force in ten days?"

"You took twenty-five ships to Tallulah," Gabor told him, his calm demeanor proof to Walkingstick in itself that the Admiral was telling the truth. "Of those, *none* are fit for immediate redeployment. *Saint Michael* is probably in the best shape, and *she* needed a full fusion-plant teardown."

The Admiral shrugged.

"We're seven days into that, and it's going to take six more for *Saint Michael* to be deployable. If you want to shift your flag to a different ship—*Idun*, perhaps?—we could have you on your way in probably two days.

"But since you already said you were sticking with *Saint Michael*, you're not leaving until the twenty-sixth. More likely the twenty-seventh."

Idun was one of exactly two *Ambrosia*-class eighty-two million, five hundred thousand cubic meter battleships in commission for the Commonwealth. The name-ship of the class, *Ambrosia* herself, had been destroyed defending TCN Central Command at Ceres, and to Walkingstick's unending frustration, the Project Hustle yards—the secret shipyards scattered through the Commonwealth—had suffered from enough supply and logistics delays that he didn't have all of the eighties he should yet.

"We're not sending any of the eighties to Weston," Walkingstick said grimly. "I gave you a wish list, as I recall."

"Four *Hercules*es, two *Volcano*es, *Saint Michael*, two *Lexington*s and three *Resolute*s," Gabor reeled off. "Seven modern and five last-gen ships. We're working on it. *Michael* is the biggest delay, but *Kilimanjaro* and *Mauna Loa* were both with you in Tallulah, and for all of her apparent failures, Waters knew to aim at the damn carriers.

"*Kilimanjaro* will be ready for deployment about the same time as *Saint Michael*, which is a damn miracle," the Admiral in charge of Sol told his boss. "*Mauna Loa* won't be. That means I had to play poker with the Vice Admirals for who gave up one of our most modern carriers."

He chuckled.

"And given that *none* of the battlecruisers you took to Tallulah are in deployable shape, we were basically doing that for your entire force. *Saint Michael* and *Kilimanjaro* are the *only* ships from your Tallulah force that we're going to be able to send to Weston, sir. So, we're pulling ten ships from Home and First Fleet for you—and while those ships were ready for *combat*, they weren't prepped for long-term deployment."

Walkingstick grunted his understanding and then sighed.

"And since *I* said I wasn't going to give up *Saint Michael*, you figured you had time for that *poker game*?" he asked.

"If you want to shift your flag to *Idun*, swap *Kilimanjaro* for *Horatio* and take two eighties at the core of the fleet? You can leave in about thirty-six hours, maybe less," Gabor told him. "Assuming we could manage to transfer your command systems to *Idun* in that time. There's a lot of staff and specialty equipment on *Michael*."

"I know," Walkingstick growled. "That's why I wanted to keep her."

He swallowed anything more actively angry. He suspected that Misra—the artificially intersex head of his intelligence and covert-operations forces—had ways to eavesdrop on the theoretically secure conversation he was having.

Either way, the silent presence of the intelligence officer kept him from critiquing *too* much. Even more so now, it was important that he criticize in private. His words as Imperator carried a dangerous weight. He didn't *think* anyone had been murdered on accidental instruction yet, but the fate of Thomas Becket hung all too high in his mind sometimes.

No one would suffer for *his* careless words. He would spill every ocean of blood needed to restore the Commonwealth, but not *one drop* by accident.

"If this had been properly explained a week ago, things might have been different," Walkingstick finally told Gabor. "But I recognize that a week ago, I was buried in the administration of the Commonwealth and barely available." The error was as much his as his subordinates', he supposed.

"At this point, it would *take* at least a week to relocate myself and my staff from *Saint Michael* to *Idun*. By which point *Michael* should be ready to deploy, correct?"

"Yes, sir."

"Then we wait. It's three weeks from here to Weston anyway. We're not saving Saskatoon, so a few more days won't make any difference."

Saskatoon was, *somehow*, still holding out. They should have run out of missiles, mines or starfighters by now, but the stubborn Republicans *still* held the inhabited planet of Regina. Even once that world fell, it would be a week or more for the Triumvirate to move on to the rest of the Republic.

"Check with the engineers," Walkingstick concluded. "I don't want to cut corners—not with my flagship!—but if there's any time we can save on *Michael* or *Kilimanjaro* to get us moving, let's find it.

"I'd rather not arrive in Weston to find that, I don't know, the *Castle Federation* has sent a battle group and rendered our help unnecessary!"

He dropped the call with Gabor and turned his attention back to Pich Misra. The Cambodian spy met his gaze impassively, their flattened and heavyset features lending themselves well to an expression of unending patience.

Misra was part of the not-quite-cult of the modern Transhumanist movement, having adopted both the visible augmentations of the group as well as the formal "gender" of being artificially intersex.

Given that Walkingstick—a relatively baseline citizen of the twenty-eighth-century Terran Commonwealth from that perspective— had somewhere around two *kilograms* of cybernetics located throughout his body, he found the whole concept amusing. By any rational standard, *every* human of their era was transhuman.

But people like Misra went further. Visible silver circuitry wrapped around the left side of the spy's head, an expansion of the regular neural implant beyond what could be easily fitted into and onto a human skull. And while many people, especially soldiers, would have some level of physical augmentation, Misra's arms were both marked with clearly visible reinforcing steel bars wrapped in more delicate silver circuitry.

"Apologies for running over, Pich," Walkingstick told the spy. "I was hoping to be on our way by now, but apparently, I use my flagship a bit too hard for that."

"There are many arguments for upgrading to one of the *Ambrosias*, I would suspect," Misra said mildly. Whether they had listened in on the conversation or not, they could clearly guess what Walkingstick's subordinates wanted.

"*Saint Michael* has been my flagship for five years, my friend." The

Imperator shrugged. "We could move enough people over to one of the new ships to help get her up to speed, but it would be months before she was truly up to the level of integration *Michael's* crew has with my staff.

"It's easier to stick with the ship I know. Sometimes, that causes issues, but it gives us time to lay groundwork, right?"

Misra chuckled, their gaze flickering around Walkingstick's office. The room certainly didn't *look* like it had been Walkingstick's space for five years, but that was part of the point.

Like so much of Walkingstick's appearance and presence, the presentation of his office with no ornamentation, no affectations or "I love me" walls was carefully crafted. The only decoration in the space was the olive-branches-and-stars emblem of the Terran Commonwealth, inlaid in gold across the steel bulkhead behind him.

This was a warrior's office on a warship. There were other spaces that might be more decorated, but the austerity of this space sent a specific message. It was also Walkingstick's own preference... he thought.

It had been a long time since he hadn't factored his intended image into *everything* he did, after all.

"Groundwork is what you have me for, isn't it?" Misra asked. There was a reason the spy didn't wear a uniform anymore. He'd originally been the intelligence officer on Walkingstick's staff. His current status was intentionally more nebulous.

All preexisting Commonwealth intelligence services had been dissolved a year earlier, after several CISS agents had attempted to assassinate Walkingstick. The Star Chamber had authorized the consolidation of all of those budgets into the blandly named Commonwealth Bureau of Information.

The grim reality was that the CBI answered only to Misra and Misra answered only to Walkingstick. That was a *problem* in the Imperator's mind, but he needed the security and control for now. Eventually, he might even tell the Star Chamber who ran the CBI.

Eventually.

"And you're here to brief me on that groundwork, I hope," Walkingstick said drily. "We were supposed to have people in the Triumvirate's forces, but the merger took me by surprise."

"That's because we were *expecting* some kind of negotiation or formal treaty," Misra replied. "I've managed to nail down when the deal was made, and *deal* is the wrong word."

"Explain," the Imperator ordered.

"They're still, from what I can tell, actually three separate nations, three separate fleets and command structures," the spy said. "Unified at the top and slowly working through the administration and logistics of merging everything all the way down.

"From the plan, though, they have time. At least eighteen years, I figure."

Walkingstick parsed that for a few seconds, then grimaced.

"A kid?"

"The Heir, capitals required," Misra confirmed. "Given that Verity's file says they have roughly the sexuality of a *rock*, I assume some level of genetic recombination was done in a lab before the fetus was implanted in Morris.

"But that's the nature of their game," they told him. "Celestine Morris is pregnant with Harendra Rao's kid, presumably with some genetic samples from Surinder Verity mixed in. Verity appears to be in command of their vanguard force... which is made up primarily of Morris's ships."

"An interesting balance of power there," Walkingstick noted.

"If it was Rao's ships, I think they'd worry that Verity would intentionally, uh, *expend* them," Misra agreed. "But since Morris's uterus is currently giving her complete control over their planned future, I think she figures she can trust Verity not to waste her ships."

"Does she feel the same after the mess that has been the siege of Saskatoon?"

Misra shrugged.

"Verity isn't wasting ships there," they pointed out. "The Governor is apparently one ice-cold paranoid bastard and didn't trust anybody —us, the Triumvirate... the Republic itself."

"The Republic is about twenty bucks and a fresh coffee from an explicit corporatocracy," Walkingstick replied. "*I* don't trust the Republic."

"Part of what makes them interesting," Misra agreed. "On the surface, at least, it looks like the corporations willingly *gave up* the ability to exert direct control of the Republic. Be fascinating to see what the reality is on the ground.

"As for Saskatoon, though, they had some nasty surprises waiting when the Triumvirate fleet showed up. The Republic held their fleet back—they must have realized that the Triumvirate was going to bring enough to crush them in a single afternoon if they tried.

"Which only makes the fact that Saskatoon has held out against a *nineteen-ship* battle fleet for two weeks more impressive." Misra grinned. "Mostly by making Verity gun-shy, from what I can tell. After the second time you walk into ten thousand preplaced missiles, you get *real* cautious."

"You do," Walkingstick confirmed. "That trick got pulled on us in the Rimward Marches a few times. That… explains a lot. We're not getting that much information from the Republic, of course."

"I've got full sensor data from the Triumvirate side for you," the spy replied, producing a data chip seemingly out of their palm. *That*, at least, Walkingstick knew was just sleight of hand. "Might come in handy."

"It will come in handy. Do we know their order of battle?" Walkingstick asked.

"On the chip," Misra said. "Biggest joker in the deck is Verity's flagship. *Custodian*—one of the Flight One *Sentinels*."

"I didn't think any of those had survived!" If the Triumvirate had a *Sentinel*—one of the eighty-million-cubic-meter carriers—that was an ugly change to his assessment.

"She shouldn't have. *Custodian* was supposed to be in the Redwall System and was *supposed* to have been destroyed in the battle over the q-com station there." Misra shook their head. "Though now that I've poked at it, the *Alliance* reports don't claim her as a kill. Her fighters were definitely in the thick of the fighting, but methinks *she* ran. Found herself in the Athas System and under the guns of one Rear Admiral

Surinder Verity, just when Verity was trying to decide what to do in the wake of the Commonwealth's loss of communications."

"And since Verity was flying their flag on a *Resolute*-class battlewagon, they upgraded," Walkingstick concluded.

"So, one of Verity's biggest contributions to the Triumvirate is that flagship," Misra told him. "Plus, well, frankly being the best tactician of the three by a long shot. Rao and Morris *started* with entire sectors, at least in theory. Verity started with one system and one task group."

Walkingstick growled at the thought. Rao and Morris had lost control of three star systems between them, out of the twelve in the Sectors they'd been supposed to *protect*. One of those systems had tried to go independent; the other two had tried to ask for help from Sol.

All three had found themselves under Verity's control, along with two systems from the Oglaf Sector.

"Not to mention that Verity was happily getting ready to slice off systems from the other two, a threat they seem to have neatly co-opted with this Heir plan."

"I don't *think* they're planning on putting everything in the hands of the kid when they turn eighteen," Misra observed. "That said, my impression is that whichever one of them is standing last is expected to pass power on to the Heir. It's going to be interesting to see how it shakes out."

"And right now? How fragile *is* the Triumvirate?"

Misra sighed and shook their head.

"I've got agents throughout the whole mess," they observed. "Hell, I need to poke gently, but I think I might have an asset on Verity's staff, and I am *almost* certain I've got two of her warship Captains in pocket. They're not going to throw away a good thing, but if the odds start going to shit, I figure I can pull as many as three or four full ship defections out of my hat."

"Almost as many as you missed coming at Dakota," Walkingstick said in saccharine tones.

Those defections, after all, had been *to* Dakota. It was Misra who'd talked him into walking away from the battle in Dakota—though it was *also* Misra who'd admitted, later on, that Tecumseh had pulled a fast one. On the other hand, if the four ships that had failed to come home had changed sides in the middle of the battle... Well, Walking-stick would have faced worse than the Pyrrhic victory the Common-wealth couldn't afford then.

"We have a far better handle on our internal weaknesses now than we did eighteen months ago," Misra said calmly. "And, frankly, that was *still* fewer ships than we'd have lost facing off against the DCN if they were prepared to fight to the death.

"Which they were."

They'd had this argument before. They'd probably have this argu-ment again. Even knowing that they'd been deceived at the time—Tecumseh had fooled them into thinking there was an entire squadron of Stellar League mercenary ships backing him up—it was still true that the Dakotans would have fought to the death.

Even victory in Dakota that day could have cost Walkingstick the Commonwealth.

"So, the Triumvirate is fragile," Walkingstick concluded, turning the conversation back to the enemy of the day.

"Not as much as we'd like. I have assets and levers we can pull, but I don't think any of them are strong enough to turn the tide of battle," Misra admitted. "If they *lose* a battle, I can pull some of those who survive. But prior to that..."

"Can we influence Verity's planning?"

That question hung in the air for a few long seconds, and then a wicked grin spread across Misra's face.

"I think so," they agreed. "I might need to go so far as to put you directly in touch with some of those officers—your name and voice carry a *lot* of weight, Imperator—but I think we can play that game.

"Some of their officers we can convince. Others we can bribe. Others, well..." Misra chuckled. "Others, we have enough access to their subordinates that we can lie to them. I can't guarantee we'll make their invasion force jump in a particular direction, but we can make it more likely."

"If we can control—or at least *learn*—where Verity strikes after Saskatoon, we can manipulate the situation to our advantage," Walk-ingstick murmured. "We can play politics in Weston, but if their fleet is weakened, well..."

"That's not necessarily something they'll miss us doing," Misra warned.

"If we use your *assets and levers*, my friend, we might be able to get Verity and their fleet to do the heavy lifting on that side." Walkingstick grinned. "Make no mistake: we're going to save the Republic... but when the dust settles, I want it to be very, *very* clear that their only safe path forward is rejoining the Commonwealth."

14

Weston System
20:00 February 17, 2740 ESMDT

AFTER TWENTY-SEVEN DAYS, James Tecumseh figured there was no one aboard Task Force Six who wasn't ready to explode. Some people found a certain joy in the strange mixed lights of the warp bubble, but most screens were set to show a simulation of the stars around them.

But humans knew it was a lie. The ability to talk to people at home and on the other ships helped, but any journey that lasted long enough to hit the Alcubierre-Stetson Drive's maximum pseudovelocity—ten light-years per day—was a strain on the crew.

He'd put the crew through intensive virtual exercises along the way and he was as confident in their capability as he could be without taking the formation into action, but, like everyone else, he was glad to see the warp bubble dissipate around them.

"Welcome to Weston," Volkov declared. "Six rocks, a gas giant and an asteroid belt." She snorted. "Do they come any more standardized than this?"

"Yes, because most planets aren't as habitable as Galen," James replied. A thought focused the display on Weston II, the inhabited planet named for some famous ancestor of the corporation that had funded the colony expedition.

Galen was a mild world, slightly bigger and heavier than old Earth and with almost no axial tilt. With minimal seasons, calm weather, and an extended growing season, Galen had a planetary population James had rarely seen rivaled outside the core sectors.

"We're picking up heavy industry above the first and second planets," Volkov reported, summarizing the reports from the Operations team. "Minimal population on the inner planet; looks like surface-level low-atmo mining. Galen herself, well."

"Over six billion people," James said aloud, pulling the data up himself. "Another hundred million scattered across the system, mostly either in the belt or around Garfield."

Garfield was the gas giant, home to dozens of space stations pulling hydrogen and helium up to fuel fusion plants across the star system. The Weston Belt was a so-called "hot belt," orbiting inside the orbit of Weston I, but the database said it was rich in easily accessible heavy metals.

"Any contact from the locals yet?" he asked. "And do we have eyes on the Republic Fleet, for that matter?"

"We don't have q-coms with them, so they might not know we're here yet," Volkov replied. "Prebensen?"

Commodore Rylie Prebensen had been Tecumseh's coms officer back when he'd commanded one task force of the Dakota Sector Fleet. Now she was his coms officer on Task Force Six—and while she hadn't served directly under his command in the intervening years, he'd still seen her in action supporting his subordinates.

There were few officers in the Dakotan Confederacy Navy Tecumseh *wouldn't* have trusted—but Prebensen was definitely in the group he trusted *more*.

"We started transmitting the codes Envoy Weaver provided as soon as we arrived," she reported. "I have a q-com relay drone on its way toward Galen to speed up coms."

"Let's keep the rest of our drones in tight," James ordered, glancing over at Volkov. "Q-probes might seem sensible to *us*, but this is *their* star system, and trying to peek around corners might seem rude."

"Speaking of seeming rude, we have eyes on a guardship formation at four light-minutes," the Ops officer reported. "Six ships, estimate three hundred thousand tons apiece. Four fighter squadrons in formation."

"Prebensen—ping them directly, advise them of our identity and intentions," James ordered. "They almost certainly have a q-com link to Galen."

Before the Rimward War, they would definitely have had a q-com link. But while the Confederacy was now at the point where the FTL network was beginning to allow broad civilian usage, he couldn't be certain that the Weston Republic was there yet.

"We're going to hang out here, nice and quiet, until they invite us in to say hello," James said aloud. Galen was eleven and a half light-minutes from its star, just outside the G3 star's gravity shadow. The planet itself cast about a four-light-minute shadow in which it was unwise to use an A-S drive—and they'd brought Task Force Six sublight sixteen light-minutes from the star and just over six from the planet.

James had taken ships, battle groups and even *fleets* in closer than this—it was called "riding the needle," keeping a ship in the careful balance between dropping out of FTL and being ripped apart by gravitic turbulence.

Today, though, that was not merely unnecessary but foolish. He wasn't attacking Weston. He was there to help them.

"We're picking up signals in Garfield orbit. Looks like another dozen guardships, with four A-S warships in the mix."

"What about at Galen herself?" James asked. "The Republic is supposed to have, what, sixteen ships?"

That made four a heavy but probably sensible defense fleet for their capital system. The rest of the Republic combined might exceed Weston in population and industry, but she was the unquestioned economic queen of this sector.

"Unless they've lost ships since Weaver's last update, which seems likely," Volkov replied. "But I'm picking up a number of orbital platforms that appear to be armed. Six appear to be *Zions* or something equivalent, but there's at least a dozen that appear to be home-design battle stations— Hold on!"

James waited calmly for a moment, poking at the edges of the datafeeds long enough to be sure they'd seen a warship in Galen orbit.

"I've got a *Volcano*-class carrier and a pair of *Resolute*s in Galen orbit," Volkov reported. "*Volcano* is *Pico do Fogo*, flagship of the Weston Sector Fleet. Formation at Garfield appears to be a *Lexington*—*Midway* —and three old cruiser thirties."

Either *Assassins* or *Oceans*. The thirty-million-cubic-meter cruisers had been an unfortunate bit of economizing on the part of the Old Commonwealth, one that had bitten the TCN repeatedly during the war—but the Commonwealth had certainly built a *lot* of the ships over the years.

Enough that the TCN had the false economy of the ships rubbed in their faces. They were only about ten, *maybe* fifteen percent cheaper than ships half again their size and at least a third again their capability.

But they hadn't been truly useful in the Rimward War, which meant they'd formed the backbone of the Sector Fleets.

"So, seven ships in this star system," James murmured. "Interesting choices."

He wouldn't judge more than that, not aloud and not without more information. But it spoke to a weakness of the Republic. They were terrified for Weston's security, but those seven ships might make all the difference in the battles to come.

"I've got a link with the guardship squadron," Prebensen reported. "They're in touch with their command at Galen and are asking us to hold position until we can establish a relayed q-com link with the President's people."

"Of course." James smiled. "I presume we're vectoring a relay q-drone over to them?"

"Yes, sir. We should have live or near-live coms with the planetary government in about thirty minutes. They seem glad to see us."

"It's nice to be welcome," he agreed. "Let's keep our eyes open, just in case. I don't *expect* a Triumvirate surprise attack, but I'd rather not *be* surprised!"

"I am Minister Mokhtar Campana," the veiled man that finally made contact with James introduced himself. "I am the head of the Republic's Foreign Ministry and, of course, the man who authorized the contact codes you are using."

"I am Admiral James Tecumseh, commanding officer of the Dakotan Confederacy Navy Task Force Six," James replied. "We are here in response to the request relayed by your Envoy Andreas Weaver."

The veil wrapped around Campana's face was translucent enough that James could see the other man close his eyes and inhale in what he hoped was relief.

"Andreas is alive, then?" Campana asked.

"He is currently setting up an embassy on Dakota," James told the local. "He, his bodyguards and I believe about half of his staff were rescued from pirates by the DCN over a month ago. While his q-com link was lost, he survived to deliver his message and the call for help."

"The last information we had from Andreas was that the ship carrying him was being boarded," Campana said quietly. "We... assumed the worst, but it looked to be weeks, even months, before we could arrange passage for a replacement Envoy. Given our current situation, we had to assume that help from Dakota would not arrive in time."

"I hope from your phrasing, Minister, that we *have* arrived in time. Certainly, Weston herself appears free for now."

"For now," Campana said grimly. "A full briefing will need to be arranged, but you understand that I am obliged to make sure of your bona fides. Your task force represents a real threat to this system if we make a mistake."

James nodded and smiled understandingly.

"I am transmitting a video message provided by Envoy Weaver, along with an encrypted sequence that he said should tell you if we've breached it," he told the Minister. "We are here to help, Minister. We can hardly do so if you don't feel you can trust us!"

"Your understanding and patience are appreciated, Admiral

Tecumseh. Your reputation precedes you, of course." Campana glanced aside, likely checking on a neural feed. "We have received the package from Envoy Weaver. If you don't mind, Admiral, would it be possible to set up a direct relay to the Envoy?

"There is not yet a reliable interlink of the q-com networks between here and Dakota."

"Of course, Minister," James agreed. "If you wish to put your staff in touch with Commodore Prebensen, we will get that sorted as quickly as possible."

"Again, thank you, Admiral." Campana paused. "Admiral Horvath's staff will be in touch shortly to provide you with a course in-system. We are expecting other arrivals today and… my understanding is that we do not wish to have your ships and those of the Imperial Commonwealth in close proximity."

James smiled thinly.

"While we are in the Republic's territory, we will honor our alliance with you and your alliance with Terra," he told Campana. "We will, of course, defend ourselves… but we are not, at this moment, at war with the Commonwealth.

"We will not seek a conflict if they do not."

———

"So, I've got one strange and unpleasant question from that conversation," Volkov told James as he passed the link back to Prebensen.

Krakatoa's flag bridge wasn't quite the spectacular over-the-top holographic universe of the new eighties, but Dakota hadn't left the flagship untouched while they'd been updating and refitting the fleet. They'd had to tear out all of the old q-com network communication equipment, after all, which had given them quite a bit of time with a bunch of bulkheads open.

One of the things they'd gained was a slightly more private zone around the Admiral, with a noise-deadening field that James could turn off or on with a literal thought. That meant that Volkov could stand next to his seat and raise points that were impolitic without anyone else hearing them.

"Other, I'm assuming, than *Where and when do the Commonwealth arrive?*" James replied. "I'll admit I'm counting on the locals to make sure we're a safe distance from the Rump when they show up. The last thing anyone wants is for someone with an itchy trigger finger to start a fight *here*."

"Yeah. If anything, the surprise is that the Rump isn't already *here*," Volkov said. "If they're in active communication, their Envoy presumably arrived intact and with working coms. They didn't have as far to go, didn't get delayed by pirates, and the Rump ships didn't have as far to come."

"Forty-two-day round trip, but they must have needed to fit ships out for endurance operations," James murmured. "Or, quite possibly, wait for Walkingstick to be around to give orders. He was fighting in Tallulah recently, wasn't he?"

"Maybe. You'd think they'd be able to launch this kind of op without him, though, wouldn't you?"

"And there, Admiral Volkov, do you find the crux of the problem the Rump faces," James told her. "But that wasn't your question, was it?"

"No. My question is much simpler: who in the stars and void is Admiral Horvath?"

James took a second to follow through the question and consider Campana's discussion.

"Presumably the system defense commander, but that's not what you mean," he guessed.

"There was no Admiral Horvath assigned to the Weston Sector," Volkov said. "No Commodore Horvath. No *Captain* Horvath. I checked, actually—there was no one with the surname *Horvath* above the rank of Captain in the *entire Commonwealth Navy*.

"Captain Alexis Horvath commanded a logistics ship in the Rimward Marches and remained with the Sitaaron Ka Saamraajy Sector Fleet when Walkingstick sailed on Terra. They're currently in service with the defense forces of the Presley System. Captain Coburn Horvath was assigned to the security forces in the Axiom System, and while we have no information on him, we can presume him KIA in the Alliance attack," Volkov continued.

"Of the nine hundred and eighty-two thousand officers and personnel of the Commonwealth armed services in the Weston Sector at the loss of communications, twenty-one men and women had that surname."

"And?" James prodded.

"Eleven were Marine Corps, three were Starfighter Corps, seven were Navy. Only two were commissioned, one Marine Corps and one Navy officer. Unless *Lieutenant Commander* Daniel Horvath has been promoted well above anything his complete lack of experience outside of an orbital platform's engineering department suggests he was qualified for two years ago..."

Volkov left the question hanging.

"Commodore Prebensen," James called, summoning the coms officer over. The slimly built woman entered the privacy zone with an aside glance that suggested she hadn't realized the sound screen was up.

"Sir?" she asked.

"You've been in touch with Admiral Horvath's staff, correct?" he asked.

"Yes, sir. I was just about to confirm the course they provided with you and Commodore Volkov." Prebensen looked back over at her team. "We've passed it on to Navigation. It seems a reasonable compromise, keeping us just outside the gravity shadow of the star and planet while well away from the direct line from Sol."

James picked the course out of the system and hung it in the air in front of him—in his implant, so no one else saw it—to review. "It looks good to me. Volkov, can you get it moving to the rest of the task force?"

"On it," the ops officer told him, her gaze going vague as James returned his attention to the coms officer.

"You had a question, sir?" she asked.

"Do you have a first name for Admiral Horvath?" he said. "For that matter, is he a full Admiral or are we looking at civilians short-handing without providing the detail first?"

"His staff was a bit clearer," she admitted. "Vice Admiral

Alexander Horvath is the commanding officer of the system defense forces, operating from Central Defense Command in orbit of Galen."

"Interesting," Volkov murmured. "Whoever Alexander Horvath is, then, he was not a TCN officer two years ago. That raises some... interesting questions."

"It's possible that someone didn't trust the TCN," James pointed out. "Which, yes, raises the question of where they sourced their officers *from*. Prebensen—let's not be obvious about it, but the more information we can get on who we're dealing with, the better.

"I assumed that the Republic, like every other Successor State we've dealt with, drew its officer corps from the Commonwealth armed services personnel in their sector. If they didn't..."

"The entire Crimea Sector is between here and the edge of the Old Commonwealth," James said quietly. "What's past that? I'm... for obvious reasons, I'm more familiar with the Rimward and Clockward borders!"

"Not much," Volkov told him, her distracted voice telling him she was deep in implant research mode. "There's a significant volume of star systems without habitable planets. A handful of single-system states surrounded by enough empty space that they can't even be bothered to fight each other.

"Past that, there's the Kaizen Shogunate. Which..." Volkov snorted. "Well, to paraphrase an old joke, the Kaizen Shogunate isn't about rapid improvement and is only a *Shogunate* because the *not-Japanese* founders thought the name sounded cool for their elected leader."

"But that's easily another hundred and sixty light-years coreward," James concluded. "Somehow, I doubt they recruited flag officers from the Kaizen Shogunate.

"So, where *did* they recruit from?"

15

FOR SOME STRANGE REASON, the Republic's Vice Admiral Horvath had decided that he didn't want *anyone* else's capital ships in orbit of Galen. He might have felt comfortable enough with James Tecumseh's four ships, who were arguably outgunned by Horvath's three ships and the orbital forts, but the *dozen* starships the Commonwealth had arrived with were a step too far.

So, James found himself studying the star system and the ships his new allies and not-quite-enemies had in play from his pinnace. The small craft was roughly the size of a standard five-thousand-plus-ton starfighter, with the same engines and mass manipulators allowing it to accelerate *far* more quickly than a capital ship, but with personnel and cargo capacity instead of positron lances and missiles.

It was the biggest non-starfighter small craft his task force had, and it was *designed* to land half an armor company—eight main battle tanks. But the TCN had long since decided that Admirals needed to travel in style and with security, so flagships carried designated flag pinnaces.

Two such pinnaces were now descending on the city of Nova-Toronto. One, James's, was heading in from Task Force Six and had been given a flight plan that would see them approach their destination from the north. The other was coming in from the Terran Commonwealth Fifth Fleet and would be approaching the destination from the south.

Except for the final approach, the two shuttles would never approach within fifty kilometers of each other. The pinnaces might not be starfighters, but they were most definitely not *unarmed*.

"One positron lance and the galaxy becomes a much better place," Volkov muttered. James's operations officer was clearly following the same sensor feed the Admiral was.

"And that, Young, is why nobody is flying anything with guns into this meeting," James told her. "Because while you and I might think the galaxy is better off without Imperator Walkingstick, *today* he is arguably our ally.

"And the Republic really doesn't want us picking fights in their skies. We need to prove we can behave or we're going to be doing a lot of long-range resupply flights!"

They had shuttles that could make the flights. And while those shuttles might be smaller than the pinnace, they could easily haul a couple of thousand tons of cargo apiece from Galen's surface to orbit and back to the fleet. The craft just managed that capacity by using much slower accelerations.

"We'll be on the ground in sixteen minutes," the pilots announced on all of their neural implants, and James glanced around the room.

There were a dozen Marines in the room, wearing medium-profile dress armor. A step down from full power armor, it still had exoskeletal muscles allowing the troops to carry the heavy penetrator rifles designed to take out power armor.

In this case, the armors' digital camouflage had been set to match their normal uniform and added an oversized version of the Dakotan Marines' coyote symbol.

Five other men and women were scattered through the mix. James assumed that the three members of Crow VIP security detail Reynolds led were probably as deadly *out* of armor as the Marines were *in* it.

Certainly, the delicate-looking carbines they carried were the same the Commonwealth had issued to the Presidential Protection Detail.

Delicate or not, those guns would go through armor as neatly as the bigger coilguns in the hands of the Marines.

The fifth ununiformed person was a surprisingly young-looking official in a plain gray business suit. The only sign that Ma'tano Littlebear wore to show he was anything but an Old Nations-descended businessman was a set of three feathers on a woven leather thong hanging around his neck.

James didn't know what birds the feathers were even *from*, but given that Dakota's Cheyenne families were the purest preservation of their culture off of Earth, he presumed they were meaningful to the diplomat and his people.

"Are you ready, Envoy?" he asked the young man.

"I understand this is mostly a military briefing," Littlebear said. "Which means I believe the main diplomatic task will be to keep you and Imperator Walkingstick from trying to publicly murder each other with your bare hands."

Ma'tano Littlebear was one of the senior members of the Confederacy's fledgling corps of diplomats and would, eventually, serve as their Ambassador to the Republic. For now…

"I am *reasonably* confident in my own self-control," James murmured. "But I suspect I may be a rather notable *irritant* to our Imperial friend." He smiled. "But we can trust in our new allies to keep the peace, I hope, rather than relying on your silver tongue."

Littlebear touched the feathers around his neck and smiled back.

"One way or another, Admiral Tecumseh, I think we will make it through today without bloodshed."

"Perhaps not tomorrow, though," James warned. "This is, after all, a council of war."

———

NovaToronto's Maple Avenue was flanked on both sides by carefully planted and maintained rows of the titular trees, imported from Earth when the colony was founded. Now three hundred years later, the trees on the boulevard provided an astonishing amount of shade as they towered in the sunlight of the local summer.

Like many diaspora capital cities, NovaToronto had been designed from the ground up to serve as an anchor of government. Maple Avenue ran north-south through the entire length of the city—with James's pinnace having landed at the main spaceport on the north end.

At roughly the center of the city, Maple Avenue intersected with Gardiner Street. Gardiner ran east-west through the width of the city, from the coast on the east side of the city to the farmland to the west.

Where the two boulevards met, they merged into a massive roundabout, circling around a park occupied by more imported trees and a building that James's implant informed him was a three-to-one-sized replica of the Westminster Parliament building in London on Earth.

They came into the Central Plaza from the north in a low-key motorcade arranged by the locals that delivered them to a broad flagstone promenade in front of the Parliament building. Their car had been driven by remote control, giving them some last moments of privacy, but they had a guide waiting for them as it rolled to a stop.

The man waiting was Black to Littlebear's paler brown coloring, but his outfit and body language had clearly been stamped from the same press as the Dakotan diplomat.

"Admiral, Admiral, Envoy," he swiftly greeted James, Volkov and Littlebear. "I am Íomhar Falk, deputy senior aide to President Frey. If you and your escort will follow me, please."

"Let's go, Major," James told Revie—trusting, *knowing*, really, that Reynolds would follow suit without explicit instruction.

The Marines and Crows spread out around the three key people, and Falk waited patiently while the security people sorted themselves out.

"There is a south promenade as well," he noted when he saw James's querying look. "And we staggered the landings. Imperator Walkingstick is due to arrive at the south entrance in about five minutes. We have time."

Not least, James figured, because there was no way the locals wanted one of them to get there *first*.

16

Weston System
09:00 February 18, 2740 ESMDT

IT WAS, without question or argument in anyone's mind, the absolute Star Chamber–mandated duty of the Imperator of Terra to see the Commonwealth restored by any means necessary. That meant that James Walkingstick had rarely encountered the governments of the Successor States in circumstances where he needed to treat them as a foreign power.

As he followed his guide through Maple Hall Parliament—what *had* been the legislature for the Galen Planetary Parliament and now served as the center of the Weston Republic's government—he maintained a carefully neutral expression.

The line he needed to walk today was a *fascinating* one. This wasn't the time for posturing and proclaiming that everyone was actually part of the Commonwealth, and that the Republic's government was illegitimate. He needed to negotiate and work with these people for now.

But he *also* needed to make it clear that he didn't fully recognize their authority and legitimacy. He would work with them as partners… but he would never work with them as *equals*.

Not because he actually judged the Republic as illegitimate. Like the Dakotan Confederacy, the Weston Republic was a relatively sane democracy with a clear social contract and popular support. If Walkingstick had to see the Commonwealth fall apart, these were the nations he wanted to replace it.

But by sacred oath, natural inclination and given duty, he was tasked to *stop* the Commonwealth from falling apart. He would bring the nations that understood the ideals of Justice, Equality and Liberty back into Unity last and as gently as possible... but there were *four* principles to the Terran Commonwealth, and Unity could not be sacrificed.

So, he followed his guide through the halls of the Republic's government like a good little ally, while hopefully radiating just enough *You are distracted children and I am here to set things right* that everyone knew who he was and what his mission was.

———

Unlike most of the people in Maple Hall, Walkingstick had been inside the Westminster Parliament building and its dozen or so knockoffs on Earth. While Maple Hall dated back to about the mid-twenty-fourth century and was hardly *new*, even a four-hundred-year-old structure paled in comparison to the sheer antiquity and weight of the original Westminster.

On the other hand, Maple Hall had been built in an era where computers, public access and *windows* were things to take into consideration. Its internal spaces were significantly airier and better lit than Westminster itself, and for all that the exterior was a carefully rendered mirror of the older building, Maple Hall had a *lot* of windows hidden away in those stone walls.

And much like the structure it imitated, Maple Hall also had a lot of secret and concealed spaces. The digital guides and maps and directions were set up to help the inattentive entirely miss the elevator his guide led them to.

Walkingstick certainly missed the elevator until his guide opened it, and he was not inattentive. It was well done—though he noted that Misra, his sole non-bodyguard companion, did not seem surprised.

"Calm, sir," the spy murmured through his implants. "They will almost certainly have us and Tecumseh arrive at the same time. Let's not say anything… precipitous."

Walkingstick's chosen right-hand woman, an officer who'd been with him since he'd been given his Marshal's mace and ordered to bring the Rimward Marches—a region of space that *happened* to coincide with the Alliance of Free Stars—into the Commonwealth, had died in Dakota at the hands of Tecumseh's main strike fleet. There was *blood* between Walkingstick and Tecumseh. Still…

"I am capable of sufficient self-control to not destroy our diplomatic endeavors here, Pich. I know Tecumseh of old. We'll be fine."

"You *knew* Tecumseh," Misra warned him. The entire conversation passed silently as the elevator rose swiftly toward the peak of Maple Hall's main tower. "You knew him as a Captain and a junior flag officer, not as the Admiral commanding an entire national navy with the lives of millions riding on him.

"That changes a man."

"Yes." Walkingstick let that hang. He knew that serving as Imperator had changed *him*. "But I know him well enough that I'm not going to try to choke him the moment I see him. Even what happened with Tasker… That was, given the path he'd chosen, his duty.

"And while the stars may leave him to the void for it, James Tecumseh will *always* do what he thinks is his duty."

That, too, was something he shared with James *Walkingstick*.

———

Despite his assurances, Walkingstick wasn't truly certain he could handle speaking to Tecumseh peacefully until the moment he saw the other officer. The Westons had timed it perfectly, and the two of them stepped into the brightly lit conference room at almost the exact same moment, both of them trailing a small coterie of guards and aides.

The last time he'd seen James Tecumseh in person, Walkingstick had been sending the younger man back to Sol in disgrace, to face a board of inquiry for losing his flagship to a pirate warlord and then allying with the Commonwealth's enemies to destroy said ship.

The last time he'd spoken to the man at all had been during the Battle of Dakota, where they'd each tried to convince the other to stand down. Both had failed, and what Walkingstick could admit had been a damn clever trick had convinced him the other man had brought new allies to the fight.

He *now* knew that two of Tecumseh's carriers had been loaded with Stellar League starfighters acquired during the battles along the former border. Then, though, the presence of the Xenophons had suggested that the small fleet of League starships the Confederacy had faked had actually existed.

There was no deception today, he judged. The Confederacy squadron was a small force but a respectable one, anchored on a *Da Vinci*–class battlecruiser. Walkingstick's Fifth Fleet had twelve ships to the DCN's four, but he hadn't brought any of the eighties. He *had* brought seven sixties, which meant he had the edge in firepower and hulls in the Weston System.

At that moment, though, Walkingstick froze on the edge of the room, his gaze locking on Tecumseh across the room. They shared height and coloring, though Walkingstick was far broader-shouldered than the younger man. Where Walkingstick's black hair was tied in braids that went most of the way down his back, Tecumseh's single braid was cut off at his neck.

It was the uniform that was the biggest change, Walkingstick realized. It was the same rough cut and black material as Walkingstick's —the core component was a shipsuit, after all—but the red sash of a Commonwealth Navy officer was missing. The lapels had been expanded and changed color, shifting from the carmine red of the TCN to a darker maroon with a silver dolphin embroidered into them.

And, of course, Tecumseh's collar carried the four stars of a full Fleet Admiral where Walkingstick's carried the single Roman aquila eagle of his Imperatorship.

"Admirals, Imperator, thank you for coming," the rotund man at the head of the table said, breaking the spell of the two men staring at each other. "Please, be seated; we have quite a bit to go over as we consider where we are and where we go from here."

Walkingstick gave his old protégé a firm acknowledging nod and then strode forward into the room, taking in the form and colors of the space. It was a large room, probably occupying the entire width of the tower, on the highest floor of the Hall's West Tower.

Almost a quarter-kilometer in the air, the massive floor-to-ceiling windows on the west side of the room allowed the bright daylight in while giving an incredible view of the western half of the city and the carefully managed parks and farmland beyond the borders of Galen's capital.

He could feel the presence of extremely modern electronics throughout the room, but the style and weight of the room clearly hadn't changed since the twenty-fourth century. The gap in the middle of the round table was no longer needed for holographic projection, but tradition endured. The table itself was of a sturdy artificial wood, as hard as steel and a quarter of the weight, that had gone out of fashion sometime in the twenty-fifth century but had been emblematic of an entire century of high-end furniture.

The rotund man—Walkingstick's files identified him as President Alistair Frey—was seated at the west end of the table, with the windows and city behind him. At his right hand was a woman of seemingly extraordinary age, with marble-pale skin and translucent white hair.

And dangerously sharp agate eyes. This, he realized, was Prime Minister May De Clerc, the other half of the Weston Republic's executive.

A handful of civilian advisors sat around De Clerc and Frey, and the east end of the table was occupied by several military officers. Unlike Walkingstick or Tecumseh, their uniform was clearly *not* a derivation of the TCN's, though Walkingstick didn't recognize the inspiration of the high-collared white tunics.

"We're glad to be here," Tecumseh said before Walkingstick could take his own seat. "We wish it was under better circumstances, of course, but there remains a connection and an obligation between the Successors of the Commonwealth."

Walkingstick didn't glare daggers at the other Admiral. Once seated, he took a careful sip of water from the glass waiting for him, then gave Tecumseh a winning smile.

"While I must disagree with the logic that the Commonwealth has or needs successors, Admiral Tecumseh's point has value as it is meant," he agreed. "I would far rather have visited Weston in calmer times, when there were no hordes at the gate."

"We would all rather not have lived to see these times," Frey agreed. "But we must deal with the times we are born into, not the times we might wish to have been gifted.

"When we sent our Envoys out, we did not know who would answer," the President continued. "The truth is that there are few remnants of the Commonwealth in a position to send ships to aid anyone. The Commonwealth in the Emerald Sector… made demands that could not be met, in exchange for their assistance. Three others begged forgiveness but had no ships to spare from their own needs and situations.

"The Commonwealth in Sol and the Dakotan Interstellar Confederacy were the only people to answer our cry for help. We called for aid… and you answered. That will *never* be forgotten."

Walkingstick was amused by Frey's dancing around the names. The Emerald Commonwealth, like the core Commonwealth, claimed to be the legitimate government. Since Walkingstick had been appointed by the full Star Chamber of the Commonwealth, before any members of it had committed themselves to their home systems' treasons and failures, he *knew* that he served the true Commonwealth.

He might only control thirty-four of the hundred and eight inhabited worlds of the full Commonwealth, but that would change. To make that change, though, he needed to sit in this room and treat the leaders of two treasonous states as allies if not equals.

"The Commonwealth was built, at its core, on the concept of defending a shared set of mutual values," Walkingstick told Frey. "*Some* may forget that, but the Star Chamber has not.

"However, rather than all of us dance around our respective opinions of the current state of affairs of the Commonwealth, should we focus on the matter at hand?" he asked. "Weston called for aid. Dakota and the Commonwealth have answered.

"We know that you are under attack, and we know that Saskatoon has fallen. Where does that leave us now?"

Frey nodded slowly, glancing at De Clerc, then gestured across the table.

"Admiral Vitali, if you can give the Admirals a briefing?" he asked.

Walkingstick looked to his left, where the man in question nodded without rising. Vitali looked as old as De Clerc, though he shared the Prime Minister's clear health and active mind. Age appeared to have simply weathered the man like an old oak—and stolen his hair, but that only drew attention to the sharp light of his jade-green gaze.

"Imperator, Admiral," Vitali greeted them with a nod. "I was retired when all of this came to pass, but De Clerc talked me back into harness for the security of our home systems."

A summary file flickered into Walkingstick's neural implant from Misra—not that the spy so much as *blinked* to suggest they'd been referencing files as names came up.

Ace Vitali had served in the TCN for fifty-two years, retiring at the age of seventy almost a decade earlier. He'd retired as a Rear Admiral, with a courtesy promotion to Vice Admiral *on* retiring, having failed to find any particular action or crisis to make his name in after the First Rimward War.

He'd served well in the Rimward War and half a dozen smaller conflicts, but his record certainly didn't suggest any reason to bring him out of retirement. There'd been equally experienced officers in the Sector Fleet who were still on active duty, after all.

No one had been asking Walkingstick's opinion, though, and the man appeared to be in charge now. A holographic map of the sector appeared in the center of the table, and Vitali gestured toward a single star blinking blood red.

"As everyone is aware, the Saskatoon System is now in the hands of the Triumvirate's Vanguard Fleet," Vitali told them. "The assault began on January eighth under the command of Admiral Surinder Verity. Governor Rawlings was apparently even more concerned about the Triumvirate's threats than the Cabinet and had spent a great deal of both Saskatoon's and *his own* money and resources assembling mine-fields, orbital forts, missile constellations and similar defenses.

"It took Verity two days to take control of Lafleche and a full *ten* to secure control of the entire star system outside the range of Regina's defenses. Some of that was due to Governor Rawlings' preparations," Vitali noted, "but much of it appears to have been due to Verity's own caution. Certainly, the *twenty-two days* it took them to secure control of Regina's orbitals appears to have been primarily due to them being extremely careful of preserving their own ships and munitions stockpiles.

"A steady stream of munitions colliers came to Saskatoon from the Qara Deñiz System along the way, which turned out to be a trap," the Admiral explained calmly. "Our forces in the Saskatoon System were always intended more for a delaying action than an actual fight, but in the logistics train Admiral Blaine thought she saw an opportunity.

"Instead, she lost four capital ships and twenty-five thousand dead, including herself," Vitali concluded. "There were no other mobile forces in the Saskatoon System, and we are now down to twelve capital ships. Thanks to your arrival, the numbers versus the Triumvirate are more equal, but Verity knew exactly the game they were playing here.

"They reduced our defenses by the use of drones and extreme-range missile fire, risking even their starfighters as little as possible. Then, when we moved to take advantage of the logistics pipeline necessary for that munitions-intensive approach, they mousetrapped and wiped out Admiral Blaine's task force."

The politics of the Triumvirate were a fascinating nest of vipers to Walkingstick. Verity was unquestionably an equal partner to the other two—they had ships that "belonged" to the other two Triumvirate states in their fleet—but he had to wonder if their taking the lead on the invasion was a sign of power or weakness among the trio.

"With Triumvirate troops in most of the cities, Rawlings ordered his forces to surrender nine days ago," Vitali admitted. "We have had very little solid information out of Saskatoon since, though it does unfortunately appear that Rawlings himself was publicly executed within twenty-four hours of the surrender."

That was just bad strategy in Walkingstick's opinion. You *needed* the Governors, the people with the authority *to* surrender, to think they'd survive surrender. If the rest of the Republic's system sub-sovereign heads of state thought they'd be shot if they yielded, they were going to be a lot more likely to order their people to fight to the bitter end.

"Assuming that Vanguard Fleet and its attached invasion forces will remain the primary mobile component of their assault, we have three systems at risk of being their next target," Vitali told them.

Three stars flashed amber on the display. Scotia, Yellowstar... and Weston itself.

"With only twelve ships to hand, we've concentrated the majority of our forces here in Weston. Scotia was a major TCN logistics facility, which has left us with significant fixed defenses in place, including no less than fourteen *Zion*-class battle platforms in two flotillas. That allowed us to move most of our forward forces to Yellowstar, where we currently have four capital ships versus one in Scotia and seven here in Weston."

Which left Halifax and Iqaluit, the other two Republic star systems, hanging in the breeze and relying on geography to protect them. It was *probably* a safe call, but Walkingstick doubted the people in those systems were happy.

"We have limited information on where Verity is planning on striking next," Vitali told them. "With your ships to hand, we have the opportunity to reinforce with significantly greater strength, but it's a guessing game... unless one of you has more intelligence?"

Walkingstick didn't even look at Misra. There were conversations they would have later, but at that moment, the choices were a matter of politics.

"My people have been in transit for over twenty days," he pointed out. "Admiral Tecumseh's for even longer. Some level of rest and recuperation is necessary, as well as review of how our forces and yours can integrate."

He coughed delicately.

"May I ask, Mr. President, Ms. Prime Minister... what happened to Governor Salazar?"

Salazar had been the Commonwealth's governor on Weston. He'd been bumbling along, following orders like the rest of the Sector, until suddenly, the entire sector had stopped responding to Walkingstick's couriers.

"Mr. Salazar resigned his post as part of the call for a general referendum on the creation of the Republic," De Clerc told him. "While he is now a private citizen, I believe I can arrange for my staff to put you in touch with him if you would like?"

"We may take you up on that," Walkingstick said. "Just in case, you understand."

He hadn't been overly *impressed* by Oliver Salazar, but the man had been the duly elected sub-sovereign head of state for this star system. It was somewhat reassuring to hear that the man wasn't in a shallow grave somewhere.

That put him ahead of roughly a quarter of the officials who *had* been Governors when the network went down.

17

Weston System
11:00 February 18, 2740 ESMDT

NOVATORONTO WAS CURRENTLY ABOUT six hours ahead of the standard time based on the Greenwich Meridian on Earth—with a twenty-four-hour-and-thirty-six-minute day, the local day slowly shifted with regards to ESMDT, with the local calendar appearing to use "months" based on that cycle rather than any local phenomena.

That meant it was on the early edge of a bronze twilight when James Tecumseh finally escaped the tension of the strategic briefing. Sitting in the same room as Walkingstick, treating the man as an ally, ignoring the fact that Walkingstick had betrayed *every* oath they'd both sworn in making himself dictator of the Rump Commonwealth... It had grown easier over the meeting, but it had been surprisingly hard.

Their guide had led them to an outdoor balcony, where he inhaled the chill air of the fall breeze. Galen didn't have truly *cold* weather any more than it had truly *warm* weather—but over two hundred meters into the air, the breeze was going to be a touch cool anywhere.

"Well?" he asked. He spoke outward, toward the wind and the city, but he knew Volkov, Littlebear and Reynolds had all joined him on the balcony, with the Marines and Crows forming an informal-but-effective barrier to give them privacy on the balcony.

"The only reason the Republic is still here is because Surinder Verity values their ships over their time," Volkov said flatly. "There were five military officers in that room, Admiral, all wearing the insignia of Admirals, and *two* were in TCN databases. One was retired. One was a *Lieutenant Commander* two years ago."

"So, who are the other three and what in void *happened* to the TCN senior officer corps here?" James asked aloud.

"The other three used to have different job titles," Reynolds said, the woman grinning at Littlebear's momentary twitch. The Envoy didn't seem surprised that she'd joined them... but he also didn't seem to have *noticed* her arrival itself.

"Lovely ones. Like *Director of System Security. Senior Trade Route Security Manager. Vice President of Special Operations.*" She let the titles hang in the air. "Since I know you lot are as pure as the driven snow in some ways, let me translate: they were corporate mercs.

"And Vitali? De Clerc is his wife's cousin. The Prime Minister's brother is the CEO of Loblaw's Interstellar Agriculture... a company that's definitely *Interstellar* if not so much *Agricultural* these days."

James grimaced.

"Corporatocracy," he spat. "I almost prefer the open ones."

He'd seen them outside the Commonwealth, at least. The *Commonwealth* had laid down the rules of the basic forms a planetary government needed to have, which had kept corporate control in the background in most places. One of the major powers of the Alliance of Free Stars, however, was the Renaissance Trade Factor, a four-system nation run as a corporation beholden to its shareholders.

Of course, becoming an RTF shareholder was as simple as being *born* there. Acquiring further shares was expensive, though definitely *possible*, but everyone born in the Trade Factor was a citizen-shareholder with a minimum of one voting share.

"I haven't had a chance to dig too much yet," Reynolds warned. "But you gotta realize that there's about eight corporations that have *always* run this sector. Loblaw's Interstellar Agriculture is the biggest, but none of them are used to having the government argue with them.

"Oliver Salazar was bought and paid for," she said bluntly. "I need to dig in more to what happened there, but…"

"All six governors resigned and called for planetary referendums on secession on the same day," Littlebear replied, then smirked as Reynolds looked at him. "We have our own focuses, Ms. Reynolds, and our own assets.

"In my case, I also have a practiced skill at speed-reading months' worth of news content for the key pieces. In this case, what happened to the Sector's Commonwealth government."

James gestured for the diplomat to continue.

"As Ms. Reynolds so cogently pointed out, every Governor in this sector was beholden to the Boards," Littlebear told them. "Money from the Weston megacorps put them in their seats and kept their planetary parliaments stuffed full of supporters.

"None of this was particularly *egregious*, mind you," he noted. "A matter of fundraising and third-party advertising, as opposed to bribes and rigged elections. Dangerous to democracy in its own way, but more on the order of poisoning it than killing it, if you follow."

"Vaguely," James replied.

"So, the Boards owned the Governors, and the Boards decided that the Sector was being screwed by the focuses of the Rump." The diplomat trailed off for a few moments of silence, then sighed. "They stuck it out until June of thirty-eight, eight months after the networks collapsed, and then decided that they needed a local government and they needed it *now*.

"Every Governor resigned June first, called a referendum for June fifteen. By June thirtieth, the First Weston Constitutional Convention was underway. *That* only lasted two weeks, long enough to establish an interim governing committee to arrange elections for the delegates to the *Second* Weston Constitutional Convention.

"By January of thirty-nine, they had a fully elected government in place. They started later than us, but they had the full deal in place around the same time. Their official provisional government only lasted six months."

Where the Dakotan Provisional Cabinet and Assembly had lasted from January 2738 through January 2739—though, *unlike* Weston, they'd been under attack by the Rump and the Stellar League in that time!

"It moved fast, which tells me that someone laid the groundwork in advance." Littlebear glanced over at Reynolds again and shrugged. "Almost certainly the Boards. And yes, people here will know what you mean if you say *the Boards* with a capital B."

James chuckled, then sighed.

"That's a lot more influence than I'd want any corporate entity to have, I admit."

"At least in this case, they seem to have realized that sometimes making sure you *have* a fourth quarter next year is more important than having a more profitable first quarter today," Reynolds said grimly. "I'm still not sure what happened to the TCN officer corps, though, boss."

"We're supposed to be getting contact lists for the Republic Navy today," Volkov noted. "That should give us some basis to see who is left. And then maybe we can quietly check into the names that are missing. Everything seems shiny on the surface, but there are enough oddities in the officer corps to make me wonder what's *under* the surface."

James nodded again before pushing off from the balcony railing. NovaToronto was a very pretty city, but his job was in space above it. Hell, his *job* was going to be in the Scotia and Yellowstar Systems, he suspected—and eventually in the Saskatoon System.

"Let's get moving," he told the others. "Sooner we're back in space, sooner we can go through the intelligence dump we've been promised."

He'd barely seen the acknowledging nods from the other three when his implant chimed with an incoming message. Sallie Leeuwenhoek was both unlikely to be calling him while he was on planet for anything *unimportant*, but he also couldn't think of any reason for his steward to be pinging him that was *important*.

On the other hand, he trusted his steward's judgment completely, so he accepted the call.

"Tecumseh."

"Admiral, we just received an invitation I wanted to pass on to you," she told him. "The *invitation* is from Vice Admiral, Retired, Androkles Nikolovski—but you're being invited to dinner at the Iron Hammer Club down the street from NovaToronto Fleet Command."

James ran the data he had and exhaled a surprised sigh.

"Androkles Nikolovski was CO, Weston Sector Fleet," he said. "Retired, huh? That's enough to get my attention, Chief, but what's important about the Iron Hammer Club?"

"It's a Chiefs club, sir," she told him. "Officers allowed on sufferance at invitation only. Nikolovski can't be a member, and *only* a member can give you an invite that will get you through the door."

"So, it's, what, a trap?" James asked.

"No. I made a call. The invite is countersigned by Senior Chief Lassana Brodeur. She *was* Fleet Chief under Nikolovski and now is the senior noncom in the WRN logistics branch."

He took a second to chew on that.

"The Admiral is retired, and the *Fleet Chief* is flying a desk in Logistics?" he asked.

"Seems like, sir. I didn't want to accept the invite without checking in, but…"

"Please accept it, Sallie. I'll send most of our people back to orbit. A show of trust means fewer bodyguards, but neither Reynolds nor Revie are going to let me go anywhere alone!"

———

The Iron Hammer Club was a squat stone structure that looked like it had *never* known what century it belonged to. There were no windows on the main floor, but sweeping arches on the upper floors revealed windows carefully positioned to block view from the ground or the nearby structures.

Just up the street, as Leeuwenhoek had said, was NovaToronto Fleet Command: a trio of bog-standard twenty-sixth-century skyscrapers built to provide administrative support for the Weston Sector Fleet. Now it acted as the administrative headquarters for the Weston Republic Navy, and the tags floating through James's implants noted that the WRN owned most of the surrounding blocks, which were distinctly *lacking* in other skyscrapers.

The Iron Hammer Club was at the edge of the semi-clear zone surrounding the military administrative center, with a park between it and the next building over: a twelve-story office building on a three-story retail podium.

Like the rest of that semi-clear zone, the Club was exactly ten meters high—suggesting a regulation imposed for long-forgotten reasons. Unlike most of the rest, though, the Iron Hammer Club actually *predated* the current NovaToronto Fleet Command Towers.

There was no entrance at street level, and if James hadn't been following downloaded directions—well, following Major Arlene Revie, who was following downloaded directions—he might have missed the stairs leading down into a dugout in front of the building. The angles and colors had been picked to help the trench avoid notice, though it was obvious once you looked for it.

There was a porticoed entrance at the bottom of the stairs, where a middle-aged woman, in an outfit that clearly aped an insignia-less TCN noncommissioned officer's uniform without *quite* breaching the etiquette rules and norms around that, gave them A Look.

"This is a private establishment, sirs, ma'ams," she told them. "Do you ha—"

The door behind her swung open before she even finished her challenge, and a broad-shouldered man of a similar ilk—middle-aged, not quite in military uniform, *definitely* ex-military—charged out.

"Please, Antonia, let's not make fools of ourselves," he told her with a chuckle. "You know who this is and you know he has an invitation."

"One officer is one thing," Antonia replied. "This is…"

"We cannot, regardless of our preferences, ask the Fleet Admiral commanding the Dakotan Confederacy Navy to enter a building on foreign soil without his bodyguards," the man said. He then turned to James and bowed slightly.

"I am Heinrich Fear, the manager on duty here at the Iron Hammer Club this evening," he introduced himself. "This is Antonia Owston, our bouncer. Her job is to remind Navy and Army officers that this is *not* their space and they do not get to charge in and give orders."

"I am an invited guest, Mr. Fear," James said. "While you are correct that I can't go anywhere without Major Revie and Ms. Reynolds and their people, I recognize the nature of a Chiefs' club. There are places in the galaxy where even Admirals must understand they are not in command.

"But I do have an invitation and I do need to bring my companions in. Will that be an issue?"

"Of course not. Come, Admiral Tecumseh. You are, of course, expected."

———

James was unsurprised to find himself ushered through the brightly lit and -colored interior of the club to a private room on the third floor— and equally unsurprised to find that he was meeting far more than just Admiral (Retired) Nikolovski and Senior Chief Brodeur. There were eleven people waiting for him in the private room—and only one of them, Nikolovski himself, was an officer.

"Chiefs," James greeted them all, then smiled in his first *actual* surprise of the night. He came to a crisp attention and saluted Command Sergeant Shakuntala Sjoberg. Sjoberg was presumably *formerly* of the Terran Commonwealth Marines, but she'd earned her Medal of Valor while a much-younger James Tecumseh had been watching.

None of them were Commonwealth military anymore, but *that* medal was still going to get him some respect.

"Chiefs and *Command Sergeant*," he corrected himself as the big Black woman returned his salute. "A long time, Sergeant Sjoberg."

"To my great distaste and confusion, that's actually *Brigadier* Sjoberg now," she replied. James had known her last TCMC rank and hadn't missed that she now wore the single gold star of a flag officer. "Of the Weston Republic Army, since higher-than-I have decided we don't want a name as *aggressive* as *Marines*."

James had some idea of how the Marines and officers of the TCMC would have taken *that* adjustment. *Poorly* was an understatement.

"Have a seat, all of you," Nikolovski instructed James and his people. "There will be food… and that's the last order and promise *I'm* giving tonight. I hung up my stars for damn good reason."

"I'll admit, when we decided to support the Republic, I was expecting to see most of the TCN and TCMC officer corps intact," James murmured.

"Oui, and we'll get to that discussion," a woman he presumed was Brodeur said in a clear French accent. Like James himself, she was clearly from Earth. "For now, let's get some food in here. I understand you all spent the afternoon in the company of the esteemed Imperator."

James followed instructions and took his seat, waiting for the locals to set the tone and pace of the conversation. No one, he noted wryly, bothered to ask his people what they wanted to eat or drink—but as the drinks and appetizers were brought in, he realized that was because someone had asked *Leeuwenhoek* in advance.

He took a sip of the iced tea they'd brought him and surveyed the room.

"A retired Admiral, a Brigadier mustanged straight from the NCO corps, and nine NCOs, mostly Navy," he observed. "I do believe I just got shanghaied by the old boys and girls network."

Brodeur chuckled and took a sip of her water.

"Exactement, Admiral," she told him. "The Republic has put ourselves in… une situation intéressante."

"Chief, I speak French and you speak French, and the Admiral has an implant, but let's not risk confusion today, shall we?" Nikolovski asked. "I can't give you orders anymore, so consider a favor for a friend. I… We… *The Republic* needs there to be no confusion."

"Fair," Brodeur conceded. "I find English abrasive, Admiral," she told Tecumseh. "My mother tongue is so much smoother. But my Admiral is correct."

James eyed the plate of boneless chicken wings placed in front of him. They smelled divine, but he needed to talk as much as eat tonight.

"What happened to the WRN?" he asked quietly. "The only senior officers I've seen are either retirees or ex-corporate security. Yet you're sitting across the table from me, so it doesn't appear that the Republic has been shooting the TCN officers..."

"I suspect some of the members of the Boards were tempted," Nikolovski said grimly. "Sense prevailed, but the Republic is..." He considered his words carefully.

"The Republic is what happens when the corporations holding the politicians' strings make common cause with the reform movements that were trying to burn those strings to ashes," Sjoberg said flatly. "Every politician in this sector was bought and paid for, Admiral Tecumseh, but the people who'd bought them realized that the Imperial Commonwealth was a weight that would drag them down.

"But the key individuals, the people who served on multiple Boards and put together a joint approach... They're students of history, Admiral. They knew damn well that the collection of venally corrupt twits they'd assembled couldn't save the Weston Sector.

"They needed real leadership, real popular buy-in, and a real long-term chance for the Republic."

"Hence the Boards' financing the Republic," James concluded.

"Exactly. But it was the reformists who did the groundwork," Brodeur told him. "And the people who'd been trying to reform the local system for the last century or so, well..." She shook her head. "They were on the wrong side of being threatened with the Navy and the Marines a few dozen times too many. Part of their price for cooperating was a microscope on the military command."

"A microscope wielded by people who find the entire concept of a uniformed military offensive," Sjoberg concluded. The ex-Marine looked exhausted. "And found the name *Marines* too aggressive. I mean, for fuck's sake, *the barbarians are at the fucking gate.* We *know* how much real weight there was behind their fears, now, and I don't blame them."

She snorted.

"Well, I shouldn't blame them."

"The Boards and the Constitutional Conventions and the first Parliament came to an agreement," Brodeur told James. "Technically, we pulled over everyone who was TCN, TCSC, or TCMC," she continued. "In practice, basically everyone over the rank of Commander was given the choice of a generous retirement package or the most boring desk the new administration could find them.

"Senior noncoms got the same offer, but I think more of us took the desks."

"They paid out every senior officer?" James asked.

"Yup. Brought in corporate-security hands used to running fighter squadrons installed on high-risk freighters and handed them task groups," Sjoberg said bluntly. "Army did better in some ways, not least because the corporate mercs *we* got know which end of a rifle the penetrator comes out of.

"Hence them managing to talk me into taking a commission. My impression is that Brodeur's people are in worse shape."

James's empty wings plate vanished as the servers made another pass through. His tea was refreshed and a delicious-smelling chicken and pasta dish was dropped off in front of him as he chewed through what the noncoms were telling him.

"So, the WRN is running with a handful of politically connected retirees, ex-corporate mercs who have never handled an A-S warship and a whole bunch of kids promoted out of their depth?" he assessed aloud. "And most of the senior noncoms are in the shore establishment?"

That, at least, gave him a surprising amount of confidence in the WRN's shoreside administration and logistics.

"Give or take. Admiral Nikolovski offered to come back after the invasion, but no one is quite willing to admit their mistakes yet," Brodeur said.

"I could have made a bigger deal of it," Nikolovski admitted. "But, frankly, Vitali is better at the top job than most. I'm not sure I could convince Parliament to recommission me as his *subordinate*, but frankly, we'd do better with me as a task force commander and him running the big desk.

"Not least because with a task force commander the President and Prime Minister theoretically *trusted*, we could get more of the fleet out of Weston." He sighed. "Which is a different problem, of course."

"I'm glad you got here first, even if only by a few minutes," Sjoberg said. "If Walkingstick had showed up with twelve starships and we'd just had seven... I'm not sure he could have resisted the urge to get grabby."

"The Imperator is here to convince the Republic to rejoin the Commonwealth," James agreed. "I... have no such ambitions. Dakota is here because you asked for help and we're hoping for allies and trade partners in the future."

"If we *were* important, you'd have brought more ships," Brodeur said bluntly. "The Triumvirate Vanguard Fleet alone outguns our entire remaining Navy, and Admiral Verity knows their job. They have different priorities now than they did as a TCN officer, but they know their objectives and they play to them."

"Everyone involved in this mess has their own priorities," James admitted. Including him—he wasn't going to *admit* that if it came down to saving his ships or saving the Republic, he'd choose his ships, but they all knew that.

Walkingstick's priorities, though...

"Priorities or not, we're glad to have you and we're glad to have the Imperials," Brodeur admitted. "We're just worried."

"And I am honored that you trust me enough to tell me this," James told her. "I am not without ulterior motives, but I mean the Republic no harm."

"If nothing else, the Confederacy is a long damn way away by the standards of our new times," Nikolovski told him. "But the food here is good, better than the Chiefs *want* their officers to realize. We invited you for dinner and we should feed you!"

18

SAINT MICHAEL WAS James Walkingstick's home. Above and beyond all of the other thousand reasons of logistics and organization and transferring his staff and all of that, *that* was why he hadn't wanted to move his flag to *Idun*. She'd been his home since before he'd accepted the Marshal's mace to go after the Alliance.

It was good to be back aboard her, where the datasphere linked to his implant and told him everything he wanted to know as soon as he needed it. Where the hardware and algorithms and subconscious artificial intelligences all knew his needs, where everything and *everyone* had been trained to back him up.

Sitting in his office, the harsh austerity replaced by holographic images of the twelve capital ships of Fifth Fleet, Walkingstick knew the status of his fleet without ever *consciously* looking at anything.

He had the level of neural-implant bandwidth that would have allowed him to be a starfighter pilot, the degree of data processing and integration that meant that he didn't need to even review information stored in his implant. He just *knew* it.

It was a useful talent, one sufficiently necessary in the fighter corps that it was rare in the rest of the Commonwealth military. It also meant that he knew Pich Misra was at his door before the spy even chimed for admittance.

"I hate it when you do that," Misra said in a rare unguarded moment—a response to the door sliding open before the spy even *could* ring the virtual doorbell.

"It saves the guards time," Walkingstick said drily. "And would you begrudge a man his few pleasures?"

There were two Marines outside his door, after all, and they could have warned him as readily as the cameras had. They hadn't, because they knew they didn't need to.

"The fact that your pleasures are as limited as they are is terrifying; you know that, right?" they asked as they strode in and took a seat without waiting for further invitation.

"I serve the Commonwealth. It does not serve me." And given the power Walkingstick had taken over the Commonwealth, that was something he needed to keep in mind.

"And you've spent two hours and thirty-seven minutes, *today*, going over reports and requests for decisions relayed from Earth," Misra told him. "This job will kill you."

"Yes." Walkingstick gave his subordinate a questioning look. "Not least because the job itself must die in the end. There cannot be a second Imperator. I will not be the Commonwealth's Sulla."

Sulla, after all, had thought he was *fixing* the Roman Republic. All he'd done in the end, though, was break the taboo against marching on Rome.

"We do what we can because we must," the spy said with a sigh. "My job is to keep you alive and support your missions until you do decide your job is done. And then I'm probably going to need to hide, because whoever comes after you is going to want to try me for war crimes or some such."

The questioning look hardened into an actual glare.

"You have a point, Pich?" he asked.

"Yeah. You want to take Fifth Fleet to Scotia and get the locals to send Tecumseh to Yellowstar."

The calm statement hung in the air like a bomb and Walkingstick sighed.

"Or we could *all* go to Yellowstar," he noted. From Misra's statement, he figured the Triumvirate was going after *that* system.

"Yep. And then you're matching—what, twenty-five?—Commonwealth, Republic and Confederacy ships against nineteen Triumvirate. Assuming you manage to mousetrap Verity, it would end the war real soon."

"They aren't particularly mousetrappable, from what I have seen," Walkingstick pointed out. "I doubt they'd make it that easy on us. Plus"—he sighed—"I can't imagine the Republic would be prepared to concentrate that much of their force in one place based on our intelligence.

"Not without proof."

"I'm not going to hand over the recordings of my conversations with Verity's officers," Misra said drily. "They might still be trying to play me, though I don't *think* any of my contacts know I'm in touch with the others. If you want more than rough intentions, though, you're going to have to talk to them."

"Me?" Walkingstick asked slowly.

"People know I *work* for the Commonwealth and they believe in the color of my money," Misra told him. "But you, right now, *are* the Commonwealth. Your word is law, your promises a coin people can spend."

"They need a deal from my mouth."

"Bingo. Two battleship captains and Verity's own operations officer, sir. They're ready to deal, if we've got the right coin... but we're not talking credits or gold here."

"They want pardons and paths home," Walkingstick guessed.

"Pardons, paths home, their own planet." Misra snorted. "I know, thanks to those three, that Verity is coming for Yellowstar next. But Verity is known to change their plans, and without a clearer lock on these people, they might surprise us."

"And if Vanguard Fleet ambushes Fifth Fleet at Scotia, Scotia's fixed defenses will not turn the tide," Walkingstick murmured. "I can match nineteen capital ships against thirteen in my head."

There was, after all, *one* solitary old battlecruiser in Scotia, according to the information from the locals.

"So, we need them on side. I want more than *information* if I'm giving them clear routes back into TCN service, though."

"I *think* that if we can get you on a link with them, we have some pull," Misra told him. "If we can cut a deal, they can make sure Vanguard Fleet hits Yellowstone. On our schedule, even. One of our potential assets manages Verity's intel stream. We can feed the information we want into it, let them pin Tecumseh's ears back."

"Given Tecumseh's eight ships versus Verity's nineteen and everyone is going to have a real bad day," Walkingstick agreed with a chuckle. "Possibly enough of one on Verity's part to even the numbers, especially if we can pin them in place to bring up the rest of the WRN."

He *could* have brought enough ships to overrun the Triumvirate in the time it took him to reach each of their stars in sequence. But while he was *reasonably* confident the Dakotans weren't going to attack the moment his back was turned, he wasn't *certain*—and he was quite certain that if he gave Emerald's Emergency Committee half a chance, they'd happily seize any systems he left uncovered.

The Commonwealth had the largest remaining fragment of the TCN and the largest number of preexisting military shipyards—but they *also* controlled the largest number of star systems, which left them with the largest defensive responsibilities.

And it hadn't been particularly polite to show up with twice as many ships as the entire Weston Republic Navy. The whole point of this affair was to get Weston to rejoin the Commonwealth voluntarily.

"Everything we can adjust about this situation to make our life better seems worth it," Misra observed. "I have people looking into the Republic's starship captains. They are… interesting."

"Competent but inexperienced, promoted beyond their age and terms of service," Walkingstick guessed. "Weston rather clearly purged the officer corps. Via retirement rather than bullets, I suspect, given the tendencies of corporatocracies like the one the Republic is pretending they're not."

"Basically," Misra confirmed. "I'm curious as to how you think they'll take Blaine's mistake."

"That can go two ways," Walkingstick told his spy. "Either they'll think she was *too* aggressive and walked into a trap, or that she should never have retreated in the first place."

The data on that piece of the Battle of Saskatoon flickered through his implant, and he smiled thinly.

"Tone of their reports suggests the latter," he observed. "I can use that. For now, though... How quickly can you set up that call with our 'assets'?"

"Give me a day," Misra said. "We can't talk to them all at once, so I'm going to *try* and get Rear Admiral Yan Shirai on a link first."

"I *know* Shirai," Walkingstick noted. "He was the assistant tac officer aboard *Steadfast*."

Steadfast had been brand-new at the time, one of the first *Resolute*-class battleships... and she'd been the last capital ship James Walkingstick had commanded himself. He had fond memories of that ship and crew.

"I'm pretty sure that's part of why he wants to talk to you, Imperator," Misra told him. "It's not a question of *if*, sir. It's a question of *when*. I will make it happen."

19

ONE OF THE advantages of not currently being "the Admiral" in command of the force he was attached to was that there *was* a ship's night for Anthony Yamamoto. As the commanding officer of Task Group *Iroquois*, ship's day on his flagship had been defined as *Anthony is up*.

And sometimes, it was nice to be able to be on a flight deck without the constant stream of activity. There was still *activity*—*Krakatoa* carried fifty bombers, one hundred and fifty starfighters, six pinnaces, twenty-four assault shuttles and thirty-plus assorted *other* shuttles and support ships. Her flight decks and shuttle bays were *never* silent.

But there was a part of the cycle that was quieter, when less work was being done. Ship's night, roughly aligned with ESMDT when Tecumseh was the Admiral, was when the parasite ships were surveyed by the deck crews and their flight engineers for work that would be done later.

Unfortunately, none of the Katanas in the carrier's flight decks belonged to Anthony. Now that they had q-probes and q-coms back, he could no longer justify putting his Vice Admiral's butt in a starfighter and flying out with his people.

He hated that part. He found the fact that he didn't have a clear spot that was "his" on the flight deck moderately inconvenient, but the real problem was that he couldn't fly with his people.

Anthony understood why. He'd set up the final policies himself. He just *hated* it.

So, instead of perching on his own fighter and watching the activities across the flight deck, he'd picked an assault shuttle that wasn't on the docket for surveys tonight and clambered on top of the spacecraft, watching the comforting buzz of activity across the cavernous void.

He knew that Reynolds *liked* sneaking up on him, so he didn't tell her when he saw her making her way across the deck toward him. In most places, the human-shaped predator he called friend could easily hide her presence and motion, a lifetime's instincts and training easily moving her through crowds and empty places alike in ways that let attention just slide off her.

Unfortunately for the assassin's lifetime of skill and practice, *Anthony* had just as much experience and skill at reading the patterns of a carrier flight deck. Anywhere else in the galaxy, she could evade his gaze, but not on a flight deck.

Especially not *this* flight deck.

"I'm assuming you aren't planning on seducing me in a flight deck with over a hundred people in line of sight," Anthony said mildly as a scuff announced her arrival on top of the assault shuttle.

There was a long pause.

"Well, *now* I'm thinking about it," Reynolds told him. She took a seat next to him on top of the shuttle. "But no, I actually need to talk shop. And this seems to be pretty private, if we want an off-the-record discussion."

"Shannon, you control every security system on this ship," he pointed out.

"And I am, in my new and all-too-white-hat role, actually obliged to maintain transparency and honesty with the Dakotan government and Navy," she reminded him. "It's part of my job to make sure that *nobody* is blanking out security systems on any of our ships, so I made a real effort to make sure there weren't any backdoors.

"Not even ones for me."

Anthony was mildly surprised.

"I'm not entirely sure I believe that," he admitted.

"Then you're smart," Reynolds said. "But I did some *hard* intrusion testing on the new systems, and my people caught me every time. So, somewhere where recording is impossible sounds good for these kinds of chats."

He sighed.

"And what trouble are we getting in today?"

"Not just us; I'm bringing a *lot* of friends into this mess," she said with a chuckle. "I took five Crows to the surface as Tecumseh's body-guards. I brought three back up."

"We are not here to launch a coup or anything like that," Anthony warned.

"No. But Walkingstick *is*."

"I wish I could believe that man had enough honor that he wasn't," he admitted with a sigh. "We all looked up to him once. He was a damn hero."

"Everything about Walkingstick was cultivated, designed and propagated through the fleet with intent," Reynolds said grimly. "He was no hero. He was a self-manufactured propaganda icon who wanted the Navy to follow him into hell for his power and reputation.

"And too much of the damn Navy did, but I never had many illusions about the man."

"A bunch of CISS followed him," Anthony pointed out.

"Because they believe, rightly or wrongly, that he is the best chance for restoring the Commonwealth we swore—like you—to protect." She sighed. "I don't regard myself as having broken that oath, Anthony, because the Commonwealth I served is gone.

"But I *fully* understand why so many of my colleagues now serve the Imperator."

Anthony could understand it too. Reynolds had initially leaned on him as a contact because she had, *correctly*, judged him as one of the last people in the Dakota Sector Fleet likely to turn on the Commonwealth.

In the end, he suspected that *Reynolds* had actually given up on the Commonwealth before he had.

"What do you need, Shannon?" he asked.

"Shuttles, a lot of them, without them drawing attention," she told him. "I've run through the numbers and the plan with Colonel Joshi, but the problem is simple: we may have a full brigade of troops, with everything from power armor to tanks to planes, but they're spread across four starships. Of course, we can't sneak heavy equipment down, but we probably don't need it."

Colonel Mahesh Joshi was the Marine CO aboard *Krakatoa*, which made him the senior Marine in Task Force Six, the man in charge of the four armored infantry battalions and their attached armor, artillery and aerospace companies.

Anthony would admit that he only really paid attention to the *transport* needs of the Marine forces attached to the fleet, but that meant he still had a good idea of what Joshi had on hand. A reinforced heavy brigade, basically, with four eight-hundred-Marine armored infantry battalions, with two more battalions' worth of "Triple A"—armor, artillery and aerospace units.

"And just what are we sneaking down and why?" he asked.

"If we can manage it before we break orbit, two armored infantry battalions," she said flatly. "We have local buy-in; don't worry. We need to get them down covertly, but we've already made arrangements to barracks and feed them."

Anthony whistled silently. Taking the shuttle they were sitting on as an example, that would be a total of roughly fifty shuttle flights.

Between pinnaces and assault shuttles, *Krakatoa* could put her entire Marine contingent on the ground in a single landing. *Krakatoa*, though, was a *fleet carrier*. If there was one thing fleet carriers had, it was space for small craft.

Iroquois was similarly equipped, though the battlecruiser's lesser Triple-A component meant she had fewer pinnaces.

Adamant and *Black Sea* both carried a battalion of power-armored infantry, but they *didn't* have the small craft capacity to land all of their Marines or their heavy support at once.

"We're not *sneaking* fifty assault shuttles down to the surface," he told her.

"Not at once," she replied. "And, hell, you're right. We're not sending them down in assault shuttles. Joshi thinks we'll pull the troops by company, two from each ship, and send them down in the supply shuttles.

"But he thinks that means *every* shuttle going down has to be rigged for troops and we have to start ASAP."

"And he's right," Anthony conceded. "I need to talk to the Chiefs, Shannon. This isn't something I can snap my fingers and make happen... and there is no way I can hide it from Tecumseh."

"I'm asking forgiveness, not permission," she said bluntly. "But I'm not trying to hide it from him, either. I just know that he'll balk at infiltrating troops onto a friendly planet, even to help *protect* them."

"We just want to make damn sure Walkingstick doesn't see them, huh?"

"Exactly. We're working with the Weston Army and Weston Security Ministry," she told him. "It's *quiet*, all of it, but the point is to put a ready reaction force near the capital that Walkingstick doesn't know is there.

"Just in case."

"I wish I could tell you I didn't think that was needed," Anthony muttered. "Instead, I'm going to tell you that if we're putting fifteen hundred–plus power-armored Marines on Galen, we *also* need to put some *actual* assault shuttles down there with them."

And he was going to poke at a few other ideas that came to mind. No one was going to trust Walkingstick, but the Imperator was going to *expect* that distrust. That meant they were going to need more surprises than the Rump was expecting.

20

THE ADVANTAGE of a virtual conference was that a lot more people could be involved in a conversation than was truly practical in person, with the subconscious algorithms supporting the meeting moving focuses and even apparent locations of people to make sure everyone heard what they needed to hear.

James Tecumseh and Task Force Six brought over a dozen people to the meeting, including all of his staff officers and the captains of each of his four starships. The Rump Commonwealth's Fifth Fleet brought twelve starship captains alone, and the Weston Republic Navy had their entire ground and intelligence infrastructure to represent.

There were over two hundred people in the meeting in the end, though only a handful were actually going to be making decisions. The rest either needed to know what those decisions were and the basis behind them—or were there to *provide* the basis on which those decisions would be made.

"We are here to support you, Admiral Vitali," James told the Westonian Admiral. "So, I guess the critical question is: where do you need us?"

"Everywhere," Vitali said drily. The old man looked around the crowd and smiled thinly. "There are three systems that we judge to be most under threat by Admiral Verity's fleet. First and foremost, most critical in many ways, is here. The Weston System itself."

A faux-holographic projection of the former Weston Sector appeared in the middle of the display. The Saskatoon System and the territory of the Triumvirate behind it were highlighted in bright red. The Weston System itself flashed green as Vitali indicated it.

"Currently, thanks to our allies, we have twenty-one starships in the Weston System," the local Admiral continued. "Vanguard Fleet, according to our latest intelligence, has not been reinforced. That said, Admiral Verity still commands nineteen capital ships, and far too many of them are modern, powerful ships: sixties and their own *Custodian*.

"Were we confident that Verity was coming here, we could hold all three of our fleets in Weston and pull our other forces in from Yellowstar and Scotia, meet her in a Mahanian battle for control of the spaceways and shatter Vanguard Fleet."

Alfred Mahan had spoken for control of the *sea*, but the long-dead strategist's arguments still applied in space.

"Their partners in the Triumvirate only have eleven ships left in their own territory, and the loss of Vanguard Fleet would likely see their control of their star systems rapidly come into question. The Triumvirate are, after all, pirates and warlords."

Two more systems highlighted in the same color as Weston. Both were closer to Saskatoon and the known location of Vanguard Fleet.

"I've examined Verity's tactics at Saskatoon," James noted. "Their past record in the TCN as well. A direct assault on Weston, attempting to lure your fleet into exactly that kind of pivotal battle, is not their style.

"If they knew the division of your forces and somehow didn't know about the presence of the Confederacy and Commonwealth fleets, they *might* move against your forces here. More likely, however, they will attempt to reduce your deployed strengths."

"Which means Scotia or Yellowstar," Vitali agreed. "It is... politically unfeasible for me to expose Weston. It's difficult enough for us to continue leaving Iqaluit and Halifax uncovered. There is little point in moving single ships into those two systems, however, and we could hardly spare more."

"There is barely more point in having just one ship in Scotia," Walkingstick pointed out. "*Phonoi* is hardly going to stand off Vanguard Fleet on her own, even with the backup of Scotia's fixed defenses."

"Unfortunately correct," Vitali said. "Without knowing which system Verity is going to move against, we almost need to provide all three systems with sufficient force to at least *delay* the Admiral from taking them until reinforcements can arrive from the other two."

"I must agree with Admiral Tecumseh," Walkingstick noted. James wondered if the words had physically hurt as the other man said them. The Imperator certainly didn't *sound* pleased. "Verity is unlikely to strike directly at Weston, not yet. Especially if they are remotely aware of the arrival of allies.

"They will continue to attempt to reduce our forces piece by piece, seeking to defeat us in detail while preserving their own force. They *will* hit either Scotia or Yellowstar unless they think we're going to somehow put twenty ships in both systems."

"Something we can't do," James pointed out. "We need enough ships in each system to make them blink. And we should be able to do that. Verity is loss-averse; they have to be! Whatever yards the Triumvirate has built over the last two years, they aren't deploying new ships for at least a year.

"It's five days from here to Yellowstar. Five and a half to Scotia... and six days to move between them. Whatever forces we send out need to be able to either make Verity back off or hold their fleet off for six days."

From Vitali's expression, James and Walkingstick weren't really treading new ground for him—but from some of what James could see among the other WRN officers, it was helping to hear it from an outside source.

"There is a logic to a nodal defense anchored on Weston," Vitali told them. "Weston is closer to Scotia or Yellowstar than they are to each other. That was part of the logic of our current deployments: as soon as Vanguard Fleet was spotted in either system, Home Fleet would be deployed to reinforce."

That was a losing proposition, in James's mind, but he could also see how it was the only option the WRN had seen. The problem was that Vitali had no way to predict where Verity would strike, and the only real chance the Republic had of winning was to put all twelve of their remaining starships in the same system as her fleet and hope.

Or at least, that had been the only chance they'd had until the DCN and TCN had arrived.

"Ten ships," Walkingstick said quietly. His volume was perfect, James noted—loud enough that the algorithms made sure everyone heard him, but quiet enough that everyone had to stop and pay attention. "Backed by the fixed defenses in each system, that should suffice to hold Verity off until one of the other battle groups can intervene."

"We have enough now," James agreed. He was no happier to agree with Walkingstick than the Imperator had been to agree with him, but the other Admiral was right. "Ten ships in each of Scotia and Yellowstar, with eight remaining here in Weston."

Icons appeared in the middle of the virtual conference, marking the twenty-eight ships of the two fleets. They had almost a fifty percent edge in numbers, volume and firepower over the Triumvirate's forward force—but they didn't know where Verity would strike.

"As of this morning, Verity was still in the Saskatoon System," Vitali noted. "Our information is limited, but we have confirmed that —we have also, however, confirmed that they have finished refueling and restocking and are almost certainly *ready* to move.

"It will be roughly the same amount of time—five and a half days —for them to get to either Scotia or Yellowstar—and if we are to get in position to meet them, we need to move immediately."

"I think we are best served," Walkingstick said smoothly, "by keeping the individual contingents of our fleets together. As Scotia has the smallest number of ships present, I volunteer to relieve *Phonoi* of her watch. If you are comfortable, I would suggest she fall back on

Weston for refuel and crew rest while Fifth Fleet takes over the security of Scotia."

That would put twelve ships in Scotia, but the value of not splitting the contingents made sense to James.

"I would gladly take Task Force Six to reinforce Yellowstar," he said. "We would come up short on the ten-ship target if we go alone, though, even with the ships already in-system."

"I could detach two of my ships to support you," Walkingstick offered, "but I am not certain that would be… wise. For anyone."

"Trust is extended, but let's not stretch it," James agreed calmly. "Admiral Vitali, would you be comfortable detaching a division of your Home Fleet to join us in Yellowstar?"

"While *I* am entirely comfortable doing so," the Admiral said slowly, "Parliament has made it clear that they are uncomfortable with weakening Weston's defenders without a clear and immediate mission."

"If I detach *Yorktown* and *Determination* to replace them, would that assuage your politicians' nerves?" Walkingstick offered. "Then I will have ten ships in the Scotia System, Admiral Tecumseh will have ten ships—four of his and six of yours—in Yellowstar and you will have six of yours and two of mine here in Weston as our strategic reserve."

"I can work with that," James said. "We'll need to sort out a command structure for the mixed fleet, but that's unavoidable. And a conversation we should, perhaps, have offline, Admiral Vitali?"

"I agree. I will have to consult with the Cabinet to be certain, people, but I believe that gives us the structure of a plan," Vitali agreed, then grimaced. "This will all take time," he warned. "We will not have immediate warning when Verity departs, which may make getting ahead of them difficult."

"We have some time, though," Walkingstick replied. "Let us have the right ships in the right places at the right time—and not the wrong ships in all of the above!"

21

Weston System
11:00 February 19, 2740 ESMDT

"Everything is ready, Pich," Walkingstick told Misra. He spent a final few seconds rolling his shoulders to stretch his spine before straightening and making sure the holographic pickups were aligned with him.

Parris had spent a good twenty minutes in Walkingstick's office before the Imperator had started and everything was set up perfectly. The Commonwealth flag would be clear in the transmission and a carefully positioned light highlighted the golden aquila on Walkingstick's collar.

Misra didn't audibly respond, but their image popped up in the corner of Walkingstick's eye. They weren't part of this call, though Walkingstick doubted Yan Shirai thought they were *truly* speaking in private.

A few moments after the spy appeared in Walkingstick's vision, the half of his office in front of his desk shimmered for a moment before being replaced with a holographic image of a very similar office on a different ship in a different star system.

Normally, the holographic projectors would do some rescaling to match the two offices together. In this case, though, the Fleet Operations Officer aboard a *Sentinel*-class carrier had much the same space as allowed for an Admiral aboard the *Saint*-class battleships.

Hopefully, Shirai's office was secure. Walkingstick had been surprised to hear that the other man had wanted a full "face-to-face" conversation, but he assumed Shirai had taken the right precautions.

He recognized Shirai, though over two decades of time had certainly worked their art across the Japanese man's features. The younger Admiral's hair had gone white around the temples and new wrinkles crossed his face, but he was still recognizably the eager young Commander who'd reported aboard *Steadfast*.

"Rear Admiral Shirai," Walkingstick greeted him. "It's been a while."

"It has. You've made yourself quite a big deal, skipper," Shirai told him. "The universe has changed around us, but here we are. And you need something from me."

"You could certainly make my life a lot easier if you work with us," Walkingstick agreed genially. "I understand that you have a list."

Shirai chuckled, his eyes barely moving, staring sharply into Walkingstick's face.

"I want a wipe of any records of my time under Verity," he said quietly. "A restoration of my TCN record at my current rank and a command of my own. I recognize the latter may take some time, so I'll be patient on that, but I'm also going to end up giving up everything I have in the Archon Sector, so… uh…"

"Money," Walkingstick concluded.

"A hundred million."

Shirai had to know perfectly well how… *minuscule* that sum was to the true Commonwealth. That was a fifth of the *annual maintenance costs* of even an older capital ship. A single percentage point of the construction cost of a brand-new eighty-million-cubic-meter capital ship.

On a personal scale, it was an immense amount of money, but if it saved even *one* of Walkingstick's ships, it was more than worth it.

"Done. You realize, of course, that we can't put you back in

Commonwealth uniform until the Triumvirate is beaten and Verity is either dead or behind bars," Walkingstick warned. "But I agree to your terms, Admiral Shirai. You will be a Commonwealth officer again."

He figured he'd give the man a task group in Home Fleet, under Gabor's watchful eye. That would give Shirai the command he'd asked for without stretching the limited account of trust his defection left him.

Shirai leaned back in his own desk, studying Walkingstick as if he was looking for the lie or the trick. The Triumvirate officer pressed his hands together absently, his focus clearly on the Imperator.

"All right. I suppose I should have known better than to expect you to haggle," he observed. "What do you need from me, sir?"

"Timing is going to be everything," Walkingstick said slowly. There was a limit to what he could tell Shirai still. He trusted Misra, and Misra felt the other officer would stay bought, but that was a guarantee that could swiftly evaporate if the war turned further in favor of the Triumvirate.

"Verity is going to lose," he told the other man. "I suspect their intelligence has already told you and them the odds you're up against. The moment the Commonwealth answered the Republic's call for aid, the Triumvirate had already lost.

"The trick, from *my* perspective, is to make that loss work for the Commonwealth. Most importantly, we need to neutralize the Confederacy—and I know where Tecumseh's fleet is going to be.

"They're delayed by organizational matters, so they will be leaving Weston in roughly twenty-four hours. If Verity leaves for Yellowstar inside the next few hours, Vanguard Fleet will be in position to ambush Tecumseh on his arrival. There will be a ten-ship force of mixed Confederacy and Republic units that you will be able to defeat in detail."

Walkingstick figured the loss of half of the Republic's remaining order of battle would set them up for his diplomatic one-two. They'd already lost four out of sixteen. Losing another six would leave their Parliament paranoid and vulnerable, open to the suggestion they already knew he was going to make when this was over.

"Verity is good," Shirai warned. "If you let them isolate ten ships, they're going to get pounded."

"That's the hope, yes," Walkingstick confirmed. "Then you're going to pass their exact plans to me and we're going to return the favor."

If he had the intelligence to hit Verity with everything the Republic and Commonwealth had left after Yellowstar, it wouldn't even matter how many of their ships Tecumseh had taken down. And Walkingstick knew that even ambushed and with forty percent of his theoretical fleet on the wrong side of the enemy, Tecumseh was still going to make Verity pay in fire and blood to wipe out Task Force Six.

"I will have to make arrangements to be somewhere other than *Custodian* that day, I suppose," Shirai said grimly. "Verity's flaws do not include cowardice. This ship will not surrender."

"We'll deal with that when the time comes," Walkingstick promised. If one or both of the *other* conversations he was going to have today worked out, he'd give Shirai a ship to make sure he *was* on when push came to shove. "Can you get them to move on Yellowstar?"

"I'll anonymize the intelligence and insert it into our pipeline," the Triumvirate officer told him. "Then I'll flag it up as priority. It's exactly what Verity is looking for. They know you've got too many ships for them to risk a head-on fight, so they're *looking* to engage the Republic and its allies in detail."

"Then let's hand them what they want."

And Walkingstick trusted Admiral Tecumseh would make the warlord choke on their own trap.

22

In Transit to Yellowstar System
12:00 February 22, 2740 ESMDT

"WELL, *that* wasn't what I was expecting."

James Tecumseh wasn't sure whether to be amused or *cry* as his two Republic capital ships found themselves in the crossfire between *Iroquois* and *Adamant*. *Bon Homme Richard*, Captain Prem Labriola's *Lexington*-class carrier, had *no* business having approached that close to the two Confederacy ships, virtual exercise or not.

And while *Momentum*, Kamilla Fujisawa's *Resolute*, was theoretically an even match to *Adamant*, she wasn't up to handling *Iroquois* on top of that.

"I think Labriola was trying something clever with the bombers, but Waterman's fighters shredded them," Volkov said, her voice forced to calm. "That was... aggressive."

"Aggression has its uses," James allowed. He'd served under Walkingstick, after all, and he'd made a point of looking up the man's work. Having fought alongside the Castle Federation's Kyle Roberts, he was *quite* certain the Federation officer had read "A Treatise on Aggression and Calculated Risk as Psychological Warfare in Modern Carrier Combat"—*Walkingstick's* primary thesis from command college.

Walkingstick had understood the impact of the carrier sooner than most Commonwealth officers. By the time of the Second Rimward War, everyone had adapted to the realization that a starfighter could carry enough antimatter to kill a capital ship, but in James's experience, the art of aggression as psychological warfare only had two masters.

Unfortunately, Kyle Roberts had no place in this war, and James Walkingstick was a dangerous ally at best. And whatever Fujisawa and Labriola thought, they weren't even playing in the same league as those Admirals.

"Well, prep for exercise debrief," James ordered, watching the two Republic ships flash death's-head icons on his screen. All four of the ships in the exercise were still in formation around *Krakatoa*, hurtling through space at one-light-year-per-day-squared with two days left of their journey to Yellowstar.

"Is it too much to hope that they learn the lessons rather than getting angry?" Volkov asked.

"It doesn't matter," James told her. "Whether they are our ships or allied ships, they are attached to this task force. That means that *making sure* they learn the lesson is my job. And yours."

"Understood, sir," she conceded. There was a long pause as the exercise wiped from the displays and *Krakatoa's* flag bridge returned to its usual display. Now they were surrounded by an illusion of the stars moving around them at a calculated estimate of their current pseudovelocity.

"Would it be *too* pointed to show up to the meeting with leashes in hand?"

In the replay during the virtual conference, it was clearer what the senior Republic Captain had been *trying* to do. Using the starfighters from his carrier as a screen, Labriola had attempted to sneak both the bombers *and* the two capital ships into *danger close* range.

Except that starfighters and bombers generally accelerated around five hundred gravities and capital ships ran at two hundred. Tier Three versus Tier Two acceleration was a question of *efficiency* rather than strict physical limitations—the tiers were plateaus in the calculated interface of mass manipulation and antimatter engines, points where fuel consumption was predictable and sustainable—but the capital ships weren't built to be able to achieve the higher thrust-to-pseudomass ratio.

So, while Labriola's *concept* had been solid, and he and his people had executed on it perfectly competently, the limited acceleration of the Republic fighter formation had given everything away early.

At which point Waterman, in command of the two Confederacy ships, had waited for the Republic ships to get into extreme lance range and then opened fire with *Iroquois*'s significantly more powerful positron lances. The starfighters could block scanners, but they couldn't stop beams of pure antimatter rated at over a megaton and a half per second.

And Labriola's aggression and determination to execute his clever idea had put his ships and his *people* into a place from which there was no retreat.

"So." James let the syllable hang in the air as the accelerated replay of the exercise ended. "Captain Labriola. Your take on the result of the simulation?"

"We were outclassed from the start and it was hardly a fair fight," Labriola said sharply. "An *Iroquois* and a *Resolute* have half again the volume of a *Lexington* and a *Resolute*. We had to be clever to make it work, and Captain Waterman suckered us once he realized we'd made a mistake."

There was… a lot to unpack in the dark-haired officer's statement, and James smiled thinly. At least he recognized that he'd made a mistake and Waterman had taken him to the cleaners with it.

"Captain Waterman and Captain Werner,"—*Adamant*'s commanding officer, who was the most junior Commodore of the three ship-commanding Commodores in Task Force Six… and still possessed of half a decade of experience over Labriola—"definitely had an edge over you, yes," James agreed. "On the other hand, *Adamant* doesn't carry starfighters at all and *Iroquois* only carries sixty, with no bomber complement.

"You had a hundred and fifty starfighters, including forty bombers, aboard *Bon Homme Richard*. I will admit I expected clever use of them, but…"

"We weren't clever," Fujisawa said, her voice soft even through the conference software augmenting her volume. "We *thought* we were clever, but looking at it, our deceit was obvious. Captain Waterman didn't need to *sucker us*. We suckered ourselves."

"Yes," James said flatly. "I'm not going to be as harsh as I might be, Captains, because you are *allied* officers."

He let that hang in the air for a second. If a *Dakotan* captain had decided to bring her carrier in directly behind her fighters in a real engagement, James would have her gold bars. In an exercise, it would *merely* have been accompanied by the type of discussion that didn't take place in the semi-public venue of the exercise debrief.

"The fundamental concept of your trick isn't bad, honestly," he told them. "The *first* problem in your execution was the clear and obvious reduction in acceleration on the part of your fighters, which made it very clear exactly what was going on.

"The second problem in your execution was including *Bon Homme Richard* in the formation at all. Once Captain Waterman realized there was a problem and put q-probes behind your formation, he was able to dial in both of your capital ships for easy targeting with *Iroquois*'s main guns."

He shook his head.

"Testing, people," he told them, addressing the Dakotan starship captains as well. "Scouting. Whether probes or even fighter squadrons, it can turn a clever idea into a genius tactic—or turn your *enemy's* clever idea into a weakness."

"Against those kinds of odds, sending our fighters in alone would have been suicide for them," Labriola argued. "Only by managing to get our full force into play did we have a chance."

"The best counter to a carrier is a battleship at close range," James said quietly. "Frankly, the *last* thing any ship wants is to be within positron-lance range of a battleship or battlecruiser, but a carrier—

especially an older carrier, like a *Lexington*—wants to stay as far away from the enemy battleships and battlecruisers as possible.

"Given the size of the ships in play, *Momentum* on her own would have been facing three-to-one odds," he reminded them. "This wasn't a battle you could win, not easily. Which brings me to an important question, Captain Labriola, Captain Fujisawa... What was the mission you were given for the exercise?"

He started a new sequence playing in the middle of the conference. This part was generated, the computers' estimate of the deployments Commodore Waterman would have engaged in once his enemies were defeated.

Starfighters lanced out across the virtual star system, chasing down the quartet of freighters Labriola had been supposed to protect. Without any opposition, the starfighters had no problem overhauling civilian ships limited to Tier One acceleration.

In the real world, *Dakotan* fighters would have ordered the civilians to adjust their course to stay inside the stellar-gravity shadow until shuttles could arrive to capture them. In the virtual scenario... Katanas only carried sixty-kiloton-per-second positron lances, but civilian ships didn't carry electromagnetic deflectors. All four freighters were destroyed within an hour of Labriola's charge.

"The destruction of the enemy was the only way I saw to secure the safety of the convoy," the Republic officer said stiffly.

"And that is not an illegitimate assessment," James conceded. The problem was neither lack of will nor a lack of basic competence. "Your maneuvers were carried out well," he continued. "I'm impressed with your people's flying, to be honest. Your starfighters managed a difficult piece of formation-keeping to maintain as much of a sensor screen as they did."

"Thank you, Admiral."

"There is a point to the argument that the destruction of the enemy is always the best way to complete your objectives," James told everyone. "*If* you can destroy the enemy, that completely neutralizes their threat.

"The question, the one we have to consider, train for and plan for, is what do you do when the enemy is too powerful to destroy in a single strike or you don't know *where* to strike?"

He was talking about more than just the exercise now. The entire plan seeing him and his ships heading to Yellowstar was one answer to that question.

"There is a term, most commonly referenced back to the planning of the First World War on Earth: *fleet in being*. Just by *existing*, you limited your enemy's options. In this case"—he gestured back to the display—"by retaining a carrier aerospace patrol around *Bon Homme Richard* and the freighters and keeping *Momentum* between the convoy and the op force, you would have reduced Captain Waterman's options significantly.

"His entire fighter strength wouldn't have sufficed to threaten your formation. He would have needed to bring *his* concentrated force after you—and every minute and hour you bought might have been enough to get the freighters out of the stellar-gravity shadow.

"While destroying the enemy is unquestionably a victory, victory itself does not require the destruction of the enemy," James said firmly. "The first question you must always ask is not *How do I destroy the enemy*. It is *How do I win*.

"Sometimes, you can win by dying," he told them. He'd been prepared to do just that in the Battle of Dakota in '38, knowing that by wrecking the Commonwealth fleet, he'd have destroyed Walkingstick's plans to rebuild the Commonwealth—even if *his* entire fleet was destroyed along the way. "Sometimes, you win by surviving. Sometimes, you win by running away and taking the civilians with you."

He surveyed the captains under his command. He knew his Dakotan officers got it—*all* of them had been at Dakota when he'd won the day with the *threat* of a Pyrrhic victory.

The two Republic officers looked thoughtful, which all he could ask for. They were his subordinates for this mission, but they weren't part of his navy. Technically, he wasn't even supposed to be teaching them.

He just figured no Admiral worth their stars could see captains that inexperienced and not *try*.

23

"You, Admiral, need to grow up."

Anthony Yamamoto rolled over to give the currently naked woman sitting on the end of his bed a questioning look.

"What exactly do you mean?" he asked. "Because I can think of a few people who would say that about my approach to relationships…"

Shannon Reynolds chuckled at him.

"I'm basically the chief spy on this ship, Anthony," she pointed out. "I keep a careful eye on everyone who is sleeping with or *trying* to sleep with our Admirals. You have good taste!"

Even with the *openness* of their friendship, that was a touch embarrassing to realize, and he sighed.

"Then what *do* you mean?" he asked.

"You were just checking your implant, reviewing the status of the squadrons slated to launch the CAP when we emerge into Yellowstar," she told him. "And if you'd been doing it two minutes earlier, I'd be *extremely* unimpressed."

He… had been doing just that, so he couldn't argue. It took a measurable degree of self-control not to *lead* the carrier aerospace patrol that would cover the Task Force in its most vulnerable moments. They had no reason to expect any trouble immediately upon arrival in Yellowstar—q-coms from the system said it was still clear.

But Vanguard Fleet *had* left Saskatoon, and no one was entirely sure when or where they were going. The fragmented nature of their intelligence in the Triumvirate-occupied system was frustrating.

So, he'd been checking. Been *working...* and as Reynolds pointed out, if he'd been doing that two minutes earlier, she'd have good reason to be actually *angry* at him, open relationship or not.

"Okay, so, your point stands," he muttered. "It's still part of my job."

"As I understand it, Anthony, making sure we *have* a CAP up within a few seconds of returning to unwarped space is definitely your job. Even setting its strength, definitely your job. *Maybe* picking the squadrons, or at least which ships they're deploying from.

"Double-checking the readiness of the individual starfighters thirty minutes before we exit Alcubierre? I'm pretty sure that's micromanaging."

"No, micromanaging would be if I was giving *instructions* at this stage," he replied... but he knew it was a weak argument. "This is just watching over my people's shoulders and hoping they don't notice."

"Because if your Colonels and Wing Colonels think you don't trust them to do their jobs, that's going to cause you some real morale issues, isn't it?" she asked sweetly, crossing her arms in an extremely distracting manner.

He opened his mouth to say something, and then sighed and gritted his teeth as he nodded.

"Now, is that coming from my *friend*, warning me I'm a twit, or the *chief spy in this task force*, telling me there's an actual problem?"

"Mostly the former," she admitted. "Helvius knows you well enough to make allowances, but it's not a good habit you're in."

Wing Colonel Helvius Ó Cochláin was *Krakatoa*'s Commander, Aerospace Group. He was both one of Anthony's most senior and trusted subordinates and about one successful mission from finding himself pulled from a starfighter himself.

When this current affair was over, Ó Cochláin was about to join the *very* short list of Rear Admirals in the Dakotan Confederacy Starfighter Corps. It was a *good* thing he knew Anthony as well as he did, but... Anthony still should trust him.

"I do trust Helvius," he said aloud, both to himself and to Reynolds.

"I know that and you know that and *he* knows that," she agreed. "But your micromanaging ways and desire to put your own butt in a starfighter are going to get you in real trouble the next time you're aboard a carrier where the CAG doesn't know you backward and forward.

"You're *Fleet CAG*. Hell, you're the CO, DCSC. You can't be double-checking that the Chiefs painted the right color of red on the starfighters you're sending out."

He sighed, giving her a very weak glare.

"It's not that bad. There's a very real job I need to do here, Shannon."

"And if you're poking through the minutiae of the CAP deployment thirty minutes before we breach regular space, you're not doing it, are you?" she asked bluntly. "You're supposed to be making sure all of the CAGs are on the same page, doing the same job and working together."

"They *are*," he pointed out. "I've been in touch with all of them, even Major Harolds on *Bon Homme Richard*. I'm doing my damn job."

"I know. And you need to trust your people to do theirs. Just like I have to trust that the agents I left behind on Galen can manage to hide *two fucking battalions of Marines* without watching over their shoulders!"

Anthony chuckled.

"You're telling *me* off because I'm doing what you *want* to do, aren't you?"

She shifted her arms, blatantly jiggling her breasts at him.

"And I think we *both* need some more distraction, yes?" she purred.

———

The *distraction* didn't take long enough that Anthony wasn't in Fleet Starfighter Control when they hit normal space. He wasn't giving orders—he wouldn't have been even without Reynolds' reminder—but at this point, he *did* need to know what was going on.

"Stetson fields are down. *Krakatoa*'s Alcubierre field is down," a Chief reported.

Fleet Starfighter Control was basically a clone of *Krakatoa*'s own Flight Control Center, a circular space a dozen meters across filled with displays and consoles. While it had been slightly rearranged to serve as a Fleet command center, the standard flight-control layout was already designed for a small group of people to support a group of deployed assets.

"*Krakatoa*-Alpha, -Bravo, and -Echo are up," another NCO declared. "*Krakatoa* Flight Control reports tubes being checked for second-wave launches."

Krakatoa had enough launch tubes to put a hundred starfighters or bombers into space in a single launch. At full speed, the deck crews could get the tubes cleared and loaded with the next wave of fighter craft in less than a minute.

Outside of active combat operations, though, they'd take any time they could get. Unexpected debris was *deadly* in a system that accelerated its contents at thousands of gravities.

"Get me a system-wide display," Anthony ordered quietly. "Mirror any data sets coming in from CIC for Tecumseh."

A map of the star system, including live visual feeds of the various planets—the ones from the two inhabited planets real-time, linked to the defensive flotilla orbiting the dual-planet system—appeared in the main display.

Some fluke of gravity and planet formation had given the star system no less than *three* such dual systems. The important one was Yellowstar IV, which held the heavily populated planet of Ulu and its sister planet, the heavy-gravity water world Imaq.

Between the two planets, there were three billion people in that dual-planet system. The Yellowstar I and Yellowstar V systems were less useful, only really notable as part of the astrographic oddity of three dual-planets in one star system. Major economic interest was focused on the two asteroid belts and Yellowstar VII—a hydrogen-rich gas giant named Mackenzie. With two habitable planets to live on, and two asteroid belts and a gas giant for extraction, the *other* nine planets in Yellowstar were mostly ignored.

"Flag reports contact is clear with WRN Task Force Three, Rear Admiral Al-Amir Tawfiq, commanding."

Anthony glanced at Commodore Peña as he reported. These days, the junior flag officer seemed to follow where he went—he'd been operations officer for TG *Iroquois*, and now he was *Starfighter* Operations Officer for Task Force Six.

As distinct from the Fleet Commander, Aerospace Group, whom Peña reported to.

"What do we have on Tawfiq?" Anthony asked. "I'm not familiar with the name."

"I've pulled his file. Commissioned into the WRN eighteen months ago at the rank of Rear Admiral. Prior to that was the chief of security for StarHydro, one of the local big megacorps. Commanded an antipiracy ship—a freighter modded to carry fifth-generation starfighters —for StarHydro before taking the job."

Anthony grimaced. He could vaguely see why the Republic had cashiered all of their senior TCN officers. He could *not* understand why they'd chosen to replace them with a pile of former corporate mercenaries.

"At least he knows which end of a starfighter the antimatter comes out of," he said drily. "He's got, what, a battlecruiser, a strike cruiser and two old carriers?"

"*Beowulf, Bay of Bengal, Gaumont* and *Torchlight*," Peña reeled off. "A *Hercules*, an *Ocean* and two *Paramounts*."

Anthony chuckled bitterly.

"And here I thought we had the last *Paramounts* standing!"

The *Paramount*-class carriers were the second generation of carrier the TCN had ever built and showed it. They were small and carried both too few fighters *and* too few onboard weapons.

"The good news is that they are fully equipped with Katanas and both of the *Paramounts* have three bomber squadrons aboard," Peña told him. "And *Beowulf* is a modern sixty."

"I doubt the Admiral is complaining about that," Anthony agreed. The question—the question he couldn't ask where his subordinates could hear him!—was whether Rear Admiral Tawfiq would recognize that Tecumseh was the more experienced officer and needed to be in charge.

Or if the local was going to give them enough of a headache that they'd have to go back to President Frey for orders.

"TF Three is in a high orbit of the Ulu-Imaq planetary system, about four light-minutes inside the gravity shadow," Peña told him. "We're on the edge of the gravity shadow and heading in to rendezvous."

"Any sign of the Triumvirate?" Anthony asked. He was pulling more information on the defenses around the three key planets—Ulu, Imaq and Mackenzie. None of them were as impressive as he'd hoped. A single TCN-built *Zion*-class platform above each planet, carrying fifty starfighters apiece. Imaq and Ulu both had cobbled-together complexes of civilian platforms that the WRN told him held another six hundred fighters between them.

Mackenzie was the interesting one, he saw. StarHydro had apparently invested in more than just armed freighters. The defensive constellation above the main cloudscoop complex was far from invulnerable, but it based the same six hundred fighters as the bases above the inhabited planets—and while they might not have been *Zion*s, the six fortress platforms were built for their role and carried real weapons as well.

Backed by what looked like a thousand single-shot missile mines, Anthony wouldn't have wanted to tangle with the corporate security force without multiple capital ships—and StarHydro had apparently sold the constellation to the WRN at a hefty discount.

One they'd more than make up from not carrying the costs of *operating* the forts, but it was still a surprisingly sensible gesture.

Not that any of the fortifications could hold off a pair of determined and properly managed capital ships with decent fighter wings. That was why the WRN's TF Three and Dakota's TF Six were there.

"Alcubierre flare!" someone snapped, yanking Anthony's attention away from Mackenzie and to the here-and-now. "Multiple Alcubierre flares—dammit, they threaded the needle! Contacts at twenty million kilometers, between us and the planet!"

The rock suddenly sinking into Anthony's stomach didn't need the details to know what had just happened, but the numbers filling in on the displays confirmed it.

Eighteen capital ships had just cut Task Force Six off from Rear Admiral Tawfiq… and there was only one force in the area with eighteen capital ships.

Admiral Surinder Verity had clearly been watching—and chosen the worst possible place and time to arrive. Or the best, Anthony supposed, from their perspective.

24

"I THINK I prefer it when I'm the one doing dangerous, clever tricks," James Tecumseh said quietly, watching his worst-case scenario begin to unfold in front of him.

"The good news is that our friend looks to have left a *Lexington* in Saskatoon," Volkov told him, new data flickering onto the displays around them as she spoke. "They've still brought five carriers, four strike cruisers, four battlecruisers and five battleships to the party."

"We can't dance with that, and neither can Admiral Tawfiq," James replied. "Vectors—ours and theirs."

"We're inbound toward the twin planets at just under one percent lightspeed," Commodore Harkaitz Zyma—the Task Force Navigation Officer—reported. "It'll take us the same twenty minutes to dump that velocity that it took us to build it, which will put us eighteen-point-five million klicks from the hostiles, assuming they do not accelerate toward us."

"And we're already *in* capital-ship missile range," Volkov pointed out. "Flight time thirty-two minutes, fifty-one seconds."

"Get the rest of the fighters up," James ordered, his tone surprisingly calm even to him. "Keep the bombers aboard. Starfighters will assume defensive formations as the Task Force inverts course. Get us out of the gravity shadow; today is not the day to fight to the death."

"Do we shoot at them?" Volkov asked—and then a spray of red icons on the display answered the question as James grunted his acknowledgement.

"Admiral Verity just answered your question about two hundred and eighty times, Admiral," James told her. "Send them back *our* opinion of their missiles, please."

If any of his subordinate Captains were surprised by the order to launch missiles, they didn't show it. If anything, he suspected that he was lucky any of them had *waited* long enough for a coordinated salvo from the entire task force.

"Sir, incoming channel from Captain Labriola… and incoming channel from Admiral Tawfiq," Commodore Prebensen told him.

"They both almost certainly have the same question; link them through together," James ordered. "Keep a silent feed to my implant of status updates."

"What are you *doing*, Tecumseh?" Tawfiq demanded harshly the moment he was connected. "The enemy is here and you are *running*?"

"What I am *trying* to do, Admiral Tawfiq, is provide cover so that your task force can get the hell out of Admiral Verity's path," James said flatly. "They're not going to go after four ships, two of them obsolete, while I have six that aren't quite running away fast enough."

Starfighters are up in Vanguard Fleet, Volkov told him silently. *Thirteen-sixty total; estimate three hundred bombers. No strike yet.*

"We cannot simply abandon another star system to the Triumvirate!" Tawfiq barked.

"My bomber pilots are wondering why they're being held back," Labriola added. "Hitting her with a bomber strike is—"

"A very swift way to get the hundred and twenty people on your bombers killed, Captain Labriola," James said flatly. "Admiral, Captain, even our combined forces are outnumbered five to three in starfighters. Two to one in missile launchers.

"If Verity pins your fleet against the twin planets with their battleships, you and all of your people are dead, Admiral Tawfiq. You need to get out of the twin planets' gravity shadow and warp space to the rendezvous point my people will be sending you as soon as we've calculated it!

"You can't fight them alone. We can't fight them together, so you *sure as fuck* can't fight them alone!"

"I thought you'd come to help us, not betray us in the face of the enemy," Labriola snapped. "I'm—"

"You will obey my orders as you were instructed by Admiral Vitali, Captain," James cut him off. "And if you look frankly at the situation, Admiral Tawfiq, we have no choices."

"We cannot simply betray our people and the system to the Triumvirate. There are thousands of pilots and flight crew prepared to fight to defend this system as we speak."

"And if I thought for one damn second they would listen, I would order them to stand down," James said flatly. "If you've made the right preparations, we can *hide* them, keep them intact until we're ready to relieve this system.

"But right now, what the people of Yellowstar need from you, Admiral Tawfiq, is for you *not* to throw your ships away in a pointless gesture. Load as many of the orbital fighters aboard as you can. Hide as many of the rest on the surface as possible.

"Verity is methodical, which means they can be slow. Making them *hunt* for the fighters rather than having them charge in pointless bravado will buy us time. Time we need. Time we can *use*, because there are *eighteen capital ships* within a week's flight of this star system."

He noted absently that Vanguard Fleet was doing *exactly* what he'd hoped. Task Force Six was shedding velocity, burning away from the planets and the enemy to try to get to the safe space where they could jump to FTL.

In response, Verity was leaving their carriers under the protection of their strike cruisers and was bringing their battleships and battle-cruisers after him at two hundred and thirty gravities. Thirty gravities wasn't *much* of an edge, but given that his velocity was already toward Vanguard Fleet, it was enough to keep the fleets closing.

"We will rendezvous one day's flight from Yellowstar," he told

Tawfiq. "Imperator Walkingstick is less than six hours out of Scotia. Once out of warped space, he can immediately adjust course and come here.

"Using q-coms and the q-probes we will need to leave behind, we can *guarantee* an aligned arrival, combining our forces to pin *Vanguard Fleet* in the planet's gravity shadow. If we fight today, Admiral Tawfiq, we might take a few of their ships with us.

"But we will die. And in the dying, we may cost the Republic their only chance of victory. I will *not* throw away my fleet today on a question of honor. Not when dealing with an enemy I know wants the planet *intact*.

"Better to yield the system for seven days and then win the war in an afternoon than to *lose* it in an afternoon today."

"And if I decline to join in your analysis?" Tawfiq demanded.

"That is your privilege as a task force commander," James allowed, swallowing down his spike of anger at the man's stubbornness. "You will lead your crews to a pointless last stand that will gain Ulu and Imaq *nothing*—likely not even time—but the choice is yours."

"And if *I* decline to join your cowardice?" Labriola asked.

"*You* are under specific orders to follow my authority," James pointed out to the carrier captain. "Which means that I'm reasonably sure I could have Vitali shoot you for disobeying orders in the face of the enemy—but frankly, if you stay, Verity will take care of that for me."

It was harsher than he preferred, but he *needed* the Republican officers to listen.

"You need to get out of there, Admiral Tawfiq, and you need to get as many fighters on the ground as you can. Leave the missiles in space, rigged as mines. *Fuck* Vanguard Fleet with them—but if you and those starfighters sortie, Surinder Verity will kill you all."

Vanguard Fleet has launched their starfighter strike, Volkov warned him. *Ten minutes to torpedo range. Twenty minutes to torpedo* impact. There was a long pause. *Even assuming we jump as soon as we clear the gravity shadow, they* will *hit us*.

"We are out of time for this conversation," James said fiercely before either of the Republicans recovered from his warning. "Triumvirate bombers and fighters just broke formation and are heading for Task Force Six. If you break formation, Labriola, they will rip *Bon Homme Richard* to pieces. I'm sorry, Admiral Tawfiq, the only way we can save Yellowstar is to give it up and come back for them."

"I will... follow orders," Labriola said grimly. "But there will be consequences for your... *choices*."

The Captain dropped off the channel before James could challenge his clearly intended ending word. For Tawfiq's part, the ex-corporate mercenary Admiral was very quiet, for longer than they could afford the time for, but James waited him out.

"I... This is my first *war*, Admiral Tecumseh. *Are you sure?*"

"I would not, for one moment, consider leaving this system to our enemies if I wasn't, Rear Admiral Tawfiq," James said gently. "We can't beat Vanguard Fleet without Walkingstick, Admiral. The fewer people who get killed proving that reality, the better—and the better off we are retaking the system when we come back."

"Won't Verity anticipate just that?"

James smiled.

"Yes. But the only way they can *avoid* it is by abandoning the system before we get back. In which case we've already won."

There was another long silence, and James breathed a mental sigh of relief as he saw that his fighters didn't sortie—unwise, given the current plan, but entirely reasonable under most circumstances—and *Bon Homme Richard* stayed in formation.

The only reason he could wait out Admiral Tawfiq's fears was because he had a good team.

"I will do what I must," the Westonian Admiral finally said. "Send us the rendezvous coordinates, Admiral Tecumseh. We will see you there." He paused. "I can fit more starfighters and flight crews on my *Paramount*s and *Bay of Bengal* than any of them can actually *operate* or even potentially sustain..."

"If you get them to the rendezvous point, Admiral Tawfiq, between your carriers, mine and Captain Labriola's, I guarantee you they will be taken care of—and every fighter we get to the rendezvous point is one more set of missiles and positron lances we can shove down the Triumvirate's throat when we get back."

"Understood. We will see you there," he repeated, then cut the channel.

James Tecumseh allowed himself the moment for one immense sigh of relief inside the semi-virtual space of his own implants, and then brought his attention fully back to reality.

He might be running... but Verity had picked their timing well, and even *running* was going to require a fight!

———

The missiles were the first problem, overhauling his fleet at over five times their acceleration. The *Dakotan* missiles, on the other hand, were heading into the teeth of Verity's Vanguard Fleet, cutting their flight time by a full six minutes versus the Triumvirate's weapons.

James's people had fired second by a few moments, but they would still have six full salvos land before the first enemy missiles arrived.

"Enemy active defenses engaging," Volkov reported. "They held back four hundred fighters for missile defense." She paused thoughtfully. "This is going to be a mess, sir. I don't know if we'll get anything through."

"First salvo usually doesn't," James reminded her. The missiles carried by capital ships were massive beasts, a good chunk of the size of a starfighter with a flight time of roughly an hour and a range most easily measured in light-minutes.

But they also carried twenty-five kilograms of antimatter in their warheads alone. And since *these* weapons were using less than half of their flight time, they were reaching their targets with almost *forty* kilograms of antimatter aboard.

The missiles were rated for a one-gigaton explosion, but with this much fuel aboard, they were closer to one-*and-three-quarter*-gigaton weapons. And Task Force Six had fired a hundred and twelve Jackhammer VII capital attack missiles.

None of the first salvo got through, but four and a half tons of antimatter created a *lot* of radiation when it annihilated with matter. The chaotic mess left behind, the *radiation hash* of modern warfare, was a critical component of long-range missile engagements.

"Do we have active links to the later salvos?" James asked. Once, the answer would have been obviously yes… but not that long ago, the answer would have been obviously *no*. They had launched at a target a full light-minute away, and a q-probe acting as a telemetry relay was a *lot* more obvious than one acting as a passive sensor platform.

"I'm holding the q-probes so we can sneak them away when we jump," Volkov told him. "We have links to salvos twelve through twenty for now."

And more than twenty salvos hadn't been worth launching. Even using q-probes as relays, the Task Force would have trouble controlling the weapons once they'd left the system—and twenty salvos was forty percent of his ship's magazines!

Their rendezvous point was unlikely to have the raw materials to fabricate a lot of new missiles, which meant Task Force Six was coming *back* to Yellowstar with whatever was left in their magazines.

"Well, then I guess we get to be clever with eight salvos instead of all of them," James said with a forced smile. "Hold those links, Admiral Volkov."

———

James Tecumseh's plans were one thing, but Admiral Surinder Verity understood their situation perfectly. They had three times as many ships as Task Force Six, and if they had seven thirties to James's one, the overall balance was unquestionably in the Triumvirate fleet's favor.

But Verity *also* had to know that Dakota and the Commonwealth had answered the Republic's call for help. That meant they *needed* to destroy every ship they could in Yellowstar before James could get the reinforcements he was running away to meet.

There was little sign of the steady and cautious approach Verity had shown in Saskatoon. Their battleships and battlecruisers rushed toward James's ships, nine behemoths armed with the most powerful positron weapons built in each of their times.

James had a few surprises tucked away for if they reached their calculated range, but there was *almost* no chance that the battle line would reach the two-and-a-half-million-kilometer range they needed for even *Saint Agricola*'s massive one-point-five-megaton lances to touch James's weakest-shielded ships.

Or at least, if the single *Saint* they'd identified in the Triumvirate fleet got close enough to think she was a direct fire threat to Task Force Six, James was going to have *much* bigger problems than the ship's positron beams.

"Missiles are incoming fast; they have full jammers up. *They're* not trying to maintain terminal control," one of the Ops Chiefs reported.

"No new orders," James murmured. "Everyone knows this game."

Six times already, his missiles had hammered Vanguard Fleet. So far, not one missile had managed to connect with their targets, but that was the game. Even a single hit from a positron lance, let alone a giga-ton-plus antimatter warhead, was enough to critically damage if not destroy a warship.

James was young enough that his entire career had been in the so-called Antimatter Era of modern war—but he'd spent the first years of his career serving under officers who *had* come up and commanded ships with sufficient armor to shrug aside "mere" nuclear warheads and *c*-fractional railgun slugs.

None of those defenses had sufficed once the weapon of choice became antimatter warheads and modified zero-point cells that unleashed beams of pure positrons.

"They might have launched more missiles than we did, people, but *we* kept all of our fighters," he reminded them. "We're fine."

He hoped no one interrogated that claim too carefully. *All* of their fighters, after all, was roughly the same number of fighters as Verity had held back as CAP to protect their fleet. They'd sent a "mere" six hundred starfighters forward with their three hundred bombers.

"Starfighters salvoing missiles in defensive patterns."

James barely even registered who made the report. His focus was on the four-hundred-plus heavy missiles surging toward his ships. They *should* be fine—the real nightmare wasn't due for, oh, about ten minutes—but the missiles were already launched.

The number necessary to penetrate a starship's defenses was mind-boggling—and mind-bogglingly *expensive*, even with antimatter produced from zero-point cells—but there was always the chance of a lucky hit.

Verity didn't get lucky this time, but the defensive fighters expended a larger portion of their missiles than James liked. The Katanas carried twelve missiles apiece—four launchers with three missiles per launcher—and every one of Yamamoto's ships had launched two of their missiles.

There were more than six salvos coming their way, which meant they were going to be in real trouble in a few minutes. Especially as the *real* attack was now drawing into range.

"Triumvirate torpedo bombers at ten-point-five million kilometers," one of Volkov's subordinates reported. "Estimated torpedo range in thirty seconds."

"And our trick?" James asked quietly.

"Executing… *now*," Volkov replied.

Even with the q-probes, they were watching the bomber-strike approach at about a two-second delay. The robotic spacecraft were still too precious to risk getting within weapons range—but with a two-second delay, Volkov had been able to recode the targeting parameters for the last eight salvos.

They were no longer aiming for the Triumvirate battle line heading toward Task Force Six. Now they were aiming for Surinder Verity's *bombers*.

The Triumvirate Admiral was better with their fighters than many officers James had seen. A starfighter was inherently expendable—the ships were far from cheap, and only about two percent of the population had the neural interface bandwidth to *fly* the things, but all of that paled in comparison with the cost of an Alcubierre-Stetson starship—but they remained a precious resource, to be used carefully and preserved if possible.

Verity understood that and had been as careful with their fighters as with their starships in Saskatoon. And while James *approved*, that also told him something critically important: Verity wasn't expecting to be able to source *replacement* fighters and flight crews.

And to attack his fleet, Verity had needed to make those fighters and bombers *vulnerable*. Now capital-ship missiles changed their courses at the last possible moment before they passed the fighter strike, diverting from the planned path toward Vanguard Fleet against *far*-closer targets.

The Triumvirate fighters had been watching the missiles and taking potshots at them to reduce the salvo before it reached their mother-ships, but eleven salvos had passed by them with total focus on the capital ships.

Three-quarters of the missiles made it into the heart of the Triumvi-rate fighter formation and detonated in furious flares of antimatter fire. And while a *capital ship* could survive anything short of a direct hit, starfighters were far more fragile.

"They're adjusting to cover more thoroughly against the follow-on salvos," Volkov reported, "but we hit them *hard*. Still estimating their losses."

"There is only one number I care about right now, Admiral Volkov," James pointed out. "How many torpedoes are they going to launch?"

"We have one more salvo going in as they enter extreme range," she told him. "Unless they rush, we're going to get more of them."

"And I can live with them rushing," James agreed. Seconds were everything, and he watched their thirteenth salvo lunge toward its prey.

Missiles and starfighters alike were minuscule by the standards of space combat, vast and heavy as a thirty-meter, five-thousand-ton starfighter was compared to air- and groundcraft. At this distance—over half a light-minute!—they could easily seem irrelevant.

But every spark on the display was thousands of megatons of explosive force. Every icon that vanished from the screen was three human lives snuffed out. Equally important, though, was that every *bomber* destroyed was four fewer torpedoes coming toward Task Force Six.

"Missiles detonating—"

"We have torpedo launch!" Volkov barked. "Triumvirate fighters are flipping their course and attempting to evade our remaining salvos."

"Get me a number and timeline on those torpedoes, people," James ordered. "I'd love it if someone told me they missed the window."

That was the other reason the Triumvirate bombers had to launch at maximum range—the window during which they could launch torpedoes and hit his fleet before they warped space was less than twenty seconds long.

"Negative, negative," one of the Chiefs declared. "Estimate flight time, five hundred ninety-five seconds. Contact will be ten seconds before we clear the gravity shadow."

"Well, then," James said grimly. "For what we are about to receive, may the stars make us truly thankful."

25

It was in moments like these, even as his entire body and soul *screamed* to be in a starfighter cockpit, that Anthony Yamamoto understood *why* he needed to be in Fleet Starfighter Control. There, linked through a virtual network with the rest of Task Force Six's command staff and the starfighter support teams, he had everything he needed.

Barely. There was no way he could have accessed and managed all of this information while flying a starfighter. To command three hundred and sixty starfighters in a mass defensive intercept, he *needed* to step back and wholly focus on what he was doing.

He tried not to think too hard about the fact that he'd done just this from a starfighter cockpit before. Instead, he focused on passing orders to entire squadrons and flight groups, laying out a massive cone in space through which the Triumvirate torpedoes *had* to fly.

"Make sure everyone has their timing and their routes locked for their fallbacks," he ordered. "Just because we have a thousand torpedoes coming at us doesn't mean we want to leave anyone behind!"

The Navy had done better with their missiles than he expected.

Three hundred bombers should have put twelve hundred torpedoes into space, a salvo with a very real chance of breaching both his defensive screen and the active defenses of the capital ships behind them.

Instead, *a thousand torpedoes* was actually rounding up. Not by *much*—the current estimate was nine hundred and eighty—but still.

With two hundred missiles, the Navy had taken at least fifty-five bombers out. It helped.

"Remember, people," Anthony said, linking into a channel that connected to all of his flight crews. "This is what we held on to your last missile salvos for. We *knew* this was coming. Clear the torps, and the Admiral is getting us all the hell out of here."

"Forward squadrons in counter-missile range in fifteen seconds and counting. Forty seconds to impact."

Anthony nodded but stayed focused on the channel to everyone.

"Fleet Control is sending you your detailed fallback routes, but once the torps are past you, run for your hangars. The Admiral isn't leaving without you, so if you drag your feet, it risks the entire Task Force! The Navy is going to owe you lot *big*, so don't give them grounds to complain!

"Fly well, shoot straight. First round when you're back is on me!"

He couldn't pick out any specific response from the chatter he got back, but the tone was what he needed. Which probably meant that he didn't *want* to pick out any of the responses—flight crew, whether pilots, gunners or engineers, were *not* known for their calm and polite commentary.

"Counter-missile launch."

It took a moment before Anthony realized that *he* was the one who'd spoken, his link into the tactical network around him so close no one had a chance to report it before he'd realized it.

The plan was simple: by creating an extended channel of fighter missiles, positron lances and missile-defense lasers, they would degrade the massive torpedo salvo step by step over twenty-plus seconds. A solid wall of fighters wouldn't have magically acquired more firing opportunities for missiles or beams, so by staggering the fighter formation, he expected to reduce overkill.

And when every missile that got through could easily wreck one of the ships behind him, *overkill* was defined as *spending munitions on a missile that was already gone*. Especially if those munitions could kill one of the missiles that *wasn't* dead yet.

True overkill, of course, was *missing* one missile while another got hit with more fire than needed. Layering the intercept wouldn't get rid of that risk, but it would make their fire more effective.

It required skilled gunners and better pilots, crews that were integrated with each other and the ships behind them. It required squadrons that trusted each other, that knew their command structure, knew their places and trusted the fallback orders they received from Fleet Command.

So, of course, the *backstop* of the entire affair was a solid block of Republic fighters from *Bon Homme Richard* that Anthony didn't know.

"First-layer intercept complete; squadrons falling back on the Task Force. Estimate eight hundred torpedoes remaining. Second layer engaging, third layer engaging. Fourth layer standing by. Final layer standing by."

The not-quite-chant from the coms and control officers echoed through the network and rattled around Anthony's skull. The first layer, now splitting up and hurtling back toward *Iroquois*, was entirely the battlecruiser's fighters—sixty ships.

The second layer, breaking off as he watched, was from *Black Sea*, with three reinforcing squadrons from *Krakatoa*. Seventy ships.

The third and fourth layers, in the thick of it as he watched the crescendo of antimatter explosions creep toward the ship *he* stood on, were both from *Krakatoa*. Sixty ships in both blocks.

Almost four hundred torpedoes broke through Anthony's fighters, and the hundred and ten starfighters from *Bon Homme Richard* got to work. The chaos of the explosions and the radiation hash made tracking everything a nightmare, but *Krakatoa*'s sensor crews knew that chaos. With six ships and a dozen q-probes to draw on, they found a clarity in the chaos that a single eye couldn't—and passed that clarity on to the starfighter crews.

Two hundred and fifty torpedoes—equivalent to capital-ship missiles in every way but range, their jammers and electronic-warfare systems singing deadly siren songs to clear a path through the defenses.

Anthony's people had done their job, the starfighters now fleeing back toward flight decks that they could only pray were still there when they arrived—and a new timer was running in the corner of his implant feed.

They were clear of the gravity well in ten seconds. The last starfighter was due aboard thirty seconds after that, which was going to be a *hell* of a strain on his people. But the next salvo of Triumvirate missiles was going to land in forty-five seconds, and they were dismantling their extended missile defense as Anthony watched.

"Please tell me the Navy's got this," he half-whispered.

Even before he finished the words, though, six starships lit up space with everything they had. Cluster-packs of starfighter missiles, loaded into capital launchers in packs of ten, filled space with smart weapons hunting other smart weapons. Decoys and jammers, dropped into space in preparation for just this moment, sprang to life with enough enthusiasm to confuse *Krakatoa*'s sensors for a fraction of a second.

And dozens of light positron lances—*hundreds* of defensive lasers—spoke into the chaos the battle group created. More torpedoes had made it past the starfighters than there had been *missiles* in the prior missile salvos, and Task Force Six pulled out the best they had.

For a moment, Anthony wasn't sure it was going to be enough—and then twelve platforms, each roughly four times the size of a starfighter and trailing barely five thousand kilometers from their four Dakotan motherships, came to life.

Decoys were a staple of modern missile combat, but these were something *else*. Built by someone who *hadn't* been distracted by the ongoing meltdown of their interstellar nation and with an energy budget few other remote-controlled systems had *ever* been provided, the Paladin-II decoys managed to *perfectly* mimic the mass and energy signatures of their motherships.

Faced with four possible targets for each of the ships they'd been sent for, the torpedoes divided themselves and then divided them-selves up again. The decoys only managed their illusion for five or six seconds—until the electronic brains realized there wasn't *nearly* enough defensive fire coming from the drones, basically—but it was enough.

"Well, that's one cat out of the bag," Anthony murmured as six of the Castle Federation–built decoys were destroyed by the missiles they'd lured—and the other six promptly self-destructed with internal antimatter explosives.

"Twenty seconds."

He wasn't even sure who had spoken, but his attention yanked back to the status of his fighters. The plan called for the ships to jump in ten seconds, and he could *feel* the vibrations of the Class One mass manipulators spinning up and *holding* that power without releasing it.

"*Iroquois* is fully loaded. *Black Sea* is fully loaded. We have eight squadrons out. *Bon Homme Richard* has five squadrons out. They can only land three at a time!"

Everything was happening at the speed of thought, and Anthony saw the problem. *Krakatoa* could land five squadrons at a time through *very* careful computer control, roughly once every ten seconds in an emergency.

Bon Homme Richard, a generation older, could only land thirty fighters at once every *twenty* seconds—and she still had fifty in space.

"Last two Republic squadrons are to divert to *Krakatoa*," he snapped. "They need to divert *now* and turn over control to landing computers as soon as they've adjusted their vector."

There was no time. For a terrifying critical moment, he thought the Republic flight crews would refuse. That the trust they'd lost running instead of fighting would damn them and they'd either lose two squadrons or, worse, *Bon Homme Richard* itself if the old carrier tried to stand off two hundred and eighty missiles on her own.

Then the icons shifted, a vector change of less than two degrees—but enough.

"*Krakatoa* Flight Control confirms landing access," Volkov told him from the flag bridge. "We've got them and they're on the ball. Touchdown in fifteen seconds."

Ten seconds. The battleships vanished into bubbles of warped space as Anthony counted down. *Black Sea* followed them, accompanied by *Iroquois* a moment later.

"*Bon Homme Richard* clear!"

The other carrier vanished, her last fighters now dependent on *Krakatoa* to survive.

Five seconds. The *missiles* were only ten seconds out, and the carrier wasn't even firing defensively. They couldn't. Even the defensive lasers might interfere with the Stetson stabilizer fields snapping into place as the fighters were yanked home by computers and flight controllers cutting tolerances to the bone.

"They're in!"

"Jump *now*," Anthony barked through his link to the bridge—and all of the potential energy that had been starting to make his hair stand on end was suddenly unleashed, crushing the universe into a tiny ball behind them.

Only then did he realize that the starfighters weren't actually on the deck. They were, literally, *in* the hangar—still in the air as the flight-deck systems strained to hold them in place.

Slowly, one by one, each of the fifty remaining starfighters flickered to dark green as they were brought down and secured.

"We did it," someone said quietly.

That was when the cheering started.

26

"WE DID NOT EXPECT this kind of blatant cowardice from our new allies! The entirety of Yellowstar, surrendered to the Triumvirate without a fight because of *that man's* betrayal!"

Walkingstick wondered if *anyone* was actually putting any weight on the rant from the Weston Republic's Minister of Industry. Rana Quigley was a useless lump of a man who only held his position by virtue of being the cousin of the CEO of Crystalline Economics, a company that, despite its name, produced roughly forty-eight percent of *all* foodstuffs in the Weston Republic.

At least, Walkingstick hadn't seen anything to make him adjust his almost certainly prejudiced opinion. Tecumseh was at least paying *attention* to the Minister—but given that the Dakotan Admiral had pulled ten starships and about sixty thousand people out of a trap that hadn't *quite* been well-laid enough, he probably felt pretty sure of himself.

"As of the last confirmations from Yellowstar's defenders, two hundred of the starfighters assigned to Ulu and Imaq are currently aboard Admiral Tawfiq's carriers," Tecumseh replied mildly. "The other four hundred such starfighters have been concealed, along with ammunition stockpiles, on the surface of the twin planets.

"Believe me, Minister Quigley, Surinder Verity knows perfectly well those fighters exist. That the orbital platforms were evacuated and left on automatic will not fool them. They are in control of Yellowstar's open space, but by no means has Yellowstar *surrendered*."

"But they *are* in control of Yellowstar, where three billion Commonwealth—I'm sorry, *Republic*—citizens live," Walkingstick said smoothly. He was *impressed* with Tecumseh at that moment—he knew the man was good, but he'd expected the other Admiral's principles to force him to fight it out.

Instead, Tecumseh had set up the Triumvirate's Vanguard Fleet to be annihilated. Walkingstick would have *preferred* to see the Dakotan and Republic task forces wiped out, preferably taking six to ten of Verity's ships with them.

"Admiral Tawfiq." He turned his attention to the Republic commander who'd been forced to withdraw. "How likely are those fighters to remain hidden for six days?"

"Unclear," the local officer ground out. The Arabic officer wasn't even *looking* at Tecumseh. He'd clearly conceded to the Dakotan officer's arguments, but it was Tawfiq who had been standing guard over Yellowstar for the last year.

The retreat had to *hurt*.

"We did not prepare significant ground positions for our fighter craft," Tawfiq admitted. "Our focus was on assembling orbital hangars to hold the force as we assembled it."

"Starfighters launching from the surface are at a severe disadvantage," Walkingstick observed.

"Their deployment and use will need to be carefully considered," Admiral Vitali interrupted, "but better four hundred starfighters that can't launch until we have opened the main engagement than twelve hundred dead flight crew and *no* fighters.

"Withdrawal is a difficult ask of any officer, Admiral Tawfiq, and your decision to follow Tecumseh's lead was the right one. With your task forces combined, we can move Home Fleet up to reinforce you and crush Verity once and for all."

Walkingstick concealed his surprise and grimace with the ease of long practice. The *last* thing he needed was for Vitali to lead Home Fleet to the relief of Yellowstar. The losses might serve his purpose, but he needed it to be clear that the *Commonwealth* had saved the Republic.

Fortunately, he didn't need to say a word.

"Surely, exposing Weston by deploying the Home Fleet is a question for the Cabinet, not merely a military call," Quigley sneered.

"There are military exigencies which can override our existing orders," Prime Minster De Clerc said, cutting off her Minister. "But... your standing orders, Admiral, are to hold back eight ships as Home Fleet."

"I believe, Minister De Clerc," President Frey replied, "that we did allow for Admiral Vitali to deploy Home Fleet at his discretion if he judged it was necessary to preserve the Republic or end this war."

In Walkingstick's opinion, the Republic had set up too many competing centers of power. By requiring both the President and the Prime Minister to sit in the Cabinet—and giving the rest of Parliament a measurable, if not *final*, say in who made up the Cabinet—they'd set up a government with too many cooks in the kitchen.

But he could use that.

"There is no need to advance your Home Fleet in this case, though," he reminded them all. "Admiral Tecumseh, regardless of his reasoning, has preserved both his Task Force Six and Admiral Tawfiq's Task Force Three. In twenty-six minutes, the Commonwealth Fifth Fleet will arrive in the Scotia System.

"If we detour immediately, we can reenter warped space in the direction of Yellowstar roughly an hour from now and arrive in Yellowstar in six days and five hours." He smiled thinly. "I presume that was exactly what Admiral Tecumseh was anticipating our next step would be?"

"Yes," the Dakotan agreed flatly. "Admiral Tawfiq and I will reach a rendezvous point around seventeen hundred hours tomorrow, roughly a quarter-light-year from Yellowstar. There, beyond the immediate reach of Verity's fleet, we will redistribute our fighters and missiles—including the extras Tawfiq retrieved from the twin planets.

"We stand a better chance against Verity deploying as a combined task force than we would separately, but the odds are still against us. With Admiral Walkingstick's fleet joining us—a convergence that should be straightforward to coordinate—we will have the advantage in numbers and any other metrics you care to measure.

"Surinder Verity and their partners want the Republic intact," Tecumseh reminded everyone. "They are extremely unlikely to engage in pointless attacks on the civilian populace. Concealing the military forces and refusing to *fight* them limits how much damage they can do."

"An easy set of excuses for a man who *ran*," Quigley snarled.

"Minister, I am here to *help*," Tecumseh said, his voice surprisingly cold. "I am not here to throw away my people's lives for *nothing*. I will fight for your Republic. I will not die for it."

Walkingstick was surprised at just *how* pleased he was at that. His protégé was all grown up—giving him a *giant* headache, yes, but it was hard not to be proud of the officer whose career he'd saved twice. James Tecumseh was his enemy now, but he'd shaped and supported the other Native American officer's career for over a decade.

He couldn't help but be proud of the man, rebel and traitor or not.

"And we will not ask you to," President Frey snapped. "Minister Quigley, if you cannot control your outbursts, we can use the q-com bandwidth for something more productive."

Like elevator music, Walkingstick figured.

"Unless the Republic sees a reason for us to hold Fifth Fleet in Scotia, I intend to immediately move to support Admirals Tecumseh and Tawfiq in Yellowstar," Walkingstick declared. "Our combined forces will have twenty ships to Verity's eighteen, and ours are bigger."

"Size isn't everything," De Clerc told him. "But in this case, I believe that we're both bringing eighties to the field."

"Thanks to Admiral Tecumseh, yes," Walkingstick confirmed.

One of the things he needed Misra to sort out was whether the Republic had the designs to build eighty-million-cubic-meter ships. They *shouldn't*, but he'd eat *Saint Michael*'s port antimatter thruster while it was active if the Republic wasn't building warships somewhere.

"Mr. President?" De Clerc turned her attention to Frey.

"Unless the Triumvirate has brought up more ships, there is only one other ship available for Verity to attack with. Even without knowing where that last ship *is*..."

"*Reprisal*, Mr. President," Vitali interrupted. "The missing ship is the *Lexington*-class carrier *Reprisal*, and we *do* know where she is. As of six hours ago, anyway, she was confirmed to be in orbit of Regina."

"Well, then," Frey said with a chuckle. "I was *going* to say that I trusted Scotia's defenses to stand off any single ship of Verity's fleet. But since we do know where *Reprisal* is, that makes the question moot.

"Please, Imperator. Take your fleet to Yellowstar. If Vanguard Fleet doesn't recognize the trap, let's *crush* them and end this goddamn war while our poor Republic can still fight!"

27

Scotia System
21:00 February 24, 2740 ESMDT

"WELL, that didn't go according to plan."

Even with an entire command staff aboard *Saint Michael*, there were a very limited number of people who knew the full extent of Walking-stick's plans and schemes for their operations there. Pich Misra was one of them—the intelligence agent currently standing at the wet bar in one corner of Walkingstick's suite.

The speaker was Vice Admiral Clarette MacGinnis, a woman who Walkingstick would have given her own fleet by now if she was *one iota* less useful in her current role as his operations officer and chief of staff. When it came to Fifth Fleet and the rest of the deployments he'd taken into the field over the last two years, MacGinnis had been forced to take over from the late Lindsay Tasker as his right hand woman.

The room's fourth occupant was inevitably equally briefed on the realities of their plan. No one there, thankfully, was likely to underesti-mate the quiet authority held by the Imperator's personal steward, and while Parris might currently be serving profiteroles—chocolate-dipped half-frozen cream puffs—he certainly had a role to play in the conversation.

"No, it didn't," Walkingstick conceded to MacGinnis as he took a pastry. "I suppose expecting perfect timing from an enemy that didn't have real-time visual of the system is a bit much. For the information we managed to put in Verity's hands, they *nailed* it. Another few minutes and they would have had Tecumseh dead to rights."

"I'm not sure they would have taken down Task Force Three either way," Misra said, bringing four wine glasses to the center of the lounge. They passed each of the Admirals a glass and then traded Parris one for a cream puff.

"Even with Tecumseh leaning on him, I wouldn't have expected Tawfiq to show as much moral courage as he did. His record suggested differently; he very much appeared to be a creature of his corporate masters," the spy continued. "Transfer to the Republic Navy appears to have been good for Rear Admiral Tawfiq."

"It's an interesting balance to walk there," Walkingstick admitted. "Frankly, Tecumseh and Tawfiq did *everything* right. They hammered the *fuck* out of Verity's fighters. The breakdown isn't clear, but after they put nine hundred–plus capital-ship missiles into that fighter formation, scan data from the q-probes suggests they wiped almost five hundred of Verity's starfighters and bombers out of the game.

"They're not going to recover from that. We're going to show up with more starfighters and bombers than Verity *started* with, and they're missing a third of her original wings. And that's ignoring the fact that Tecumseh has tucked an extra two hundred fighters aboard his new combined fleet—God only knows how he's going to manage arming and deploying them, but let's not bet against him and Tawfiq *managing* that.

"Surinder Verity is doomed. And because we have played our cards the right way, it didn't *matter* that Tecumseh did everything right. He can't win the day without the Commonwealth. Only *we* can save the Republic.

"And we need to make sure they realize that. That's our balance," he repeated. "On the one hand, we need to use the golden opportunity

Tecumseh has set up to win the war. But we *also* need to make certain he gets none of the credit."

"Easy enough, I think," Misra said thoughtfully. "You already hit the right tack in the meeting, I believe. Tecumseh takes the blame for the retreat. You take the credit for the victory."

"We need to make sure that you are in command, Imperator," MacGinnis warned. "Vitali isn't foolish enough to exert authority from Weston, even with the q-coms online, but can we trust Tecumseh to recognize you as his commander, however temporarily?"

"He will follow my orders so long as I do not order him to do anything *stupid*," Walkingstick said. "There is no way in any stars that he will integrate his ships into a tactical network with ours. The presence of those decoys he used against Verity's torpedoes tells me that Tecumseh has secrets he's not admitting to anyone just yet."

"I suspect we weren't supposed to see those," MacGinnis guessed. "We got the sensor records from the two Republic ships in company with his Task Force Six. They knew we would, so they didn't hide their presence, but any commands to the decoys are missing from the tactical-network log we received."

"Of course they are." The Imperator grimaced and took a large gulp of his wine. "Do we even know what the hell those things *were*?"

"No," Misra said flatly. "And that makes me nervous, Walkingstick. I thought we had a solid lockdown on the new ships and weapons produced by the Confederacy. Those are a small, relatively simple system… but they're one we didn't know existed."

"So, we don't know what else we might have missed," Walkingstick said grimly. "May I suggest that you get your agents on that, Misra?"

"The orders are already going out," the spy agreed. "I have a guess as to where the decoys came from, though, and I don't like it."

"The Federation," MacGinnis guessed.

"The Federation," Misra confirmed. "We don't have nearly the penetration of the former Alliance that I'd like. Our focus has been in what *was* our own territory. I can tell you that the Republic is only building one warship class and they're *not* eighties. I can tell you that the Dakotan Confederacy has more than doubled their shipyard capacity and is building the Project Hustle designs. Except that Project Hustle didn't include twenty-thousand-ton decoys anchored on a Class Two mass manipulator!"

"That does sound like something coming out of the Castle Federation," Walkingstick said grimly. "Which leaves us with an uncomfortable question, I suppose. Just how much *did* the Federation give Tecumseh?"

"It would explain why they had military q-coms as quickly as we did and *more* widely available initially," MacGinnis observed. "We had the Phobos entangled-particle fabrication plant, but all of the records say that Phobos was the *only* backup the Alliance didn't wreck."

While the Alliance attackers had *tried*, the focuses of their attack had been on the q-com switchboard stations elsewhere in the star system. Phobos, inside the Martian defensive constellation and separated from the switchboard station, had only taken minor damage from long-range missile fire.

The Phobos fabrication plant was primarily a research lab, which meant it had taken months to get enough production scraped up to even give Walkingstick q-com-equipped command ships. The Confederacy, on the other hand, had clearly had q-coms between most or all of their ships at the Battle of Dakota.

As MacGinnis said, the Federation providing the entangled-particle blocks would explain a lot of that.

"I want you to dig into everything we have on the current Federation Navy tricks," Walkingstick ordered Misra. "If Tecumseh has more surprises in store for us, I need to know."

He smiled coldly.

"That way, I can make him use them on the Triumvirate instead of saving them up for us!"

28

"WESTON REPUBLIC NAVY TASK FORCE Three, arriving!"

James Tecumseh wasn't entirely sure where the choice of a new instrument to replace the traditional bosun's pipe the Commonwealth Navy used had come from. By the time it had reached his desk, the humble wooden recorder had the full backing of the Dakotan Navy Chiefs... which had made *his* opinion basically irrelevant.

The Admiral, Commanding, of the Dakotan Confederacy Navy knew who *really* ran things. That meant that as Rear Admiral Al-Amir Tawfiq came aboard a Dakotan ship for the first time, he was met by a trio of recorders playing a musical greeting.

It appeared that someone aboard *Krakatoa* had assumed *someone* from the Weston Republic would come aboard sooner or later, and the three-woman band had taken the time to learn the tune to the Republic's national anthem.

With properly made Dakotan-greatwood-and-ivory construction, James had to admit that it sounded better than any bosun's pipe *he'd* ever heard, and he held his salute to Tawfiq for an extra moment out of respect for the musicians.

"Admiral Tawfiq, welcome aboard *Krakatoa*, flagship of the Confederacy Navy," James told the Weston Admiral. "I appreciate your willingness to meet in person."

"I appreciate your willingness to invite me. We have nothing but time, it seems, and there are matters to discuss."

Several other officers had accompanied Tawfiq, falling in step behind him, but he'd brought only a single Army NCO for security. That worthy, however, was one of the largest men James had ever met, a towering individual well over two meters tall, wearing a Sikh's orange turban to go with the long dark-green tunic of his dress uniform.

"Gunnery Sergeant Vikramjeet Singh." Tawfiq indicated the bodyguard. "Head of my personal security. Commodore İnci Cingolani, my operations officer. Commodore Odarka Abels, my Fleet CAG."

"Vice Admiral Anthony Yamamoto, our Fleet CAG," James returned the introductions, indicating Yamamoto. "Rear Admiral Young Volkov is my operations officer. Agent Shannon Reynolds heads the civilian side of my security detail."

From the momentarily surprised look Tawfiq gave in response to being introduced to Reynolds, he had a good idea what the woman was—or had used to be, anyway—but he controlled it swiftly.

"Come, Admiral, we don't want to have these discussions standing in the flight bay!"

———

Leeuwenhoek had, of course, done James proud. He gave his Chief Steward a thankful nod as she gestured them into a small meeting room, comfortably large enough for the eight of them, and took a second to uncover a surprisingly diverse array of foodstuffs.

"Before anything else, Admiral Tecumseh, I find I must apologize for my government," Tawfiq said stiffly. "I did not expect Minister Quigley to be quite so…"

"Minister Quigley has two daughters, three sons-in-law and two grandchildren on Imaq," James told the other Admiral as he trailed off, searching for words. "He would be a poor parent if he was not distressed at the current situation. I do not blame either him or your government for concerns and harsh words.

"The decision we were forced to make is not one anyone wants forced on them. You were not incorrect in your arguments. Minister Quigley is not incorrect in his fears. We have placed the fate of too many of your citizens in the hands of Surinder Verity."

James took his seat at the head of the table, claiming a steaming-hot cup of tea from Leeuwenhoek, and gestured for everyone else to sit.

"The alternative, unfortunately, was to accept the destruction of our fleets and the deaths of sixty thousand or more military personnel *for no benefit*," he reminded the Westonian Admiral. "The Dakotan Confederacy and the Weston Republic are both very young. We cannot afford to sacrifice thousands of our people on the altar of anyone's honor."

"You do not have to face the people of Yellowstar once we have retaken the system," Tawfiq said grimly. "I will."

"What is the old saying? *Victory has many fathers, but defeat is an orphan?*" James pointed out. "We will return to Yellowstar with our friends in tow, and we will shatter Vanguard Fleet. I suspect, Admiral Tawfiq, that the realities of the war will buy you more grace than you fear!"

"And we gave you no choice," Volkov pointed out brightly. "Feel free to blame us."

"I spent a long time in corporate security, Admiral Volkov," Tawfiq reminded them. "The first task of any good manager is to make sure *blame* is irrelevant. *Responsibility* may be important, but the *goal* is to make sure the issue doesn't happen again."

"I do not believe the Weston Republic will be able to support a large-enough fleet to make sure none of your systems are *ever* taken by an enemy," James warned. "Even the Old Commonwealth, with over a hundred star systems, couldn't guarantee that. You'll need to upgrade your fleet—we all will—but part of the *problem* we're facing is that every Successor State has at least one old Sector Fleet to draw on. Hundreds of TCN warships remained after the collapse."

"And all too many of their crews chose to follow assholes," Tawfiq said grimly. "We did the Weston Sector Fleet a disservice, I suspect, in requiring the resignations of so many officers... and yet I look at the Triumvirate and I understand *why* we did it."

"Hard for you to argue against it, either way," Yamamoto said in his incongruous Scottish accent. "You *weren't* a Navy officer until after the forced resignations."

"I benefited from it, but I see some of the issues now," Tawfiq conceded. "But as I said... *blame* isn't important. The goal is to make sure the issue doesn't happen again. For us, today, that means making the best use of the resources available to us to make certain we retake Yellowstar before Verity does anything foolish."

James nodded, then sighed.

"While we are in far better shape combined than we were before, we are still ten ships versus eighteen," he reminded the others. "While it might be *politically* beneficial for us to liberate Yellowstar without Commonwealth assistance, it is impractical unless Admiral Verity withdraws their forces."

"Which is not impossible if their intelligence is solid enough for them to know what's coming," Commodore Cingolani suggested. "They knew, to within a few minutes and a few million kilometers, when and where your task force would arrive. It seems likely Verity will realize the axe is about to fall on them."

"It's possible," James agreed. "I can't see a way out of the particular trap Verity is in that doesn't involve retreating immediately to acquire new starfighters in Triumvirate space."

He smiled.

"We have left enough q-probes in place in Yellowstar that if Verity withdraws, we will know," he reminded them. "At that point, we can return to reclaim the system in twenty-four hours.

"We would need to be careful," he warned, watching Yamamoto lean forward out of the corner of his eye. "Verity already tried to ambush us once. I wouldn't put it past them to attempt to trick us into bringing the Task Forces *back* into Yellowstar where they could ambush us."

"Our largest immediate concern is the reallocation of starfighters across the combined force," Yamamoto said, his attention clearly on his counterpart. "How many fighters did you manage to cram aboard?"

"Forty bombers, one hundred and eighty-six Katana starfighters," Commodore Abels said instantly. "Half of the bombers are aboard *Beowulf* and *Bay of Bengal*, which don't even have torpedoes to arm them with—and to fit them aboard, they're not carrying torpedoes."

James hoped that his impressed surprise showed on his face. The Republic officers *needed* to know they'd pulled a miracle off managing that.

There'd only been sixty bombers and two hundred and thirty Katanas aboard Task Force Three in the first place. Loading the bombers aboard without torpedoes would have helped, but that was over twice as many starfighters as he'd expected them to bring along.

"All right, I'll admit it," he told Abels. "I'm impressed. As Admiral Yamamoto notes, allocating them is going to be a pain—and as Commodore Abels notes, I don't think any of our battlecruisers can arm bombers."

"Nor can *Bay of Bengal*," Tawfiq warned. "I know your *Black Sea* has the gear, as does the Republic's own *Tasman Sea*, but *Bay of Bengal* was never refitted Before the Collapse, and since… Well."

"We didn't have the bombers to spare for her at the start," Abels said grimly. "And by the time we did, we wanted them for the orbital forts and, well, it didn't seem worth putting effort into an *Ocean*. The *Bonaventure*s were supposed to be online quickly enough that we'd be replacing *Ocean*s with them and using the *Ocean*s' Class Ones for new, modern ships."

"I've heard the name *Bonaventure* before, but I appreciate the reason in no one telling us quite what the Republic is building," James admitted.

"Not as much as we'd like," Tawfiq replied. "*You* may have half a dozen eighty-million-cubic-meter starships swanning around, Admiral Tecumseh, but *we* didn't even have the design parameters to build Stetson fields that large."

The bubble of warped space created by current-generation Alcubierre Drives was roughly fifteen hundred meters across—approximately two *billion* cubic meters. The main focus of the Stetson stabilizer fields was the *external* Stetson field that limited the impact of the bubble on the rest of the universe around it—but without the internal field, the inside of the bubble was utterly destructive to humans and machines alike.

Ten years Before the collapse, the TCN had developed the parameters to build a sixty-five-million-cubic-meter internal field—and assembled an entire generation of ships: the *Saints*, *Hercules*es, and *Volcano*es at the sixty-four-million-cubic-meter size point.

Three years Before the collapse, a breakthrough had given them an estimated *eighty*-five-million-cubic-meter internal field—resulting in the new Project Hustle designs that the DCN had just finished building their first wave of.

"That kind of technological exchange may be on the table, depending on the terms of the agreements our governments negotiate," James said quietly. That was Ma'tano Littlebear's job to sort out, not James's.

Thankfully. Though the oddity of the situation was that *Littlebear* was expected to phone home via q-com… and *James* had been given full plenipotentiary authority, if he ended up feeling he needed it.

"For now, I am told we have engineered a seventy-million internal field, and while we don't have the construction schematics of even the last-generation ships, we do have the actual *ships* on hand—and several dozen of the people who designed them."

"That's part of why Scotia is so well-defended still," Cingolani admitted. "A third of our new yards are there. Several of the new *Bonaventure*-class carriers are under construction under the shield of those forts. They're still a year from completion, though."

"Even with the additional ships you and Walkingstick brought, the Republic remains vulnerable until the new carrier fleet is online," Tawfiq conceded. "We cannot show weakness in the face of the Triumvirate. They are bullies and must be forced to back down.

"Our retreat from Yellowstar puts us in a dangerous position. If Verity waits for Walkingstick to leave Scotia and then moves on the shipyards there themselves, they can destroy a third of our entire construction program in an afternoon. The defenses are powerful, but they cannot stand off Vanguard Fleet."

"So, I guess the question is whether Verity has that much information, that solid an idea of how the Republic will jump... and if we can see where they go if they leave Yellowstar," James noted.

"Because while those defenses might not stand off Vanguard Fleet, our combined Task Forces couldn't stop them, either. Trapping them *between* us and those defenses, however... That is a distinctly more promising proposition.

"One way or another, we *will* bring Vanguard Fleet to bay," James promised. "Whether it is in Yellowstar, in Scotia—or if we have to chase them back to Saskatoon or even Qara Deñiz in the Crimea Sector. We will bring the combined might of three nations into play against these warlords.

"The Republic and the Confederacy alike have sustained the ideals of equality, justice and democracy, Admiral Tawfiq. We will not allow murderers and tyrants to set the tone of what replaces the Commonwealth. Not today.

"Not ever."

And if Tawfiq recognized that James was including one of their *allies* in that second grouping, well, he certainly didn't argue the point.

29

Deep space en route to Yellowstar System
12:00 February 26, 2740 ESMDT

"ADMIRAL VERITY KNOWS you've moved. They're seriously considering abandoning Yellowstar and moving on Scotia, intending to take down the logistics and shipyard facilities there."

"That can't be allowed to happen," Walkingstick told Admiral Shirai firmly. "Do you think you can convince them to stay? Or do we need to get more drastic?"

"Right now, the Admiral figures you've got twenty ships coming their way and that you're going to be able to coordinate with the ships that bailed," the Triumvirate officer told him.

It was a private call, just the two of them—though Misra was, of course, listening in. MacGinnis would be briefed on the contents of the call if anything impactful came out of it, but Walkingstick would humor the illusion, at least, of secrecy between himself and Shirai.

"Honestly, they think they can take your fleet on its own. But with fighters based on the surface of the twin planets, they can't leave Ulu and Imaq alone long enough to neutralize Mackenzie, and they aren't as convinced they can take your fleet when the locals are going to shove half a thousand starfighters up our arse the moment we turn our back."

"I take it you haven't had much luck locating the Republic fighter bases?"

Shirai snorted.

"There *aren't* any Republic fighter bases, Imperator; that's the damn problem. They landed the starfighters anywhere that had a storage shed and some nearby water to launch from. Especially on Imaq, there are over *ten thousand* covered docks large enough for them to stuff a starfighter into."

And while starfighters, unlike star*ships,* wouldn't float without help, they shared the bigger vessels' lack of atmosphere-safe fusion or chemical thrusters. As Walkingstick understood it, using the mass manipulators to minimize a starfighter's mass could allow it to launch with a *minimum* level of thrust from their antimatter engines, but that was still something most safely done over water, a long way from anything fragile.

"I'm surprised that Verity hasn't decided to just level every one of those docks to be on the safe side," Walkingstick observed. It was what *he* would have done in her place.

"Too much collateral damage, and, well, a fishing trawler can't make money to pay taxes if you put an orbital-strike munition into it!"

Walkingstick chuckled.

"Keep your ears open," he instructed the other man. "For our purposes, the Republic's fighter forces are *entirely* expendable. If we get you the locations of those fighters, will Verity be able to move on them?"

"Aye," Shirai said slowly. "It can't be too perfect—they'll get suspicious—but if we can even narrow it down to two thousand docks that might hold those four hundred–odd fighters, I think I can talk them into the strikes. Those will only hold us up for a few hours, though."

"Then you need to convince Verity that the destruction of the Star-Hydro facilities at Mackenzie will be just as crippling to the Republic as the loss of the ships under construction in Scotia," Walkingstick instructed. "With the new alliances, the Triumvirate can't just run over the Republic. They need to think longer-term—Verity isn't going to be able to hang on to Yellowstar, but taking out twenty-three percent of non-antimatter fuel production is going to put a major crimp in their operations."

"And might keep them here long enough for you to arrive," Shirai agreed. "Once the fighters at the twin planets and Mackenzie are out of the picture, Verity will be more willing to fight, too."

He paused, then raised his hand palm-up in a half-shrug, half-warning.

"I don't have any levers to pull to alter the course of the battle, Imperator," he warned. "But if you can get me that intel on the Republic's fighters, I can make sure they don't run before you get here."

"Oh, leave the battle to me, Admiral Shirai," Walkingstick said calmly. "Just find a way to make sure *you* survive. I promised you a command in the TCN, after all."

And while it would make his life notably easier if Rear Admiral Yan Shirai died in the fighting, Walkingstick would put *some* effort into making sure that didn't happen. He had, after all, made the man a promise.

———

Misra and MacGinnis were both in Walkingstick's office twenty minutes later as he finished laying out the situation.

"Pich, I know you were listening and you've got your fingers in a lot of pies here," he told the spy. "I want options."

"I doubt anyone is surprised that I *have* what you promised Shirai you could give him," Misra replied drily. "There were sixty-two squadrons based in orbit of Ulu and Imaq, including four of bombers. All forty bombers and nineteen of the starfighter squadrons managed to squeeze onto Tawfiq's ships.

"I can tell you, with about ninety percent certainty, where the locals have concealed roughly four hundred Katana starfighters," the spy concluded. "A lot of them, as Shirai guessed, are concealed in fishing docks and ship sheds across Imaq. What Vanguard Fleet appears to have missed is that there *is*, actually, a concealed fighter base in one of Ulu's mountain ranges. It's the only surface facility that has torpedoes on hand, but they don't have any bombers to launch them.

"That said, there are still twelve squadrons in it. With support personnel... probably twelve, fifteen hundred WRN officers and ratings."

"Most of the rest are, what, two or three ships in a spot? Minimal support personnel, just the missiles in their onboard magazines?" Walkingstick asked.

"Exactly. What are you thinking, Imperator?"

"As I told Shirai, the WRN's fighter forces are completely expendable. Hell, I'm hoping Tawfiq is going to ask for a position at the front of the line for his battlecruiser, at least. It feels like the man is struggling with a hell of a guilt over withdrawing, and I'm happy to let him assuage it by dying bravely.

"Make the intelligence on the sites we know feel less certain," he ordered. "Hell, add at least one more potential fighter base. Triple the number of smaller sites; make them all look similarly likely. Then let's dump that intelligence to Shirai and let him anonymize it into their datafeeds.

"Let Verity decide if that's close enough or if they want to narrow it down—the fighters *are* there, so they *can* narrow it down. I don't much care either way."

Unless the Republic flight crews had been *extremely* careful shutting down their zero-point cells and weapons systems, a fighter hit from orbit was going to go up like a multimegaton nuclear warhead no matter what anyone did.

"So, we hand Verity the fighters on the twin planets, but what then?" MacGinnis asked. "Do you really think Shirai will be able to get them to go after Mackenzie? I mean... that's a bleeding *war crime* if they blow the cloudscoops."

"There are ways to do it cleanly," Walkingstick pointed out. "I suspect Verity will demonstrate at least one; they seem uninclined to be *utterly* destructive. But the careful ways take more time. That's to our advantage.

"I need them to remain in the system for at least two and a half more days. A day to scan and bombard the surface of the twin planets won't take us all the way. We need Shirai to convince them to take down Mackenzie, remove the threat of the starfighters and fortresses there before they face us.

"Even then, though, the timing may flex on us. Verity might think Vanguard Fleet can face our combined allied forces, but they also might lose their nerve. This fleet is their main political card in the Triumvirate—not just command of Vanguard Fleet but the fact that Vanguard Fleet contains basically *every* ship of Verity's own command.

"They may choose the preservation of the Fleet over a chance of victory." Walkingstick wouldn't have—but he suspected Tecumseh might. *Walkingstick* knew that aggression was the key to victory. Tecumseh, in his mind, was sometimes too concerned with *not losing* to win.

"We need a final check to make sure they don't leave," he concluded. "Misra, I need you to get back in contact with Commodore Salzwedel. I know we have her tentatively agreed to stand *Hrothgar* down when Vanguard Fleet starts getting hammered, but I need her to go one step further.

"She needs an Engineering casualty, something that will keep her trapped in system."

Walkingstick smiled coldly as he saw his people catch up.

"*Hrothgar* is a *Hercules*-class battlecruiser," he observed. "One of Verity's five truly modern warships. They are *not* abandoning her in Yellowstar. To save a *Hercules*, they'll wait.

"To save *Hrothgar*, whose crew is already half on our side, Surinder Verity will fight. And when they fight, they will lose."

30

Deep space near Yellowstar System
10:00 February 27, 2740 ESMDT

"IS EVERYONE CLEAR ON THE PLAN?"

James Tecumseh was struck by the odd familiarity of sitting in a briefing led by Walkingstick. The Imperator might be a lot of things these days, but he was still a fleet commander at heart, and nothing had changed in the mannerisms or calm competence he brought to fleet command.

"We need to remember that all of this will change," the Dakotan officer warned the handful of other senior officers in the virtual briefing. "While we know exactly where Verity and Vanguard Fleet are at this moment, we are still over eighty-five hours from arriving in the Yellowstar System.

"Everything can change in three and a half days."

So far, everything had stayed surprisingly constant in the three days since his ships and Tawfiq's had withdrawn from Yellowstar. Verity had moved their fleet into a high orbit around both of the twin planets and ordered the planetary governments to surrender—and stand down *all* of their forces, including the starfighters that had hidden themselves on the planets.

The governors had surrendered their civil forces but were claiming helplessness with regard to the Republic forces. That was, from what James understood, a fictitious helplessness, but everyone recognized that those several hundred starfighters might make all of the difference in the coming days.

"Of course it will," Walkingstick agreed. "We need to *have* a plan before we can deviate from it, though. You know that."

"I didn't say otherwise. As plans go, this is relatively basic, but that's all we *need*," James replied. "My only suggestion is to keep a close eye on the feeds from the q-probes left in Yellowstar. While dividing our forces is unquestionably risky, it may be necessary to prevent Verity escaping with too much of their fleet."

"Thankfully, we *have* those probes," Tawfiq observed. "Admiral Tecumseh's people and mine both seeded the system with a number of them. Verity's people have shot down more than a few, but I don't think they even *begin* to realize how many they've missed.

"Still, there is one parameter that I believe needs to be established that all of us have carefully avoided raising," the Republic Admiral continued. "And that, gentlemen, is chain of command. Imperator Walkingstick, of course, has the largest of the three forces we are bringing to Yellowstar. No one is questioning that you command the entire allied force, sir, but I believe the status of *second-in-command* needs to be clearly established in case something goes wrong."

James forced himself not to tense. There were a *lot* of potential problems that could come out of that particular nightmare.

"I believe there is only one logical option, Rear Admiral Tawfiq," Walkingstick said smoothly. "These are *your* star systems we are fighting to defend, and you have the second-largest fleet."

That depended on how the numbers were drawn. James had passed Captains Fujisawa of *Momentum* and Labriola of *Bon Homme Richard* over to Tawfiq's command, though, which made the argument technically correct.

Of course, Tawfiq had two *Paramount*s and *Lexington*s; one major shortcoming was their lack of missile launchers, which meant that

James's Task Force Six had more missile launchers on roughly the same volume as Tawfiq's Republic contingent. And over a quarter of the Republic *starfighters* were operating off Dakotan ships—*Krakatoa* was simply that much bigger than any of the Weston carriers.

"I could accept that argument," Tawfiq said calmly, "except that I am merely a Rear Admiral handling an oversized force due to the complexities of our situation. I do not have the *staff*, as much as anything else, to handle taking over command if something happens to you.

"Plus, I believe asking a full Admiral of *any* navy to take the orders of a Rear Admiral is... rude," the WRN officer continued. "I believe, Imperator Walkingstick, that Admiral Tecumseh is the correct choice to act as second-in-command of this fleet."

There was a long silence until James coughed delicately.

"There is a question, bluntly, of trust," he told Tawfiq. "The Dakotan Confederacy is the Republic's ally. The Terran Commonwealth is the Republic's ally.

"We are not *each other's* ally. While we are prepared, due to the necessities of the moment, to share certain tactical networks and systems with the Republic, we are not prepared to give the Commonwealth *any* such access. We are, frankly, better served acting as a division of the Republic Navy acting in alliance with Walkingstick than sharing any kind of direct command relationship."

It wasn't that he didn't think he was the right person to be the second-in-command. He entirely agreed with every argument that Tawfiq had made and would have made most of them himself were the situation slightly different.

If Admiral Vitali, for example, was in overall command, James would argue for the second spot. As it was, the degree of network-sharing necessary to act in that role wasn't something he could accept with the TCN. He simply did not trust Walkingstick or the man's people that far.

His honesty appeared to have thrown everyone else off, and the virtual conference was quiet for a few seconds—and then every Admiral in the room twitched as emergency alerts hit their implant feed.

222 | UNBROKEN FAITH

"I... am connecting the feed from the q-probes to this meeting," Tawfiq said slowly, his voice sick.

James could see it in his own implants, but the data update swiftly filling the center of the virtual space turned nightmare into brutal reality.

Two *Resolute*-class battleships had moved into closer orbits of each of Ulu and Imaq. Both planets had surrendered, so that in itself hadn't been enough to draw the attention of the Operations staffs and trigger an interruption.

Not until they'd opened fire. Not, in truth, until the first ground-penetrating nuclear warheads had struck Ulu's mountain ranges.

James could read the datacodes without even pulling up the extra information. Three entire *mountains* had been obliterated on Ulu as hundred-megaton bombs detonated underground, converting hundreds of thousands of tons of rock into ash and debris that would scatter across the entire planet.

The secondary explosions of starfighters losing antimatter containment were already lost in what was a clear ecological *catastrophe*—but while that was the largest strike, it was only the beginning.

"Analysis is estimating thirty one-hundred-megaton ground-penetrating weapons were fired at three separate locations in the mountain ranges on Ulu," Tawfiq continued, his voice fading from *sick* to *dead*. "One was the main surface fighter base. The others..." He swallowed. "One was a civilian geothermal plant. The other wasn't *anything*.

"Low-yield kinetic strikes are continuing across Ulu and have started on Imaq. We... We can't be certain, but we're estimating over two hundred of the concealed starfighters are gone... and we have no idea of the civilian losses."

James stared at the red dots speckling the two globes.

"Stars preserve us," he whispered. "I didn't... I couldn't..."

No one spoke into the silence he and Tawfiq left until the apocalyptic bombardment ceased.

"We... We need to confirm if any of the starfighters survived," Walkingstick said quietly. "And make arrangements for as much humanitarian aid as possible to arrive once we've retaken the system."

"This wasn't..." There was a long silence as James forced himself to meet Tawfiq's eyes.

"You could not have known," the Weston Admiral ground out, each word sounding like he was tearing out his own teeth. "We had to judge based off their record and their actions in Saskatoon. This..."

"I *knew* Surinder Verity," İnci Cingolani growled, drawing everyone's attention to the *very* junior Weston Commodore. "I served on their staff as a very junior officer, yes, but I *knew* them. This... *senseless slaughter* isn't like them."

"No," Volkov said grimly. "It doesn't fit their profile, except..."

"Young?" James prodded his ops officer.

"They would accept collateral damage if they thought they were guaranteed to take out the fighters," Volkov said. "They didn't hit *every* mountain or *every* warehouse that could conceal a starfighter. While not every place they hit was a hiding spot, their success ratio is too damn high.

"They weren't guessing, sirs. They *knew* where our starfighters were. Not with a hundred percent accuracy, but still too high for random fire. Someone gave Verity *everything*."

No one even checked in with the Admirals before the feed shifted, the view of the two planets shrinking off to one side to be replaced by the image of an androgynous-looking officer with black wings tattooed around their eyes.

Thanks to the nature of the virtual conference, Surinder Verity was front and center to everyone on the call—but they were *addressing* the governors of Ulu and Imaq.

"I believe, Governors, that I have removed the apparent barrier to your full and proper surrender," they said in tones of utter friendly innocence. "With the Republic forces that you claim you have no authority over removed, I now expect your full and unconditional surrender.

"I will return to Ulu and Imaq in seventy-two hours. If, by that point, I have not received said surrender, I will take whatever means end up being necessary to bring you and your populaces into compliance with my orders.

"Think carefully. My patience has already been expended."

The transmission ended and James's attention shifted back to the ships.

"They will *return*..."

"They're heading to Mackenzie," Tawfiq said flatly. "Twenty-three hours each way. They'll hit them early tomorrow. We *have* to reinforce the forts! If Verity only sends part..."

Even as Tawfiq was arguing for the mission, they all saw the reality. The *Resolute*s that had carried out the bombardment had moved first, but the rest of the fleet started moving quickly enough. The velocities would match up in deep space, but there would clearly be no moment where Vanguard Fleet was separated.

"They're taking everything, Admiral Tawfiq," James said quietly. "The math is very little different now than it was three days ago. We hurt their fighter wings, they're down to maybe a thousand starfighters, but you and I only have a thousand starfighters between us."

Nine hundred and eighty-six, exactly. And launching the extra two hundred–odd they'd taken from Ulu and Imaq was slowing down their *entire* launch cycle. Adding an extra twenty-five percent to the deployment numbers more than *quintupled* the overall launch time.

Normally, James would expect to have the fighters in space and sorted out in two or three minutes. Now he'd be looking at twenty or more. They couldn't count on surprise.

"And Verity is a battle-line commander at heart regardless," James continued. "They *will* bring the battlecruisers and battleships into our faces. They'll use their fighters to tie up our fighters and make it a lance duel.

"A lance duel we *will* lose."

That... wasn't as cut-and-dried as he made it sound to Tawfiq, of course. Even ignoring James's secrets, *Iroquois* had heavier beams than anything in the enemy fleet except *Hrothgar* and *Saint Agricola*—and positron-lance range was a terrifying calculation of beam strength, deflector strength and the size of the target.

"MacGinnis, can you get us details on the Mackenzie forts?" Walkingstick asked, holding up a hand to forestall the conversation.

The gas giant appeared at the center of the call as a three-dimensional display. Three relatively small moons and no rings left limited useful anchor points for civilian infrastructure, so Mackenzie Valley Station served as the sole real site of human habitation around the planet.

MVS was a relatively ordinary sprawling complex of refineries, docks, fueling stations and tankers. It was about four kilometers wide and twice that tall, but the actual volume of *station* was probably only on par with a few carriers.

Certainly, the central station was effectively unarmed. Icons around the perimeter marked laser systems designed for debris or worst-case-scenario "traffic management." Those weren't even useful against missiles, with range measured in thousands of kilometers at best.

The *real* security lay in the seven fortresses orbiting in a rough half-sphere above the station. A TCN-built *Zion*-class battle platform anchored the whole affair, with its fifty starfighters representing a significant threat to anyone foolish enough to challenge the star system's fuel infrastructure.

Of course, the six ex-StarHydro fortresses were even bigger. Unlike the *Zion*, they had more than purely defensive weapons as well, with twenty missile launchers apiece to support the six hundred starfighters they carried between them.

The rest of the defensive constellation consisted of minimally mobile satellites controlled from the *Zion*. Single-shot missile mines and relatively capable antimissile laser satellites made up most of that, though with almost four *thousand* platforms in the constellation, it was worth paying attention to.

Against eighteen starships with a thousand starfighters, though...

"It's *possible* your combined task forces could turn the tide at Mackenzie," Walkingstick said. "But it is not likely. I will not stop you from going to the rescue of your people, but Fifth Fleet remains eighty-five hours from Yellowstar."

"If you go, I can't join you," James told Tawfiq quietly. "I can't commit Task Force Six to a battle we are likely to lose. My first responsibility is to my fleet. We can hope that Mackenzie can hold on their own, but—"

"Sir! *Bon Homme Richard* is moving away from the task forces and preparing her Alcubierre Drive!"

James tried not to bite through his own tongue. Prem Labriola might have reached the end of her patience, but there were *six thousand people* aboard her ship that she was about to get killed.

"I believe, Admiral Tawfiq, that either you need to take your fleet after Captain Labriola or rein her in," Walkingstick said drily. "The choice, I suppose, is yours."

Something in his tone rubbed James the wrong way. The *words* were right, but there was a touch of sardonic taunting to it that felt out of character for the Imperator.

"I will talk to her," Tawfiq said flatly. "But this, too, sits on *you*."

He was looking *directly* at James before he dropped from the conference.

31

Deep space near Yellowstar System
13:00 February 27, 2740 ESMDT

VANGUARD FLEET WAS BEING WATCHED, but there was nothing James Tecumseh or anyone else was going to be able to do. Tawfiq seemed to have talked Labriola off the brink of a mad rush to *save the day* that would only end in catastrophe.

And James was left wondering if he'd made the right call. The accelerated time-frame simulation running above his desk told him that he *could* have won. *If* Tawfiq and his people played their roles right. If the WRN's collection of over-promoted junior officers and ex-corporate-security managers managed to keep up with the solid veterans of the DCN and stand up to the Triumvirate's blooded pirates.

If all of the cards fell right and Verity pressed their attack without concern for *their* losses, the combined task forces could have taken Vanguard Fleet. He would have lost half of the ships he took back to Yellowstar and potentially *still* not have stopped the destruction of Mackenzie Valley Station, but he could have destroyed Vanguard Fleet.

Instead, they'd wait for Walkingstick and *crush* Vanguard Fleet, probably with relatively light losses. And James Tecumseh wasn't entirely certain he hadn't just been manipulated into a mistake.

"Sir!" He looked up as Volkov stepped into his office. "May I have a moment?"

"Please. Sit, grab a drink. I'm just staring at a potential Pyrrhic victory I could, potentially, have justified for the sake of making us look good to the Republic."

His Operations Officer obeyed instructions and glanced at the simulation. His implant told him she'd downloaded the precis of the results, and then she snorted as she sipped her coffee.

"Yep. Pyrrhic victory, all right—one that would have left us and the Republic crippled and vulnerable when Walkingstick showed up in the system with ten fully refreshed and equipped warships. That would be that for the Republic, I suspect, with an open question of whether *we* managed to extract *anything* from the mess."

"I don't..." James trailed off. "No, I'm not sure I can even *say* that I don't believe Walkingstick would betray us that quickly. I had faith in the man once. Now..."

Now he wasn't entirely sure *what* he had faith in. The Confederacy, he supposed. It was easier to honor the faith people had in him than to have faith in others, at this point.

"Walkingstick wants to look good to the Republic so that he can make a pitch for them to rejoin the Commonwealth without a fight," Volkov said bluntly. "If he can get anyone to sign back up voluntarily, that will make a lot of the smaller Successor States get real thoughtful about how bad things could really be."

"For all of the problems with what Walkingstick has done, much of the core infrastructure of the Commonwealth's democracy remains. For now," James said grimly. "The problem is that even if he succeeds in laying down the aquila when he's fixed what he can, he's set the precedent that the Imperator role *exists* and can be *seized*."

"The Commonwealth is fucked," the woman in his office told him harshly. "You've read the same reports from the Crows that I have. Walkingstick has set up a balance of factions that only works because they all are loyal to *him*. The Burnses don't like Gabor or vice versa. Hell, this new Commonwealth Bureau of Information is fucking *terri-*

fying and is probably going to do more damage than anything else before it's done."

"I'm *hoping* it can survive him," James admitted. "I'd like the Commonwealth to survive. I've spent all but two years of my adult life its sworn servant; I don't *want* the Commonwealth to fail. And for all that's wrong with the Rump, it's not Emerald's Terran Commonwealth Emergency Committee."

"Which is neither Terran, in service of the Commonwealth nor acting in an emergency anymore," Volkov said, repeating the latest version of a very old joke. "Fortunately, my understanding is that the systems under Alliance protection are watching them, and the Committee does *not* want to tangle with the Alliance of Free Stars."

The Alliance of Free Stars had fought the Commonwealth to a standstill at the peak of Terra's power… *twice*. And then they'd *broken* the Commonwealth, in a way that James still couldn't quite wrap his mind around.

He understood intellectually that the Terran Commonwealth's flaws had been legion and omnipresent, but the sworn officer of the Commonwealth he'd been had never quite realized how fragile the whole edifice was.

He certainly hadn't expected it all to break apart at the first real blow the way it had—and *he* had been one of the first to toss aside a Marshal's mace provided by Walkingstick in pursuit of liberty.

"If I may make a suggestion, sir?" Volkov asked.

"Fire away, Admiral. It's nineteen more hours until Verity reaches Mackenzie," he said drily. "Fifty-eight until we need to move to meet with Walkingstick.

"Call your wife," the junior Admiral told him. "You've been married for two months and have spent most of it in space. I *know* how often you've been phoning home, boss, and it is *not* enough. We give everyone personal q-com hours for a reason, you know."

"Point taken, Admiral," James conceded. He realized he was staring at the main decorative paperweight on his desk—the pieces of the Marshal's mace Walkingstick had sent him, sliced in half to destroy the electronics and then set in Lucite to serve as weights.

"What's happening in Yellowstar is not your fault, sir," Volkov said quietly. "But I know you won't hear that from me. I figure you might just believe it from the First Chief."

"So, call your wife," she repeated. "It'll be good for both of you, for a long list of reasons."

James chuckled.

"Voice of experience?"

"Bitterly earned, sir. *I* got a *Dear Jane* letter three months before the coms went down. Learn from my mistakes, please."

"All right, all right. Point taken."

———

One *minor* issue with being married to a sub-sovereign planetary head of state was that Abey Todacheeney was just as astonishingly busy as James himself. Still, her staff knew how limited *his* time was and told him they'd make something happen.

He even managed to not spend the forty-odd minutes it took Abey to get free watching Vanguard Fleet's steady transit across the Yellowstar System. It was already far too late for the two task forces sitting a day's travel away to intervene.

Of course, that meant he spent the time doing datawork. There was no limit to the forms, reports, messages and decisions to be reviewed or made by the commander of even a four-ship Task Force.

Leeuwenhoek made sure he had a fresh tea and a sandwich moments before the computers informed him that he had a q-com link request. The timing was sufficiently suspicious that he gave the Steward a long look.

"You had them hold the call until you fed me, didn't you?" he asked.

"Steward's secrets, boss," she told him. "Say hi to the missus for me."

"Say hello yourself," Abey told Leeuwenhoek as her holographic image flickered into existence across the desk from James. The two offices didn't quite overlap as the holograms came online, with the computers adjusting positions of furniture to overlap Abey and her chair over the seat in front of James's desk.

"Your Honor," the Chief Steward greeted Abey with a tiny bow. "Good to see you."

"If you call me *Your Honor* in private again, I *won't* let you hang out with Sherlock next time James is staying with me," Abey said sweetly. "And he'd be *ever so sad*. So, behave."

"Yes, Abey," Leeuwenhoek said with a chuckle. "I'll leave you two to it."

The Steward vanished from the room with a speed that James *swore* disproved the claims that teleportation was impossible.

That left James alone in the room with the hologram of his wife.

"I'm sorry to pull you away," he told her. "Your staff sounded… harried."

"James, my dear, we were married for *twelve fucking days* before you vanished to the other side of the Old Commonwealth," Abey reminded him—for only, oh, the two hundredth time since that decision had been made. "The only thing that will make me drop everything faster than you calling is you coming home. At which point I'm locking you in my bedroom for a week and we're having a *very private* second half of our honeymoon."

"I look forward to it," he said quietly. Abey was younger than him, but she'd still celebrated her fortieth birthday before their wedding. Even a decade-plus age gap didn't feel that serious at their respective ages—and neither of their ages seem to be slowing down their desire for each other.

"How is Dakota treating you?" he asked. "I'm getting basic news reports, and everything seems quiet on the home front."

"You *should* be getting the confidential minutes from the Cabinet meetings," Abey noted. "In which case you'd *know* about the headache."

James prodded his implant directories for a second, scanning for any such files.

"I… am not," he said. "I… didn't realize I was supposed to be getting those."

"Even at the other end of the Old Commonwealth and at war, you *are* a member of the Confederacy Cabinet, James," his wife said sharply. "I will have to ask some pointed questions—mostly because if *Chapulin* finds out you aren't being briefed, heads will roll."

Prior to becoming the First Chief of Dakota and now the President of the Dakotan Interstellar Confederacy, Quetzalli Chapulin had been a Terran Commonwealth Marine Corps Colonel with twenty years of experience. Heads probably wouldn't *literally* roll if something she'd thought was happening wasn't… but *careers* might end.

"I chose not to attend meetings by q-com to keep everyone on both sides from sticking their fingers in active business," he reminded her. "Someone may have taken that a step further than any of us meant, but it's probably innocent."

"Probably," she echoed. "But I am going to make *certain*." Abey chuckled grimly. "Or, more accurately, I'm going to have *Reynolds' people* make certain."

James didn't bother to conceal his expression. He understood the necessity of the recon organization, but having a covert-ops organization bothered him.

"The Crows handle counterintelligence, James," she reminded him. "If this is more than a slip-up, it is their job."

"I know."

There was a long silence.

"The headache that *you* should know about—and I'll have my staff put together a position paper on for to bring you up to speed—is that Brillig and Blyton have both applied for membership in the Confederacy," she said simply. "The Kipling Directorate is making threatening noises around what they'll do if we *accept* their applications—and, very, very quietly, the Shakespeare System's government has let us know that if we *'deal with'* Director Loan Mai and her little two-system empire, they will consider signing on as well."

James whistled near-silently.

"Okay, yes, I needed to be paying more attention," he said. "Because some of that is *definitely* in my area."

"You're a long way from home and Vice Admirals Voclain and Modesitt are talking quickly," Abey said with a chuckle. Madona Voclain commanded the Dakota Fleet and Jessie Modesitt commanded the Meridian Fleet, the two main "home guard" formations James had left behind.

"The Cabinet has informed the Parliament Foreign Relations Committee, as required, but for the moment, we're keeping our cards close to our collective chests while we decide whether the Brillig Sector is worth fighting for," she said bluntly. "What's left of the Sector Fleet is split between Brillig and the Directorate, and Director Mai has the lion's share of it.

"If it comes to a slugging match, Mai can't stand us off, but she can make annexing Brillig or Blyton more than painful if she wants to get nasty."

James knew Mai had four ships. The Kipling Directorate existed because Loan Mai's sister had been the second-in-command of the Brillig Sector Fleet. When the sector had disintegrated, Rear Admiral Tuyêt Mai had taken her ships to "visit" her planetary governor sister... and never returned to Brillig, where Vice Admiral Dzianis Ivanow had completely failed to adapt to the realities of the new world.

He'd lost four ships to Mai's desertion and one to piracy—*becoming* a pirate, not destroyed by pirates. That left him with a "Sector Fleet" of an old strike cruiser and a somewhat-younger battleship, answering to the planetary government of Brillig as the rest of the sector went their own ways.

"Given what I know of the sector, can we get the systems *without* Governor Ellis or Admiral Ivanow?" he asked. James Ellis was the Governor of Brillig, and between him and Ivanow, they'd frittered away every chance they'd been offered to keep the sector together or, say, prevent the Mais conquering the Keats System.

"You are not the first to say that," Abey told him. "If I'm being honest, we're going around in circles. There's too many potential pros for us to ignore the request and too many potential cons for the Cabinet to come down cleanly on one side or the other.

"*I* recommended we put the decision to the full body of Parliament and let our democracy have its say. Which is what we're going to do, sooner or later, but Chapulin would like to send it to Parliament with a recommendation."

Abey smiled and James nearly forgot what they were talking about.

"Quetzalli thinks she can get the Cabinet to agree on something," Abey noted. "I am... less optimistic. But she was a soldier and I have always been a politician. We see things differently and that's a *good* thing."

"It is," James agreed, taking the moment to just... luxuriate in her presence and her smile. "I'm looking forward to getting home. You don't *need* me for these discussions—my subordinates know the situation—but that all seems so much simpler than our current mess."

She was silent for a moment, then reached out across the desk. It was only an illusion—they couldn't *actually* touch—but he placed his hand under hers and drew strength from her.

"I'm not an Admiral," she said quietly. "But I am a student of history and politics. You made the right call, but no one in Weston is going to appreciate it."

"I know and I know," James conceded. "I'm more worried about Walkingstick using it against us... and a lot of people just *died* because I made the wrong call."

"Your staff is better at making sure the classified reports get to us than vice versa," she said quietly. "I saw. Any estimates on the damage?"

"Ulu is going to go into nuclear winter outside of major climate intervention," he told her. "Along with three fishing ports basically just... gone, probably a hundred thousand already dead and millions suffering. Imaq is both worse and better—worse because the bombardment hit a far larger number of sites but better because all of those sites were all hit with smaller weapons and the population is more widely distributed anyway."

"You didn't know. You *couldn't* know."

He frowned but nodded.

"Maybe not, but a quarter-million people are dead because I misestimated Verity," he told her. "And yes, that's part of my *fucking job*—both making the call and dealing with it when you get it wrong—but I'm not blaming anyone here who puts the weight of that on me."

"And Walkingstick?" Abey asked.

"Walkingstick is the consummate warrior politician who can't wage war without waging politics at the same time," James said slowly. "He's *damn* good at both, so it's not always clear which he's doing, but there's a few things he's said and the way he's said them... Tawfiq, the senior Weston officer in the immediate mess, is hurting. He withdrew because I left him no choice—but he can't bring himself to just blame me.

"He feels as much or more responsible for what has happened as I do, and I swear to stars and void that Walkingstick is needling him. Prodding him to see if he can make Tawfiq make a mistake."

"And what happens if he does?"

"Abey, he almost took six ships to fight eighteen to try to save Mackenzie," James said quietly. "The *best*-case scenario—if I'd gone with him—was a Pyrrhic victory that handed the Republic to Walkingstick.

"I don't *want* to lose Mackenzie. Even if Verity just takes down the forts, that's another ten thousand dead." He shook his head. "Worse, if they vent the fuel stocks, *I* have to take Task Force Six back to Weston once we retake the system.

"*Black Sea* and *Adamant* paid for their refits with their fuel capacity. We can generate positrons and electrons from ZPCs until the heat death of the universe, but we need hydrogen for the engines and water for the crew.

"And while I *can* feed the crew recycled ration bars, everybody knows what we're eating at that point," he reminded her. "There is an immediate and clear loss of morale and efficiency within twenty-four hours of going on recycled rations.

"We've already moved supplies over from *Krakatoa* and *Iroquois*, but if Mackenzie isn't operational when we retake Yellowstar, I have to miss the next stages of the war to get my ships restocked."

Not least because he'd drained the bigger ships' supplies to keep the two older ones operational. He couldn't even take *Krakatoa* and *Iroquois* to the next fight.

"You cannot control Surinder Verity," his wife told him. "You need to stop blaming yourself for what other people do and focus on what you *can* do: kicking that piece of shit all the way back to Qara Deñiz, where they can tell their new spouses how bad an idea screwing with you was!"

Her sudden fierceness took him by surprise, and he was shocked into a laugh.

"I love you," he told her quietly.

"And I love you and I want you back here," she told him. "I *don't* want the Confederacy fighting two wars at once, and I'm selfish enough to want my new husband in the same star system as me. Deal with Verity, James. Deal with Walkingstick.

"Save the Republic for its people, and then come back home.

"Understood?"

"Yes, ma'am!"

32

WALKINGSTICK HAD to salute the officers and spacers of the Weston Republic Navy. The defenders of Mackenzie had been dealt an awful hand, without even the ability to load their starfighters aboard a starship and flee. While people would have complained, he suspected no one would have truly *blamed* them if they'd laid down their arms and surrendered in the face of Vanguard Fleet.

Instead, they fought. Six hundred starfighters and a few thousand mines against an entire battle fleet.

Verity knew their business too. They'd shown again and again in the Battle of Saskatoon that they knew when to push and when to scrape—and the first ten hours of the engagement above Mackenzie had been *scrape*.

Battleships and starfighters had trawled at extreme range, flinging capital-ship missiles into the region of Mackenzie Valley Station to clear mines with gigaton-range antimatter explosions. The missiles were carefully enough aimed to make sure they didn't hit the space station itself, but the station wasn't their target.

As the WRN spacers realized quickly enough, they didn't even have to be very effective at clearing the missiles and laser platforms. Verity's ships had to have limited munitions—they'd fired enough at Tecumseh to need to watch their magazine levels—but Walkingstick wouldn't have guessed it from their fire rates.

Any given missile was only going to take out two or three of the weapons in orbit of Mackenzie, but every defensive weapon they destroyed was a weapon that was utterly useless to the defenders. Verity's people took out around a hundred of the torpedoes and capital-ship missiles preplaced in Mackenzie orbit before someone finally gave the order, launching every single one of those missiles *back* out at Verity's fleet in a tsunami of antimatter hellfire.

Except Verity had been waiting for that, and there was a *reason* they'd only let *Hrothgar* and *Saint Agricola* get close. The two newer ships had a thirty-gravity acceleration edge on the older *Resolute*s that had provided the fire support, and they now used every scrap of it to pull out of the effective range of the missiles.

Walkingstick knew the dance Verity's people were following, and they hit the notes *perfectly*. A thousand missiles flung themselves at half a dozen starships, but the starships dragged out the flight time further and further... and further, allowing hundreds of starfighters and their own defenses to shred the missiles with terrifying ease.

Their fighters didn't manage any better. It took Verity eleven hours to draw out and annihilate every weapon that could defend Mackenzie Valley Station from range.

"They've summoned MVS to surrender," MacGinnis reported. The two of them stood on *Saint Michael*'s flag bridge. That limited how much they could talk about other aspects of the mess, but it let them watch the situation unfold with the best possible display. "I expected the defenders to hold out longer."

"I didn't," Walkingstick replied. "Verity is very good at what they do. I'm not entirely sure where they picked all of it up—they never served under *my* command—but they may be one of the best siege commanders I've seen in our generation."

"Huh." MacGinnis was quiet for a few moments, studying the display. "You can still take them, of course."

Walkingstick chuckled.

"They're *not* as good as an open-space commander," he observed. "*Tecumseh* has them beaten there—and while Tecumseh is no slouch, well…"

Walkingstick knew, with no real false modesty, that he was a better commander than Tecumseh. He and Tecumseh had the shared advantage of knowing how the other man thought, which had been enough to turn the last battle between them Tecumseh's way, but Walkingstick knew that given equal forces, he'd smash the other Admiral.

He also knew that Tecumseh would make him bleed for the privilege, and *that* was what had tipped the balance at Dakota. Walkingstick hadn't been able to pay the price then.

"Update from MVS," MacGinnis said in the silence. "Verity is ordering them to evacuate the entire station."

Walkingstick *heard* his chief of staff swallow.

"Admiral?" he asked.

"Station administrator said they couldn't. Verity told them they have twelve hours and then the station will be vaporized regardless of who is still aboard."

"They know we're coming," Walkingstick said softly. "They know we're coming and they don't want distractions."

Shirai had done his job well, Walkingstick judged. Mackenzie's destruction was a strategic victory for the Triumvirate, but while it would hurt the *Republic*, the cost to the *Commonwealth* was negligible. Losing that large a portion of their purified-hydrogen production would be a drain on the Republic's economy, one they could easily make up by returning to the Commonwealth.

Another piece of the foundation laid for what would, he judged, be an inevitable decision shortly.

"Forty-eight hours until we arrive," he said aloud. "If Verity opens fire on the station in twelve hours, I am assuming they can still make it back to the twin planets by the time we get there?"

"Yes, sir. They could be anywhere in the star system by that point." MacGinnis shrugged. "Or halfway back to Saskatoon, for that matter."

"No." Walkingstick shook his head. "No, they won't run. They're clearing the battlespace for the fight they want to have. They figured my plan involved the starfighters from the planets hitting them from behind, and so they neutralized that threat. They want to make the Republic ships angry, so they took down Mackenzie."

The Republic crews *were* angry. It could be a problem… except that it was *exactly* what James Walkingstick wanted.

The goal was to save the Republic, yes… but it was also to convince the Republic to stand down.

———

Later, alone in the dark in the meditation chamber attached to his quarters, Walkingstick could count the cost. He tried not to, but his own self-honesty required him to face the demons he'd created.

The meditation chamber served many different purposes in his experience, depending on the Admiral. It allowed for a fully immersive virtual-reality environment. Some used it for communications; some used it for its official purpose of meditating.

But if he was being honest, Walkingstick had to admit that most of the Admirals he'd known had used it for porn. He had never quite seen the point. For him, its main value was that it was a truly sound-proofed space that he could set to block his implant and meditate in.

He couldn't *sleep* in the space—he couldn't justify blocking his implant coms for more than ten minutes at a time, really, but it gave him precious moments of quiet surrounded by a recreation of the stars *Saint Michael* was passing through.

And in that quiet, he ran through the information he'd downloaded into his implant before entering it. Give or take, a quarter-million people had died in the Yellowstar System in the last twenty-four hours.

Every one of them due to intelligence he'd provided and pressure he'd arranged. Verity might have made the decision and their people might have pulled the triggers, but Walkingstick wasn't going to pretend he hadn't put those fingers on those triggers.

Hard times called for hard men. He didn't want to *be* one of those hard men, but those were the times he'd been given. A broken Commonwealth would rob the promise and the future from untold millions of potential future citizens.

The lives he sacrificed today *were* a sacrifice. A painful one, hardest of all for those who fell and those who loved them, but the Terran Commonwealth had lifted more people out of poverty and given them a future than any organization in history.

Unity begat Equality, begat Justice, begat Liberty. Without Unity, without humanity standing together as one against the darkness, it was a constant struggle to avoid sliding into barbarism. He was seeing that in the years since the Alliance had destroyed their coms.

Two-thirds of the Commonwealth had collapsed into chaos and anarchy, with their best unity provided by warlords and the occasional Admiral with more honor than sense. Without the guiding light of the Commonwealth, there were now *thirty* different states struggling to survive in the anarchy they'd created.

That was what had brought war to the stars of the Weston Sector. Without the Commonwealth Walkingstick had sworn to protect and sworn to restore, only chaos and bloodshed lay ahead for the so-called Successor States.

So there, in the darkness, Imperator James Calvin Walkingstick faced his dead with squared shoulders. They had died for a reason. He would make certain they had not died for nothing.

The best way to avoid spilling oceans of blood was to be willing to shed a lake at a moment's notice. When he was done, the citizens of the Commonwealth would sleep peacefully at night once more.

And if he would stain his own soul forever in the doing, that was no sacrifice at all compared to what he asked of others.

33

"WE HAVE LOCKED in emergence parameters with all four ships," Volkov reported.

A rumble of conversation and discussion underlay her calm words. Every member of the flag staff aboard *Krakatoa* knew that *this* was the play for all the marbles.

Plus, James knew, they'd run away once and that stuck in everyone's throat. *Nobody* liked running away, especially not when the flight had left their enemy to commit a horrific war crime on the planets they'd abandoned.

"I don't suppose anyone is going to mind if we *don't* keep Admiral Verity around for the war-crimes trial, are they?" he asked aloud, chuckling bitterly. "Matter-antimatter annihilation might be too good for some people, but I will admit it is *damn* convenient."

The answering chuckles were equally bitter.

"Verity has pulled their fleet in around the twin planets," Volkov told him. Holographic globes of Ulu and Imaq hung in the center of the flag bridge, the focus of every eye and most of the work going on around the space as the analysts worked through the data being gathered by q-probes.

The probes were sneaking ever closer now. Everything James was looking at was less than thirty seconds old. There were aspects of it that were even newer, basically real-time data relayed from sensor platforms on the planetary surface.

Those were coming through now–Vice Admiral Tawfiq's ships. The Republic officer had received an all-too-necessary promotion from the Republic Cabinet while they'd prepared for this operation.

James doubted it had soothed the man's wounded pride or anger.

"They want us to come to them," James told Volkov. "Or, if they feel the odds are more against them than they can afford, to pull the exact same retreat that Admiral Tawfiq did."

"It's a four-light-minute gravity shadow, give or take, and Vanguard Fleet is in *deep*. Three hours and change once we exit warped space."

James nodded silently.

"We've confirmed they *have* received what appears to be a munitions collier from Saskatoon," Volkov warned, highlighting the nineteenth ship. "We have to assume that Vanguard Fleet is fully restocked on missiles."

"The question is whether that collier brought starfighters," James noted. "Because if they've replaced *all* of the toys, this gets a lot messier." He smiled coldly. "Not messy enough to save Verity, of course, but enough to make our day harder."

"No one on the surface has seen any starfighter transfers, according to Tawfiq."

"And I'd love to take that as unquestioned truth," James agreed. "But for now, let's operate on the assumption that Vanguard Fleet has made up their fighter losses."

From *where*, he didn't know. He suspected part of the reason Verity had left *Reprisal* in Saskatoon was to spread the *Lexington*'s fighters across their other carriers, bringing their fleet back up to full fighter strength on the ships they'd brought to Yellowstar.

If Verity had replacement fighters, James would have expected them to arrive aboard *Reprisal* herself. Which suggested that they *didn't*, but he couldn't assume that.

"*Saint Michael* has sent over final arrival vectors," Prebensen reported. "Passing them over to Ops to set up for our ships."

"He's keeping all three fleets a full half-million kilometers apart," Volkov observed as the data propagated.

"And with the Westons between us," James agreed. "I think he's feeling twitchy. Worried we might be tempted to put a few hundred kilos of antimatter through *Saint Michael* if he lets us get close."

"We're going to be a bit busy. Exiting warped space in twenty minutes, sir. Assuming no maneuver by Vanguard Fleet, we will make a zero-zero entry into the Ulu-Imaq planetary system three hours and twenty-one minutes after that."

"And missile range?" James asked.

"Roughly eleven minutes. Less if they come out to meet us—but that's a full hour's flight time. Accuracy will suck and, well, *we* don't have the missiles for that."

"But both Walkingstick and Verity do," James replied. "We'll hold fire until the range is closer, and I *presume* Tawfiq will do the same, but Fifth Fleet has a hundred and eighty launchers of their own to play with."

He considered the situation, looping Yamamoto into the conversation with a silent call and response.

"Time for fighter launch?" he asked the CAG. "I saw some ugly estimates bouncing around to get our guests off the decks, so I'd love to hear something better," James said.

"The Chiefs are *promising* me fifteen minutes," Yamamoto replied. "I don't like it any more than you do, sir, but we did stick a *lot* of extra fighters on the decks."

"And we're going to be pleased to have every damn one of them, Anthony. My compliments and gratitude to your Chiefs in advance, Admiral. Those extra birds may make all of the difference today."

"I've been telling them that all week, sir. They'd probably have done miracles anyway, out of sheer determination not to be shown up in front of the Rump, though!"

"Do you have coordination with the Republic and Rump fighters?" James asked.

"Decent with the Republic, basic with the Rump. Time will tell once we're in space—it's not like we'd have had q-coms for the fighter strikes at any point."

"Fair. Are you ready?"

"To strap on a fighter and do something stupid? Probably. Am I going to do my job instead? Yes."

"I never flew a starfighter, so I don't get the urge," James admitted with a chuckle. "But given how much I like sending people into trouble ahead of me, I suspect I'm closer than I might think."

"At the end of the day, a lot of this battle is going to be set by what happens with three hundred and fifty bombers," Yamamoto said. "And believe me, sir, this is probably the first time in the last few years that I've wished the Rump brought *more* bombers to the party!"

———

Despite her role as James Tecumseh's bodyguard, Shannon Reynolds was a rare-enough presence on the flag bridge of *Krakatoa* that he knew the moment she entered the room, his spine stiffening in tension.

Here, today, the ex-assassin was his bodyguard. Except that his bodyguard had no business stalking across the metal floor to his command station... and the Director of the Dakotan Commonwealth Reconnaissance Organization very easily *could* have said business.

"What have you got for me, Reynolds?" he asked as she reached his chair.

"Something that stinks real bad," she replied grimly, keeping her voice quiet. "I don't have the people in Vanguard Fleet I'd like, and the handful I *do* have don't have q-com access. You follow?"

"So far," James said. He checked the time. Ten minutes till they exited warped space. He *knew* Reynolds understood the timing and the importance of the situation, which meant she wasn't bothering him right now unless it was actually critical.

"*Somebody*—I'm presuming one of my agents—pinged one of our q-probes with a pulse transmission twenty minutes ago," Reynolds said. "It took your coms people ten minutes to pass it on to Bevan's people."

Vice Admiral Ove Bevan was the head of DCN Naval Intelligence. He'd sent a solid subordinate—Commodore Dallas Kovats—on this mission, but James wasn't surprised that Reynolds still regarded the Intelligence section of his staff as "Bevan's people."

"And?" he prodded.

"*Hrothgar* just had a major engineering failure," she said quietly. "Zero-point resonance cascade in her primary cells."

James winced.

"Did she *survive?*" he asked. A primary zero-point cell produced several gigawatts' worth of electrons from one "pole"—and an equivalent *mass* of positrons from the other. A resonance cascade could easily result in containment overload in *multiple* primary cells, which would destroy *anything*.

"They caught it in time but had to shut down all of her primary cells. I'm not as familiar with that as you, but my impression is that booting those from cold shutdown is…"

"Six hours," James told her. "Except that *cold* shutdown isn't *emergency* shutdown. So, more like sixteen—or even *sixty*. In which she can barely fly and, more importantly, *doesn't have deflectors*. Or most of her defensive lasers, for that matter," he finished thoughtfully.

"I was expecting the six," she admitted. "And that was stinky enough. She lost her primary defenses thirty minutes before we enter the system? And Commodore Salzwedel served under Walkingstick in the Rimward Fleet, back before the collapse."

"You think he's turned her."

"I don't *think*, Admiral. I *estimate* about four-in-five odds that Salzwedel has turned her coat. And, according to my little birdie, *so does Verity*."

James shivered. Verity had just killed a quarter-million people to avoid risking a few hundred starfighters stabbing them in the back. He wasn't sure how they'd respond to potential treachery, but he doubted it would be pretty.

"According to our data packet, Rear Admiral Shirai, two hundred fifty Marines, and fifty staff just transferred to *Hrothgar*," Reynolds told him. "The Admiral is taking command of something they're calling *Task Force Bravo* and taking *direct* command of *Hrothgar*. Salzwedel has been relieved... but it doesn't change anything. Without her primary cells, *Hrothgar's* stuck."

"Not as much as you might think," James warned. "She can't fly particularly *fast* sublight without that positron supply, but she can get Tier One acceleration. Fifty *g*s. Enough to run—and if they run every other power source they've got into the capacitors, they can *probably* charge the A-S drive in about ten hours."

He shook his head.

"Make sure Volkov and the rest have the info about *Hrothgar*," he told her. "That won't change much in the plan, I don't think, but that's one battlecruiser we're not fighting today."

And *Hrothgar* was a *Hercules*-class battlecruiser, with megaton-and-a-half positron lances and modern deflectors. Taking her out of the main line was going to have interesting impacts on Verity's plans.

"And keep an eye out for other packets from your birdie," he ordered. "The more information we have from inside Vanguard Fleet, the cleaner this will get."

"Think I can get Walkingstick to hand over the intel *he* has?" she asked drily. "If he's turned one of Verity's top captains, he's got to have a lot more info than I do!"

"Whatever links Walkingstick has in Vanguard Fleet, he hasn't shared with us," James observed. "And if he has his hands inside their command structure..."

There were possibilities in that concept, and James Tecumseh didn't like *any* of them.

———

"Ten. Nine. Eight. Seven. Six. Five. Four. Three. Two. One. *Emergence!*"

There were few circumstances under which even the Book called for a verbal countdown, but emergence into an expected battlespace was definitely one of them. The Chief gave a steady, measured count right up to the moment where the universe shivered back into existence around *Krakatoa*.

"Report," James barked. "Get me the datadumps."

The first stage was the mix of q-com and lightspeed updates from Task Force Six. *Krakatoa* was the first to update, since he was *aboard* her, but the other three were only moments behind. All four Dakotan ships had emerged exactly on target, roughly five hundred kilometers between them as coms and sensors relinked and their electronic eyes peered into the rest of the star system.

"Task Force Three is off position," Volkov barked. "Fifth Fleet is as expected, one million kilometers to starboard. Task Force Three is *not present*."

"Prebensen," James said smoothly. "Do we have a link with Tawfiq's people? Where the *hell* are they?"

"They dropped out early; no one is giving me a *reason*, but given their formation, I have a guess," the communications officer told him drily. "Relinking the telemetry to Ops."

James winced as the data came up. The six Republic ships had completely screwed up their formation, spreading six ships that *should* have emerged in a bubble ten to twelve thousand kilometers wide across six *hundred* thousand kilometers.

Worse, they were spread across a *particular* six hundred thousand kilometers that was *nine million* kilometers from where they were supposed to be.

"They jumped the gun on emergence by thirty light-seconds," Volkov said grimly. "*That* is going to cause us a giant headache, isn't it?"

"Yes." James shook his head. "We do what we can. Get our fighters and bombers into space and hold position until we get an update from Walkingstick.

"Like it or not, *Saint Michael* is the flag for this mess, which means Walkingstick makes the c—"

"*What in the void?*"

James held his tongue for a moment, giving Volkov and her people the time to convert a junior expression of surprise into something actually useful for decision-making.

"They were watching us," he concluded aloud as he caught up with the data. "They had a solid idea of where we had to emerge, and there's got to be quite a few q-probes out here now."

"Yeah, well, now there *aren't* any of *our* q-probes near Ulu and Imaq," Volkov told him grimly. "They just hit *every* probe within five light-seconds of the planets with long-range lance fire. It'll be almost twenty minutes before we have new probes in position."

"We were expecting the ones we left behind to be useful, but Verity knew that," James said. "They must have spent *days* nailing down the location of our probes—and they left them alone until we were here to make sure we didn't realize they'd pinned the probes down."

"I'm not entirely sold on sneaky fuckers on *my* side, let alone the enemy's," Volkov told him. "And it looks like Verity has pulled another trick out of their hat."

James saw it as Volkov spoke. Even from seventy-plus million kilometers away, there were a lot of details a fleet's sensors could pick out. Now, though, new jamming platforms were waking up and making a hash of everything.

Artificial heat signatures, radiation sources, coms transmissions... the works. There had to be at least a hundred different platforms, and they were making a *mess* of the scan data on Vanguard Fleet.

"Get me as much information on those jammers as you can," he ordered. "I suspect that q-probes close in would render them pointless, but that's still an interesting toy in Verity's box."

"Working on it," Volkov ordered.

"Sir, instructions from Fifth Fleet Flag," Prebensen told him. "TF Six and Fifth Fleet will advance at fifty gravities while TF Three catches up in real space at two hundred. Fighters will form up until all are in space, but the forward components will maintain half thrust until TF Three's can catch up."

"Make it happen, people," James ordered.

The numbers were flickering through his implant as the Ops team and Yamamoto's people updated them. It would take over an hour for the fighters to consolidate into a single strike force, though they'd be twelve million kilometers closer to the planet by then.

How close they were to Vanguard Fleet depended on what the

Triumvirate ships did. The ships that James's people were no longer able to track.

"We can't share telemetry with the Rump, but I don't suppose they have a better angle on Vanguard?" he asked.

"They're sending us some data that we're heavily sanitizing," Prebensen told him. "It doesn't look like they're seeing any better than we are, though."

Task Force Six had left q-probes in the system when they'd bailed. Losing those q-probes put them on an even keel with the Terran Fifth Fleet, which was… aggravating.

"And Task Force Three?" he asked.

"They lost their q-probes the same time we did. Tawfiq *may* have some sources on the surface that aren't sending to us, but my impression is that their main surface sensor *and* coms arrays were in the base Verity's people blew up," Volkov said grimly.

"So, we wait and see just what the Triumvirate decides to do," James concluded. "Let's focus on getting the fighters up, people. I'm holding Yamamoto's Chiefs to that fifteen minutes!"

34

ANTHONY YAMAMOTO WAS BARELY able to track individual *squadrons* in the sheer number of starfighters forming up around the allied fleet. The three hundred–odd Dakotan starfighters and bombers were now backed by another hundred Republic ships they'd crammed aboard TF 6's ships—and all of them were in space.

He swallowed the temptation to order his people to head forward at full thrust. *Yes*, the main weight of their force was the seven hundred starfighters and bombers of the Commonwealth Fifth Fleet and the four hundred fighters and bombers directly answering to him, but the plan was heavily dependent on their unquestioned starfighter superiority.

Task Force Three carried a hundred bombers and four hundred and fifty starfighters, and they needed every one of them. So, Yamamoto's fighters limited their acceleration, loping forward at an easy two hundred–odd gravities.

And if every one of *his* pilots and gunners had their Commonwealth counterparts locked in—just in case—Anthony suspected that the Commonwealth pilots and gunners were doing the same.

"We still don't have clear eyes on Vanguard's fighters," Peña reported, the young Commodore sounding more irritated than anything else. "Their jamming zone is expanding, which suggests they're moving the platforms out alongside their fighters."

"Clever, but not as clever as they think," Anthony replied. He pulled data on the display in front of him with a gesture and a thought, running the analysis in a blink of an eye.

"That's interesting," he murmured.

"Sir?" Peña clearly hadn't followed his analysis, but he could feel him poking into the scenario through his implant. "Oh. That is strange."

He'd caught up. That was faster than Anthony had expected.

"Two hundred gravities," he said aloud. "Pass that on to the flag bridge, please. Either they're moving the battle line forward with the jammers and we're just not *seeing* their fighters, or their starfighters are moving slowly."

"We can get visual confirmation if we take a few minutes," Peña suggested.

"Do it," Anthony ordered. Something itched at the back of his neck, and like any good starfighter commander, he wanted to know where his counterparts were. He was allowing for Vanguard to be back up to thirteen hundred fighters and bombers, but he only really *expected* a thousand.

Once he *knew* how many ships his Triumvirate opponent had in space, he could adjust his plans.

"TF Three fighters will catch up to the fleet in thirty minutes, sir," someone reported.

"Thank you, Commander," he told the analyst, his focus on the analysis of the lead edge of the jamming field. The field wouldn't blind them for long—q-probes were already on their way to spread the fleet's eyes around Vanguard Fleet's cloak of shadows—but it was creating a few uncomfortable minutes.

It would be even longer for TF 3 to catch up to the main fleet body than for the fighters to rendezvous, he judged. That wasn't his problem, thankfully. *His* job was to coordinate with the TCN and WRN Fleet CAGs.

Weston's Odarka Abels, he noted absently, was partially incommunicado. *She* had decided to strap herself into a Longbow bomber and was with the fighter strike.

Walkingstick's Rear Admiral Kade Farago, on the other hand, was aboard *Kilimanjaro*. He and Anthony were using basically identical controls and software to exert control over fighter groups made up of the same types of fighters.

That wouldn't last. The Dakotan Confederacy Starfighter Corps had rolled out prototypes of their own starfighters and starbombers on Confederacy Day. Anthony had left behind a list of items to review and correct when they'd left, but he expected to see Wolves and Ravens replacing Katanas and Longbows before the end of the year.

"There's the visual confirm, sir," Peña told him. "We're limiting our data interface with Fifth Fleet, but we've got decent links with Task Force Three, and we're getting *some* telemetry over from the Rump."

"Interpolation complete, and we have *some* information."

The very front of the expanding jamming zone became clearer. Hundreds of Katanas formed a slightly curved wall in space, with what Anthony suspected were the jammer platforms interspersed with them.

"Do we have eyes on the bombers?" he asked.

"Negative, we have no clear visual on anything behind that front screen," Peña said. "They know what they're doing. They could have the entirety of Vanguard Fleet tucked in fifty thousand klicks behind them and we wouldn't be able to see crap."

"Which is unlikely both because their jamming stretches all the way back to Ulu-Imaq orbit *and* because it's bloody stupid," Anthony pointed out. "Holding their fighters up like this is giving up a starfighter's best advantage."

"So, the question is *What does Verity think they're getting in exchange?*"

Anthony didn't *quite* jump at the sound of Tecumseh's voice in his ear. The Admiral was entirely capable of eavesdropping on Fleet Starfighter Control—or *Krakatoa*'s bridge or most key positions across the entire fleet for that matter—but Anthony expected some warning when his commanding officer digitally linked into the conversation.

Which, he observed wryly, his implant had *given him*. He'd just been very focused on the datastream on the starfighters. Neural implants and other cybernetics aside, humans were still human. The hardware just allowed them to make human mistakes faster and, perhaps, with more confidence.

"I'm not sure, Admiral," he told Tecumseh, making sure that Peña was linked into the conversation and consciously minimizing his Scottish burr to make sure of clarity. "They're giving up over half of their acceleration. They're moving slowly enough that they *could* be trying to tuck their battle line in behind the fighters, but that's… just a quick way to run the battleships into our torpedoes, really."

"And we *want* their battle line in torpedo range sooner rather than later," Tecumseh agreed. "So, I think the question is…" The Admiral haloed the unknowns on the display, the shuttle-sized spacecraft Anthony was assuming were the starfighters.

"If these are the jammer platforms—and the data I'm seeing says they *are*—how fast are *they*?"

"Going out on a bit of a limb, I'm going to say they're running Tier Two acceleration around two hundred gravities," Peña said. "And they're holding the fighters back to stick with them. They're hiding *something* with those jammers—something they figure we'd see without them."

"A fighter screen on its own can hide a lot of things," Anthony pointed out. "But taking out the q-probes and limiting the fighters to the jammers… Someone thinks they're being clever."

"Somehow, that does not reassure me," Tecumseh said grimly, then paused. "Command conference coming in via q-com. I'm looping you in, Yamamoto. Virtual link.

"Let's see what our allies make of this."

———

"Admirals, our situation has grown rather interesting," Imperator Walkingstick declared as they all linked in.

Anthony took a quick look around the virtual space. Three officers each from Task Force Six and Fifth Fleet, the usual selection: the commander, the operations officer and the CAG. Task Force Three only had Vice Admiral Tawfiq and Commodore Cingolani.

Commodore Abels wouldn't have reliable q-com access from her bomber, after all.

"Task Force Three has sorted themselves out and is catching up," Walkingstick continued, his tone sufficiently dry to make *Anthony* want to shiver, and it wasn't even aimed at him.

"We are approximately twenty-five minutes from the starfighter forces assembling, which will be suitably close to the front of the Triumvirate's jamming field for us to plan for heavy action," he observed. "By then, we will have a better idea of what our friends are hiding."

"Surely, they'll sortie forward prior to that," Volkov said. "They need to get their bombers into range of us as well, whatever they're hiding."

"Assuming they have a material number of bombers *left*," Admiral MacGinnis observed. "You made a *nasty* mess of their fighters when they chased you all out of Yellowstar. It's not clear from our information that Verity has even a hundred bombers left. Given their resources, they may be planning for an old-fashioned in-our-faces fighter strike or just using the starfighters for cover."

Anthony concealed a grim chuckle. *An old-fashioned in-your-faces fighter strike* basically summed up *their* plan, with a few flourishes as the bombers and capital-ship missiles came into play.

"You are all missing a key point," Tawfiq said flatly. Something in *his* tone warned Anthony that the Republican officer hadn't missed Walkingstick's half-concealed barb earlier. "Verity is hiding something, and it makes no sense for them to limit their fighters to this acceleration.

"If they're short of bombers, the only tools they have to hurt us are their starfighters and their battle line. Four *Resolutes* and a *Saint*, if we don't know they're coming, will do immense damage at close range.

"But we can turn that around on them," Tawfiq continued fiercely. "Task Force Three is still outside the gravity shadow of the twin planets. We can warp space from here and ride the needle down past their fighter screen.

"They think they have the advantage of surprise, but we can put six capital ships in their teeth while they still think they're safe!"

Anthony tried to mentally count all of the ways that was a terrible idea—not least that three of those capital ships were *carriers* and another was an *Ocean*-class strike cruiser, which was only *slightly* better equipped for a close action than the carriers.

The old *Paramount*-class carriers might actually carry *more* positron lances than the newer *Lexington*, but the two old ships paid for that by being *completely* unarmored, even by the standards of the antimatter age.

"Admiral, your courage is admirable," Walkingstick told Tawfiq. "But you don't have the ships or the firepower to handle Verity's main striking force, even *with* complete surprise—and riding the needle is a difficult task even for well-trained, battle-hardened crews."

Walkingstick didn't finish the statement with *who can manage to emerge in formation with the rest of the fleet* but Anthony knew he wasn't the only one who heard it.

Tawfiq looked… calm. Surprisingly calm. *Worryingly* calm, to Anthony's mind.

"We don't need to take risks," Anthony interjected to hopefully head off an argument. "We have the edge in fighters and firepower."

"Exactly," Walkingstick said with a firm nod. "The worst thing that Verity can do right now is take their ships and run. So long as they fight us here in Yellowstar, this war will basically be over by lunchtime.

"They may have some clever ideas, they may have some tricks, but *we* have the Commonwealth Fifth Fleet. There are few more experienced or well-trained formations in the galaxy, my friends.

"Combined with your task forces, there is no question of the result today. We will prepare our missile salvos to support the bomber strikes, and we will use our q-probes to locate the enemy. We will *not* guess. We will *not* take foolish risks."

For a man who seemed to be saying the right *words*, Walkingstick's emphasis and tone were ever so slightly off. It didn't feel aimed at

Anthony, but it made his skin itch. There was no way the other man could *miss* how badly he was prodding the pride of his allies, right?

"We will continue with the plan. Verity's cloak of jamming will not even buy them time. Bring up your task force, Admiral Tawfiq. We will fight as one fleet today."

35

Yellowstar System
00:20 March 2, 2740 ESMDT

WALKINGSTICK HAD WATCHED Tawfiq's face as he'd spoken, and he judged he'd landed his arrows well. No recording or transcript of the meeting would suggest he'd ever said a thing wrong. Only the handful of people *in* the call might be able to put together his tone with Tawfiq's weaknesses.

"Do you think he's going to bite?" MacGinnis's voice said in his ear.

With the bridge full of his flag staff, they couldn't talk aloud, but their implants allowed a private conversation even as dozens of people buzzed around them.

"He has about ten minutes before he has to either follow orders or do something *really* stupid," Walkingstick replied. "If he was ex-TCN, there'd be no question. Anyone inclined to let their emotions compromise them doesn't make Captain, let alone flag rank."

There were enough emotional undertones to the implant link for him to know that MacGinnis didn't *quite* buy that.

"That is, at least, the *theory*," he conceded. "But regardless of what might or might not happen in the Commonwealth Navy, Vice Admiral Tawfiq spent his entire career in corporate security. The only starship he ever commanded before two years ago was a freighter that gave up a few million cubic meters of cargo space to pack in a handful of obsolete starfighter squadrons.

"It is only in the last few days that he has truly begun to discover what it means to be a naval officer. His trial by fire hasn't been one I would have wished on any officer of mine." Walkingstick considered the display marking the position of Task Force Three.

"Tawfiq is lost and grieving and angry," he observed on their private channel. "He is under pressure from his civilian leadership to show that the Republic Navy can stand on its own two feet—and from the officers under his command to do *something*.

"His people and his nation look to him to do something more than follow in our footsteps, and in this trick of Verity's, he thinks he sees the way to expunge the shame of his retreat." Walkingstick smiled thinly, watching the distances tick away as Task Force Three continued toward the gravity shadow.

He might be wrong. Tawfiq might have seen right through him—if there was one thing the corporate boardroom should have taught the man, it was how to avoid being manipulated.

And who knew? Tawfiq might be *right*. Verity might be using the jammers to conceal their entire fleet. Walkingstick doubted it, personally, but the Triumvirate leader was certainly doing *something* they thought was clever.

"Sir! We have Stetson field formation on Task Force Three!"

And there he goes.

"Get me confirmation on that," he barked at the analyst who'd reported. "They shouldn't be going anywhere!"

"It's confirmed," MacGinnis said briskly. "We have exterior Stetson fields and initial Alcubierre Drive bubbles on all six Weston ships.

"Get me Tawfiq on the coms," Walkingstick ordered. "He can't make this assault on his own, and no one else can reinforce him."

"No response, sir," a com tech reported. "We're still receiving telemetry, and *Beowulf* is definitely *getting* the channel request.

"Drive bubbles complete," MacGinnis's analyst reported. "Task

Force Three has warped space, vector aligned with the front of the enemy formation."

"And still no com response?" Walkingstick asked, his tone soft.

"No, sir. Telemetry channels and so forth remain online, but we have no active channels with anyone in the Weston fleet."

"They all followed," MacGinnis said on their private channel. "I... honestly expected he'd have at least one ship refuse."

"The pressure to act was coming from his Captains as much as anything else," the Imperator replied.

"Time to emergence?" he asked aloud.

"Seven and a half minutes. The Triumvirate ships will see them disappear before they arrive."

That was the problem with the Alcubierre-Stetson Drive as a tool for tactical faster-than-light travel, Walkingstick reflected. Assuming the Republic ships held together for a seven-and-a-half-minute flight *into* a pair of overlapping planetary-gravity shadows—the presence of the twin planets made threading the needle that much harder—the A-S drive didn't actually make the trip faster than light for them.

Faster than any *other* form of travel available—over *six hundred times* the acceleration of the fighters they were trying to drop behind—invisible and invulnerable to weapons fire until they arrived, but still not faster than light over this distance.

"MacGinnis, relay orders to the Fleet and to Task Force Six," Walkingstick finally said. "Main force will accelerate to two hundred gravities. We... Well, we aren't waiting for the Westons to catch up anymore, are we?"

"And Task Force Three, sir?" MacGinnis asked.

"Even if Admiral Tawfiq starts taking our calls again, it's too late. He can't turn back now, morally or physically. He's committed."

And even if the Weston Admiral was *correct* as to Verity's plan, Walkingstick figured Task Force Three was already dead.

But it was time to wait and see what happened.

———

The q-probes were still far enough back that everything they saw directly was delayed by at least ten seconds. Despite the refusal to answer Walkingstick's calls, though, Task Force Three was still relaying full telemetry to the other allied fleets.

That gave the Imperator a front-row seat to just what Surinder Verity's surprise had been supposed to be.

The jamming platforms were new and interesting—he was hoping they would capture at least one intact, as he could think of half a dozen uses for them—though they were *mostly* a brute-force application of existing technology.

Still, they'd bought Verity a zone roughly thirty light-seconds wide that the attackers were blind in. Walkingstick figured they had to be near the limits of what the jammers could actually hide—mostly, it was that the fighters and their platforms were putting up a solid wall he couldn't see through and his q-probes hadn't gone far enough out to see around them.

Yet.

Now, though, Task Force Three's six capital ships plunged back into reality roughly two hundred thousand kilometers past the front starfighters, expecting to find the Vanguard Fleet battle line either right there or at least within lance range—roughly a million kilometers for the older ships firing at each other.

Instead, Tawfiq arrived in hell.

"That's a *lot* of fucking missiles," MacGinnis cursed, staring at a display that was almost *solid* with the red icons of capital-ship missiles. "Verity must have *emptied* the magazines of everything they had left."

"CIC makes it *ten thousand missiles*, plus/minus ten percent," a flag bridge analyst reported.

"So, yes, every missile from their carriers, strike cruisers and older battlecruisers," Walkingstick confirmed aloud. "That was going to be a nasty surprise, wasn't it?"

"Some of Tawfiq's ships must have *interpenetrated* with missiles on emergence," MacGinnis said. "Their Alcubierre Drives swept a zone clear on arrival; even capital-ship missiles wouldn't survive being close to a starship punching out of the needle."

And all of Task Force Three had *survived* the three-and-a-half-light-minute micro-jump too. They'd even arrived in something resembling formation, if one with far larger gaps than Walkingstick would have tolerated.

It wasn't going to save the Republic Task Force... but Tawfiq might just have saved the *rest* of the allied fleet.

"Torpedoes launching," MacGinnis observed. "Somebody panicked. Six hundred–plus in the air."

"That's not going to make a difference," Walkingstick said calmly as the first crescendo of antimatter weapons descended on the Republic ships. Every weapon Tawfiq had was firing at its maximum rate, even the heavy one-point-five-megaton lances on *Beowulf* pressed into service as antimissile guns.

Vanguard Fleet's bombers *shouldn't* have launched their torpedoes. But, like MacGinnis has said, someone had panicked.

"Those missiles are packed way too closely for proper attack runs," his ops officer said. "At this stage in the run, they were focused on hiding them."

"Verity wanted us deeper into the gravity shadow before they showed their hand," Walkingstick agreed. "The accuracy degradation from trying to control that many missiles would be more than painful—they must have been planning to pass it off to the fighters, another reason for tying them to the starfighters and jammer plat-forms—but that many missiles at once... We'd have had a very bad day."

Any missile the Republic ships hit took a dozen other missiles with it as it detonated. Hundreds—*thousands*—of missiles were torn apart in fratricidal fire before the first weapon ever hit any of Tawfiq's ships.

First to die, of course, were the *Paramount*s that had no business in a close action anyway. In a slugging match with the Vanguard battle line, the sixteen six-hundred-kiloton lances the two ships carried between them might have been worth something. In this catastrophically sprung ambush, even a near miss was crippling to the old ships.

The other four ships endured for a few seconds longer. *Bon Homme Richard* was third to go, followed swiftly by *Bay of Bengal*. *Momentum* and *Beowulf* both took hits, but their layers upon layers of reactive armor did their job, blowing warheads and antimatter clear before they could wreck the ships.

It didn't buy them long... Just long enough to...

"They're firing missiles?" Walkingstick asked, surprised.

"Yes, sir. They... Yes, we have them! The Vanguard battle line split the difference and is coming up behind the starfighters at one hundred *g*s, Tawfiq got... three salvos into space, aimed at the battleships."

And that was *all* the Weston Vice Admiral managed in the end. *Beowulf* and *Momentum* fought hard, but they had never stood a chance. A missile swarm intended to take out the entirety of the allied fleet had crashed down on one component of it and utterly annihilated it.

"Get the q-probes wider and closer," Walkingstick ordered. "We need to know how many of those missiles survived."

He'd just watched thirty-five thousand soldiers and spacers die. Arguably, he'd doomed them as effectively as if he'd ordered Tawfiq to make the jump—but the record would forever show that Tawfiq had made the attack in *defiance* of his orders, not because of them.

And, in so doing, had reduced the entire Weston Republic Navy to six starships.

"What do we do now, sir?" Rear Admiral Farago asked.

Fifth Fleet's overall CAG was theoretically in command of the entire allied fighter force, though Walkingstick had *definitely* noted the man deferring more to the Vice Admiral running Tecumseh's planes.

Tecumseh might only have brought four ships, but he'd brought most of his A team in terms of fleet officers. If Walkingstick thought for one second that he could pull off walking Tecumseh into the kind of meat grinder Tawfiq had charged into, he'd have tried.

But that same list of A-tier officers that he'd like to *eliminate* would make it impossible to pull the same trick. He wasn't going to easily manipulate that lot, and he knew it.

"MacGinnis, let's close up the side distance with Tecumseh's task force," Walkingstick ordered. "Enough of those missiles may have survived to give us a nasty headache. Farago, tighten your link with Yamamoto and make sure the Republic fighters aren't going to try anything like their Admiral did.

"*My* plan rides on those bombers and matching missile velocities with them—but if there are still a few thousand missiles in space heading our way, I'm going to need the starfighters to cut the salvos down to size.

"We may have lost a third of our hulls, but Verity doesn't have the missiles to make up for what Tawfiq just took out—*and* he got their bomber pilots to panic. Vanguard's fighter force's main bolt has been shot, and *we* now know where their battle line is."

Walkingstick studied the display and let an honest smile grow on his face.

"If Verity wants to think that because they cut us from twenty ships to fourteen, they've changed the weight of this battle, let them," he told his people. "Our plan always relied on our fighters and bombers, and they remain untouched.

"The next stage is on your people, Admiral Farago."

36

ANTHONY JUST FELT SICK. The Starfighter Corps Admiral couldn't *show* it. Not surrounded by the entire command staff for Task Force Six's fighter wings. Not linked in to the overall tactical command network for the entire Task Force.

He could not, with all those eyes on him, show the sickening feeling of watching thirty-five thousand people die because Al-Amir Tawfiq had let Walkingstick provoke him.

Anthony *knew* he'd never be able to prove that—just as much as he *knew* it had happened and *knew* that Tecumseh had picked up on it too.

"Times," he said aloud, glancing at Peña.

Amos Peña shivered, then refocused.

"Ten minutes until we're in fighter-missile range," he said shakily. "Missile impact two minutes thirty after that. Four minutes after that, our bombers will range on their battleships and battlecruisers. Assuming that Verity doesn't decide to make up their mind one way or another."

Anthony growled in the back of his throat.

The Vanguard Fleet "battle line"—three *Assassin*-class battlecruisers, four *Resolute* battleships, *Saint Agricola* and the *Sentinel*-class carrier *Custodian*—had been advancing behind the same shield of jamming that had concealed their missiles. They'd been taking it slow, at a "mere" hundred gravities of acceleration.

Once the Weston Task Force had wrecked *that* whole plan, they'd reversed course. They'd stuck to the same hundred gravities of acceleration, though, as Verity was clearly trying to keep their options open as they assessed the new situation.

That meant that the fighter strike was barreling toward the Triumvirate ships at five hundred gravities and the enemy were *dawdling* away at a fifth of that thrust.

"Missile intercept?"

"They did loose them. About three minutes before the missile swarm passes our fighter group." Peña shrugged. "Current estimate is about eighteen hundred birds. We've got thirteen hundred and sixteen Katanas between them and the fleets.

"Some will get through, but not enough to threaten the fleets. Probably."

"And that's the hard part done?" Anthony said drily. "Or are we going to *stop* taunting the demon Murphy?"

Peña chuckled grimly.

"The hard part done. Right." He met his boss's gaze. "Now all we have to do is stop our Commonwealth allies from stabbing us in the back, our Republic allies from charging off blood-mad and, oh, the *actual enemy* from killing us before we finish putting the boot in.

"Easy. Of course."

"Oh, good, we understand the problem." Tecumseh's tone was dry enough to peel paint as he sounded in the back of Anthony's mind. "There are still enough missiles in play, Anthony, that we're closing up formation with Fifth Fleet.

"Which means we're not just in range of the big guns anymore. I *know* Walkingstick has the Twenty-Seven-Thirty-Six Refit standard on all of his older ships, so he's probably counting us all as having the same deflectors."

Anthony checked the plots for how close the two fleets were and nodded silently. The range of a positron lance was a wobbly thing, depending on the power of the beam, the power of the deflector, and the size of the target.

Against the 2736 Refit standard applied to the Rimward Fleet during the war, the big one-and-a-half-megaton lances were more limited by near-lightspeed delivery than they were by the deflector fields of the older ships. Both fleets had a *lot* of one-megaton and six-hundred-kiloton lances still in play, though.

And against the 2736 standard, those beams had a range of about a million kilometers—and Fifth Fleet was now only eight hundred thousand klicks from Task Force Six.

They *still* weren't close enough for real mutual support against the missiles. Just close enough to divide the missile salvo so it didn't descend on just one of the two forces.

Assuming the fighter strike left any missiles for the fleets to worry about, of course.

"That would be a sensible analysis on his part, given that we didn't even have the Thirty-Six Refit on half of our older ships," Anthony replied. "We'll do our best to make sure you don't have too many suicidally intelligent visitors."

"There are still enough missiles left to leave us writing a lot of *Dear Mrs. Jones* letters, Anthony. Do what you can—but remember that I don't want to write those letters to your *pilots'* families any more than I want to write them to my spacers' families."

"We know the drill, sir," Anthony replied.

He was using q-probes to watch the key enemy groups and to relay coms to his subordinates. He had *all* of the information and all of the tools to manage it. His doing it from *Krakatoa* was going to save lives; he knew it.

But the main thing keeping Anthony Yamamoto out of a starfighter at that moment was that the starfighters were all ten million kilometers away.

———

The scale of the tidal wave crashing down on Anthony's subordinates put the size of Surinder Verity's sucker punch into perspective. Over eighty percent of the capital-ship missiles that the Triumvirate had concealed behind their shield of starfighters and jammers were gone, but what was left was enough to remain a real threat to the fleets.

The defensive intercept started with the starfighters salvoing their own missiles. With three rounds per launcher, the starfighters could afford to expend one salvo against the missiles—and between the starfighters and the bombers, they put over *seven thousand* missiles into space to try to shoot down the enemy fire.

Acting as a counter-missile was one of the roles the Javelin VII fighter missile had been designed for. With a closing acceleration of over twenty kilometers per second squared, the distance between the two missile swarms vanished rapidly—but the same acceleration and speed made direct hits all but impossible.

A wall of fire filled space as the lighter, shorter-legged and unquestionably *stupider* fighter missiles tried to kill their larger cousins. Even a near miss was often enough, given that for all of their comparative shortcomings, the Javelins carried the same one-gigaton antimatter warheads as the bigger missiles.

At this range and timing, even the q-probe relays couldn't give Anthony live control. He'd given his orders, and now all he could do was watch.

Seven thousand missiles met eighteen hundred, and enough antimatter to power a star system for a year converted itself to explosive energy.

Perhaps a third of the Triumvirate missiles survived, desperately lunging forward to make a mutually deadly rendezvous with the main fleets—but the fighter pilots and gunners had already lost too many friends today.

Positron lances and defensive lasers sliced through the air in a deadly pirouette, and more missiles died. New icons flared into existence on the display, and Anthony held his tongue for a long moment as the *Weston* starfighters sent another salvo of Javelins into the teeth of the capital missiles.

Then it was over, the last scattered handfuls of weapons still blazing toward the fleet while the starfighters continued on toward *their* mission.

"All Weston starfighters fired a second salvo," Peña confirmed before he could ask. "And no, Farago didn't pass on any orders you didn't."

"If they *all* fired, Abels almost certainly ordered it," Anthony observed. "I guess she wanted to make sure we were all still here to give them a ride home. Any losses?"

"We lost eleven fighters. The Commonwealth fourteen and the Republic twelve. All escape pods appear to have functioned properly, and we've got beacons on all thirty-seven lifeboats."

Anthony sighed and nodded his gratitude.

"Nail those beacons down tight," he ordered. "Get SAR into space as soon as we're sure they're clear."

The lifeboats, at least, were no longer accelerating toward the clashes still to come. Their limited engines were designed to shed velocity slowly and efficiently so they could land the escape pods on a convenient planet.

Sometimes, they just shed velocity to be easy to pick up. In Yellowstar, though, they'd definitely be able to get any of his people that got missed onto one of the planets. Anthony just preferred to pick up the pods himself.

"Fighter-missile range in ninety seconds, sir," Peña reminded him.

"Triple-check the formations; make damn sure the bombers are hanging back," Anthony ordered. "I don't want to lose anyone we can avoid, but we *need* the Longbows to survive."

"Ours are," his ops officer confirmed. "Looks like everyone else's too, but I'm half expecting to find out that the Republic crews have spent the last half hour strapping new engines to their bombers while we weren't looking so they can go faster."

"Would you blame them?" Anthony asked. "Verity just hit the absolute top of everybody's shit list."

As he spoke, new icons began to sprinkle the display around the allied fleets. This was the second part of Walkingstick's clever plan, though weakened by the loss of the launchers aboard Task Force Three. Hundreds of their own capital-ship missiles were being fired to arrive shortly before and in coordination with the bomber torpedoes.

If the missiles Tawfiq had launched had done so much as scratch Vanguard Fleet's paint, Anthony hadn't seen any sign of it. All nine heavy capital ships continued their slow withdrawal toward the planet.

The Triumvirate bombers were somewhere in between, desperately hauling ass toward their own carriers. Anthony *understood* why the starfighters weren't, even if he wondered if these pilots were really *that* ready to die for Surinder Verity.

"Missile range in thirty seconds. Lance range in two minutes," someone announced.

Anthony's fingers twitched unconsciously as his hands and implants tried to give orders to a fighter he wasn't flying.

"Squadron commanders," he said aloud instead, linking in with all of his key people. "We can't be certain the Commonwealth or the Republic planes know their jobs as well as we'd like. So, let's make sure we do ours.

"Missiles down the center—everything we've got—to clear a path. Hit the edges with your lances; widen the hole. No matter what happens, the Triumvirate starfighters aren't getting away and *they know it*. Do not take them for granted and do not take them lightly.

"We have the advantages here. Let's use them and clear the road for the torpedo bombers."

———

Anthony's closing instructions were probably unnecessary—but he figured his people deserved to hear his voice instead of just receiving electronic instructions. It was a distraction in the moments where they could do nothing *but* undermine themselves with their own fears.

It carried them into the battlespace, where his people executed on his orders perfectly, flinging over a thousand missiles at the center of the Triumvirate formation. So did the *rest* of the fighter wings, all three fleets' fighter forces operating in smooth synchronicity, entirely unlike Anthony's fears.

They'd lost more fighters in the missile intercept than he liked, but the combined fighter and bomber force launched seven thousand missiles into the teeth of the Triumvirate fighter strike—and, of course, the Triumvirate calmly put three thousand into space back at them.

While the Weston Republic fighters were out of missiles now, Anthony knew that *his* ships—and the Commonwealth ships—were keeping a full salvo in reserve for when they caught up to the battle line. The torpedoes and capital missiles were *supposed* to do the dirty work there, but he needed his people ready to finish the job if it wasn't enough.

The Triumvirate fighters had no such restrictions. They weren't planning on tangling with Fifth Fleet and Task Force Six, and they emptied their triple magazine as quickly as possible. After forty-five seconds, there were *nine* thousand missiles in space, heading toward the allied fighter wings.

"Inform the squadron COs they're clear for Mirror," Anthony murmured. He should *probably* have cleared that with Tecumseh—but even as he thought that, he felt the mental message arrive agreeing with him.

Paladin, Mirror and Rampart were the three key modifications they'd made to the DCN—with help from the Castle Federation. *Paladin* was the Paladin-II decoys, powerful platforms the Confederacy couldn't build and still had to buy from the Castle Federation.

Mirror was an entirely domestic development, pulling tech from both the Federation tech transfers and the Project Hustle systems. It was the initial version of the system that would truly separate the new Wolf and Raven fighters from their Commonwealth counterparts.

His ships had given up a full quarter of their antimissile lasers to carry it, and he figured that the TCN had already noticed that. Now that Walkingstick knew they had *something* up their sleeve, Anthony figured they might as well pull the trigger on it.

The missiles were almost two-thirds of the way through their flights when the two starfighter groups entered lance range of each other and the onboard weapons began to speak in earnest. Beams of pure antimatter connected ships across less than a light-second of space, and there were no real surprises there.

Everyone in the Yellowstar System was flying Katana-type starfighters, with the same lances and electromagnetic deflectors. Those were two systems that Anthony had left off upgrading until the next-generation ships—a decision he regretted now as dozens of the icons marking his people flashed red and then vanished from the display.

"Sir, the Republic ships!"

Anthony winced as he saw what Peña meant. Part of him had been expecting it, so he wasn't even all that *surprised* to see the Weston Republic Navy fighter squadrons find a few extra gravities of acceleration and put themselves in front of everyone else.

In the same way the fighters were shielding the bombers with their own hulls, the WRN starfighters were now shielding their allies. Commodore Abels was, it appeared, determined that Yellowstar was getting liberated today—and knew that the bombers and the missiles in the other starfighter forces' magazines were the only hope of pulling that off.

"That will not be necessary, I don't think," Anthony said calmly. "Mirror?"

"Just about... now."

Of the not quite thirteen hundred surviving Katanas in the allied formation, fewer than three hundred and fifty were Dakotan.

But at the moment Mirror activated, they were the only ones that mattered. Mirror, in the form mounted on Anthony's fighters, would be useless against anything *except* a Javelin VII fighter attack missile. It had been hard-coded to engage on specific frequencies, hit specific receivers with specific amounts of energy.

Against those receivers at those frequencies, the resonant energy was catastrophic. The wideband energy pulses from the Mirror projectors weren't powerful enough to take out missiles directly or even be *remotely* useful as energy weapons in their own right.

Instead, they blinded every sensor on the first wave of incoming missiles. Ten seconds later, they did it again to the second wave. Then the third. Then they hit the *first* wave again to make sure that none of the three thousand–odd missiles descending on Anthony's people had a working sensor left between them.

"I really hope we manage to work out a way to make that work against missiles we *don't* know the full technical specifications of," Anthony said drily as nine thousand super-intelligent seeking missiles were reduced to blind ballistic projectiles, easily evaded and even more easily destroyed by the fighters they were targeting.

Their missiles were still fully functional as they crashed down on the Triumvirate ships. The allies lost ships—mostly Weston-piloted Katanas, when all was said and done—to the enemy positron lances, but Mirror rendered the enemy's main weapon helpless.

"Even against Javelins, we figure we'll lose forty percent effectiveness once the people firing them know Mirror exists," Peña reminded him. "Which we just told Walkingstick, of course."

"Of course," Anthony agreed. "But I think we can safely say that was *more* than worth it today."

Now it was down to the bombers, and he watched the Vanguard Fleet battle line increase their acceleration as the timers ticked toward zero. There was time left for Surinder Verity, he judged.

He just couldn't see anything they could *do* with it.

37

"Final downloads received from *Saint Michael*. Missiles launching."

Krakatoa shivered softly around James Tecumseh as Volkov spoke, the carrier's dozen missile launchers flinging the massive weapons into space. More icons appeared on the displays and tactical feeds around him as well. *Black Sea* put another dozen missiles into space. *Adamant* added twenty-four—and *Iroquois* launched *forty*.

Task Force Six alone put eighty-eight missiles into space, hurtling toward Vanguard Fleet at a thousand and fifty gravities. Fifth Fleet added another hundred and eighty-two, for a total of two hundred and seventy missiles in each salvo.

"Remind me of the plan," James told Volkov.

"Three salvos, standard dispersal, set to arrive prior to the bomber strike," she told him. "Make a hash of their defensive systems. We might get a few hits, but we're not counting on it.

"Three salvos, accelerations varied to stack a single-time-on-target arrival with the bomber torpedo strikes. Four salvos, standard dispersal, for cleanup. We're keeping probes close to those four, for retargeting or self-destruction if whoever is left surrenders."

"And Vanguard's missiles?"

Verity's battleships and battlecruisers must have used a *lot* of their magazine capacity for the swarm Task Force Three had unknowingly sacrificed themselves to destroy. Combined with the bombardment of Mackenzie Valley Station, James was surprised they had any munitions left.

Regardless of *his* estimates, though, Vanguard Fleet's battle line had opened fire again when the fighters had ripped apart their main salvo. They didn't have an exact number—"less than two hundred" was the best his people could give him from the sensors—but given the ships involved, it was probably around a hundred and eighty to a hundred and ninety.

Three *Assassins*, four *Resolutes*, a *Saint* and a *Sentinel* had a hundred and eighty-eight missile launchers, after all.

"They're intentionally trying to play coy, but I will bet a week's pay they're aiming at the fighters. Contact will be approximately forty seconds before the bombers can launch. It's *possible* they might be able to take out some of the bombers."

"Anthony's people just shredded two *thousand* missiles," James pointed out. "Possibly, yes, but I think the odds are in our favor for the plan."

Enough had been sacrificed to get here that they'd *better* be.

Krakatoa shivered softly as more missiles plunged into space, and James leaned back in his seat. At this point, he had given or agreed with the orders for *this* battle. His job now was to watch for things *changing*—for Verity pulling something else out of their back pocket, or for Walkingstick deciding to fire on Task Force Six and say the losses were from the Triumvirate fleet.

Verity had to be trying to find another trick in their toy box. James had to watch for a threat there—but when the dust started settling, he was going to have four capital ships in the system to ten under Walkingstick's command.

The only real defense his command had against treachery at *that* point was Walkingstick's need to at least *appear* to still be a good and honorable man. If the Commonwealth turned on the Confederacy in victory, it would probably destroy any chance of Walkingstick winning the Republic without firing a shot.

"Triumvirate missiles are reaching the fighter force," Volkov announced. "Damn shame we can't calibrate Mirror to take out Jackhammers."

"Even if we did, capital missiles are too capable to be disabled by an installation we can fit on a fighter," James reminded her. "Even Javelins, once the people launching them know Mirror exists, have a dozen options to reduce the impact. A Jackhammer is smart enough to take those options *on its own*."

"The Weston fighters are out in front again," Yamamoto told him from Fleet Starfighter Control. "I *tried* to tell Abels we really didn't need them to do that. She isn't listening."

"Would you?" James asked softly, watching as positron lances and lasers cut apart the incoming missiles. In some ways, it was *easier* for the starfighters to engage missiles targeted at them. The angles and vectors were easier—but on the other hand, the missiles had a *lot* of electronic-warfare capabilities that they unleashed as they approached their final targets.

"In her place, I'd be about ready to use my *starfighter* as a bloody missile," Yamamoto admitted. "I'm doing the best I can to keep her people out of *that* kind of desperation."

"We're bringing them home, Anthony. We owe the Republic that much."

"Yes. We do."

"Missiles are clear," Volkov reported. "No starfighter losses."

"And now we… *blossom*," Yamamoto said, leaving James to smile at the all-too-accurate piece of poetry.

For the last hour, the Katanas had formed a barrier in front of the Longbows, protecting the bombers from all of the missiles and lance fire and whatever else Verity had thrown at them. They'd paid for that protection. Paid *hard*—*Krakatoa*'s crew were tracking over two hundred ejector-pod beacons in the wake of the starfighter strike, and only about two-thirds of the fighters had managed to save their crews.

In exchange, every one of the three hundred and forty bombers the allies had brought to the Yellowstar System had survived. Now the starfighter formation opened, squadron after squadron peeling aside to create uneven "petals" of starfighters spreading out from the bomber wings.

Gaps were left between the petals for the capital-ship salvos to fly through, but the key point was to expose the bombers. For about fifteen critical seconds, those thirty-four bomber squadrons had nothing between them and Surinder Verity's battle line.

They'd spent the entire flight laying in their targeting data, launch plans written and revised in the Fleet Starfighter controls based on q-probe sensor data and then relayed out to the starbombers by the q-probes closest to them.

Most, if not all, of the flight crews of those bombers would have gone over and revised the targeting plan themselves, right up to the moment they fired—but at that moment, there was no delay, no hesitation.

Almost fourteen hundred torpedoes launched in the space of a second. Nine hundred more missiles were coming up behind them at carefully calibrated speeds and acceleration that would bring them to Vanguard Fleet at the same time.

"Bombers are salvoing Javelins," Volkov reported, a slightly confused tone to her voice. "Admiral Yamamoto?"

"Counter-missile mode, Admiral Volkov," Yamamoto replied. "We've been sparing with the bombers' missiles since the first salvo, but now they can return the favor to the Katanas."

"And get the hell out of the way," James said firmly.

"Yes, sir."

Yamamoto's confirmation lined up with the display. The star-bombers had the same three-round magazine as the fighters, and they'd only used up one salvo so far, taking down the Triumvirate's massive missile swarm. Now, four thousand missiles appeared on the displays, surging forward to take down the capital-ship missiles aimed at their starfighter guardians.

And the bombers themselves flipped in space, going from gaining five kilometers per second of velocity every second to *losing* five KPS each second. It wouldn't really keep them out of the fight, not with a base velocity closing on seven percent of lightspeed, but it would put space between them and the enemy.

"First road-sweeping salvo will reach the enemy in eight minutes," Volkov reported. "Second and third at forty-second intervals after that."

She coughed delicately.

"Triumvirate ships have increased their acceleration to two hundred gravities. They are now most definitely trying to get out of here—we have motion on the ships in orbit as well! They are maneuvering at fifty gs; looks like they're aiming to put the planets between us and them while they run for the edge of the gravity shadow."

"Let them run," James said. "Those carriers have no fighters and no missiles. Walkingstick can clean them later."

Task Force Six certainly wasn't going to. With what his ships had given up in supply capacity for some of their new tricks, plus hanging out in deep space for a week... Without the ability to refuel at Mackenzie, he had to fall back to Weston.

The space between the fighters and the Vanguard Fleet ships was filled with fire now. The bombers' missiles ripped apart the Triumvirate capital-ship missiles as they tried to reach the fighters, but the Triumvirate ships were starting to take their own toll on the fire heading at them.

The first three salvos, the missiles from Task Force Six and Fifth Fleet, weren't even truly intended to *hit* their targets. No one was going to complain if they scored hits or even took out an enemy ship, but their real purpose *was* to be destroyed before impact, filling the area around Verity's ships with the stereotypical radiation hash of antimatter warfare.

"Road-sweeping complete, no hits. Though I think we still got a piece of one of the *Resolutes*," Volkov observed. "She just dropped twenty gs of acceleration. Rest of the battle line is matching her for now, but the hammer is dropping... now."

The closest q-probes were a full light-second away, and they could barely make out anything as a storm of antimatter hellfire descended on Surinder Verity. James and his allies had put over a thousand fighters in the path of two thousand missiles to cover the capital ships, knowing that those two thousand missiles would devastate fourteen starships.

Verity had no starfighters *left* at this point. There'd been a desperate attempt at the end to use their capital-ship missiles as defensive weapons, but there'd already been too much radiation hash for that to work for them.

And they'd only brought forward their battle line, their nine most powerful direct combatants—excluding *Hrothgar*, currently limping away with the carriers under the command of one of Verity's top officers.

A well-built capital ship could, on average, survive two or three antimatter missile hits and remain mostly mission-capable. She *might* survive as many as five and still be able to get most of her crew to safety.

It wasn't clear how many missiles hit *anything* in Verity's formation. When the immediate chaos passed, though, it was clear that none of the remaining four ships were mission-capable.

"Who's left?" James asked grimly.

"We aimed for the biggest and the smallest could take the least hits," Volkov told him. "First-cut analysis says three *Resolute*s and one *Assassin* survived. *Custodian* is gone. *Saint Agricola* is gone."

With the *Sentinel*-class flagship and the big battleship gone, not only was Verity themselves almost certainly dead, their second-in-command was probably gone too.

"The crippled *Resolute* just cut acceleration and is transmitting a surrender signal," Prebensen snapped. "ID says Captain Yevgenviy Bogdanov, aboard *Steadfast*— She's standing down— Wait, no, they're *all* standing down."

"Volkov, you know the drill," James ordered. "Divert all remaining salvos. Stand by for further orders. Prebensen..." He paused, then sighed.

"Get me a channel to Walkingstick. We need to *talk* about what happens next."

———

"Admiral."

"Imperator."

The single-word titles hung in the virtual air like tombstones for several silent seconds. It was just James and Walkingstick in this conference, which felt... strange. And dangerous.

"I suggested detaching my battlecruisers to secure the remainder of Verity's battle line," Walkingstick finally said. "The *Hercules*es are more than capable of handling three battered *Resolute*s and an *Assassin* if they decide to be foolish. We have every reason to believe their surrender is honest, but I see no reason not to be careful."

"We could slow the entire fleet to handle that and pick up our starfighter ejectees," James pointed out. "It's not like we can catch the carriers now. They're going to get away, presumably to Saskatoon if not all the way back to Triumvirate space."

"They'll head to Saskatoon," Walkingstick told him, with a certainty that sounded odd to James's ear. "*Reprisal* was light on fighters, but more were likely supposed to be brought up from the Triumvirate. Their only real chance now is to reinforce with as many fighters as our surviving Triumvirate members can scrape up.

"Unless they want to bring up the ships they held back, and they *need* those ships to keep a lid on their systems." Walkingstick shrugged. "We'll let Shirai run with the carriers for now, but we will pursue to keep his mind sharp."

"Task Force Six will not be able to pursue them to Saskatoon," James warned. "I could theoretically refuel from Mackenzie directly, but I think everything is better served by using TF Six to escort our prisoners and captures back to Weston.

"After... today... the Republic needs those ships."

A lot of the emotional side currents of an implant conversation were suppressed for this kind of virtual conference—more so than usual, given that neither James nor Walkingstick trusted each other. Even so, James picked up that Walkingstick wanted to argue whether the ships *should* go to the Republic.

"That will be for discussions in the future, I suppose," Walkingstick finally allowed. "For now, let's finish the task in front of us. If you are prepared to provide cover, I will task my carriers alongside your Task

286 | UNBROKEN FAITH

Force for relief of our ejected pilots and the capture of the surrendered Triumvirate ships."

He smiled coldly.

"In that case, of course, I will retain my *Hercules*es alongside my battleships as I pursue Admiral Shirai and Vanguard Fleet's survivors.

"I don't expect to have any great problems, but Verity's people have surprised us once already. Today was expensive, Admiral Tecumseh, and we must take care it does not become even *more* so."

"Just shedding velocity and reconcentrating our ships and fighters is going to take us most of the day," James warned. "I'll play mother hen while you go hunt."

That worked well enough for everyone. The main thing James needed *now* was to get back to Weston and start laying some political groundwork. He had his suspicions as to how Walkingstick was going to play this, and both his own long-term strategic needs and his respect for the Republic required him to counter the other man's steps.

The war was all but over… but the *political* conflict was only just beginning.

38

Yellowstar System
21:00 March 2, 2740 ESMDT

IMPERATOR JAMES CALVIN WALKINGSTICK needed a shower, a drink, and twelve hours of sleep.

He wasn't entirely sure when he was going to get those, but he was more grateful than he'd dare admit for the fact that the virtual conferencing software automatically removed such minor details as the wrinkles in his clothes and the five o'clock shadow on his face.

"Well?" he asked the man on the other end of the call.

"What do you *expect*?" Yan Shirai asked. "A whole lot of my colleagues are dead. My own fucking staff is dead—though, let's be honest, most of the ones I *liked* are here on *Hrothgar*."

"None of this is any surprise," Walkingstick said flatly. "There was a reason you transferred to *Hrothgar*, and it was so that you would live while Surinder Verity died. *That*, Admiral Shirai, has been handled. You have more than earned your promised rewards. Though I would have *preferred* some warning about that godawful missile-storm plan they rigged up."

"*I* wrote the damn plan," Shirai said flatly. "But by the time I realized Surinder was going with it, there was no way I could covertly access a q-com to contact you. I figured you could handle it."

And had also, Walkingstick suspected, been perfectly willing to play both sides. If Verity's plan had worked, Shirai would have been a senior officer on the winning side—and the loss of Fifth Fleet along with the Weston and Dakotan Task Forces would have seen the Weston Republic fall neatly into the Triumvirate's hands.

"And now you are in FTL with half of Verity's fleet answering to you," Walkingstick observed. "So, tell me, Admiral Shirai, what happens now? You know I'm coming after you."

"And you know perfectly well that this 'fleet' of mine has no fighters and no missiles," Shirai said drily. "I have pretty much exactly six days left to lay the groundwork with the Captains. If you make a decent offer for us turning our coats en masse, I'm about eighty percent sure I can give you this fleet on a platter."

"Can you even fight?" the Imperator asked.

Shirai laughed.

"No, and you know it," he admitted. "We're not *defenseless*, but *Hrothgar* has only four hundred missiles aboard, and that's the *entire* missile count of what's left of Vanguard Fleet, Imperator. We can't fight you, but we can make you destroy these ships.

"What are ten intact capital ships, crews and all, worth to the Commonwealth?"

Walkingstick said nothing. Shirai knew the answer to that. That was half a wealthy star system's entire annual gross domestic product. Four of the ten were *Ocean*s, obsolete but not worthless… but there were a *Hercules* and two *Volcano*es, sixties all.

"Well, Admiral Shirai, if you want your Commonwealth commission back, I suggest you find out what your Captains and crew are prepared to accept as payment to reenter TCN service," he told the traitor. "We'll have to break up your crews and move them around once we get you home—and none of you will ever serve in the stars of the soon-to-be-*former* Triumvirate—but I'm prepared to buy their surrender and defection."

"I'll lay the groundwork," Shirai repeated. "But unless there are a *lot* more resources waiting for us in Saskatoon than I'm expecting, I'm pretty sure you can *buy* this fleet when you get there."

———

Money wasn't *nothing*, not even to the Imperator of the Terran Commonwealth. But versus the scale of ten capital ships, Walkingstick could justify spending a great deal of it. That it would save lives—on both sides!—and put the Triumvirate fleet's ships and people on the right side of history didn't hurt.

Why, then, did the whole affair feel quite so dirty?

"Pich," he said aloud, knowing that the spy was still listening on the channel he'd closed. "Get in here."

It would take Misra a few minutes to arrive, so Walkingstick took a few of those minutes to scrub his face and find the drink he'd promised himself. By the time the spy arrived, the Imperator had wine waiting for them.

"Hell of a day," Misra told him, taking the wine without question. "You want MacGinnis in on this?"

"MacGinnis is asleep, well-deservedly so," Walkingstick pointed out. "I am enough older and enough more of an insomniac to keep going for a while yet."

"The wine will help, I hope," Misra said quietly, an edge of worry in their voice that surprised Walkingstick.

"Not really," the Imperator admitted. "I've been awake for twenty-seven hours, though, so that'll handle itself in due time."

He gestured at the screen consuming an entire wall of his suite's lounge. Currently, it was showing the estimated astrographic positions of the key players.

The remnants of Vanguard Fleet had left Yellowstar twelve hours earlier after a long stern chase across the system. Fifth Fleet, for their part, was now comfortably ensconced in Ulu-Imaq orbit, with Terran Marines on the surface carrying out desperately needed humanitarian relief.

The Dakotan Marines were doing the same, with Task Force Six carefully positioned with... Well, *both* planets between the two fleets.

The last *key player* was the Weston Home Fleet, the last remaining six ships of the Weston Republic Navy. Currently positioned in Weston itself, standing guard over their government.

"Our pursuit needs to get moving inside the next twelve hours or so," Walkingstick observed. "Which leaves all kinds of complications in play. Like Tecumseh's claim that his fleet needs to resupply at Weston."

"My impression is that it has to do with those decoys they deployed when they retreated," Misra told him. "It looks like they fit them into their older ships by giving up fuel capacity. I wasn't under the impression a modern fleet *needed* much in resupply."

"A fleet needs either supplies or time to create those supplies," Walkingstick admitted. "And, let's be honest, Tecumseh isn't going to run his magazines or his fuel tanks dry with us around. He doesn't trust us."

"That's probably wise," Misra said drily. "I could certainly make arguments *right now* for ambushing and destroying his Task Force."

"And were matters here in Yellowstar the only factor in play, I would even listen to those arguments." The Imperator studied the display. "But if we manage the next two weeks *right*, I think I can talk the Republic into lowering their flags and returning to the Commonwealth without further fighting."

"At the end of the day, the megacorps around here are the reason the Republic exists," Misra observed. "They stepped back and handed control over to a purely civilian government because they saw *that* as the most stable option. If the corporate sponsors behind the Republic come around to thinking that the *Commonwealth* is once against the best deal in town for long-term stability... we win."

"That's the plan," Walkingstick agreed. "They've lost two-thirds of their fleet. They lost a third of their *star systems*. We've retaken Yellowstar and we'll shortly move on Saskatoon."

He considered the icons of Task Force Six again.

"It honestly serves my purposes in a lot of ways to leave the Dakotans behind," he observed. "If the liberation of Saskatoon is unquestionably, one hundred percent Commonwealth, that gives us ammunition when we make our pitch.

"But I *don't* want Tecumseh on the ground in Weston before I'm there."

"So, find something else for him to do," Misra suggested. "What are the limitations we're looking at? He can't make an FTL jump without knowing he has fuel at the other end, and he doesn't want to run out of missiles with us around."

"Tecumseh suggested he escort our captures back to Weston. I am *not* letting that happen," Walkingstick stated. "If *he* delivers them to Weston, he's going to hand them over to the locals and we'll only regain control of them once we regain control of the Republic. Plus, even four battered starships change the numbers back in favor of the Republic.

"We need them feeling weak, which means *we* need to hang on to those ships."

"I think the answer is already right in front of us," Misra said, gesturing toward the twin planets. "Between us and the Dakotans, we've got, what, ten thousand Marines running humanitarian support? Dozens of shuttles? Hell, someone needs to make an A-S jump out to Mackenzie to pick up the people that *did* get evacuated from there."

The reminder of the catastrophe he'd helped create sent a cold chill down Walkingstick's spine, but he also saw Misra's point.

"We go after Shirai," he murmured. "But we put the captures under guard of one of our ships here in Yellowstar and task Tecumseh with managing the humanitarian operation. There is more than enough work here to keep his ships and crews occupied for the week it will take us to deal with Shirai."

"And then everyone shows up back at Weston at the same time," Misra agreed. "Tecumseh, carrying the blame for the original flight from Yellowstar and Tawfiq's sacrifice. *Maybe* he can swing things to take credit for the four wrecks he shows up with.

"*You*, on the other hand, show up with ten captured starships and having liberated both star systems that the Republic lost to the

Triumvirate. It won't take much to turn *that* into a hero's welcome. They'll listen to what you have to say."

"They will listen no matter what," Walkingstick said grimly. "I'll look to you to make sure of that."

He chuckled bitterly.

"Well, you and the Terran Commonwealth Marine Corps!"

39

"IROQUOIS REPORTS they've located the evacuation fleet from Mackenzie Valley Station," Prebensen informed the command conference. "Captain Waterman says they're a touch grumpy to see *us* but glad to see anyone able to provide help at all."

"Do they need further assistance?" James Tecumseh asked. "*Iroquois* should be able to provide most supplies I can think of, but we don't really have a way to transport anyone from Mackenzie to Ulu and Imaq until further support arrives."

A flotilla of half a dozen big freighters was on its way from Weston, but they'd only left after the battle was over. It would be four more days until they arrived, at which point they'd be able to take over a lot of the humanitarian work and do such minor things as *load an entire evacuation convoy into their cargo bays to move them to Ulu.*

"Waterman says they're in decent shape, but they have a wish list he's burning through his inventory to fill out," the coms officer noted. "I'll get a list from his people of what they've used up and what the evacuees might still need and make sure we fill in any gaps."

"We only have so many supplies of our own," Volkov warned.

"We have enough for any assistance they'll need," James said. "Or we'll borrow them from the planet, or we'll buy them from Weston when we get back there. What those people need, they get."

"I wasn't arguing *that*, sir," Volkov conceded.

"Verity paid for their atrocities, but it certainly hasn't left this system in great shape," he continued. "We will do everything we can to keep things together until the Republic relief fleet arrives."

"How long are we staying here?" Yamamoto asked. "I was under the impression you wanted to get back and support Littlebear."

"I do," James conceded. "But Walkingstick found a task to hang around our necks that I can't really argue with. Our Marines are saving lives down there, people. Salvaging Ulu's atmosphere and climate is going to take actual terraforming equipment, gear we don't have—but that Weston is sending.

"Once the relief fleet is here, we should be able to begin pulling our people back aboard and getting everything sorted, but we're not heading to Weston for another five or six days at least. Until we know we've done everything we can."

"Can't argue that," Volkov said quietly. "I know this wasn't our fault, but..."

"But we feel responsible, and we will work to fix it," James replied. He knew the demons his people were wrestling with. He was wrestling with them himself in his darker hours. He knew, intellectually, that he wasn't responsible for the fate of Tawfiq's ships or the fire Verity had rained on Ulu and Imaq.

But he'd helped create the situation where those decisions had been *made*, and he bore some of the weight of them.

"I have a meeting with Admiral Vitali in a couple of hours," he reminded his people. "No Walkingstick this time, which leaves me curious about what our Weston friend has to say.

"That said, what are *Roland* and her crew up to?"

Roland was the *Hercules*-class battlecruiser Walkingstick had left behind to stand guard over the captured battleships and their imprisoned crews.

"What they're supposed to be, so far," Volkov told him. "Sitting in orbit of the Yellowstar V planetary system with their captures, running distant remote admin for the Marines they left here while managing the rescue ops on those battleships."

"Those ships got the crap kicked out of them," Yamamoto added. "I can't say I feel bad about that, though."

"Let's not remind the locals too loudly, but it's the ships that *survived* that bombarded Ulu and Imaq," James said quietly. "For now, we'll hang responsibility for that on Verity, but if Weston starts making noises about war-crime trials for the Captains and gunners who launched those missiles…"

He shrugged.

"We aren't letting them walk away," he told his people. "*We* are too far from home to carry out those trials, and I will argue that the trials shouldn't take place here in Yellowstar… but those trials *must* take place, and the people who plotted those firing plans and pressed those buttons *must* face justice."

A quarter-million innocent dead required nothing less.

———

James spent longer than he was going to admit to anyone staring blankly at the wall in his office. If asked, he'd have said he was staring at the wallscreen showing the status reports of the hundred different deployments of his Marines and spacers across two planets.

It hadn't missed his notice that he was *missing* a third of the Marines that should have been aboard his ships. For most of what Task Force Six was getting up to, the missing sixteen hundred or so sets of boots hadn't been relevant.

For *this*, though, they—and the shuttles that were *also* missing— would have been very, *very* useful. Colonel Joshi wasn't exactly *stonewalling* him on where they were… She'd just told him he was going to want plausible deniability.

There had been a time that James would have refused to take that as a reason to let two battalions of Marines go missing. Sixteen hundred Marines, with power armor and assault shuttles, could cause a *lot* of damage.

The difference now was that he *trusted* Mahesh Joshi. He even trusted Shannon Reynolds, who he *knew* was involved in anything where the *Admiral* needed plausible deniability. So, he'd let them keep the secrecy they wanted... even as he had a *damn* good idea where those two battalions were and just how realistic *any* "plausible deniability" was when it came to the task force commanding officer who was *also* the uniformed commanding officer of the Dakotan Confederacy Navy.

It wasn't like he could conjure those Marines back aboard his ships by being frustrated at his officers. Or like the two battalions he had *left* —backed by the battalion's or so worth of Marines from the Triple-A companies and another two thousand or so Naval personnel—weren't doing an exemplary job of disaster relief.

Hopefully, they didn't share their Admiral's enduring feelings of guilt for the disaster they were rescuing people from. James knew, intellectually, that the responsibility for the orbital strikes rested with Surinder Verity, but he *also* knew that he was the one who had told the locals to hide their starfighters on the surface.

As he watched, three orange icons on the display slowly shifted to green. A thought to his implants checked in on the details—those strike locations *had* stored Weston starfighters, which meant they'd had antimatter annihilation blasts to deal with on top of the impact itself.

Firestorms had been tearing through the surrounding areas, driving civilians and even planetary firefighting crews ahead of them helplessly.

Now, with Dakotan assault shuttles hauling the civilians to safety and power-armored Marines providing muscle and will to back up the firefighters' specialty gear and expertise, the fires were going out. People had lost their homes, many had lost their lives, but thanks to the hard work of the locals and James's people, *no more.*

He was vaguely aware of the door to his office sliding open. Only one person could get past his security team without being flagged, and that same person also didn't necessarily need to announce herself.

"Sir, you're not answering your com," Chief Leeuwenhoek told him.

"I... wasn't aware I was receiving calls," James murmured. He prodded his implant and saw that he had, in fact, received one from the Chief. No others in the hour or so he'd spent staring at the display, but he wasn't entirely sure how he'd missed Leeuwenhoek's.

Alerts that rang inside his head were generally hard to miss!

"That is roughly where I figured you were," the Chief Steward told him. "And what I told Abey. So, I have strict orders from Greater Authority."

James gave his keeper a not-quite-glare.

"Neither of us is going to pretend *your wife* isn't a Greater Authority than you these days," Leeuwenhoek told him brightly as she shut down the wallscreen and made a surprisingly efficient pass of his desk for abandoned cups and plates. Along the way, she somehow managed to magically reorganize four tablets and twelve hard copy folders into an arrangement that was both significantly more orderly looking *and* made just as much sense to James's eyes.

He supposed she had a lot of practice in understanding how he thought at this point.

"What is all of this, then?" he asked. "Abey's orders?"

"Stop you brooding, feed you and then tell her when you're ready to talk like a human being," Leeuwenhoek told him. "Well? Have any requests for dinner, or should I just fill a bowl with dry pasta and watch what happens?"

"Whatever is being served in the mess is fine, Sallie," James said with a chuckle. "And yes, I'd be delighted to talk to Abey."

"Yeah. You should be," his keeper said firmly. "And I will point out, sir, that this is *not* Rank Hath Its Privileges. You're calling your wife less than we encourage our damn *ratings* to talk to their spouses via q-com.

"I'd say it's not my place to tell you how to manage your marriage, but it sure as hell *is* my place to manage the rest of your life, so I'm going to anyway," Leeuwenhoek told him firmly. "You're going to talk to Abey. It'll be good for both of you.

"And then *I* am going to *schedule* a bloody call for the pair of you with *her* staff so that both of you stop worrying about interrupting the other's Highly Important Work!"

The capitals were very, very clear… and so was the Steward's point.

And her assessment of why James had not called home as much as he would have liked.

"I am not so foolish, Sallie, as to argue with the Steward who runs my life," he told her. "And... thank you. I appreciate the reminders. We all need them sometimes."

Volkov had made similar comments, he remembered now.

"Let's get that dinner moving," Leeuwenhoek told him. "And once you can pretend you're human, I'll connect Abey." She smiled. "And, given the timing, *Sherlock*."

———

Sherlock was the first part of the holographic link to make himself very, *very* obvious. The virtual merger of James's office aboard *Krakatoa* and the back office tucked away in Abey's official residence wasn't quite perfect, but the software could handle the German Shepherd seeing James and *leaping* across the room.

He moved to absorb an impact that didn't actually happen and heard Abey laughing at the poor dog's confusion as Sherlock passed through him, paused on the floor, and then tried again.

"Come here, Sherlock," she told the dog. There were a few pitiful whines and attempts to paw at what was actually empty air, and then the dog slinked back to Abey, who ruffled his ears.

"Someone misses you," Abey told James.

"I miss you both," he said. "No offense to Sherlock, but he definitely falls second on that list."

"I miss you," she said. "And I worry."

"*I* worry." He glanced past the illusory merging of the offices to where he'd been staring at the wall. "We needed to do this, for the need of the Republic and for the soul of the Confederacy, but it's... It's hard.

"I want to bring my people home, Abey, and I don't think I'm going to be able to bring them *all* home, even in the best case. We're going to have to leave at least one ship as a sign of our commitment going forward. Assuming, of course, that the Republic still exists in two weeks."

She sighed and reached across to put her illusory fingers on his.

"That bad?" she asked.

"Walkingstick needled and prodded and poked Admiral Tawfiq until he could give an order and know the man would do the opposite," James murmured. "I didn't realize how intentional it was until it was too late, love. Over thirty thousand people died because our *ally* had something other than just victory on his mind."

"We can't let him win."

James nodded his agreement and stared down at where his hand merged with the hologram of hers.

"He gets the glory of the victory," James said softly. "He has liberated Yellowstar. It would take a miracle for the Triumvirate to hold Saskatoon—and we don't *want* them to hold Saskatoon. I want him to succeed, but come the fifteenth, he's going to be back in Weston.

"And he's going to ask them to drop their flags and rejoin the Commonwealth. They will be weak, because of him. They will be afraid, because of him. And they will look to him for salvation... against the weakness and fear *he* created."

Abey took a moment to pet Sherlock's ears before looking up and meeting his gaze.

"We really should have more quiet *us* conversations, you know," she said. "So that we're not talking about the fates of worlds and nations *every* time I talk to you like this."

"Sallie says the same," he agreed with a chuckle. "And she's right. I know *I* was worried about interrupting you. You have a lot going on back home."

"And I don't exactly want to jog the shoulder of a man fighting a war, however far away he is," she admitted. "I want you here, James. Stars know we've enough of a headache with our own problems. We needed to intervene with the Republic, but I think I underestimated how much having *you* gone would suck.

"For me, mostly, though I know the Cabinet is twitchy over anything that looks like starting a war while you're gone."

James snorted.

"I left you good people," he told her. "The Kipling Directorate?"

"Yeah. Basically, we've sorted out enough with the rest of the Brillig

Sector to know that if we remove their threats and posturing, they will all sign on. I'm not entirely convinced the *Confederacy* benefits from bringing the Brillig Sector into the folder, but *they* certainly will.

"But the Directorate has made it clear that they *will* fight. They can't *win*, but a lot of people will die."

"Modesitt and Voclain have already told you the solution, haven't they?" James asked.

"Take half the fleet and *sit* on Kipling until the Directorate gets the point, basically. We have almost as many eighties as they have *ships*. Voclain wants to take all five of them, plus the *Saint*s and *Vesuvius*, on a 'courtesy visit' to make the point."

"We're not going to conquer the Directorate," James said. It wasn't a question. "But sending eight heavy capital ships to visit a nation that only has seven capital ships total definitely makes a point. We don't need to conquer them to make them realize they don't want to cause their neighbors issues."

"That was Modesitt's argument," Abey said with a chuckle. "You're a good influence on your people."

"I'm *an* influence on my people, at least," he said wryly. "I hope my support of their advice helps."

"It does, actually." She held his gaze for a few long quiet seconds. "I'm not sure I have anything as useful for you with regards to the Republic, though."

"Littlebear has been laying groundwork. I know what his plan is," James admitted. "That's our best shot, I think. But to make his plan work, the Republic has to be prepared to defy Walkingstick—because I don't think he is going to lightly stand by and let us make the Commonwealth *obsolete* as well as broken."

"And they're not going to be?"

James shook his head.

"I don't think so. Like I said, Walkingstick will be coming back to Weston covered in glory—most of it legitimate. I, for my decisions, bear the weight of withdrawing from Yellowstar. And while the orbital strikes were Verity, there will be people who blame me. Not entirely without justification, either."

"The whole situation seems to have worked out very neatly in the

Imperator's favor, hasn't it?" Abey murmured. "From which system Verity attacked to Tawfiq making his damn fool jump. Something doesn't smell right, love."

"And you can tell that from Dakota," he said grimly. "Unfortunately, on the ground I think it's harder. You and I and our people? We don't trust Walkingstick; we're *looking* for the hidden blade.

"But the Republic sees him differently. There are definitely people who don't trust him. The Republic *exists*, after all, because the Sector felt they weren't getting the support and protection they needed from the Commonwealth as run by him.

"His argument, though, is that when the shit hit the fan and they called for help, Terra answered. Regardless of their treason and secession, Terra answered."

James smiled sadly.

"Hell, the argument works *on me*," he admitted. "That he was here, himself, with a large-enough fleet to turn the tide against the Triumvirate? That's more than I ever expected from the Imperator. If things didn't smell quite so fishy, I'd be considering suggesting warmer diplomatic relations with the Commonwealth. While I'm never going to argue for rejoining while there's an Imperator of Terra, the high level of what's happened here would open that door more than I've considered in a long time."

"And yet what you're saying is the opposite," Abey said. "You not only aren't ready for reconciliation with Terra, you're considering the Republic's possible reconciliation not only a failure on your part but an active threat to everyone."

She paused, meeting his gaze through the hologram and looking deep into his soul in the way only she ever did.

"You think the whole invasion was a setup."

Eight words. Eight words James would never have said himself, that he'd never even consciously *thought*.

Eight words that tore the ground out from underneath him because she was *right*.

"I do," he admitted steadily. "I think Walkingstick is working with key elements of the Triumvirate—that he's betrayed them as thoroughly as anyone else, but that he set this up! Everything from their invasion plans to the surrender of the surviving battleships here in Yellowstar.

"His refusal to turn those ships over to the Republic is a small thing, and yet... it's telling."

They were both silent for a long time, then Abey exhaled a long sigh.

"That gives me a place to start," she told him. "I'll talk to Littlebear. And others. There are levers we can pull, strings we can draw. Talk to Reynolds about it, too," she suggested.

"This isn't your type of battlefield, my love. This is diplomacy and lies and shadows." She smiled coldly. "And you *never* thought I was *just* a secretary when you met me."

40

THERE WAS a palpable sense of relief on *Krakatoa*'s bridge as *Antonia Gloria* disgorged the largest piece of her cargo. At two hundred and fifty meters long, the terraforming ship *Did Ya Miss Fresh Air?* was only barely small enough to *fit* inside any interstellar freighter, and it had taken several hours to clear enough of the other cargo out to allow *Fresh Air* to make her way out into deep space.

Not that she *stayed* in open space, as the terraformer's crew knew exactly what she was needed for.

"They spent the entire trip planning their work, didn't they?" Volkov asked, watching as the relatively small ship dove into Ulu's darkening atmosphere. Boson signatures flared around the ship as her crew settled her into a technically impossible orbit inside the planet's upper atmosphere, manipulating mass of ship and fuel alike to lock her into place.

"It's what we would have done," James agreed. Data tags were flickering off the icon of the terraformer at a speed he'd rarely seen from anything that *wasn't* a warship. "And the crew of a ship like that are even *more* experts and specialists than we are."

Did Ya Miss Fresh Air? wasn't supposed to be used for this kind of process. She was designed to set up near-breathable atmospheres over the course of a decade, doing everything from dropping ice asteroids to deliver oxygen and water to filtering toxic chemicals out of the target's air.

It was the last purpose she was serving today. Massive scoops unfolded from her sides, expanding until the ship sat at the center of a cone almost ten kilometers wide and deep. Gravity and vacuum alike began to suck in untold billions of liters of Ulu's atmosphere.

One ship, however capable, couldn't filter out the damage done by the vaporization of entire mountains. But *Fresh Air* didn't work alone, and a second terraformer—*Green Is Good For Ya*—drifted out of *Antonia Gloria*.

"Loblaw's Interstellar Agriculture apparently owns ten of these guys," Prebensen observed as the rest of *Krakatoa*'s flag staff watched the ship dive down into the atmosphere, aiming for the opposite side of the planet from *Fresh Air*. "There are six in the convoy. The other four are needed to keep their current project stable."

One of Halifax's planets sat just outside the liquid-water zone, as James understood it, and LIA had been working to inject enough of a greenhouse-gas effect to warm it up sufficiently to support Terran-grade food crops. An entire planet, after all, made for a lot of farming space if the agricorp didn't have to argue with people who were already living in chunks of it, or try to preserve a preexisting ecosystem.

"We're running a double check on their analysis now," Volkov told James. "But LIA Terraforming figures there will be a noticeable but non-harmful temperature decrease over the next six weeks or so, followed by a return to normal over the following six weeks.

"In three months, it will be like those impactors never hit."

"At least according to Ulu's atmosphere," James murmured. "Won't bring the mountains, homes or lives back."

"No," Volkov agreed. "There's a reason the Republic wants the battleship COs and tactical officers for trial."

"Yeah." James grimaced. "*That*, thank you for reminding me, is my next meeting. Because Walkingstick's people are getting stroppy, and I need to present a compromise that *doesn't* require us to storm a Commonwealth battlecruiser on the Republic's behalf."

Despite what her Captain seemed to think, *Roland* was more badly outclassed than an initial look at the *Hercules*-class battlecruiser would suggest. The *Resolutes* under *Roland*'s guardianship were empty husks, only the repairs necessary to keep them from breaking apart having been completed, but the TCN had moved all of the *officers* aboard *Roland* herself.

The Republic had the crews and NCOs in a prison camp on the surface—with line of sight to the gaping wound that *had* been the generally accepted most beautiful mountain in five or six star systems. But the Commonwealth had kept the officers.

The very people the Republic wanted to prosecute for war crimes.

"Imperator Walkingstick, frankly, your attitude with regards to these ships and their crews is becoming quite concerning," President Frey said sharply less than five minutes after James logged into the virtual meeting. "They were captured in a Republic system, having committed war crimes against Republic citizens.

"Those ships belong to the Republic, and their officers *will* face the Republic's justice for their crimes. Why do you continue to blockade the surrender of those ships and personnel?"

"Those ships were taken by Commonwealth troops operating in the aftermath of a battle we can all agree was won *by* the Commonwealth forces," Walkingstick said calmly. "We remain responsible for both the warships—with all of the risk inherent in both a warship and a damaged starship!—and for the personnel aboard them.

"While I recognize the Republic's legitimate concerns around the actions of the Triumvirate personnel of Vanguard Fleet and the atrocities carried out under Surinder Verity's command, the policies, doctrines and *laws* of the Terran Commonwealth Navy restrict me from turning over my prisoners if I cannot be certain they will receive fair and just trials.

"While I have a degree of faith in the systems of the Republic, we must all acknowledge that they are very *young*. And with the crimes in question, it is all too easy for popular outcry and the emotions of the justices and lawyers involved themselves to get in the way of true justice."

"The Republic will not permit kangaroo courts," De Clerc said firmly. The Prime Minister sat at her President's right hand, presenting a unified front along with Admiral Vitali.

James had to wonder how Captain Zheng Jaromir, *Roland*'s commanding officer, felt about being the most junior person in the call by several light-years. Three Admirals, one a head of state in his own right, plus two people who acted as head of state together.

And one Captain, with a battlecruiser a long way from any kind of support but tasked to stand guard over the captured ships and crews.

If Zheng was less of a stubborn prig, James might have had more sympathy for the man.

"I think the answer is relatively straightforward," James interjected, giving Walkingstick his calmest gaze. Now that Abey had brought his realization and suspicions about the Imperator's role in the Triumvirate invasion to the fore, he was surprised at how evenly he was managing to deal with the other man.

"Agreed. The personnel should remain in the custody of the Commonwealth and face trial in the courts of a neutral third party: the Commonwealth," Walkingstick said firmly. "Or do you mean to tell me that none of you have faith in the courts of the oldest legal system in human space?"

Given that said courts had upheld the Imperatorship, James didn't, actually. He wasn't going to *say* that, though.

"The prisoners have the right to a speedy trial as well as a fair one," he told the Imperator. "Transferring them to the Commonwealth will not enable that. Also, bluntly, their crimes did not take place in the Commonwealth.

"They *must* face Republic justice. I do, however, agree with the Imperator's basic concern about heightened emotions," he continued before Walkingstick could argue with him. "My recommendation is that the Republic come up with a list of individuals that need to face war-crimes trials as opposed to standard POW treatment.

"I judge that in about two days, Task Force Six's personnel will no longer be needed to complete the humanitarian work needed here in Yellowstar. At that point, we will return to the Weston System to resupply—and we can easily transport those individuals, under secure guard by, as Imperator Walkingstick suggested, a *less*-impacted third party to Weston.

"Once in Weston, they can face a fair and proper trial under Republic law under the care of justices and lawyers with as much separation as possible from the immediate impact of their crimes."

"That does not necessarily—"

"The DCN, like the TCN, also has rules around handing over people when we are uncertain of their fate," James interrupted Walkingstick smoothly. "I think both of our legal obligations would be met if the Republic was prepared to commit to taking the death penalty out of the equation?

"While I recognize that *just following orders* is an insufficient defense in the case of the use of weapons of mass destruction, the core weight of the blame must fall on Surinder Verity, and… Well, in their case, the highest penalty has already been taken care of, hasn't it?"

De Clerc and Frey exchanged a look, then both glanced over at Vitali. James could readily recognize the signs of a silent implant conversation—one that ended in a single choppy nod from Frey.

"We are prepared to work with those terms," De Clerc said. "We will provide a list of the key individuals we believe must face charges, based on the recordings we've already received from the captured ships, and we will formally commit in advance that none of them will face execution for their involvement in Surinder Verity's crimes."

James moved his attention to meet Walkingstick's gaze again and shrugged slightly.

"I know the TCN regulations on this, Imperator," he reminded the other man smoothly. "Unless they've dramatically changed in the last two years, that *does* cover your legal obligations towards *our* prisoners."

He still half-expected Walkingstick to argue—he was sure the man could come up with *some* reason to keep stonewalling—but he also knew that he'd just put the Imperator on the spot in front of people Walkingstick *needed* to believe he was the just and honorable leader.

"It does," Walkingstick agreed, his tone flat but calm. "Captain Zheng, see to the transfer once we have that list of individuals.

"As we speak, I am approximately ten hours from entering the Saskatoon System," he continued. "I anticipate no material difficulties in liberating that system from the remains of Vanguard Fleet. Admiral Shirai is not Surinder Verity nor, indeed, is he even a member of the Triumvirate. His hold on that fleet is fragile, and the arrival of Fifth Fleet will destroy whatever courage they retain.

"I have every confidence that I will be speaking to you all tomorrow as the liberator of the Saskatoon System from the Triumvirate. Soon after that, I look forward to seeing you all in person once more.

"This war will soon end. We will shortly need to outline the nature of the peace and the future that we all desire."

41

Yellowstar System
20:00 March 6, 2740 ESMDT

"Director Reynolds is waiting to see if you're available, sir," one of James Tecumseh's Marines said in his implants the moment his q-com conference ended. "She, uh, seems agitated."

"Send her in."

He hadn't even finished the second word in the sentence before the doors slid open and the woman-shaped predator stalked into the room.

"Reynolds," he greeted her calmly. "What did you *do* to my poor Marines?"

"What?" she snapped.

"The Lieutenant called you *Director* Reynolds," James pointed out. "Last time I checked, you only used that title when you were playing Chief Crow. So, either you were Top Spying at the poor young man, or you pissed my Marines the hell off.

"Which one was it?"

Reynolds grimaced and consciously, *visibly* re-exerted control of her emotions. That she'd shown as much irritation as she had spoke volumes about her trust of one James Tecumseh, he judged.

"Both, probably," she admitted. "Someone decided to both dangle the biggest carrot I've ever seen in front of me *and* be the biggest prick I've spoken to in a while."

James grimaced.

"I take it you want the carrot in question?" he asked.

"And, unfortunately, I suspect our little bird's price at least tripled because I refused to fuck him. Somewhat rudely," Reynolds added. "Just because I *have* slept with him didn't mean I was going to do so again. Especially when he's now on the other side."

James considered that mouthful for a moment, then sighed.

"Money is not something I spend freely," he observed. "On the other hand, I am *far* more prepared to spend it than to tolerate harassment of my people.

"So, why don't you start at the beginning?"

He gestured her to a seat and sent a silent message to Sallie Leeuwenhoek to bring tea for him and coffee for the spy.

"You know we got an information pulse from a little birdie on *Custodian* during the battle," she reminded him. "While I didn't want to draw too much attention to it at the time, I didn't think we actually *had* any assets on *Custodian*. And, well... we didn't."

"You said the contact used one of your codes?" James remembered.

"I lied," Reynolds said flatly. "In the middle of the battle, the complication of the fact that my birdie used a *CISS* encryption code would have left you questioning the intelligence more than the data was worth."

"A CISS code," he echoed. "So, your birdie was another ex-CISS agent?"

"Daniel *fragging* Feldman, as it turns out," she said grimly. "The first agent I ever senior-partnered for. In that lovely gap between being senior enough to be the senior of the pair and being senior enough to not be assigned a partner at all unless I wanted them.

"I don't know if Feldman was supposed to be Verity's assassin the way I was supposed to be yours or was just undercover on one of the ships that became part of the Triumvirate when things went to hell."

"If he was supposed to control or eliminate Verity, I think it's a safe call to say he failed," James said. "And not with good reason, from what I can tell. I understand *your* reasons for failing to knife me in the back. I'm not sure why anyone let one of the Triumvirate live."

"Feldman was always..." Reynolds bit her lip thoughtfully. "*Pragmatic*, I suppose. *Mercenary* might be a better word. From what I can tell, he was working on Verity's flag staff aboard *Custodian* but had at least three different exit strategies planned. So, when a missile storm headed for *Custodian*, he wished the good Admiral Verity an unfond farewell and got the hell off ship.

"He clearly figured he wanted in on the side of whoever won this mess, so he sent a few pieces of useful but not *key* intelligences in the battle," she continued. "So, now he figures we won, he apparently doesn't want to touch Walkingstick with a twenty-foot pole, and he wants to deal."

"And apparently get back in your pants," James noted.

"Apparently. My ego is tickled, but that's not all he was aiming for." She sighed. "It took me fifteen minutes to finally get out of the man what it is he has for sale, and if he'd *started* with that, he might have got everything he wanted.

"As is, I threatened to kick him in the nuts and, probably related, his price became five hundred million Commonwealth dollars."

James whistled.

"That's a lot of money, Reynolds. And he pissed you off enough that *you* pissed all over my Marines because they made you wait. What the *hell* does he have for sale?"

"Recordings of Imperator James Calvin Walkingstick's q-com conversations with Rear Admiral Yan Shirai."

James froze, and his office was deathly silent as Leeuwenhoek delivered the pair of hot beverages. He took a sip of the tea, burning his tongue and hissing at his distraction.

"Tell me he has a way to prove that," he finally told her.

Reynolds didn't say anything aloud. She linked into the holoprojectors and started a file.

It was an odd feeling, watching both halves of two holographically merged offices from the outside. It formed a diorama on James's desk, about a meter wide, showing him the two men. He didn't know Yan Shirai on sight, but he *did* recognize Walkingstick.

"*Rear Admiral Shirai,*" the miniature Walkingstick said. "*It's been a while.*"

"*It has. You've made yourself quite a big deal, skipper,*" Shirai replied. "*The universe has changed around us, but here we are. And you need something from me.*"

"*You could certainly make my life a lot easier if you work with us,*" Walkingstick agreed genially. "*I understand that you have a list.*"

The recording froze, that twenty seconds of exchange clearly all she'd been sent.

"*This* doesn't have a date stamp," she observed. "But Feldman has promised me that all of the recordings were through *Custodian*'s systems and have the appropriate date stamps."

"There is no way that either of them had this conversation through *Custodian*'s systems."

"Not that they knew about, no," Reynolds agreed. "I'd have to see the full unedited files to be sure, but I suspect that we're looking at is the security-system recordings from Shirai's office—from recorders that Shirai almost certainly turned off and that Feldman had rigged to record for *him* if Shirai did so.

"He'd be able to set that up, especially if no one knew there was a CISS agent aboard."

James grimaced.

"He sounds like a problem."

"He *is* a problem," Reynolds agreed. "But for half a billion dollars, he's apparently prepared to give us the proof of how deep our dear Imperator had his fingers in the Triumvirate invasion of the Republic."

"I take it you don't think this is coincidence," James murmured.

"No, I've been looking for the link between Walkingstick and Vanguard Fleet for a bit," she told him. "Even before Abey put the word out in the shadows that that was our suspicion. I'm not *entirely* sure he was involved prior to showing up, if I'm going to be honest.

"But there's no way in hell everything kept coming up Walkingstick since he got here by fluke." She pointed at the frozen diorama. "And if he turned Verity's ops officer, even if he didn't have anything on Verity themselves, he had eyes in the operational planning of Vanguard Fleet from well before the attack on Yellowstar.

"And instead of using that to win the war in one fell swoop, he used it to set up everyone like pawns on his little chessboard."

James stared at the frozen diorama, disturbingly solid proof of his worst fears.

"We'll find the money," he promised Reynolds. "Make the deal."

42

Saskatoon System
04:00 March 7, 2740 EMSDT

VICTORY HAS MANY FATHERS. *Defeat is an orphan.*

The hoary old phrase rang silently in Imperator James Walkingstick's head as he strode onto *Saint Michael*'s flag bridge in full regalia. Officers and ratings snapped to attention, giving crisp salutes before immediately returning to their duties.

There was a ceremony and a weight to all of this—but part of what made Walkingstick's particular style of leadership and, well, cult of personality *work* was that he needed his people to do their jobs and *respected* that his people needed to do their jobs.

So, they acknowledged him with full ceremony and then immediately got back to work without him saying a word. He'd flown his flag from *Saint Michael* for the better part of a decade, as Admiral, Marshal and Imperator.

This crew knew how he worked. They were also the parents of his victories, and today, they expected to add another to the list.

"Emergence in thirty minutes," MacGinnis reported. "We have no

316 | UNBROKEN FAITH

clear information on the status of Saskatoon. Any change to the emergence plan?"

There was very limited flexibility to the course once a ship entered warped space. The complete lack of ability to see the outside universe forced a starship to navigate by, effectively, dead reckoning. The *angle* of the jump was completely unchangeable. The only things that could be adjusted, really, were the turnover point—already days in the past for this trip—and the moment of emergence.

Cut the emergence *too* early and the released energy could destroy the starship. Cut it too late and the ship entered gravity shadows, and *not* being yanked into real space took a massive amount of skill.

"There's no need for us to ride the needle, and our information suggests Vanguard Fleet's survivors are above Regina," Walkingstick reminded her. "We will emerge at the edge of Regina's gravity shadow as planned."

And they weren't going *into* the gravity shadow until Shirai had fulfilled his promises. Starfighters and bombers—Fifth Fleet had been reinforced to full strength with Weston flight crews and ships Walkingstick wasn't planning on giving *back*—would dive toward the planet to finish the job if Shirai had lied. The capital ships would remain outside the gravity shadow, where they could use their A-S drives to go *around* the planet and cut off the Triumvirate fleet if they tried to run.

Despite what MacGinnis said, even *officially*, they had pretty decent information on where Shirai and his ships were. The Republic might have lost *control* of the Saskatoon System, but they'd left agents and q-coms behind. Their plans for this situation hadn't been particularly *good*, but they'd *existed*.

That put them ahead of a lot of people, in Walkingstick's experience. And because of those plans, he knew that all ten surviving ships of Vanguard Fleet were in Regina orbit.

Thanks to Shirai, of course, he knew even more. He knew that they hadn't replenished their starfighters beyond what they could build out of onboard parts. Even with *Reprisal* added to the ships Shirai had left Yellowstar with, they had less than two hundred fighters and a mere ten bombers to deploy.

They had missiles—those were relatively easily fabricated out of onboard resources—but they'd emptied their magazines in Yellow-star, so they didn't have nearly as many as they would like. And since *Lexington*s like *Reprisal* didn't have missile launchers, they didn't have any more ability to *launch* missiles than they'd had in Yellowstar.

If the Republic's allies were the parents of victories, Shirai was a man orphaned by defeat.

Walkingstick, on the other hand, had nine of Fifth Fleet's best ships —with three-quarters-full magazines, though Fifth Fleet's spare-parts inventory was looking just as bare as Vanguard Fleet's—five hundred starfighters and a hundred and thirty bombers.

Plus, he had *three* battlecruisers and three battleships, four of them modern sixties, to Shirai's single modern battlecruiser and four old strike cruisers.

Even if he *hadn't* laid the groundwork for a completely different path, any *battle* in Saskatoon was a foregone conclusion.

"Status reports on all ships?" he asked, settling into his command chair and carefully adjusting his long braids.

"Everything is turning over at ninety-five-plus percent efficiency," MacGinnis told him. "We are running low on capital missile compo-nents, though we can *probably* cannibalize starfighter missiles for parts if we need to."

That would require them to be in regular space, Walkingstick reflected. Most of the starfighter missiles were on the carriers, but it was *Saint Michael*, *Perseverance* and *Endurance*—his two *Resolutes*—that needed capital-ship missiles the most.

"No, we'll be leaving part of the fleet here and returning to Weston to coordinate rearming before we go into Triumvirate space," Walking-stick replied. "The first stage of this campaign was always to liberate and defend the Republic."

So far, everything was proceeding close enough to plan that he was *quite* confident that he wouldn't need to worry too much about appear-ances when he moved against the Triumvirate. He could only bring so many ships to protect a secessionist state that asked for help.

Once the Republic rejoined the Commonwealth, there would no longer be a political reason not to bring up Seventh Fleet as well.

Twelve capital ships had turned the tide of the war without great difficulty.

Thirty would crush the Triumvirate and make it clear that joining the Commonwealth wasn't just the best game in town; it was the *only* game in town.

———

Reality rippled around Walkingstick, and *Saint Michael*'s ongoing violation of conventional physics came to an end in the usual burst of harmless radiation.

"Range to Regina is four-point-five light-minutes," a sensor tech reported.

"Scans are confirming the presence of starships above the planet," another analyst said. "No weapons platforms or new fortifications, just warships."

"Any civilian transport?" Walkingstick asked. The largest possible danger, a surprise that might have led Shirai to feel that he could lie to them, would have been civilian shipping arriving, carrying stored fighters. Fully restocked with parasite craft, the carriers and strike cruisers that made up the bulk of Vanguard's survivors would go from relatively helpless to terrifyingly powerful.

If Shirai had replaced Vanguard Fleet's starfighters, this went from a massacre to an even fight. Walkingstick was confident he would still *win*, but the loss of the sense of weakness would undermine his main plan.

"Just one transport, sir. Looks like it may be the same ship that was at Yellowstar."

Walkingstick nodded. That made sense—with the q-com network restored, Shirai hadn't needed to use the ship as a courier to tell the two surviving members of the Triumvirate what had happened.

"We've resolved hull numbers and identifications," MacGinnis reported. "One *Hercules*, three *Lexingtons*, two *Volcanoes* and four *Oceans*. It's Vanguard Fleet, all right."

She smirked.

"Or what we've left of it, anyway."

"Execute on ops plan Alpha-One," Walkingstick ordered. "Get our fighters into space and spread the fleet out. We need to make it clear to Shirai and his people that we can catch them if they try to run."

"Yes, sir."

It took a few minutes for everything to shake out—more than enough time for the light from their arrival to reach the ships in Regina orbit. Walkingstick didn't have real-time sensor data or communications yet, but it was time to start the game.

"Ready to transmit?" he asked.

"On your order, sir."

"Record."

Walkingstick knew where the holographic pickups and video pickups were and adjusted his posture ever so slightly to give them the best angles. Then he leveled his calmest, most imperial demeanor on the primary pickups.

"Triumvirate warships," he greeted the people he was there to see. "I am Imperator James Calvin Walkingstick, currently commanding the Commonwealth Fifth Fleet and charged by the Star Chamber of the Terran Commonwealth to restore the unity of our fractured nation.

"You are rebels and secessionists... and you have already lost one battle to me. You have received no resupply, no new fighters, no new missiles. I have received all three of these things.

"If you fight, I will destroy you. Since I would prefer to avoid risking damage to Regina or the rest of the Saskatoon System, I am prepared to consider your surrender."

He smiled thinly.

"You have until my bombers reach you to make up your mind."

His message was sent and his fighter strike started moving at the same time. Down to the second.

No one had ever claimed Walkingstick didn't know how to turn battle and politics alike into theater.

———

Until the q-probes were closer and Walkingstick was prepared to risk one as a relay, the round-trip communication between him and Shirai was a bit less than ten minutes. The *actual* response took about twelve, but there were some allowances to be made for Shirai not being solidly in command.

The familiar appearance of the aging Japanese Admiral appeared in the center of Walkingstick's bridge. An interesting gesture, the Imperator recognized—sending the three-dimensional hologram was a gesture of confidence, since he was spending the bandwidth to transit the hologram, but also of an odd weakness.

After all, if Shirai had sent him a video feed, he'd have seen half or more of the man's flag bridge. The three-dimensional hologram only showed the Admiral himself.

"I am Rear Admiral Yan Shirai," Shirai introduced himself. "I served you once, long ago, aboard *Steadfast*. With the death of Admiral Surinder Verity at the hands of you and your allies, the Captains of Vanguard Fleet have accepted me as their commander."

From some of their previous conversations, Walkingstick suspected that it had been a near-run thing. Shirai had *officially* been the second-in-command, but he'd also unquestionably been Verity's man... and most of the surviving ships belonged to Admiral Celestine Morris.

They had a lot of reasons to choose getting back to their pregnant mistress and reinforcing her power base in the Triumvirate over fighting a lost battle.

"While I will not correct the failings of your intelligence," Shirai told them, "I have discussed your offer with my Captains. We are prepared to yield the Saskatoon System without a fight in exchange for free passage back to Triumvirate space.

"No blood need be shed today, Imperator Walkingstick. We await your reply."

The hologram winked out and Walkingstick smiled.

"Admiral MacGinnis," he called softly. "Do we think it's a good idea to let Celestine Morris have her carriers back?"

He suspected that if Vanguard Fleet made it back, even the surviving Verity loyalists would hitch their flags to Morris. If Vanguard Fleet *didn't* make it back, Walkingstick suspected Celestine Morris was swiftly going to find her uterus a more critical piece of her power base than she'd thought.

He had to wonder how Rao had talked the other two members of the Triumvirate into leaving most of *his* ships behind while they sent most of *their* ships into the Republic.

They'd been planning for victory, he supposed. They should have known better.

"I imagine it's not, sir," MacGinnis answered the question. "Carriers without fighters are vulnerable, but Morris and Rao can replace those fighters. Those carriers will never be as vulnerable again—and there are two *Volcano*es over there."

"Thoughts?"

This, too, was theater.

"Those *Volcano*es are worth a lot," MacGinnis observed. "If we can take them intact, that's two modern sixties added to the TCN. *Hrothgar* is more dangerous right now but still worth something if we can take her."

"The *Lexington*s, too, are worth some effort," Walkingstick agreed. "I don't much care for the *Ocean*s either way, but I don't want Morris to get them back."

"What are you thinking, sir?" MacGinnis asked.

"These are crews who followed an Admiral who's now dead," Walkingstick told her. "They followed Verity for loyalty, for pride, for money. They didn't break with the Commonwealth for ideology and principles.

"They broke for money. Now they understand the power of the nation they defied. The navy they deserted. But."

Walkingstick let the word hang in the air.

"But we can use their ships. We might even be able to use *them* and their skills. And if they broke with Terra for loyalty and money, well… Surinder Verity is dead and I have money to spare."

He gave the coms technician a firm nod and leaned forward.

"Admiral Shirai. I remember a precocious young tactical officer by that name," he told the other man. "A man I wouldn't have expected to betray the Commonwealth. You followed Verity. It seems they were good at getting people to follow them.

"But Surinder Verity is dead and the Commonwealth stands. You and your comrades broke from Terra… but Terra endures. The

Commonwealth has not fallen. It is not broken. *It stands* and it calls upon your loyalties once more.

"Lay down your flags. Return to the service of our shared Unity. Bring your ships with you, and we can pretend the last two years never happened."

He smiled.

"And to sweeten the deal, perhaps an ancient Roman tradition: the donative. If the last two years never happened, you are all owed back pay. Recognizing the value of your ships and your skills, I am prepared to pay every spacer, marine and officer five years' salary."

The deal had already been negotiated. The terms the captains would accept had already been set. *Eight* years' salary—what he was actually going to pay—for the crews of ten capital ships was an astonishingly large amount of money… but it was also less than the cost of building *one* capital ship.

It was a price Walkingstick was prepared to pay and one, thanks to Yan Shirai, he knew his soon-to-be-former enemies would accept.

43

"HE... BOUGHT THEM?"

"Exactly," Reynolds confirmed, looking around the senior officers of Task Force Six at Volkov's surprised exclamation. "For eight times the annual salaries of the crews of ten starships, he convinced them all to rejoin the TCN. Ten ships removed from the Triumvirate and added to his own numbers."

"And Saskatoon liberated," James finished. "Which is a win, don't get me wrong, but one more weight on the scales when Walkingstick returns to Weston."

"We'll get there first," his ops officer said. "Everything is in order, and the last of the Marines are coming back aboard the ships tonight. We'll break orbit at about oh two hundred hours, jump to FTL at oh five thirty.

"We'll be back in Weston late on the twelfth."

"Littlebear will be waiting with bated breath," James said with a chuckle. "We didn't leave our diplomat nearly as many people as he'd like. That he knows of."

About half of the meeting clearly didn't know what James meant. Reynolds and Colonel Joshi both very definitely *did* and looked vaguely uncomfortable at his drawing attention to it.

"I'll talk to Vitali before we leave," James continued. "The next stage of this is probably offensive operations, and I frankly don't think *we* need to be involved in that. It's outside the scope of the help we agreed to provide and, unless I missed something, the scope of the alliance Littlebear has been trying to negotiate."

And unless they could get Walkingstick to release the four captured battleships to the Republic, it wasn't like the Republic had the forces for offensive operations on their own. A counterstrike into Triumvirate space was dependent on the Republic having more than the six ships that made up their entire current order of battle.

It would probably be welcomed by the people under the Triumvirate's rule, but James knew the reality: the only force capable of liberating Triumvirate systems from their dictators was the Commonwealth.

And while the Rump Commonwealth was a better deal than the Triumvirate, he wasn't sure that really counted as *liberating*.

"The last of the agreed-upon prisoners are being transferred aboard at nineteen hundred hours," Captain Patricia Jack reminded everyone. "We will be expected to surrender them to civilian Republic constables once we arrive."

"Part of the deal," James agreed with a nod. "We will be the last military personnel with custody of those officers."

The list had consisted of sixteen names in the end. Officers one and all, men and women and others aboard the battleships with the ability and authority to say "I will not obey an illegal order" to orders to bombard civilian targets.

The bitter irony, James knew, was that the *worst* damage—the damage six terraforming ships were working overtime to attempt to repair—was from the only strikes that *hadn't* been war crimes. There was no question that a planetary starfighter base constituted a legitimate military target.

It was the fishing trawler dockyards and shipping sheds, less than a third of which had contained starfighters and all of which had been in cities or towns, that had been illegal targets. *Those* were orders that should have been refused, and the Captains, executive officers and senior tactical personnel should all have refused.

James was honest enough to admit that even in the TCN, that refusal would probably have seen the officers brigged and the orders carried out anyway. But he would have expected at least one of the sixteen officers in question to have at least *tried*.

"The surrender of the ships at Saskatoon only adds to the complications," Volkov said grimly. "That's a *lot* of people who aren't necessarily innocent in the Republic's eyes... but now they're all TCN personnel, per Walkingstick."

"The Imperator is many things," James noted. "But he is *not* an idiot. Those ships are going right back to Commonwealth space, probably with most of his Marines aboard them."

"A lot of his Marines," Joshi said flatly. "Not all. We all know he's going to keep enough Marines to repeat the goddamn Star Chamber if the Republic doesn't capitulate."

"We *fear* that," James corrected. "We do not know. I would like to think better of the Imperator than that."

"You served under him. Had your career shaped by him, by what you shared—and not just a first name," Volkov replied. She sounded hesitant, but James could tell that she was speaking for everyone on his key staff. "You knew him better than any of us, and you give him more credit for all of those reasons.

"But I have to remind you, sir, that Walkingstick *did* land Commonwealth Marines on the Atlantic Elevator Platform. He *did* respond to a summons from the Assembly and Senate of the Terran Commonwealth by seizing control of the Star Chamber.

"And he *did* seize control of the Commonwealth at the point of a thousand rifles. This is not a man you should *think better of*, sir. He has shown the galaxy who he truly is.

"Perhaps, sir, you should believe his actions and not your hopes."

James was silent for a few long seconds. The whole room, a small conference within twenty seconds' run of both the flag and command bridges of the carrier, was silent, as if his people were holding their breath.

"Allow me my false hopes, Young," James finally told Volkov. "I will not let them influence my choices. Regardless of what I think James Walkingstick *was* or *should be*, he *is* the military dictator who overthrew the state I swore to serve.

"We *know* now, beyond a doubt, that Vanguard Fleet danced to his tune for half of this campaign," he continued. While the files they'd acquired from Feldman remained tightly held, his Flag Captain, Fleet CAG, ops officer and Marine CO had all watched them.

"Are we prepared for what that may mean once he returns to Weston?" Yamamoto asked, the CAG speaking for the first time in the meeting. "This is a situation he believes he has complete control over. We have ways to undermine that, but when he is ready to move... he will not take a loss of control lightly."

"We have countermeasures in place," Reynolds said flatly. "We will have *more* countermeasures in place by the time he speaks to Parliament."

"Has that been scheduled yet?" Volkov asked.

"No, but I have enough little birds in place to know he's laying the groundwork." The Chief Crow shrugged. "There will be a grand speech proclaiming his victory.

"I think we all *fear*"—she echoed James's word choice emphatically —"where he is going to take *that*."

———

It didn't look like the last few weeks had been particularly kind to Ace Vitali. The Admiral of the Weston Republic Navy looked utterly exhausted as his office linked to James's for the virtual conference.

"It's... over, basically, isn't it?" he asked James. "What's left of the Triumvirate Navy isn't enough to both maintain their own security and threaten us."

"I don't know if Rao and Morris will sue for peace," James warned. "They didn't exactly officially declare war, either. They just issued an ultimatum and then invaded."

"I'm not sure Parliament would *accept* peace," Vitali said. "There is a lot being said over that ultimatum, Tecumseh. Treacherous neighbors, perfidious monsters. There are a lot of angry words being exchanged on our news networks and on the floor of Maple Hall.

"And yet I, more than anyone else alive, I suspect, am all too aware of the weakness of our Navy. Not just the lack of material strength. You saw."

"I saw," James allowed. "But there is only one way to get past that weakness, Admiral Vitali. The Republic Navy must survive. Grow. Learn. Experience can be made up for with enough training and practice, to a point, at least."

"You wouldn't take our Navy to war if you had a choice, would you?" Vitali asked.

"You don't go to war with the navy you'd choose; you go to war with the navy you *have*," James said, the quote rolling off his tongue far too neatly. "Left to my choices, Admiral, I'd never go to war. I think we've both seen enough of it by now."

"I served through the Rimward War and enough other bloody messes to never wear a uniform again," Vitali said grimly. "But De Clerc asked, so here I am. I'm too damned old for this, Tecumseh."

"I don't think anyone is ever the *right* age for a war of any kind," James replied. "No, Vitali, you are the man your nation has. And if you think you can't fight this war, you need to tell your Cabinet and your Parliament that.

"And they need to trust you."

"Our politics are complicated. More so than an outsider sees, let alone understands," Vitali told him. "My nation was born of an alliance between political reformers and the very megacorporations they wanted reforms to protect *against*.

"They cleaned up the military officers the reformists feared, but we still need a Navy, so suddenly, all of my officers were corporate mercs." Vitali shook his head. "I think the reformers might have trusted us *more* if we'd kept the old TCN senior officers, and *they* were the ones who wanted to be rid of them.

"I'm six months from a fleet of carriers that could withstand any threat, Tecumseh, but I never told you that," Vitali warned. "I don't have the crews or the pilots I'd want for that fleet, but we've got the hulls and we've sourced the Class One mass manipulators.

"The *Bonaventure*s will be physically complete in six months. I can't even guess when they'll be *combat*-ready, but I fear the only way we'll find out is the hard way."

"You know as well as my people do what Walkingstick is going to say when he gets back to Weston," James murmured.

"That would solve the problem with crewing *Bonaventure* and her sisters, wouldn't it?" Vitali observed wryly. "Of course, *you* don't want a dozen seventy-million-cubic-meter warships joining Walkingstick's fleet, do you?"

"My biases and priorities aren't Weston's," James conceded. "I don't necessarily want the Rump—the Imperial Commonwealth, as you call it—to fall, either. I just want them to recognize that they aren't the Old Commonwealth."

"Maybe they should be," Vitali said. "Maybe now that the q-coms are back up, we *can* rebuild and reintegrate. How much of the Commonwealth has to sign back up for Walkingstick to put away the eagle and become just another Admiral?"

"It's not that simple. We both know it's not that simple. Sulla thought he was saving the Roman Republic, after all. It almost doesn't *matter* whether James Walkingstick means everything he says and does everything he says he will.

"What matters is that he has told future Commonwealth Admirals that the Imperatorship *exists* and can be seized. The Commonwealth you and I swore to serve died the moment that became true."

The other Admiral was silent for at least twenty seconds.

"I know," he conceded. "But I am sworn to serve the Parliament of the Weston Republic now. They will make their choice and I will abide. I am neither inclined to become a dictator nor to keep fighting, if I am frank.

"I am very, very tired, James Tecumseh. But you want something, not just the minutiae and administration discussions of your journey here and what happens when you arrive. I don't disagree with your suspicion of the next stage in Walkingstick's plan, but…"

Vitali stared blankly off into space for a few more seconds, then sighed.

"To the victor go the spoils, Tecumseh, and Walkingstick has won the day for us," he told James. "He has smashed the Triumvirate's Vanguard Fleet and liberated our star systems. The loss of Tawfiq's task force only makes his point stronger.

"We need the Commonwealth."

"Even if everything you just said was theater?"

Vitali's silence was less exhausted this time. More... frozen. He didn't know what James meant, but James could *see* in his eyes the horrified suspicion.

"What do you mean?"

"I..." James trailed off in thought, then swallowed and nodded. "I am going to send you a series of secured files. They *cannot* be widely distributed; the very fate of your Republic may depend on it.

"But I need you to watch them and understand the *truth* of the events of the last month. And I need you to give those files to the best cybertechnicians you have, Admiral Vitali, because I *need* you to know, beyond any doubt, that I am not deceiving you."

"I'm going to hate you, aren't I?" Vitali asked, the exhaustion in his voice bone-crushing. "I'm going to hate someone else *more*, I suspect, but I wanted an easy answer. I *had* an easy answer. And you're taking that away from me, aren't you?"

"I can't apologize, Admiral Vitali. I can't give you an apology I don't mean," James said levelly. "All I can give you is the truth."

"Damn you, James Tecumseh. Send me your files. Confirm, then, the fears I'd buried as the whispers of angry ghosts."

44

"MEMBERS of the Weston Republic Parliament, I give you the Liberator of Saskatoon and Yellowstar: Imperator James Calvin Walkingstick!"

Walkingstick wasn't *quite* up to arranging trumpets to accompany his entrance into the main Parliament Chamber in Maple Hall, but the crescendo of applause that met the announcement of his arrival more than made up for it.

A pair of Parliamentary Constables, unarmed security officers, led him along the green-carpeted artificial gully between the two rows of seats that ascended back to the east and west. The Republic governed over fourteen billion human beings, and he suspected many felt the fourteen hundred–odd MPs gathered around him weren't *enough* to truly represent those people.

He was the center of attention today as he walked toward where Prime Minister May De Clerc waited for him at the end of the hall. It was Speaker Gregers Anker who'd introduced him, a broad-in-every-way man standing behind the raised podium at the north end of the Chamber.

There was a clear section for "guest" seating in front of the podium, and Walkingstick would have preferred most of the two benches' occupants be somewhere else. Ace Vitali was seated at the far eastern side, with President Frey and a bodyguard east of him. On the western side, James Tecumseh had the far seat, with Envoy Ma'tano Littlebear and a suited civilian woman Walkingstick assumed was an aide to Littlebear next to him.

De Clerc was standing at the base of the stairs to the podium waiting for him. Her seat was on the western side of the Chamber as an elected Member of Parliament, after all.

"Imperator," she said, bowing slightly. "You wished to address Maple Hall. We await your news."

He smiled and returned the slight bow, following her gesture toward the stairs and up to the dais. Anker stood aside, clearing his way to the lectern and the center point of several million dollars of acoustic equipment.

Recording pickups were focused on him from every angle. Everything that took place in the Parliament Chamber of Maple Hall was recorded, broadcast live to the six worlds of the Weston Republic via the rebuilt q-com network.

We have control of the broadcast. Misra's words were silent, sounding only in Walkingstick's implant. *Shouldn't be necessary, but we can shut down the transmission on your order.*

And the fallback plan?

That's more with Brigadier Hall. The spy's mental voice was sardonic. They both knew they had the information to hand. *One battalion on the ground with concealable gear. Two more standing by within five minutes' action.*

The rest on the ships. That was a problem. Even now, even having liberated a third of the Republic from their enemies, the Republic hadn't allowed him to bring his ships into planetary orbit. They at least hadn't let the *Dakotans* into orbit, either, which put the two fleets orbiting Weston itself, ten light-seconds behind Galen.

And exactly six light-seconds apart. *That* range had been arranged *very* carefully. Against anything except the Confederacy's single *Da Vinci*–class battlecruiser, *Saint Michael* and the *Hercules*'s one-point-five-megaton lances had a range of, well, a touch over six light-seconds or more.

Surprise would be key if it came to that, but Walkingstick had arranged everything. He was there to *ask* for what he wanted, but he had set things up for if people decided to say no.

When the Commonwealth called for its debts to be paid, after all, *no* wasn't an acceptable answer.

———

"Members of the Parliament of the Weston Republic," Walkingstick began, projecting his voice such that he didn't need the audio equipment aimed at the podium. "Guests from other powers. Citizenry of the Weston Republic."

He smiled and raised his hand palm-up. Some parts of oratory never truly changed.

"You know me." It was barely egotistical to say that, given that he'd been formally introduced on entering Maple Hall's Parliament Chamber. "I speak for Terra and the Terran Commonwealth. I am a soldier, first and foremost, tasked to guard the battered boundaries of the nation we all once called home.

"I also act, at the charge of the Star Chamber of the Interstellar Congress of the Terran Commonwealth, as Imperator: the voice and symbol of our unity in these difficult times. Yet, as I am but a soldier, when the call came from the Weston Republic for aid, *my* answer was clear:

"These people turned aside from Terra. They betrayed the oaths they swore to us. What did we owe to them?"

He let that accusation hang in the air, then smiled softly.

"But I know that I am only a soldier, so when others spoke, I listened," he told the Parliament. "For they asked me an important question: *whose oaths matter to Terra?* The oaths of the worlds of our diaspora, stretched to the breaking point by the pressures and horrors of the darkest of times?

"Or *our* oaths? The oaths of the Star Chamber and the Terran

Commonwealth Navy… and of the Imperator? The oaths *we* swore to protect *all* of the Commonwealth, not just the core sectors?"

Silence again, and he knew every ear in the immense room was hanging on his words.

"Our oaths were what mattered. The worlds of the far sectors might have broken faith with us, but *we* were the Commonwealth. *Our* will was unbroken. *Our* faith, unbroken.

"The worlds of the Weston Sector felt it necessary to secede to see to their own safety in this dark hour. They broke their oaths to Terra and the Commonwealth."

His accusation was very broadly aimed. He could have named specific names—seventy percent of the forty-five members of the First Weston Constitutional Convention were in this room as MPs. Eighty-three percent of the three hundred members of the Second.

All too many of the politicians and bureaucrats who had betrayed the Commonwealth were in this room.

"But you were not alone in this," he allowed. "The Commonwealth teetered in the wake of the Alliance of Free Stars' vicious attack on our interstellar communication infrastructure. We wavered, and many of the sectors wavered into secession.

"And even those of us on Terra, whose faith and will remained unbroken, understood that this was not truly treason. With the communications network gone, with the deployment patterns for security task forces in tatters, the outer sectors *needed* to look to their own security.

"But we believed—*we believe!*—that this security would always have been best served by a unified front, by a Terran Commonwealth that never fractured. Never broke."

He lowered his hand and shook his head sadly.

"And if I were to honor the oaths we swore and the beliefs we held, then there could be only one answer when Weston came to us for help," he told them. "If the Terran Commonwealth was to be what it should always have been, we needed to *prove* our truth. To you.

"To prove our unbroken faith in our shared dream, our shared nation."

Walkingstick waited a few more seconds, then leaned forward, grasping the sides of the podium.

"Members of the Parliament of the Weston Republic, it is my duty and my privilege to report to you that the Triumvirate fleet has been driven from your stars," he told them. "Mere hours ago, the last hold-outs of the landing forces on Saskatoon Two—Moose—laid down their arms after a thirty-six-hour bombardment by artillery detachments of the Terran Marine Corps.

"Your stars are once more free from the threat of invasion and conquest. Those warlords and traitorous Navy officers who brought violence, fire and bloodshed to your worlds have been defeated: killed or captured.

"Unto you, once citizens of the Commonwealth I serve, *I*, James Calvin Walkingstick, have delivered victory."

He made as if to continue speaking, but he was *expecting* the crescendo of applause that answered that. He'd primed them with fear, with the reminder that he had come even when he perhaps shouldn't have. He'd readied them, in many ways, for *bad* news—even though every person in the room knew what news he *was* delivering.

"*Once* citizens," he repeated. "*Former* citizens. This is the choice you and your people made. But when the darkness came for you, you came back to us. The Commonwealth answered your call in your time of need.

"In exchange, I demand nothing. I *ask* that you consider this: what happens the next time a warlord or outside invader arrives on your doorstep? What happens if the Triumvirate does not sue for peace and, in a year or two, their fleets return to conquer you again?

"Will you call to Terra for aid once more? Will you lean, *again*, on a bond you repudiated? I promise you your call will be *heard*... but as the Commonwealth struggles to manage the conflicts around us with far-reduced resources, I cannot promise it will be answered."

This time, his pause was filled with shouts and arguments and objections, and he held up a hand to silence them.

"We will hear you if you call and we will, if we can, answer," he promised. "But there is a way to make certain the Terran Commonwealth Navy stands ready to defend you, against any enemy at any time! A way to make any possible foe quail from the thought of *ever* risking these stars.

"You know the answer, in your heart of hearts. There is only one way to guarantee you stand behind the shield of the Commonwealth Navy, and it is truly very simple.

"I do not demand anything," he repeated. "But I would ask this Parliament to consider coming home. To lay down the flags and ceremonies wrapped around an action taken of fear of the dark.

"Rejoin the Commonwealth, citizens of the Weston Sector, and no enemy will ever dare threaten your skies again. On *that*, you have my word."

45

THE CHAOS on the benches of the Parliament Chamber had to be heard to be believed. James had been expecting it, though, and he glanced past Reynolds to meet Ma'tano Littlebear's eyes.

"We're ready," the diplomat said softly, backing up his words with a silent implant message to make sure it got through. "I don't know how he'll take it."

Littlebear jerked his head up to where Walkingstick still stood at the podium like some kind of conquering angel.

"You or me?" James asked.

"Has to be you," Littlebear told him. "Most of them know the pitch. But today, at this moment, it has to be you."

"Okay."

James sent a silent message up to Speaker Anker, who had been waiting for it.

"Excuse me, excuse me," Anker bellowed. "I *will* have decorum and I *will* have the silence of the Chamber!"

The Speaker didn't *quite* elbow Walkingstick out of the way, but James suspected he'd made the Imperator jump more than the man had expected.

"It is a very... daring statement that Imperator Walkingstick has laid before this Chamber," Anker said slowly. "One with many implications that I suspect many of us would like to bury in committee for, oh, a couple of human lifetimes."

The Speaker's humor seemed to calm the gathered representatives.

"Apologies, Imperator Walkingstick," he addressed the Terran man as Walkingstick tried to step forward again. "We have another request to speak to the Chamber, one that I feel will be relevant to all of our thoughts in response to your... *request for consideration.*"

Anker waved James up, gesturing him to the big man's left as part of the stage *split.* New platforms rose out of the speaker's dais, revolving out to create two platforms clearly intended to face each other while still allowing speech to the Chamber.

James nodded to the Speaker and strode up to the eastern platform, leaning on a lifetime of experience of starships to avoid even the tiniest hint of surprise as a full duplicate of the main dais and podium the Speaker now occupied unfolded around him.

"Thank you, Speaker," he said loudly once he was sure enough of the system was online for his words to be carried across the Chamber —and, for that matter, the entire Republic.

He suspected that more people than usual were tuned into the live feed of Parliament's deliberations today.

"You should all know," James began, "that Imperator Walkingstick and I go back a *long* way. Much of my career has been on ships under his command, and I will, unhesitatingly, give him credit for saving my TCN career at least twice when I chose honor over the perhaps military *expedient* course of action."

Walkingstick hadn't yet been directed onto the western platform, he noted as he met his old mentor's gaze and gave the other man a nod of respect. Whatever had happened between them, James would never begrudge the acknowledgement of what he *owed* Walkingstick.

Turning his gaze back to the rest of the Chamber, he realized the Imperator was actually being physically *blocked* from taking the western platform, a solidly built Parliamentary Constable standing in front of the access and watching Walkingstick impassively.

"That part of my past career is not as much common knowledge, of course, as what has occupied my last three years," he said with a wry smile. "I believe, though even now I cannot be certain, that the Dakotan Interstellar Confederacy may have been the first of the Successor States to take formal shape.

"I *know* that we were the first to deliver a Declaration of Independence to the floor of the Star Chamber of the Terran Commonwealth. I speak to you today as someone who has walked the same path you walked. But where Weston *chose* this path, Dakota found it forced upon us.

"Forced upon us *by* Imperator Walkingstick." He shrugged. "I won't bore you with the details. You know or can easily learn them. Important, though, is that when our delegation delivered our Declaration of Independence on the floor of the Star Chamber, *Walkingstick ordered them arrested.*"

He let that hang.

"Those representatives," he said quietly, relying on the audio equipment to carry his words through the Chamber, "have never been released. Some of them are bureaucrats who were intended to negotiate the details of long-term trade and diplomatic negotiations. Many were people like the Members of this Parliament, elected to speak for the star systems they represented.

"And for *daring* to honor the wishes of the people who elected them, the Representatives and Senators of the Dakota and Meridian Sectors were thrown into prison, and our attempts to negotiate their freedom have been ignored."

James paused, genteelly ignoring the shouted calls and complaints as he surveyed the Parliament.

"That is the *faith* Walkingstick speaks of," he reminded them all. "To him, faith is to be kept with the Commonwealth. There is no other course. The Commonwealth cannot fail. It cannot *have* failed. Its disintegration in the wake of the Alliance attack can only be a result of treason and Alliance saboteurs."

He smiled thinly.

"Who in this room was an Alliance saboteur?" James asked. "I won't ask who is a traitor—by the standards of the Commonwealth, I think everyone here *except* Imperator Walkingstick is a traitor.

"Democracy. Freedom. Justice. Unity," he echoed. "Four simple words. Four simple pillars on which our forefathers built a nation that endured over half a millennium.

"A nation that, by the time the Alliance struck its death blow, was rotten from within."

James *had* to pause now, as the angry shouts—agreeing and disagreeing alike—filled the hall while Speaker Anker demanded order.

And Imperator Walkingstick glared daggers at him.

"*We know this,*" he told them. "The Weston Republic was born from *preexisting* political movements, ones that recognized and struggled against the clear guardrails present in the Commonwealth's democracy. So long as you played by Terra's rules, you had a voice. If you broke those rules, you were broken.

"You know this," he echoed, and he could *feel* the chill silence as memory took hold in the room. "And Weston was a mid sector, not on the borders. You weren't worlds conquered by the Commonwealth Navy within living memory.

"I have walked those worlds," he told them. "I knew then what our campaign for Unity cost. I should have known then that that cost *could not be borne*. Not forever. The fall of the q-com network was the blow, but the lines along which we fractured already existed."

The silence was fading now, but he still had the Chamber's attention—and could *feel* Walkingstick still glaring daggers at him. Only the looming presence of the Constables—three more had appeared silently on the Speaker's dais near Walkingstick—seemed to be keeping him contained.

Or perhaps James was only seeing what he expected to see.

"Imperator Walkingstick has asked you to rejoin the Commonwealth," James told them. "I have… an alternative suggestion. The Weston Republic is far from helpless. The Dakotan Confederacy wields significant power of our own. The current Commonwealth, whatever we want to call it, remains a valued neighbor and one we would gladly call friend.

"Others: the Emerald Commonwealth, the Kipling Directorate, the Colina Republic, the Icon Sector—and a dozen single-system nations who feel vulnerable but are prepared to *fight* for the independence they have gained. The Successor States of the Commonwealth are no longer *flags and ceremonies wrapped around an action taken of fear of the dark.*"

He echoed Walkingstick's words with intent and knew he'd landed a hit.

"We share a common heritage and a common dream," he reminded them all. "But we broke apart and away for good reasons. I know Ma'tano Littlebear has spoken to many of you about this—and other Envoys of the Confederacy are present in capitals across the Old Commonwealth, raising the same concept.

"We can no longer be one nation. We perhaps never *should* have been. But that does not mean we cannot keep the faith of that old ideal." He gestured around him. "This is not my home, but officers and spacers under my command died to protect it.

"Weston called for aid. Terra and Dakota answered. If we lay the groundwork and treaties for a grand alliance, then, as the Alliance of Free Stars guards their worlds without ever imposing rule on any nation, we can engage in shared security while guarding our individual sovereignties."

He raised his hands.

"We can recognize the realities of today while keeping faith with the dreams of yesterday. We do not need to lay down our flags and the nations born in sacrifice. We *can* stand together. Dakota will stand with you."

Unspoken, of course, was that Dakota was arguably still *at war* with the Terran Commonwealth. No war was declared, so it could be argued they were at peace, too... but no war had been declared before the Terran Expeditionary Fleet had invaded Dakota.

If the Weston Republic rejoined the Commonwealth, Dakota would *not* be coming to their aid in the future. From the rumblings throughout the Chamber, many of the MPs realized that—but it was Admiral Ace Vitali who rose.

"The Speaker recognizes Admiral Vitali, Chief Naval Officer of the Weston Republic," Anker declared loudly.

Instead of generating a new platform for Vitali, a swarm of drones descended on the Admiral. Clearly, this was how the MPs would normally speak in the Chamber, as a holographic projection of the old Weston officer appeared on the south end of the Chamber of Parliament.

"Both of you speak of paths forward," the Admiral declared. "Walkingstick speaks of old oaths and promises kept. Tecumseh speaks of new futures, sovereignty maintained and *new* oaths and promises.

"Yet I must speak to the challenge being raised by dozens if not more of our esteemed members of parliament. Admiral Tecumseh, when *you* met the Triumvirate's Vanguard Fleet... you ran. You forced Admiral Tawfiq to retreat and yield the Yellowstar System to our enemies.

"It was only in company with Imperator Walkingstick's fleet that you returned—and it was under *Walkingstick's* command that Vanguard Fleet was defeated.

"The Commonwealth, many here feel, has proven the worth of its word," Vitali reminded him. "But while your fleet has contributed, yes, there are many who will say that the Commonwealth would have saved us *without you*."

Walkingstick had stepped up to stand next to Speaker Anker and was whispering fiercely.

"Admiral Tecumseh, do you have an answer for Admiral Vitali?" Anker asked, not quite ignoring the Imperator.

"War is not a neat and simple thing," James said. "Admiral Tawfiq understood that. We withdrew from Yellowstar because ten ships could not fight eighteen. With the Commonwealth ships, well... *twenty* ships can fight eighteen.

"But if the Commonwealth had not been here? How many ships were here in Weston, Admiral Vitali, that would have joined us to retake Yellowstar?"

"Six," Vitali said instantly. He *probably* shouldn't have had a microphone, James knew, but Anker was finding some fascinating ways to play favorites.

"Sixteen ships, backed by the starfighters of Mackenzie Valley Station and the surface bases on Ulu and Imaq, *would* have been able to fight Vanguard Fleet," James told the Chamber. "Imperator Walkingstick won the Battle of Yellowstar, yes—but if he *hadn't* been there, *Admiral Vitali* would have."

There was a lot more shouting now, and James couldn't even make sense of what the sides in the argument were. Some were pro-Commonwealth, some were pro-alliance, some were simply pro-Vitali —or just anti-Commonwealth.

"The Speaker recognizes the Imperator of Terra, James Walkingstick," Anker said, finally gesturing the Constable aside and allowing Walkingstick to stride up to the platform facing James. Similar audio equipment now surrounded both men, though James suspected Anker had tight control over who could speak and whether it was transmitted.

The hologram of Vitali shrank into nothingness as the Weston Admiral was seated, leaving the two foreign officers to challenge each other across an open void of space.

"You have always been naïve, James Tecumseh," Walkingstick said, his tone surprisingly gentle for the daggers he had been glaring earlier. "How many of those *other nations* you speak of answered Weston's call?

"Look around you. You and I alone, of all of those who could have answered the call, kept faith with Weston. And you, my all-too-young friend, have *always* chosen honor over sense. The first time I know of that you *didn't* was to withdraw from Yellowstar."

That wasn't as true as Walkingstick hoped, James suspected, but it was true enough. *More* than true enough for the moment, and he could almost feel the balance in the Chamber shifting back toward the Commonwealth.

"And how many died on Ulu and Imaq for that choice?" Walkingstick asked, his words sending a chill through the Parliament—and a spike of nearly uncontrollable anger down James's spine.

James *knew* who had set that in motion now, and only years of command and the absolute *need* to say the right things kept his lips sealed in that moment.

"The truth is simple: the Republic owes a debt not easily paid to the Commonwealth," Walkingstick continued. "You should never have seceded, but when you called, we came anyway. We have shed blood, fought together and liberated worlds together.

"I ask you to stand with us again, to acknowledge the debt and pay it in the only coin spendable amongst brothers: that of family and family bonds."

There was no visible sign that James Tecumseh had an active microphone again, but he knew and he leaned forward as he searched for the controls he needed.

"A debt," he whispered, allowing the audio equipment to carry his soft words through the hall. "Because, of course, it wasn't Fifth Fleet that found itself ambushed by the entire strength of Vanguard Fleet. Because, of course, the starfighters that would have rendered Fifth Fleet's contributions lesser were gone by the time you arrived, murdered alongside tens of thousands of innocents.

"Has anyone in this Chamber *not* wondered why everything seemed to work out so neatly for Imperator Walkingstick? I could argue that it was my and Tawfiq's withdrawal from Yellowstar that truly delivered victory against Vanguard Fleet, but that's not the point, is it?"

He turned his gaze to Anker, ignoring Walkingstick's momentary confusion.

"Speaker, may I have permission to play a recording that has come into my possession?" he asked.

"Granted."

James linked into the holographic projectors and activated the same diorama of the conjoined offices that Feldman had sent him to prove the worth of his intelligence. It was even the same recording, though from much later in the conversation.

Of course, on the holographic projectors of the Chamber of Parliament of the Weston Republic, the figures of Walkingstick and Shirai were basically life-size.

"*Timing is going to be everything,*" Walkingstick declared loudly, pulling the attention of every eye in the Chamber. "*Verity is going to lose. I suspect their intelligence has already told you and them the odds you're up against. The moment the Commonwealth answered the Republic's call for aid, the Triumvirate had already lost.*

"The trick, from my perspective, is to make that loss work for the Commonwealth. Most importantly, we need to neutralize the Confederacy — and I know where Tecumseh's fleet is going to be."

Angry and confused rumblings began to echo through the Chamber, but James kept the recording playing. He'd been tempted to edit this section down for length, but playing the full unabridged sections was key.

He needed, after all, to be very clear about the truth of what he was showing.

"They're delayed by organizational matters, so they will be leaving Weston in roughly twenty-four hours," Walkingstick's past self declared. *"If Verity leaves for Yellowstar inside the next few hours, they will be in position to ambush Tecumseh on his arrival. There will be a ten-ship force of mixed Confederacy and Republic units that you will be able to defeat in detail."*

"Verity is good," the Triumvirate officer replied. James figured half the room knew who Yan Shirai was—and the *rest* recognized the uniform of Verity's personal fleet. *"If you let them isolate ten ships, they're going to get pounded."*

"That's the hope, yes," the hologram of Walkingstick confirmed. *"Then you're going to pass their exact plans to me, and we're going to return the favor."*

Angry shouting overran the room until Anker slammed a physical gavel on his microphone, the augmented crash silencing everyone.

"Imperator Walkingstick was in communication with key members of Vanguard Fleet's command staff from before he left Weston," James said calmly. "And since the Imperator wishes to hang the dead from Verity's orbital strikes on me, I have one more recording to play."

"Play it," Anker ordered, even as Walkingstick tried to shout something—and James realized that the same audio equipment that could *project* sounds could also, it turned out, *muffle* them.

The diorama flickered. It was clear that it wasn't the same recording, but it was the same two offices and the same two men.

"For our purposes, the Republic's fighter forces are entirely *expendable,"*

Walkingstick's past self condemned him in his own words. *"If we get you the locations of those fighters, will Verity be able to move on them?"*

"Aye," Shirai confirmed. *"It can't be too perfect—they'll get suspicious —but if we can even narrow it down to two thousand docks that might hold those four hundred–odd fighters, I think I can talk them into the strikes. Those will only hold us up for a few hours, though."*

"Then you need to convince Verity that the destruction of the StarHydro facilities at Mackenzie will be just as crippling to the Republic as the loss of the ships under construction in Scotia," Walkingstick replied before James let the recording end.

"Imperator James Calvin Walkingstick provided Surinder Verity with the intelligence that led to the orbital strikes on Ulu and Imaq," James said loudly. "He arranged for their staff to convince them to destroy the Mackenzie Valley Station and the attached refinery facilities—half a *century* of investment.

"Every aspect of this war since he arrived in Weston has been choreographed, designed and controlled. Admiral Tawfiq was provoked and manipulated, needled in every meeting until the only option to regain his honor in his mind was a suicide charge into the heart of Vanguard Fleet."

He spread his hands.

"*This* is the man who speaks to you of *debt*, Members of Parliament. The very blood he claims debt for, *he* arranged to shed. And if you hesitate to believe the data I have provided... Admiral Vitali?"

The drones swarmed the Weston officer again, and his holographic self looked *exhausted* as he gazed at the Members of Parliament.

"Admiral Tecumseh provided us with the files in question a week ago," Vitali admitted. "His desire was for us to confirm, beyond *any* doubt, that the files were correct, original and unedited. He has unquestionably chosen *inflammatory* pieces... but the recordings are true.

"And there is no context to excuse what was said and arranged."

James was about to challenge Walkingstick directly when a moment of feedback tore through the system, leaving him cringing back as the piercing sound silenced everyone.

And then Reynolds' voice sounded silently in his head.

System-wide broadcast cut off the moment you started playing the hologram, she hissed. *Walkingstick just took control of the whole damn A/V system—I guess he wasn't expecting to need that, but right now, the Imperator owns every computer built into this fucking room!*

46

Surprise and shock had turned to determination and a burning anger like Walkingstick had rarely experienced in his life. He wasn't sure *how* Tecumseh had acquired those recordings, but he had to assume—had to *hope*—they'd been sourced from Shirai's side.

If the carrot and the leash weren't enough, then the stick and the sword remained.

"You won't believe me if I tell you those recordings are lies," he proclaimed as Misra's people gave him full control of the Chamber's systems. The holographic projectors now created an illusory duplicate of him at the other end of the chamber, easily ten meters tall. He hadn't expected to need control of the Chamber's internal systems—but he hadn't expected the degree to which Speaker Anker had clearly been ready to subtly but firmly limit his ability to argue back.

He now realized that Anker, like Vitali—and probably Frey and De Clerc!—had seen those recordings. To *him*, they weren't as damning as the Westons seemed to be taking them... but he'd admit they looked bad.

"I have a duty," he told them. "To protect the Commonwealth. The true Commonwealth. What you call the *Old Commonwealth*, like the nation we fought and bled and died for is already gone. Already on the dump heap of history.

"I spent my entire adult life fighting for Unification. Knowing—not believing, *knowing*—that we brought the light of civilization and prosperity with us. Knowing that the worlds we brought into Unity were better for it.

"And then people like you and like James Tecumseh *shattered* that Unity. Faced with a momentary bump in the road, you betrayed *everything* we of the Navy fought and sacrificed for."

He glared around the room, knowing that the holographic image of him at the other end of the Chamber would do the same.

"But when you found another momentary bump in the road, when you struggled to meet the barriers your own choices created, you came crawling back to us. And the very ideals I fought for demanded that we help you."

He growled in the back of his throat, letting the excellent audio equipment *fill* the room with his anger.

"So, yes, we came to help you and to convince you to come home. And yes, there were choices made of cold pragmatism to turn you in that direction. But your childish naivety cannot be afforded anymore. The Commonwealth *must* be reunified.

"A debt is owed. Of honor and blood and faith—and even treasure. The Republic has always been a lie, built on the sacrifices of the Commonwealth and resources *stolen* from the Commonwealth.

"That debt *must* be paid. The time for childish games is over. This Chamber could have returned to the fold of your own free will and everyone would have benefited... but to deny the debt owed, to seek a path beyond that which is inevitable and necessary... That will not be permitted."

Updates suddenly slammed into his implant feed as the Marines made their move. He'd sealed the galleries when he'd started speaking this time, and half of the people inside the security systems were *his* people.

His people were moving—but even *he* was surprised when the first gunshots echoed through Maple Hall. The Parliamentary Constables, it turned out, were *not* as unarmed as they looked.

"We are all trapped in here now," he told them. "My Marines are coming. This only ends one way now. The surrender of your ships, your stations and your worlds—the correct and necessary return of the Weston Sector to the fold of the Commonwealth."

"And if we refuse?" Speaker Anker snarled. He apparently still had enough control to activate his own microphone.

"What part of what I just said suggested this was a discussion or a request?" Walkingstick replied. The doors behind his holographic counterpart at the other end of the room *exploded* inward as if to accentuate his ultimatum.

Except that instead of the steady ranks of armed Marines he was *expecting* to march through the door, he saw the rapid fire and maneuver of Marines under pressure. Lacking armor or any weapons they couldn't conceal, the Marines he had infiltrated into the building were unusually lightly armed—though selected from the more heavily *augmented* members of the battalions aboard his ships.

And while they weren't *losing*, they certainly hadn't secured control of Maple Hall as quickly or easily as he'd expected. The Constables had apparently been equally armed with concealable weapons… and, from the accuracy of the fire as they pushed his Marines into the Chamber of Parliament, equally *augmented*.

"Maybe the fact where your Marines are having their treacherous asses kicked by Parliamentar—"

Walkingstick hadn't shot the Speaker himself, but he would have if he'd thought of it. A squad of Marines had emerged from one of the more covert entrances into the Parliament Chamber, moving up to secure the Imperator as one of them ended Anker's traitorous proclamations forever.

Half of those Marines were dead before they'd dealt with the Constables around the main dais, and Walkingstick forced himself to control his expressions. Everything he did was still being duplicated at five times scale at the other end of the Chamber, even as the Members of Parliament bolted from the main entrance and the ongoing battle.

Second wave arriving, his Marine CO said grimly in his head. *We now have heavy weapons and armor. The Constables are better than we expected, vets to a one for all that our data says only two in ten are Marines.*

Their reaction force is moving, but I think we'll cut them off before they get to you. We'll hold, but reinforcements from on high might be more necessary than we expected.

"End this bloodshed, President Frey," Walkingstick said to the President as he lowered the platform toward where his Marines had secured the Weston leadership. "You can order this all to end."

"So can you," Frey said flatly, ignoring Walkingstick to stare at the slumped corpse of Speaker Anker. "This is all your doing and your choice. It ends on your word."

"I have a duty," Walkingstick declared.

"So do I." Frey glared back at him.

"It's not going to end the way you think," Admiral Tecumseh said softly.

Walkingstick had half-forgotten Tecumseh was even *there*. He'd kept the other man's platform locked in place, five meters in the air with no safe exit, and now he looked up at the other Native American man.

"Your fleet is outgunned and in range of mine," Walkingstick pointed out. "The order for their surrender is already going out. It's over, Tecumseh, and the sooner you and yours lay down your arms, the easier it's going to be for everyone."

"Nothing here is as you believe it is," Tecumseh told him. "Your Marines are not the avenging angels of justice. Nor are they the only force coming to relieve Maple Hall. Your fleet isn't the unstoppable armada you think it is. *You* are not the paladin of righteousness you think you are.

"All of this is on your hands. The blood you have shed will *never* be worth it. Everything you try to reclaim, you taint with the death you inflict in the trying.

"In trying to take Weston by force, you have already failed."

The updates Walkingstick was receiving from his Marines were a *lot* more reassuring than Tecumseh's fiercely calm words. The Constables' rapid reaction force *had* been intercepted by his Marines, and while Misra's people didn't *yet* have control of the Hall's defenses, they'd made sure no one else did.

"My people are a long way from failure, James Tecumseh, and like Frey... you would be better served by orderi—"

He didn't even recognize the sound at first. A strange canine *yipping*, projected from powerful speakers that he realized had to be attached to assault shuttles. Not *his* assault shuttles.

No TCMC assault shuttle was rigged to broadcast the yipping of a hunting coyote at maximum volume!

47

"ADMIRAL YAMAMOTO, we need you on the flag bridge *now*."

Anthony's usual battle station wasn't on the flag bridge—as the Fleet CAG, he was supposed to be in Fleet Starfighter Control. It took him a good several seconds to remember *why* he'd be getting summoned to the flag bridge.

James Tecumseh was on the planetary surface, and Vice Admiral Anthony Yamamoto was senior to Rear Admiral Young Volkov. That meant he was the senior officer aboard Task Force Six and put *him* in command.

"I'm on my way," he told the officer who'd contacted him. "*My* office is farther than the Admiral's; brief me as I move."

An overlay dropped onto his vision as he crossed to his door. In theory, there was nothing stopping him from virtually accessing the flag bridge and commanding the battle group from there—nothing except the risk of losing connection and the fact that people worked better when they could see each other, at least!

As he walked briskly toward the command center, the overlay

picked up the assorted tactical and informational feeds that the flag bridge would provide, and Anthony caught at least one of the problems immediately.

"Fifth Fleet has been carefully and quietly adjusting their orbits since they were slotted in," Volkov told him, the operations officer taking over for her staff. "I think they thought they were being sneaky, but we were keeping an eye on them all along.

"Range is now six light-seconds, pretty much exactly. We're all still three million klicks from Galen, but one-point-eight million klicks is the standard range for a *Saint*'s positron lances versus, oh, a *Volcano*-class carrier's electromagnetic deflectors."

"Did they really think we wouldn't notice?" Anthony asked.

"Everything was *supposed* to be all diplomatic at this point," she replied. "Fifth Fleet are theoretically our damn allies—or at least *Weston*'s allies."

"But if they take us out, that makes a point to the Republic without attacking Republic assets," Anthony said grimly. "And they're in range of everybody but *Iroquois*."

Project Hustle had included an impressive arrangement of new electromagnetic deflectors in all of their new ships. So, *Iroquois*, the shiniest and newest battlecruiser for a lot of light-years in any given direction, would be shielded from the Terran beams at notably closer ranges than anyone else.

"And what are they doing right now?" Anthony asked.

"Drifting toward us at about two hundred klicks a second—but we just lost contact with the Admiral. They're using the older ships to screen *Saint Michael* and the *Hercules*es, but..."

"But they're doing that so we don't realize they're charging the one-point-fives," Anthony declared. He was still over a minute from the flag bridge, and a minute might be too damn long.

"Activate Rampart, Admiral Volkov, on my authorization," he told her, shifting to an outright *run*. He could have been in Fleet Starfighter Control. "I'll be there in sixty seconds, but we don't have time. All ships to *maximum deflection*."

Because the Dakotan Confederacy Navy had possessed *all* of the designs and schematics for Project Hustle, including the revised hardware and layouts for the new electromagnetic deflectors. Installing them in the older ships had been a *nightmare*, one that had cost the ships with the Rampart upgrades massive amounts of supplies.

But even *Black Sea*, an obsolete thirty-million-cubic-meter *Ocean*-class strike cruiser that had barely been able to fit the new projectors, wasn't *actually* inside the weapons range of the Commonwealth Fleet.

And Anthony barely gave the order in time. He was still twenty seconds from the flag bridge when the Commonwealth formation shifted, opening up like the shields retracting from around a concealed weapon, and thrusting the five modern warships to the fore.

Ninety-six heavy positron lances spoke without warning, each flinging enough antimatter across space to trigger one-point-five *megatons* of destructive force every second. At six light-seconds, Task Force Six detected the shots about sixty milliseconds before they hit.

Or would have hit.

A hundred of the most powerful antimatter beams ever built by mankind hit the electromagnetic deflectors shielding the Dakotan fleet just as Anthony Yamamoto charged onto *Krakatoa*'s flag bridge. Kilograms of pure antimatter were flung aside, the beams curving away from the DCN ships to vanish uselessly into deep space.

"Sir!" Volkov greeted him as he reached the central dais. Despite everything, she sounded calm enough as she gestured him to the seat at the heart of the flag bridge.

"*Iroquois* and *Adamant*," Anthony said levelly, watching a second salvo of beams tear across space—probably fired before the Terrans had even seen the failure of their first shots, "target *Saint Michael* and return fire."

The other half of Project Rampart had been an attempt to upgrade the main guns of the older ships. It... hadn't worked as well as planned. *Black Sea* had ended up giving up two of her six six-hundred-kiloton beams in exchange for the improved deflectors.

Adamant, on the other hand, had seen half of her reactive armor stripped away to install the deflectors. *Her* lack of supplies had been due to eight of her eighteen main positron lances being upgraded to fifteen hundred kilotons per second.

Now, combined with *Iroquois*'s heavy beams, thirty-two positron lances answered Fifth Fleet's ninety-six. The Commonwealth had sent more modern ships to answer Weston's call, but even their newest ships hadn't been updated to match Project Hustle—and their handful of eighty-million-cubic-meter ships with the new deflectors had been needed elsewhere, Anthony presumed.

None of Fifth Fleet's beams struck home. *All* of Task Force Six's did, and *Saint Michael*, flagship of the Terran Commonwealth Navy, vanished in a blaze of stark-white matter-antimatter annihilation.

————

Anthony stood at the command seat, his hand on the back of the chair that would always be Tecumseh's to him, refusing to sit in it as he watched chaos unfold. It was clear that not all of Fifth Fleet's Captains, even, had known what was coming. They'd followed their maneuvering orders, but they hadn't expected to see their five heaviest combatants open fire on theoretical allies.

The Dakotan ships might have lost contact with James Tecumseh, but the Commonwealth ships were clearly still receiving orders from the surface. Orders Anthony might have refused or at least questioned —firing on allied forces without warning was a bad look at the best of times!—but it seemed Walkingstick hadn't shaped a fleet that would argue with him.

"Open the range," he ordered. "Full acceleration, all ships."

"Do we keep firing?" Volkov asked.

"Negative, hold fire for now," Anthony snapped. "We just killed over six thousand people. Let's give the *other* sixty-odd thousand a chance!"

If his worst-case scenarios around the loss of communications from Tecumseh were true, the numbers were probably lower than that—at least aboard *Saint Michael*. If *Anthony* had been infiltrating Marines into a friendly power's capital to overthrow their government, he'd certainly have pulled them from his flagship!

To be fair, his impression was that *Tecumseh* had pulled Marines evenly from all four ships, but Anthony also trusted that Tecumseh hadn't put boots on the ground around NovaToronto with the intent of *overthrowing* the Republic's government.

"TCN ships have continued firing," Volkov reported. "Deflectors are functioning to spec. No hits, but… there's enough antimatter coming our way that the odds of a fluke are going up every moment."

"Understood." Anthony was silent, studying the display.

"TCN is launching starfighters as well," another analyst said. "No missiles yet."

"They don't have any more fucking missiles than we do," Anthony said drily. "And at this range, starting from rest? Missiles are going to take too long and be too vulnerable to be worth spending the ones we've got.

"That said, get *our* fighters into space," he ordered. "Full missile-defense spread. If they decide to get clever, let's shut them down."

More antimatter blazed around his ships, and a chill ran down his spine.

"Give me warning shots," he told Volkov. "Bracket every single one of those *Herculeses*—*Saint Michael* should have made the point, but let's add an addendum before I talk to them."

Krakatoa's guns didn't have the range for this. It was one of the key design flaws in the *Volcano*-class carriers, in his opinion, that they mounted the one-megaton lances of the previous generation of battleships. Either they should have carried the heaviest lances available, or they shouldn't have mounted heavy lances *at all*. The mass and cubage could have been spent on defenses or more fighters, anything except an energy weapon that was only useful against other carriers and older capital ships.

Still, *Adamant* and *Iroquois* carried enough positron lances to make the point. Six lances bracketed each battlecruiser in a perfectly distributed hexagon, one that made it clear their deflectors weren't strong enough to survive.

"Commonwealth ships," Anthony addressed the video pickup. "You have misjudged your advantages, and you are outranged and outclassed. If you push this, I will destroy your *entire fleet* to protect the ships under my command."

He had enough starfighters to hold off Fifth Fleet's counterparts.

Especially given that there were hundreds of Weston "loaners" still on the Terran ships—a major part of why he didn't *want* to fire on the Commonwealth carriers.

"No responses, sir," Prebensen reported. "They are continuing to close at two hundred gravities."

"And we are continuing to *retreat* at two hundred gravities, I hope," Anthony said drily.

"Yes, sir," Volkov confirmed. "Range is closing at several hundred kilometers per second, but…"

"They have two hundred thousand kilometers to close," the Vice Admiral said. "Dammit, are they trying to *make* us kill them?"

"We… probably killed their second-in-command," the operations officer pointed out. "Chain of command says there's *someone* over there with the authority to stand down, but standing down eleven ships to four—"

"Requires someone to have epically fucked up. Which they did," Anthony ground out. "We're not letting them run to launch a fighter strike. If they start launching bombers, the gloves come off."

"And until then?" Volkov asked.

"We give sixty seconds, then one last chance," he said. "But if they launch bombers or missiles—or, gods forbid, actually *hit* us—we open fire."

At which point Anthony Yamamoto would deal with the ghosts. Because his *first* duty was, without question, to the officers and spacers of the Dakotan Confederacy Navy's Task Force Six.

48

THE CHAMBER of Parliament had never been intended to be a battlefield. The *roof* was gone, cut away by *relatively* careful laser fire as the Dakotan shuttles descended. Benches intended for MPs and staff had been turned into impromptu cover as gunfire had torn through the room and Dakotan Marines had dropped from the air to retake the room from the Terrans.

James wasn't sure where Reynolds had gone. She'd definitely been making sure he and Littlebear were safe at the start, but then she'd disappeared.

"Sir, over there," one of the Marines told him, pointing to a panel opening in the side of the Speaker's raised dais.

Escorted by a single, visibly wounded Parliamentary Constable, President Frey and Prime Minister De Clerc slowly and carefully exited an armored chamber James figured *they* hadn't known existed.

James strode across the space to meet them.

"Mr. President, Madame Prime Minister," he said. "Thank the stars you're alive. My people are coordinating with yours, but we have only tentative control of Maple Hall. We have confirmed the presence of other formations of Commonwealth Marines in NovaToronto, reinforcing and working with what appear to be elements of the Republic Army.

"Most formations of your Army are, of course, working with us and providing primary direction. NovaToronto is—"

"A warzone," Frey said grimly. "Our city. Did Walkingstick really think this would help his cause?"

"He thought he could win," James said. "He… *knew* he would win. The thought of failure wasn't part of his ultimate plan—parts of his plans could always fail, but he always had another backup, another line of attack.

"*Failure* wasn't in his vocabulary, sirs."

"What about in space? He has more capital ships and you and us combined!" De Clerc exclaimed.

"Thanks to Admiral Vitali being sensible, Fifth Fleet is not in a position to actively threaten your orbital fortresses or anchorages," James reminded them. He paused, looking around the Chamber. It was hard to tell much of anything in the ruins of the place—both of the raised podiums he and Walkingstick had pontificated from were twisted wreckage now, for example—but he realized he was missing someone.

"Where *is* the Admiral?" he asked.

Frey and De Clerc both darted pained looks back at the safe room, and James shivered.

"He…" De Clerc trailed off and swallowed. "He had a heart attack. There were *three of us* in there, Admiral. We… We couldn't do anything."

James let a chill wipe away his grief as the Prime Minister struggled with her own emotions. One more death on Walkingstick's account.

And where *was* the damn man?

He twitched as his implant suddenly chimed with a signal.

"Jammers are down," Major Revie's voice said in his head. "Where the *hell* are you, sir? We do not have eyes on you."

"I'm about five meters from where I was giving a speech, Major," James told his bodyguard. "I should be on the tacnet if it's back up."

"I see you," Revie confirmed. "Stay where you are, sir. We're on our way to you."

His bodyguards had waited outside the Chamber, trusting his immediate security to Reynolds. Usually a safe call—Reynolds, for all her unassuming appearance, was unquestionably deadlier than any single Marine in his security detail.

More data flowed into James's implant. He'd had *some* information coming in from the Marines, but the short-range frequency-hopping communicators the Marines used to overcome the jammers only allowed for local networks.

Now he was getting full updates from the shuttles—and promptly managed to establish a link with the Task Force.

"Sir, you're alive!" Volkov's voice echoed in his head.

"Not for lack of the Commonwealth trying," he replied. "Our Marines have secured Maple Hall, but the place is a wreck and I have no idea how many of the MPs were saved or caught in the crossfire. Headcount is going to take some time.

"Status report up there?"

"Fifth Fleet opened fire on us," Yamamoto joined the channel. "They didn't know about Rampart; they missed their range calc and can't hit us. We returned fire. *Saint Michael* is no more, but the battle-cruisers are trying to close the range, and the carriers are sticking with them.

"We can wipe them all out, sir—they have to know that—but they're still coming, and I suspect they're prepping bombers and missiles." There was a long pause. "I don't think Walkingstick told everyone the plan, and I suspect their Weston loaners are giving them problems."

James pulled the status update he had on the ships. With the Rampart upgrades, his people wouldn't be in range of the Common-wealth's beam weapons until they were within seven and a half light-seconds. The hundred and fifty thousand kilometers they needed to cross to *reach* that range was only a short distance by the standards of space combat—and with Task Force Six keeping the range open, Yamamoto wasn't understating the situation.

Thinking that *they* had the perfect ambush, Fifth Fleet had walked themselves into a trap. If they tried to fall back to open range for missile or fighter strikes, Yamamoto would have to destroy them—but they wouldn't *survive* closing to their actual lance range.

His datafeed, showing the "battle" ten seconds earlier, marked another round of ranging shots from Fifth Fleet. The *Hercules*-class battlecruisers weren't giving up. They weren't prepared to face the consequences of surrendering to a force a third their size when Walkingstick found out.

"I need Walkingstick," James said aloud. "Living or dead, he's the only one who can get them to stand down."

"His people moved to retrieve him the moment they were through the door," Revie told him, the Marine not even out of breath despite clearly having sprinted the full length of the Chamber of Parliament. "None of the Marines have had eyes on him since."

"Get a search protocol up," James ordered. "If we can't find Walkingstick in about the next two minutes, we may have no choice but to destroy Fifth Fleet."

He would. Helpless as the enemy was at the range *they'd* chosen, it wouldn't even bother his sleep much—not when they *kept* firing uselessly at his ships. But the acrid smell of smoke and blood in what should have been a place of governance and discussion told him there had been enough death today.

"This way."

James hadn't even registered Reynolds' reappearing, and the connection to his cybernetic arm gave him a spasm of pain as he twisted too quickly to look at her.

Both his right arm and right leg were mechanical replacements, a legacy of the last mission he'd carried out under Walkingstick's direct command. Most of the time, he didn't notice, but if he moved *too* sharply, it became hard to ignore.

"This way to…?"

"You said you needed Walkingstick," she told him. "Well, this way if you want to talk to him. But you need to hurry."

James Tecumseh's snap judgment was that if they were *currently* standing in a fully equipped medbay with a ready supply of high-end cybernetics, Imperator Walkingstick would have had a fifty-fifty chance of making it.

As it was, the only reason he wasn't *already* dead was that Walking-stick had clearly rigged a brutally efficient tourniquet at the top of his right thigh, only a palm's breadth from the gaping wound where someone had shot his leg out from under him.

The Imperator of Terra was alone, surrounded by a half-dozen dead Commonwealth Marines who clearly had tried to get him to safety before everything went to shit.

Walkingstick's leg wound was the most obvious injury, the one that had clearly cost him the most blood and was probably going to kill him, tourniquet or no. He had his hand pressed to his torso, a chunk of his uniform jacket roughly shaped into a compress over an injury that was either into his lungs, his guts... or both.

One eye flickered open as James and Reynolds approached, and Walkingstick growled like a cornered animal.

"Finish it, then," he snarled. "If you have the guts."

"I need *you* to," James said quietly, crouching down by his old mentor. "Your Marines and ships are still fighting, James. In your name, they'll fight. By your orders, they will not surrender. But this fight is already over.

"Your ships misjudged our defenses. They aren't in range of mine, and mine are in range of them." James sighed. "*Saint Michael* is gone, James. And if your people don't stand down, we'll have to destroy them all."

"Fuck... you," Walkingstick ground out.

"It's not about me right now, James," he told the dying man. "It's not even about you, is it?"

Walkingstick coughed bitterly.

"No," he conceded. "What do you *want*... James?"

For all that their shared first name had been a source of amusement and connection for a decade, James Tecumseh wasn't sure they'd *ever* called each other by it.

"I need you to order your people to stand down," he told Walkingstick. "Because they'll fight for you if you don't, but the only thing anyone will gain from that will be a larger escort when you enter hell."

Walkingstick spat at him, a gob of bloody spittle that didn't make it across the barely a meter of distance.

"I have enough training for this." He nodded vaguely down toward his wounds and their rough dressing. "I know what this looks like. You can't save me."

"No one can," James agreed. He was honestly surprised the man was still *alive*—the rough-and-ready first aid had done something, but Walkingstick was spending seconds he didn't have.

"But you can save sixty-odd thousand Commonwealth military personnel," he whispered. "You owe them that, don't you? A chance. Fuck, James, I'll even make sure the Republic lets them go home."

Without Walkingstick, the Rump Commonwealth was going to change dramatically. And there was no question that it was going to *be* without Walkingstick.

"I don't have coms," Walkingstick whispered, shifting his head slightly to allow James to see the injury he'd *missed*. Built-in safety protocols had kept the man alive so far, but a bullet had cracked his skull and damaged his implant.

"Here," Reynolds said softly, holding out what James realized was probably the helmet from one of the dead Marines. "It's linked to your planetary coms. You should be able to get everyone, on the ground and in space."

Walkingstick snorted. James wasn't sure whether it was amusement or gratitude, but it brought bubbles of bloody froth onto his face.

Still, he took the helmet and, with the hand not holding his torso together, tapped a command.

"All units, Marines and Navy," he said in a firmly steady voice. "This is Imperator Walkingstick. Authentication. Lakota. Cherokee. Lambda. Nine. Nine. Washington. Six. Blackfoot.

"Stand down. All Commonwealth military forces are to stand down. Passage home will be negotiated… but we are surrendering. It's over."

Walkingstick tapped a second command, closing the channel before the helmet slipped from suddenly nerveless fingers and hit the floor.

His hand was equally limp, and James could tell there wasn't much time left.

"Damn you," Walkingstick murmured. "You, James Tecumseh. You should have just followed orders. We could have saved the Commonwealth, you and I.

"All you had to do was trust me."

"I would have followed Admiral or Marshal Walkingstick into hell and back again," James told the dying man. "You were my guiding star, my mentor, my commander.

"But the day you became Imperator Walkingstick, the man I served died alongside the Commonwealth you destroyed."

Walkingstick didn't respond… and James realized the man hadn't even heard his words. He was gone.

The Imperator of Terra was dead.

49

"How are the Westons taking it?"

Quetzalli Chapulin's question wasn't an easy one to answer, James reflected.

His office had been subsumed into a virtual recreation of the Cabinet meeting room in Táála'í'tsin. The entire Cabinet was gathered for this. He probably wasn't the only one attending virtually via q-com link, but everyone else was at least in the Confederacy.

"Better than I would have expected," he finally told them. "Which isn't saying much." He shook his head. "I was expecting to force a vote and for the vote to go against Walkingstick. *That*, I knew, was going to have consequences.

"I will admit that even I did not expect Walkingstick to move as quickly, as violently or as ruthlessly as he did." He paused in thought for a moment, grateful for the rest of the Cabinet's patience.

"If we had not, through prior agreements with the locals, infiltrated two battalions of our Marines onto the surface, it might have worked," he admitted. "Walkingstick's people had co-opted enough of the

Republic Army that it came within a few wrong words of outright civil war—and that was *after* the TCMC had stood down.

"So, the Republic's leadership and people are shaken… but they are unbroken."

Most of them. There had been fourteen hundred and eighty-three elected Members of Parliament attending Maple Hall when Walkingstick moved. Two hundred and eighteen were dead.

"Obviously, there is no chance that the Weston Republic will now apply for reabsorption into the Commonwealth," James concluded. "While they have honored my promise to allow the Terran personnel to return home, they claimed a high price for the privilege."

The Fifth Fleet that was returning to the Terran Commonwealth was a far smaller formation than had *left* the Commonwealth. While the overall ship losses were in the TCN's favor, given that Walkingstick had sent his ten captures directly to Terran space, Frey and De Clerc had kept the *Hercules*es and the *Volcano*es as their pound of flesh.

And with James's fleet sitting calmly but *pointedly* in the half-light-second area where they could blow said Terran ships to hell without being touched in turn, the surviving Commonwealth command structure had acquiesced. Five ships would be leaving within the next few hours.

"With the captures from Yellowstar, the Republic Navy is now back up to sixteen capital ships. A force that will more than suffice to force peace with Morris and Rao."

"It will," Hjalmar Rakes confirmed. The Minister for Krete and Intelligence nodded to James, silently asking permission to interrupt.

James nodded back, more than willing to yield the floor while he got his thoughts in order.

"Their Majesties King Harendra and Queen Celestine—both the First, presumably!—formally declared the Star Kingdom of Archon this morning," Rakes told everyone. "They retain all fourteen star systems of the former Triumvirate, and all of Verity's planetary governors appear to have signed on as new Grand Dukes under the system.

"They have summoned a constitutional convention, one that I imagine will have some very strict guidelines, but are clearly planning for the long term. That long term will *require* peace."

"Because the alternative to peace is that the Republic waits six months to commission their new carriers and then overruns the Star Kingdom with a two-to-one advantage in hulls," James concluded.

"In any case, our primary objectives here are complete," he told the Cabinet. "Envoy Littlebear will remain here with *Adamant* and *Black Sea*—the two warships as symbols as much as anything else—and finish hashing out the details of our alliance."

"Others will join quickly now, I think," Abey added. Despite the formal circumstances of the meeting and both of their determination to be professional, her gaze was focused on him. That *might* have been an illusion of the holographic conferencing software, he supposed, but if so, he didn't think it was one she'd mind.

"The Rump Commonwealth is going to go through an interesting time," Chapulin said grimly. "With Walkingstick dead, who rules on Terra now?"

"I don't know," James admitted. "I'm not sure *they* know—actually, after barely two days, I am one hundred percent certain they *don't* know."

"Walkingstick left behind several counterbalanced centers of power," Rakes warned. "They may cooperate, but their loyalties were to *him*, not to each other."

"Knowing Walkingstick, I suspect that all of them have at least some loyalty to the concept of the Commonwealth as well," James pointed out. "That may be their only saving grace in the end. Because, if nothing else, I've *met* Mihai Gabor."

He let that sink in.

"Gabor *hates* politicians," he warned. "The man with all of the guns and starships in the Solar System hates the civilians he has to work with to sustain the Commonwealth going forward. *If* he can come to an agreement with the Senators, he has the physical power to hold things together.

"Unfortunately, I'm afraid he might just break everything, trying on his own."

"All too possible," Rake agreed. "Worse, though, are some of the conversations I've had with Director Reynolds. Despite the Crows' best efforts, we are quite certain that Pich Misra survived the Battle of Weston and has almost certainly found their way to safety.

"The power of the Commonwealth Bureau of Information is subtle but no less real for it. Misra represents an entirely separate power base from the political or the military. Their disappearance, well…"

"Suffice to say I believe the Commonwealth is going to be heavily wrapped up in their own affairs for quite some time," James concluded drily. "With the reduction in the forces of the now–Star Kingdom and the new additions to the WRN, I feel comfortable leaving a smaller force under Rear Admiral Volkov to provide a presence and support mission for our new allies."

"Good. We need you here," Chapulin said firmly. "And not *just* to keep the First Chief of Dakota from vibrating out of her skin from barely suppressed frustration!"

Both James and Abey flushed at that, but the chuckles answering Chapulin's joke were warm and good-natured.

"Twenty-seven days," James reminded them all. "It will be a day or two here still before we're ready to come home. *We* didn't get any shiny new starships out of the deal, though, so once Fifth Fleet is gone, we won't be needed for much longer."

"I look forward to it," Abey said throatily, then flushed again as everyone looked at her. "I mean, *we* look forward to it. My *personal* desires aside, the situation in the Brillig Sector is only growing more complicated. Kipling, it seems, has gone to Emerald for help."

"We can manage that," James said calmly.

"We know," Chapulin said. "But instead of merely needing to intimidate a two-system power into letting its neighbors make their own choices, we now face the prospect of having to *fight* a *nine*-system power. And the question of whether three star systems are worth it."

"If Parliament decides to stand aside, I won't go waging wars on my own," James said firmly, "but my opinion is simple.

"If there is one principle for which we must fight, one standard for which we must stand, the standard that sent us here, the standard that drove us into secession in the first place, it is this:

"People must make their own choices. As individuals, as nations, as star systems. If Brillig, Blyton and Shakespeare wish to join the

Confederacy, then the *only* decision that matters is whether we wish to expand at all.

"We cannot allow others to impose their will on those nations. Otherwise, we break faith with the ideals we forged our own nation from.

"And I have shed too much blood for those ideals to let them go without a fight."

"For once, we are all on the same page," Chapulin said, glancing around the Cabinet. "This matter has now passed *far* beyond what this Cabinet can decide on its own, but we at least have a recommendation to give the Assembly when we present the whole matter to them.

"And I know most of the Assembly will be reassured to know you are coming home, Admiral," the President noted. "We have faith in our other Admirals, but if the Confederacy must go to war again, we want The Admiral in command."

"I will be home soon," James promised—to both Abey and the rest of the Cabinet. "And if the Confederacy must stand in defense of others and their right to choose, that, my friends, is why I wear the stars you gave me.

"So. Let's be about it."

JOIN THE MAILING LIST

Love Glynn Stewart's books? Join the mailing list at

GLYNNSTEWART.COM/MAILING-LIST/

to know as soon as new books are released and for special announcements.

ABOUT THE AUTHOR

Glynn Stewart is the author of *Starship's Mage*, a bestselling science fiction and fantasy series where faster-than-light travel is possible–but only because of magic. His other works include science fiction series *Duchy of Terra, Castle Federation* and *Exile*, as well as the urban fantasy series *ONSET* and *Changeling Blood*.

Writing managed to liberate Glynn from a bleak future as an accountant. With his personality and hope for a high-tech future intact, he lives in Canada with his partner, their cats, and an unstoppable writing habit.

VISIT GLYNNSTEWART.COM FOR NEW RELEASE UPDATES

CREDITS

The following people were involved in making this book:
Copyeditor: Richard Shealy
Proofreader: M Parker Editing
Cover art: Sam Leung
Typo Hunter Team
Faolan's Pen Publishing team: Jack and Robin.

facebook.com/glynnstewartauthor

OTHER BOOKS
BY GLYNN STEWART

For release announcements join the
mailing list or visit **GlynnStewart.com**

STARSHIP'S MAGE
Starship's Mage
Hand of Mars
Voice of Mars
Alien Arcana
Judgment of Mars
UnArcana Stars
Sword of Mars
Mountain of Mars
The Service of Mars
A Darker Magic
Mage-Commander
Beyond the Eyes of Mars
Nemesis of Mars
Chimera's Star
Mage-Captain (*Upcoming*)

Starship's Mage: Red Falcon
Interstellar Mage
Mage-Provocateur
Agents of Mars

Starship's Mage Novellas
Pulsar Race
Mage-Queen's Thief

DUCHY OF TERRA
The Terran Privateer
Duchess of Terra
Terra and Imperium
Darkness Beyond
Shield of Terra
Imperium Defiant
Relics of Eternity
Shadows of the Fall
Eyes of Tomorrow

SCATTERED STARS

Scattered Stars: Conviction
Conviction
Deception
Equilibrium
Fortitude
Huntress
Prodigal

Scattered Stars: Evasion
Evasion
Discretion
Absolution

PEACEKEEPERS OF SOL
Raven's Peace
The Peacekeeper Initiative
Raven's Course
Drifter's Folly
Remnant Faction
Raven's Flag
Wartorn Stars *(upcoming)*
Honor & Renown: A Peacekeepers of Sol Novella

EXILE
Exile
Refuge
Crusade
Ashen Stars: An Exile Novella

CASTLE FEDERATION
Space Carrier Avalon
Stellar Fox
Battle Group Avalon
Q-Ship Chameleon
Rimward Stars
Operation Medusa
A Question of Faith: A Castle Federation Novella

Dakotan Confederacy
Admiral's Oath
To Stand Defiant
Unbroken Faith

AETHER SPHERES
Nine Sailed Star
Void Spheres *(upcoming)*

VIGILANTE
(WITH TERRY MIXON)
Heart of Vengeance
Oath of Vengeance

Bound By Stars: A Vigilante Series
(With Terry Mixon)
Bound By Law
Bound by Honor
Bound by Blood

TEER AND KARD
Wardtown
Blood Ward
Blood Adept

CHANGELING BLOOD
Changeling's Fealty
Hunter's Oath
Noble's Honor
Fae, Flames & Fedoras: A Changeling Blood Novella

ONSET
ONSET: To Serve and Protect
ONSET: My Enemy's Enemy
ONSET: Blood of the Innocent
ONSET: Stay of Execution
Murder by Magic: An ONSET Novella

STANDALONE NOVELS & NOVELLAS
Children of Prophecy
City in the Sky
Excalibur Lost: A Space Opera Novella
Balefire: A Dark Fantasy Novella
Icebreaker: A Fantasy Naval Thriller